# THE SIN EATER

*Recent Titles by Sarah Rayne*

TOWER OF SILENCE
A DARK DIVIDING
ROOTS OF EVIL
SPIDER LIGHT
THE DEATH CHAMBER
GHOST SONG
HOUSE OF THE LOST
WHAT LIES BENEATH

PROPERTY OF A LADY *
THE SIN EATER *


* *available from Severn House*

# THE SIN EATER

## Sarah Rayne

This first world edition published 2012
in Great Britain and in the USA by
SEVERN HOUSE PUBLISHERS LTD of
9–15 High Street, Sutton, Surrey, England, SM1 1DF.
Trade paperback edition first published
in Great Britain and the USA 2012 by
SEVERN HOUSE PUBLISHERS LTD

British Library Cataloguing in Publication Data

Rayne, Sarah.
  The sin eater.
  1. Occult fiction.
  I. Title
  823.9'2-dc23


ISBN-13:  978-0-7278-8162-5 (cased)
ISBN-13:  978-1-84751-425-7 (trade paper)

*All Severn House titles are printed on acid-free paper.*

Severn House Publishers support the Forest Stewardship Council [FSC], the
leading international forest certification organisation. All our titles that are printed
on Greenpeace-approved FSC-certified paper carry the FSC logo.

Typeset by Palimpsest Book Production Ltd.,
Falkirk, Stirlingshire, Scotland.
Printed and bound in Great Britain by
MPG Books Ltd., Bodmin, Cornwall.

# ONE

Benedict Doyle had always known that if he ever entered the house that had belonged to his great-grandfather, the ghost that had shadowed most of his own life would be waiting for him. If it had been possible to avoid coming to the house today, he would have done so – in fact he would have travelled to the other side of the planet if he could have managed it.

But the visit could no more be avoided than tomorrow's sunrise. In a couple of weeks he would be twenty-one, and Holly Lodge, that tall, frowning old place, would become his.

'You'll have to go through all the stuff that's in there,' his cousin Nina had said, with her customary bossiness. 'I shouldn't think you'll want much of it yourself, although my mother used to say there were some quite nice things in the house.'

It was all very well for Nina, whose life had been entirely ordinary, and who, if she ever encountered a ghost, would most likely breezily tell it to sod off.

Still, Nina was right about the house's contents needing to be sorted out before it was sold. The solicitors, who had administered the trust fund left by Benedict's parents, had let Holly Lodge to a series of tenants over the years, but it had been empty for the last two years. They assumed Benedict would want to sell it, rather than live in it. Would they be right?

'Yes,' said Benedict, who would not have lived in Holly Lodge if he had been homeless and starving. He said he would sort out the contents and sell the furniture, and agreed that the house must not stand empty through another winter. Yes, he would see to it. No, he was not putting it off, but he was busy at the moment. This was his third year at Reading and there were exams looming, revision – his finals were next year. You did not acquire a decent degree in law and criminology by sitting around doing nothing. He would go up to London at half-term, or perhaps Christmas . . .

Inevitably it was Nina who pushed him into it. If nothing else, he should have the contents valued by an antique dealer, she said. As it happened, she knew someone who might help. Nina always knew someone who might help – she was constantly offering people to all her friends, from doctors and acupuncturists, to marvellous little boutiques who sold designer clothes at a fraction of the cost. Benedict thought he might have guessed in the present situation she would offer him an antique dealer.

'Her name's Nell West,' Nina said. 'She lived in London until her husband died, but she's based in Oxford now. I expect she'd travel to London for what's practically a house clearance though. She won't rip you off, either. I'll phone her, shall I?'

'Well, all right.' It was already the beginning of December and Benedict knew he would have to face up to entering the house. 'Make it just before Christmas. Say the eighteenth.'

It was to be hoped Nina's antique dealer contact would not turn out to be one of her butterfly-minded friends, playing at running a business. A young widow might be anything from a mournful workaholic to an extravagant dragonfly, squandering insurance money and trailing strings of lovers.

At first 18th December was far enough away not to matter, but as it got nearer Benedict was aware of an increasing nervousness. He woke on the morning of the 18th to find his stomach churning with apprehension.

London was a seething mass of Christmas shoppers. Benedict eyed them and wished his day could be as normal as theirs. He would far rather grapple with Oxford Street in the Christmas rush than enter an empty old house where God knew what might be waiting for him.

He had not been sure he would remember the way from the tube station and he had been more than half prepared to find himself lost and have to ask for directions. But when it came to it, he recognized the landmarks from twelve years ago – the clusters of shops, the scattering of restaurants, the jumble of house styles, interspersed here and there with single modern office buildings. But he thought that in the main this part of London, which was a kind of satellite suburb of Highbury, would not have looked much different in his great-grandfather's day.

Here was the road now – a polite-looking street, with large dwellings, some fronting on to the pavement, others standing behind hedges. Most of them looked as if they had been divided into flats and some had brass plates indicating they were doctors' or dentists' surgeries. Holly Lodge was halfway along – one of the few private residences left. The gardens were unkempt and the holly hedge that gave it its name was thick and spiky.

Benedict stood looking at the house for a long time, telling himself it had been empty for nearly two years, and that any old, empty house would look gloomy and forbidding on a grey December day. Twelve years ago he had believed in ghosts; these days he did not. There would not be anything waiting for him inside the house.

But there was. He knew it the minute he stepped inside.

Benedict's parents had died shortly after his eighth birthday, in a car crash which had also killed his grandfather who had been travelling with them.

Even now, he could remember the cold sick feeling that had engulfed him when Aunt Lyn, tears streaming down her face, told him what had happened. He had not really understood why his parents had been driving through an icy blizzard that day – he had supposed there was some important grown-up thing they had to do. Aunt Lyn, angrily dashing away tears, had said it was irresponsible of them to go haring across London in the middle of a fierce snowstorm with the roads like ice rinks and visibility virtually nil, and it was as well that Benedict, poor little scrap, had some family left who would take care of him. He would, of course, come to live with her and his cousin Nina.

Benedict had been too sick and numb with grief to care where he lived. He had not known his grandfather very well, so that part was not too bad, but the loss of his parents was devastating. He had to pack his clothes and go to Aunt Lyn's house. Aunt Lyn was kind and comforting, but she was not Benedict's mother and her house was not his house. He had stayed with her sometimes, because Aunt Lyn and Nina were supposed to be the lively ones of the family and Benedict's mother said he was apt to be too quiet and something called introverted. It would do him good, said his mother, to stay with Lyn and be with Nina who was always so sparky, and see if he could imbibe some of that spark.

'He won't,' said Benedict's father, who was quiet himself and liked Benedict the way he was. 'He'll retreat from the world into his books.'

'The way you retreat from the world sometimes,' said Benedict's mother. Benedict, who had been only a quarter listening to this exchange but who had been getting slightly worried in case his parents were going to have one of their very rare rows, heard the smile in his mother's voice and relaxed and went back into the book he was reading, which was *Alice Through the Looking Glass* and which he could read properly by himself now. It was just about the best book in the whole world.

After the crash he could not believe he would never hear his mother teasing his father like that again, nor could he believe he would never see the familiar faraway look on his father's face which his mother called retreating, but the rest of the family said was useless daydreaming.

That first night Aunt Lyn gave him the bedroom he always had, and Benedict closed the door and sat on the bed, refusing to go downstairs or join Aunt Lyn and Nina for a meal. He did not want to talk to anyone and he did not want to see anyone. He said this very politely, but he kept the door closed for the next two days, only going out to the bathroom. Aunt Lyn carried up meals on trays and did not seem to mind that he did not speak to her. Benedict had brought *Alice Through the Looking Glass* with him and he read it all the way through, then turned to the first page and read it all over again.

The funeral was four days later. Aunt Lyn came up to the bedroom to tell him about it, tapping on the door before coming in. It would be at the local church, she said, but Benedict need not go if he did not want to. Nina, who was fourteen, came up later to say if he had any sense he would stay in the house. Funerals were utterly gross. There would be coffins and stuff like that, and everyone would cry. She was going, said Nina importantly, because everyone else was and there was a grown-up party afterwards.

'It's not a party,' said Aunt Lyn in exasperation. 'I keep telling you it's not a party.'

'I don't care what it is, it's at a big house I've never been to, and there'll be food and I can wear black and that's seriously gothic.' Nina was into being gothic at the time.

Benedict did not want to go to a party that would have his parents in coffins and at which people would be seriously gothic, but the night before the funeral his grandmother, who was his mother's mother, came to the house in floods of tears and said he must go, because he was the one scrap of her beloved daughter she had left, and only his presence at her side would get her through the terrible ordeal.

'That's unanswerable,' said Aunt Lyn to Benedict afterwards. 'I think you'll have to go. I'm really sorry about it. But it'll only be about an hour.'

'I'll sit by you and hold your hand if it'll help,' said Nina.

'I don't want anyone to hold my hand. I'll be all right,' said Benedict. After they went out, he tried on the black tie which Aunt Lyn had given him and which was what people wore to funerals. He put it on and stared at it in the mirror. The tie looked horrible and Benedict hated it. He hated everything and he wished he could do what Alice had done, and step through the mirror into another world. Alice only had to say, 'Let's pretend,' and her mirror had dissolved. The world in the looking glass sounded pretty scary, but Benedict thought any world, no matter how scary it was, would be better than this one.

He was about to turn away when something moved in the mirror's depths. Benedict looked back and his heart skipped a beat. Looking out of the mirror, straight at him, was a strange man. As he stared, the man smiled and Benedict glanced over his shoulder into the room, thinking someone had come in without him hearing. There had been people coming and going all day, vague relatives Benedict hardly knew, and friends of his parents. Some of them had come upstairs to tell him how sorry they were; this man must be another of them.

But the bedroom was empty and the door was closed.

Benedict looked back at the mirror and this time his heart did more than skip a beat, it lurched and thumped hard against his ribs. The man was still there, standing very still, watching him.

Benedict was not exactly frightened, but he was confused. His mind felt as if it was opening up and as if thousands of brilliant lights were pouring into it. He could see the man clearly – he could see that he was about his father's age, and for a marvellous moment he thought it actually was his father. Supposing dad had come back, just to say goodbye? But even as he was thinking it, he knew it was not his father. It was someone who had very vivid blue eyes, and dark hair. Benedict could not see the whole of the man's face because he was standing slightly sideways, but he could see the remarkable eyes and he could see the man was wearing a dark coat with the collar partly turned up. Behind him was this bedroom, looking exactly as it did here, except for being the other way round.

But people did not live inside mirrors, not unless they were people in books. Might it be a dream? He took a tentative step closer to the mirror and he thought the man put out a hand to him. Benedict hesitated, wanting to put out his own hand, but fearful that he might feel the stranger's cold fingers close around it.

Then from downstairs came Aunt Lyn's voice, calling something about closing the bathroom window, and the man lifted a finger to his lips in a 'hush' gesture. Benedict glanced over his shoulder to the door, and when he looked back at the mirror, the man had vanished.

He did not know if he was relieved or upset, but he did not think he would tell anyone about the man. Aunt Lyn and Nina might think he was going mad – he might actually be going mad. In any case, it had probably not happened or, if it had, it was something to do with his beloved Alice from his book. He had never heard of people being able to call up the worlds that lived inside books, but that did not mean it could not be done. For all Benedict knew, it might be something people did quite often, but that nobody ever talked about. This was such a comforting thought that he felt better for the first time since the car crash.

\*    \*    \*

Benedict had never been to a funeral before and he did not know what to expect. It was dreadful. His grandmother cried all through the service, and clung to his hand, and one of the aunts fainted halfway through and had to be taken outside and given brandy from somebody's flask. The three coffins stood in front of everyone – Benedict managed not to look at them because he was afraid the lids would not be on and he would see his parents' bodies all dead and mangled up from the crash.

The vicar read a piece from the Bible that said the dead did not die, only went to sleep. The thought of his parents sleeping inside a coffin deep in the ground was so terrifying Benedict was not sure if he could bear it. He bit his lip and stared at the ground and thought about all the worlds in books that he might escape to when this was over, and wondered if the man who had looked out of the mirror at him had been real or just part of the nightmare of his parents dying in a dreadful tangle of metal and glass on the Victoria Dock Road.

He thought he could go back to Aunt Lyn's house after the service, but it seemed everyone was going to his grandfather's old house, and Benedict had to go with them.

Aunt Lyn came with him in one of the big black cars. She was surprised he had never been to Holly Lodge. 'It was your grandfather's house,' she said. 'Are you sure your father never took you there?'

'No, never.' Benedict did not say his mother had suggested it once, but that his father had said, quickly, 'Benedict mustn't ever go to that house.'

'Why not?'

'You know why not.'

'Oh Lord, you don't think it's still there, do you? Not after all this time?'

Benedict, listening, only just caught his father's reply. 'Yes, it's still there,' he said. 'You've never really believed it, I know, but I promise you, it's still there.'

As the big black car slid through the streets Benedict looked through the windows, waiting for the moment when he would see the house, which his father had never wanted him to enter. I'm very sorry, he said silently to his father's memory. You didn't want me to go inside this house, but I'll have to.

Aunt Lyn was saying something about an inheritance. 'When you're twenty-one, Holly Lodge will be yours.'

It sounded as if she was promising him a huge treat, so Benedict said, 'Yes, I see,' even though he did not see at all. He was trying to pretend that the rain sliding down the car's windows was actually a thin silver curtain that he could draw aside and see sunshine beyond and his parents still alive and everything ordinary again.

But it was real rain, of course – a ceaseless grey downpour. When the cars drew up outside Holly Lodge it dripped from the dark gloomy trees surrounding the house and lay in black puddles on the gravel drive.

Benedict had not known what to expect from this house, but his father had talked about something being in there that he, Benedict, must never meet. Clearly it was something really bad, so it would not be surprising to find Holly Lodge looked like the terrible castles in *Jack the Giant Killer*, although he supposed you did not get many castles in East London and you certainly did not get any giants, or, if you did, people kept very quiet about them.

When they got to it, he saw it was an ordinary house in an ordinary street. But as they went inside, he had the feeling it had never been a happy house; he thought quite bad things might have happened here, or – what was worse – might be waiting to happen in the future. It was quite a big house, though, which was good because a lot of people were here. Aunt Lyn had arranged for tea or coffee and sherry to be offered, and people wandered around sipping their drinks, eyeing the furniture and the pictures and ornaments. It appeared that hardly anyone had been to the house before; aunts murmured that it was all in better condition than they would have expected; uncles peered dubiously at paintings, and a bookish cousin, with whom Nina tried unsuccessfully to flirt, discovered a collection of works on Irish folklore, and was seated on a window sill reading about creatures with unpronounceable names and sinister traditions, who had apparently haunted Ireland's west coast.

There were a few framed photographs on the walls which must be pretty old, because they were all black and white and

some were even a kind of dusty brown like the faded bodies
of dead flies on a hot window-sill. The older aunts inspected
these photos with curiosity.

'None of Declan Doyle,' said the one who had fainted in
the church. 'Pity. I'd be interested to see what he looked like.'

'I think there are some of him upstairs,' said someone else.

'Are there? Then I might have a look presently. My grandmother said he was one of the handsomest men she ever met.'

'Handsome's all very well,' said one of the uncles. '*I* heard
you couldn't trust him from here to that door.'

'Declan Doyle was your great-grandfather,' said Aunt Lyn
to Benedict. She was handing round sandwiches and she looked
flustered. Benedict wondered if he was supposed to help her.

He felt a bit lost. Everyone seemed to be huddled in little
groups, all talking very seriously. He still did not like the
house, but he was curious about it, mostly because of what
his father had said that time.

'*It's still there . . .*'

Whatever 'it' was, his father had seemed to find it frightening, but his mother had not believed in it.

Benedict slipped out of the room, wondering if he dare
explore. But if it would be his house one day, surely he was
allowed to see the rest of it.

But to begin with, the rooms were not especially interesting.
Benedict looked into what must be a dining room and into a
big stone-floored kitchen. The nicest room was on the other
side of the hall: there was a view over the gardens and bookshelves lining the walls. A big leather-topped desk stood under
the window. It could have been his grandfather's study; people
who had big houses like this did have studies. Benedict tried
to picture his grandfather sitting in one of the deep armchairs
reading, or writing letters at the desk. Old people often wrote
letters. They did not text like Benedict and his friends did, or
email, because there had not been texting or computers in their
day. Benedict thought it must have been pretty fascinating to
have lived in that long-ago world, although he would miss
texting and computers.

There was a calendar in a brass frame on the desk and a
big desk diary with a page for each day of the week. On both

of these the 18th January was marked in red and a time – three p.m. – was underlined. Whoever had done it had not just drawn a circle round the day, but had made an elaborate shape like a little sketched figure. Benedict stared at the marks, feeling cold and a bit sick, because the 18th was the day of the crash and three o'clock was the time it had happened. Aunt Lyn had said so. Benedict could not bear thinking about that, so he went out of the study, closing the door firmly, and hoping no one would see him.

He paused for a moment in the hall to listen to the sounds from the long room where everyone was eating and talking. One of the aunts was trying to find out where Benedict's parents had been going in the middle of an icy blizzard, insisting there was something peculiar about it.

'Because I can't imagine what was so important as to send them on a car journey in the depths of winter. Half of London had ground to a halt and all the television news programmes were warning people not to travel unless absolutely necessary.'

'Like in the war,' said an elderly man, who was wandering around with a bottle of brandy. '"Is your journey really necessary?"'

'Yes, and I don't see how that journey could have been, do you? They were very insistent that it couldn't be put off, and they were very secretive about it as well.'

Benedict went up the stairs. There would not be much to see up here, but anything was better than hearing people say horrid things about his mother and father.

There seemed to be a lot of bedrooms, with ceilings spotted with damp and faded wallpaper, and furniture draped in sheets so you imagined people crouching under them. Had his grandfather lived here on his own, with all these rooms and dusty windows and the drifting cobwebs that reached down to brush against Benedict's face like thin fingers?

At the end of this landing was a second flight of stairs. Benedict hesitated, but he could still hear people talking and no one seemed to have missed him, so he went up the stairs, which creaked as if the house was groaning. There was another landing at the top; it was very dark and, as he looked doubtfully about him, a door on his right swung slowly open.

Benedict froze. Was someone in there? He took a deep breath and went up to the door, but the room was empty except for an old dressing table and a desk pushed against one wall. Or was it empty? As he stood uncertainly in the doorway, the long curtains billowed out as if someone was standing behind them, and something seemed to dart across his vision. He gasped and was about to run back downstairs when he realized that what he had seen was only the glint of a silver photograph frame on the dressing table. There were several photos, but this one must have caught the light when he opened the door. He let out a whooshing breath of relief, then went up to see the photo. It was one of the faded brown ones, but Benedict could see the man in it had dark hair. He was wearing old-fashioned clothes and he was only partly looking at the camera so that half of his face was hidden.

Benedict stared at the man, his mind whirling and panic gripping him in huge wrenching waves.

The man in the photograph was the man who had looked at him from his bedroom mirror four days earlier.

# TWO

After a long time Benedict picked up the photograph and turned it over. Photographs often had things written on the back to tell who the people in them were. His hands were shaking so badly he almost dropped the frame, but eventually he managed to peel off the sticky tape on the backing and take out the photo.

There was nothing. The back of the photo had splodgy brown marks, but no one had written on it to say who this was or when or where the photo had been taken. Benedict sat down on the window sill to think. This was his great-grandfather's house and the aunts had said there were photographs of him up here. So there was only one person this could be. Declan Doyle, his great-grandfather.

Benedict put the photograph back in its frame and replaced it on the dressing table. He wanted to run out of the room, but he did not want any of the people downstairs to see him shaking and on the verge of tears. He would stay here a little longer until he felt better.

The mirror on the dressing table was reflecting the photograph of Declan. It was odd how reflections changed things. Even this room looked different in the mirror – it was smaller and the walls were darker. If you narrowed your eyes, you could even think you were seeing a fire burning in a small grate. Benedict quite liked seeing this, because people did not have fires like that any more. He kept his eyes half-shut for a while, then he opened them, expecting to see this bedroom reflected in the glass. But it was not. He could still see the fire-lit room. There was a bright red rug in front of the fire and a small table and two chairs. Standing by the fireplace, its leaping light behind him, was the man from the photograph. Declan.

Benedict shrank back against the window pane. He would not be frightened. He could not be hurt by somebody who was inside a mirror. But he ached with the pain of wanting Mum, because she would have put her arms round him and told him he was safe from everything bad in the world. Dad would have said, in his quiet way, that all you had to do with things that tried to frighten you was make a rude face at them and they ran away like the cowards they were.

Was that fire-lit room where Declan had lived? Aunt Lyn had said Declan was Irish – would the cottage be in Ireland?

At once a soft silvery whisper seemed to hiss into the room.

'Yes, it's in Ireland, Benedict, it's on the very edge of Ireland's west coast, near the Cliffs of Moher . . . They're wild and dark, those cliffs, and the Atlantic Ocean lashes against them forever and there's the cold music of the sidhe inside the ocean, and the sound of screeching gulls, like wailing banshees, or souls shut out of heaven . . .'

Benedict looked round the room in fear, but there was no one there.

'And there's an ancient watchtower built by one of Ireland's High Kings, and they say the devil himself prowls that stretch of the cliffs . . . That's where it began, Benedict, inside that dark tower, reeking of evil . . . One hundred and twenty years ago, near enough . . .

'We'd make up stories about that watchtower, Benedict – wouldn't any child do that? We'd say to one another, "Let's pretend . . ." '

Let's pretend . . . There it was, the spell that had taken Alice to that other world.

'We'd pretend it was the ruinous halls of the High Kings, the last magical stones from the ancient kingdom of Tara . . . Or a giant's castle – you know about giants, Benedict, you know how they have to be killed . . . And wouldn't any child with half an ounce of spirit or adventure want to go up there, to find out what was really inside that old tower? I did, Benedict, I and a good friend I had, a boy I grew up with.'

The voice had a way of pronouncing things Benedict had never heard, and the words were broken-up like a crackly old radio, or as if they were coming from a long way off.

Greatly daring and having no idea if his own words could be heard, he said, 'Did you do it? Go up to the tower?'

*'I did. Oh, I did, Benedict. I and my friend went up there. We thought we might find giants and ghosts, or princesses that had to be rescued from evil sorcerers and black enchantments. I'd have hacked my way through brambles and thickthorn hedges for a princess even at that age. Wouldn't anyone?'*

'Did you find those things? The giants and the kings and the princesses?'

'No,' said the soft voice. *'We found something far worse.'*

*Ireland 1890s*

Declan Doyle and Colm Rourke had always known they would one day brave the ancient watchtower on the Moher Cliffs. From the time they were very small, growing up in the tiny village of Kilglenn, they had agreed it was a mystery that must one day be solved. And then wouldn't they be the toast of the entire village and half the villages around! Wouldn't they have made their fortunes and have enough money to be off to London town, where it was said that you might almost dig up gold in the streets.

'We'll be out of here as soon as we're properly grown-up,' said Colm, and Declan, who followed Colm in most things, said they would, for sure, and they'd take Romilly with them.

Romilly. Colm's cousin, a year younger, the most beautiful creature either of them had ever seen, although, as Declan pointed out, they had not in fact seen so very many girls, because anyone who was even half good-looking usually left Kilglenn for wider worlds.

'We'll leave as well, but not until we've managed to get inside the watchtower and see if we can make our fortunes from it,' said Colm, grinning.

'Even if we got in there, all we'd find was Father Sheehan, living there like a hermit. And I don't want to meet him,' said Declan firmly. 'My father says he's very wicked and the Church excommunicated him because of a woman.'

'If you listen to them in Fintan's bar of an evening, they'll tell you it was nothing to do with a woman,' said Colm. 'They say Nick Sheehan met the devil one morning on the cliff tops and traded his soul, and that's the real reason he was excommunicated.'

'People don't trade their souls, except in books. And what would the devil be doing in Kilglenn anyway?'

'I don't know, but they say he challenged Nick Sheehan to play chess and Nick Sheehan won, and the devil had to give him the chess set. But he locked it away in the watchtower because it's so evil it'd frizzle your soul if you so much as looked at it. That's why he lives up there – keeping guard over it.'

'I don't believe any of that,' said Declan firmly.

'I don't either, not really, but I'd like to meet Nick Sheehan and make up my own mind,' said Colm thoughtfully. 'And it's a grand story, isn't it? I bet it's told in every house in Kilglenn round the fire every Christmas.'

'If we stay here long enough, we'll be telling it as well, in about a hundred years' time.'

'Not us,' said Colm. 'We're not staying in Kilglenn for a hundred years. We'll be off to London long before that.'

*London, late 1990s*

Benedict could still hear the grown-ups talking downstairs, and somebody was calling to know whether there was any more coffee, but the sounds seemed a long way off. What was much nearer and much more real was the small Irish village where two boys had grown up, and where an ancient watchtower looked out over the ocean.

He wanted to ask Declan what he and the other boy – Colm – had really found in the watchtower, but he was starting to feel very frightened, and one of the things that was frightening him most was the way Declan was standing with half of his face turned away. But his father would want him to be brave, so Benedict got down from the window ledge and went towards the mirror, to get a better look at Declan and the fire-lit room. At once, the image seemed to flinch; Declan did not step back exactly, but he turned his face away like a man suddenly faced with a too-bright light.

Why had he done that? Benedict was trying to decide if he dared say Alice's *Let's Pretend* spell after all and see if the mirror let him step through it, when the fire-lit room with the dark figure shivered, then splintered, and all he could see was the reflection of this room with its dusty walls.

It's all right, thought Benedict. He's gone. I don't know what that was, but I don't think those two boys and that village and that stuff about the devil's chess set was real. I'll go downstairs, and I won't ever tell anybody about this. It won't ever happen again. I'm safe.

But he never did feel safe, not through all the years he was growing up in Aunt Lyn's house. He had the feeling that Declan was waiting for him, somewhere just beyond vision and just outside of hearing, waiting for his chance to talk to Benedict again.

Once, when he was eleven, travelling back from staying with relatives of his mother, half asleep because it was late and the journey was a long one, he thought Declan looked at him from beyond the darkened window of the train. He sat bolt upright in the seat, peering through the window in panic. But the outline dissolved and Benedict tried to think that ghost images often did look back at you from a train window in the dark. They usually turned out to be the guard coming to check tickets, or somebody walking along the aisle.

By the time he was twelve, the pain of losing his parents was not as severe, and on his thirteenth birthday he realized he had to concentrate to recall their faces. He felt so guilty about this, he looked out several photographs and asked Aunt Lyn if they could be framed and put on his dressing table. He knew he would never forget how he had felt when they died, but Aunt Lyn was kind and loving and made no difference between Benedict and Nina, and Nina appeared to regard him as a younger brother she could organize.

But if his parents' ghosts receded, the memory of what he had seen in his great-grandfather's house did not. *I'll outgrow you*, he said to Declan's memory. *I'll go away – to university if I can – and leave you behind.*

By the time he got to Reading University at eighteen, he

thought he had succeeded. He found law absorbing – and he thought he might even try for a PhD in criminology. He made friends – in his second year he shared a rambling old house with three other students – and there were one or two girlfriends. Life was interesting and full.

And then, a few weeks before his twenty-first birthday, he received the solicitor's letter, saying that under the terms of his parents' will, the ownership of Holly Lodge would shortly pass to him, and that unless he wanted to live in it himself, which they thought he did not, they recommended he sell it. If he decided to do so they could arrange a house clearance, but Benedict must, of course, first go through the house's contents to see what he wanted to keep.

I'll have to go back, thought Benedict, the remembered dread stealing over him. It's been eleven years, but whether I sell it or keep it, I'll have to go back to Declan's house.

# THREE

Nell West had been pleased when Nina Doyle asked her to value the contents of a family house near Highbury. It had belonged to an elderly relative, said Nina, showering information on Nell in her customary pelting way, and it had been rented for about ten years, but there were most likely some quite nice things stored away. It was her cousin Benedict's grandfather who had originally owned it; he had died in a car crash along with Benedict's parents years ago. It had all been frightfully tragic, said Nina, because Benedict had only been eight at the time.

Nell said how appalling for an eight-year-old to lose both parents at once.

'Well, the poor lamb seemed to come out of it unscathed, although in my experience, people are never entirely unscathed, are they? And Benedict can occasionally be a bit introverted. He sometimes seems to retreat mentally, if you know what I mean.'

Nell said she did.

'I dare say you find that with your Oxford don,' said Nina. 'Academics often tend to be a bit other-worldly, don't they? Ivory towers and all that.' The words and tone were studiedly casual, but Nell had the feeling of being mentally pounced on.

She said, offhandedly, 'Michael isn't mine.'

'Would he like to be, though? Would you like him to be? Because honestly, Nell, I know you were utterly torn to pieces when Brad died, but it's been more than two years.'

Nell was not going to discuss Michael Flint with Nina Doyle; in fact she was not going to discuss him with anyone. Instead, she brought Nina back to the question of when she could see the Highbury house and inventory the contents. It appeared that Benedict had put forward 18th December as a suitable date, and Nell thought it would be worth braving the seething crowds of Christmas shoppers to see what was inside the house.

'I haven't been there since I was in my teens,' said Nina. 'I don't think Benedict has, either. But he's twenty-one in a few weeks, so everything can be sold. I don't know what's likely to be there, but I shouldn't expect Dutch masters in the attics or Sèvres in the cellars.'

Nell was not expecting either of these things, but there might be a few nice pieces of furniture which she could display in her shop. Oxford had antique shops every twenty yards, but she was trying to make hers fairly distinctive. The setting helped: it was in Quire Court, near Turl Street, almost in the shadow of Brasenose College. There were several small businesses and shops in the court, but none was in direct competition with Nell's so it had been easy to get planning permission for antiques. Her shop had a deep bow window, and she had recently sold a small Regency desk which she had displayed there, and had taken Beth to London for the day on the proceeds.

Beth, who was nine, had loved the Christmas lights in Oxford Street; there was a Victorian theme this year and she had stared at everything with solemn and silent delight as if she was storing it all up to relive later. She was wearing a brown velvet coat with a hood which had been a birthday present from Michael, and which gave her a slightly old-fashioned look. With tendrils of brown curls escaping from the hood and little fur boots and mittens, she might have been a child from the Victorian age herself. Nell watched her, smiling, and, as if sensing this, Beth looked round at her mother with a grin of happy conspiracy. A pang of sharp loneliness sliced through Nell, because Beth's dead father used to look like that when something delighted him and he wanted to share it with her. For a moment, the pain of loss was so overwhelming, Nell almost started crying in the middle of Selfridges. That was the trouble with ghosts; just when you thought you had got them under reasonable control, they came boiling out of nowhere and reduced you to a jelly. It was not unreasonable of Brad's ghost to still do this, more than two years after his death, but it was annoying that it should choose Selfridges during the Christmas rush.

As she sat in the train from Oxford to Paddington, she wondered if there were likely to be any ghosts in Holly Lodge. Michael would have said most old buildings had ghosts – the ghosts of the happinesses and sadnesses that had left imprints on the bricks and stones and timbers. Nell smiled, thinking how serious and absorbed Michael looked when his interest was caught.

It was nice to be part of the buzz and life of London again, although the noise and the crowds were slightly disconcerting after the relative calm of Oxford. In the jam-packed tube, Nell had a sudden reassuring image of Quire Court and its serene old stones, and the faint sound of chimes from one of Oxford's many churches politely and unobtrusively marking the hours.

Benedict Doyle's house was fairly near to the tube and the streets here were not quite so busy. Nell, following Nina's directions, enjoyed the short walk; she liked speculating about the people who lived or worked here, and who shopped at the smart-looking boutiques or ate in the restaurants. She was interested in meeting Nina's cousin, whose parents had been killed when he was the same age as Beth had been when Brad died.

Here was the road, and halfway along it was Holly Lodge. Clearly this had once been a fairly prosperous residential area, but only a few of the houses seemed to be still privately owned. Holly Lodge looked a bit forlorn, but Nina had said it had been empty for two years, so Nell supposed it was entitled to look forlorn. But as she went up the short driveway, she realized her skin was prickling with faint apprehension. This was absurd and also annoying. She had encountered more than one vaguely sinister old house in the course of her career, and if Holly Lodge seemed sinister it was only because most of the curtains were closed and the shrubbery at the front was overgrown, obscuring the downstairs windows.

Nell pushed back a wayward holly branch and thought if Michael were here he would start to weave improbable stories about the place for Beth, and the two of them would egg each other on, and end up with a fantastical modern-day version of

Sleeping Beauty. But as far as Nell was concerned, this was nothing more than a large Victorian house, which might yield some useful and profitable things for her shop.

There was no response to her knock, but she was a bit early and Benedict Doyle might not have got here yet. Or he might be here working at the back of the house and not heard the door knocker. Nell made her way through an iron gate at the side and along a narrow path which had weeds growing through the cracks. She peered through the downstairs windows, then stepped back, shading her eyes to see the upper ones. Was there a movement up there? Yes. And he had seen her. Nell waved and he beckoned to her to come inside.

'Well, can you unlock the front door and let me in?' called Nell, pleased to have found him, although feeling a bit ridiculous to be standing in the middle of a garden, shouting to someone she could barely see. 'Or is there a door open somewhere?'

He pointed downwards to the French windows. Nell gestured an acknowledgement, and tried the handle. It turned, the door swung open, and she stepped inside.

Benedict had managed to keep Declan Doyle out of his mind for almost the entire journey from Reading. Instead, he concentrated on Christmas: on the parties he would be attending, and on an essay he had to write over the Christmas holiday on unusual and unpublicized crimes in the nineteenth century. If he could find some really quirky cases, and if he did try for a PhD later on, it might form the basis of his doctorate.

He had allowed sufficient time to have a couple of hours on his own at Holly Lodge, and had bought a pack of sand-wiches and a can of Coke at Paddington so he could have some lunch while doing some preliminary sorting out.

It was midday when he reached the house. Over the years he had built up an image of it in his mind, until it resembled a cross between Sauron's Mount Doom in *Lord of the Rings* and a *pied à terre* belonging to the Addams family. But standing outside now, he saw it was perfectly ordinary – perhaps a bit more decrepit than it had been twelve years earlier, but nothing that could not be cured by a few coats of paint and several sessions with a mower.

As he unlocked the door he reminded himself that his mirror ghost was nothing more than an unusual experience during a tragic time in his childhood. A rogue image, half-seen in an old glass, created by any number of peculiar, but explicable, circumstances.

As he stepped into the big hall, the house's empty staleness breathed into his face. Ghost-breath, thought Benedict. No, it's more likely to be damp or mice. But the sensation that something inside the house was breathing and living increased. Declan, he thought, and unease stirred his mind, like hundreds of glinting needle-points jabbing into it.

The furniture in most of the rooms was shrouded in dust sheets, making them seem eerie and slightly menacing. Benedict's footsteps echoed as he walked through them, recognizing them from that long-ago afternoon. Here was the big drawing-room where Aunt Lyn had dispensed sherry and coffee that afternoon, and people had speculated as to why his parents had been driving through the blizzard that last day. Behind the drawing room was the study where he had seen his grandfather's calendar and diary, with the 18th marked so vividly and so strangely. He had always thought he would one day try to find out what that appointment had been, but he never had.

He went up to the first floor. As he reached the main landing there was a blurred movement at the far end, as if someone who had been standing there had darted back into the shadowy recess of a deep, tall window. The curtains moved slightly, and Benedict's heart came up into his mouth. Someone here? Maybe it was an ordinary, down-to-earth burglar. Given a choice, Benedict would rather meet a housebreaker than a ghost. He took a deep breath and went forward, reaching out for the curtains, and snatching them back before he could beat a cowardly retreat down the stairs.

There was nothing there. There was just the window, smeary with dust and damp with condensation. Or was there the faint imprint on the faded window seat, as if someone had been crouching there? And had someone traced a faint 'D' in the moisture on the glass?

Benedict looked down at the monochrome gardens, then

stepped back from the window. The doors of the main bedrooms were all open, and nothing stirred within any of them. He would look at them in more detail later; for now he would go up to the second floor, where the solicitors had stored the valuable contents of the house. They had sent Benedict an inventory, along with the keys for the two locked rooms. Initially, they had wanted all valuables to be removed; however much care was taken over tenants, there was still a risk that valuable contents might get damaged, they said. But no one in the family had room to store them, and professional storage for the years until Benedict was twenty-one would have been ruinous, so this compromise had been agreed. The solicitors visited the house two or three times a year to make sure none of the tenants had loaded the entire contents on to a van at dead of night and made off with it to the nearest fence.

There were four rooms on the second floor, including the one where Declan's photograph had been. Benedict had intended to leave Nell West to explore the room's contents and take whatever might be valuable to sell in her shop, but now he was here, he was aware of a strong compulsion to see what the room might yield. There might be clues to his great-grandfather's life – things that might prove, or disprove, those details about Ireland and the ancient watchtower on the Cliffs of Moher. As he unlocked the door his heart was beating furiously; he thought if he had been seeing Holly Lodge as Tolkien's Mount Doom all these years, he had certainly been seeing this room as Bluebeard's seventh chamber. Or would it turn out to be Looking-Glass land after all?

But the room was bland and ordinary and, if there were any ghosts, they were keeping a low profile. There were five or six large boxes and tea chests, and a few pieces of furniture. He would go through the boxes with Nell when she got here, but he already knew he would not want any of the furniture – he particularly would not want the big dressing table with its triple mirror which had given that disturbing reflection all those years ago. But there was a small bureau which was rather nice. He pulled an old kitchen chair across and sat down to take a closer look. The front flap was stuck with the accreted dust of years, but it eventually dropped down into a writing-desk-top, and the scent of old wood and dust drifted up.

Inside the bureau were several pigeonholes, some containing yellowing notepaper with the Holly Lodge address, others with envelopes and books of old stamps whose value was a penny and twopence. There was also an old inkstand and a small blotter, but that seemed to be all. Benedict, who had been half-expecting to find locked-away secrets, was disappointed, but as he was about to close the bureau, he saw several sheets of newspaper folded at the back. Probably they were only makeshift drawer-liners, but he might as well glance at them.

They were not drawer-liners. They were cuttings from some long-ago newspaper or magazine, and the dates were the late 1890s. Declan's era, thought Benedict, reaching for them. He unfolded the first and saw that the headline referred to a *cause célèbre* in the late 1890s – a series of killings which had apparently been known as the Mesmer Murders.

This sounded interesting, and Benedict thought he would read it while he ate his lunch. The articles would not have any connection with Declan, but they might be useful for the criminology essay. And the name bestowed on the killer was unusual enough to warrant a further look. He retrieved his sandwiches from his jacket, and returned to the bureau.

There had been, it seemed, five victims of the Mesmer Murderer – three men and two women. One of the women's bodies had been found in her own house, but the others had been found in Canning Town, near the river, close to an old sewer outlet. One theory was that the killer had intended to dispose of those victims in the river but had been interrupted. The newspaper would not distress its readers with the details, but the killings had been violent.

Benedict thought Canning Town was a part of London's docklands that had not been much developed yet. Bodies in Victorian docklands did not, on the face of it, seem to form much of a base for an essay, never mind a doctoral thesis, but somebody in this house had thought it worth keeping these. He reached for another sandwich and unfolded the next cutting, which focused more on the victims than on the police investigations. Benedict took a large bite of his sandwich and read on.

A curious fact linked the victims. Immediately before their deaths they had all referred to an appointment that must be kept – an appointment about which they refused to disclose information. 'He cancelled everything to keep the appointment,' said the sister of one victim. 'Even an important church meeting that had been arranged for months.'

All the victims, without exception, had marked on their calendars or diaries the date on which they had met their death.

'And very elaborately marked, as well,' said the sister. 'Red ink and curly scrolls. Entirely out of character. A plain note in his diary was what he'd make if he had a business appointment at his work, not something a child might draw on a calendar for its birth date.'

The paper's editor had added a note at this point, to say that the business concern in question was a small printing firm in Islington, of which the man had been general manager.

A female victim, described as an actress and artists' model, had apparently told a female friend that she had an engagement which she thought might bring her a good sum of money.

'That's all she would say,' the friend was quoted as saying. 'But she was in a kind of dream about it – like those people you see being mesmerized in the music halls. Afterwards I found her diary, and she had drawn a picture round the date and the time, as if she thought it was going to be a really important day for her.'

The wife of a third victim described the calendar markings in more detail. 'Every single calendar and diary in the house was marked,' she said. 'It sounds a bit fanciful, but my brother plays chess, and the outline my husband drew on the calendars looked exactly like a chess piece.'

A chess piece. Benedict stared at the page, his sandwich forgotten. That's what I saw that day, he thought. That was the outline on the calendar and the desk diary in this house all those years ago. One of my parents – or my grandfather – sketched the outline of a chess piece on that date on the calendar. Only I didn't recognize it then.

There was not much point in searching the house for the calendar and the desk diary, but Benedict did not need to. He could still see them clearly. A chess piece – perhaps a pawn

– drawn around the date in red ink. And a smaller, similar, sketch around the time of three p.m.

Just over a hundred years ago, five people had been hell-bent on keeping a mysterious appointment on that date and at that time. They had drawn the outline of a chess piece on their calendars. All five had died. Twelve years ago, Benedict's parents and his grandfather had done the same thing and they had died as well.

But the people in the 1890s were murdered, he thought. My parents weren't murdered.

*'Weren't they, Benedict? Can you be sure of that? A driver can be forced to swerve on an icy road because he thinks he's seen someone standing in the road . . . Someone who never came forward to give evidence and who was never traced . . .'*

The words came raggedly, as if time had frayed them, but it was Declan's voice, soft and with that recognizable Irish lilt. Benedict frowned and tried to push it away. This was sheer nerves, nothing more; it was purely because this house had such bad memories for him. Declan no longer existed; he had been dead for more than fifty years.

But these newspapers existed, and the facts in them were real. He continued reading. The article, having finished reporting on the victims' families, next seized on the remark about mesmerism, and told its readers that one theory suggested the killer had made use of this contentious practice; that he could have somehow planted in each victim's mind the command to be at a specific place on a specific date. This did not give a motive, but when did a madman need a motive?

The police, it appeared, did not exactly support this theory, but had gone so far as to say if anyone noticed relatives or friends becoming preoccupied with an appointment about which there seemed to be unusual or worrying secrecy, police advice should be sought immediately. There followed a slightly schoolmasterly explanation about mesmerism and hypnosis, most of which Benedict skimmed, moving down to the closing paragraph which had the air of wanting to give a dramatic finale. It warned readers that there might still be undiscovered victims and pointed out that if that was so, the tally for the

Mesmer Murderer might be higher than that achieved by the notorious Whitechapel murderer dubbed Jack the Ripper.

Benedict foraged for his notebook and jotted all this information down, including the date of the newspapers. Then he reached for the third, final cutting.

This was much shorter, and was dated a couple of weeks after the first one. It described how the police had been admirably vigilant and energetic in their endeavours to lay the Mesmer Murderer by the heels. The killer had apparently been arrested and a trial set up. However, he had escaped from police custody while being transferred from Newgate Gaol. Police had refused to release his name, but the paper's reporter – by dint of ingenuity and one of the brand new Eastman Kodak 'Brownie' cameras – had managed to obtain a photograph of the killer.

Staring from the page of slightly smudgy newsprint was the face that had haunted Benedict for the last twelve years. The face of his great-grandfather. Declan Doyle.

# FOUR

The closing sentence of the newspaper article stated that the police had no more leads and, at the time of going to press, the Mesmer Murderer had not been recaptured.

Of course he wasn't, thought Benedict, sitting back, his mind in turmoil, the grey and black image on the page burning deep into his brain. He never was recaptured.

The mention of Victorian serial killers always brought to people's mind one iconic image: the silhouette of a black-cloaked killer, only ever known as Jack the Ripper, forever surrounded by the swirling mists of a Victorian London 'pea-souper', a case of glinting surgical knives at his side . . . But Jack, it appeared, had had a rival for the dark title and that rival had been Declan Doyle.

Declan had been the Ripper turned respectable. After the killings, he must have gone to ground somewhere and later bought Holly Lodge – although God knew how he afforded it, thought Benedict – then married and settled down into prosperous, middle-class London society. Who had he married? Benedict did not know anything about his great-grandmother, Declan's wife, although he had a vague impression she had died young. But whoever she was, had she known she was married to a murderer?

He could feel the familiar needle-jabs of apprehension scratching at his mind again, and, after a moment, he forced himself to look across at the old dressing-table mirror. Did something move in its depths? Something like a piece of old cine film struggling to come into focus?

And then, between one heartbeat and the next, he was there. The man who had walked in and out of Benedict's mind for the last twelve years, the man whose face had stared out of the old newspaper. Declan Doyle, who had apparently prowled Victorian Docklands and slaughtered five people. Three men and two women, thought Benedict, unable to look away. Declan was standing as he always did, slightly sideways on so that one side of his face was partially hidden, but Benedict could see details he had never seen before. The vivid blue eyes, the tumble of dark glossy hair, the soaring cheekbones . . . You might have been a murderer, thought Benedict, but you must have been a knockout, you really must.

'*I was . . . There was many a lady, Benedict . . .*' There was an unmistakable note of amusement in the silvery voice now.

The last thing Benedict wanted was to respond, but he could not help it.

'Why did you leave Ireland?' he said softly.

'*Because of Romilly.*'

Benedict was not actually hearing the words, he was feeling them etch themselves into his mind. He thought if anyone else had been in the room they would not have heard them.

'*She was a wild one, that Romilly. You'd think butter wouldn't melt – you'd think the saints themselves would trust her with their salvation, but she was as bold as a tomcat under all the fragile innocence. Red hair and skin like polished ivory. And eyes that would eat your soul. There are some eyes that can do that, did you know that, Benedict?*'

'No,' said Benedict shortly. 'In any case I don't believe you.'

'*But one day, Benedict, you will, because one day you'll walk with me along those cliffs on Galway's coast, and we'll see the devil's watchtower together, and you'll understand what happened that day and why I can reach out across the years like this . . . There are chords deep within the mind, Benedict, and they can resonate far longer than anyone realizes . . .*'

The glinting needle-points dug harder into Benedict's mind, splintering it into jagged, painful fragments. He gasped and put up his hands in an automatic gesture of defence. As he did so, he felt, quite distinctly, a hand – a dry, light hand – close around his and pull him down into that place he had glimpsed all those years ago . . . The place where there was a wild lonely coastline with black jagged cliffs and the ancient watchtower.

The place where the devil walked . . .

*Ireland, 1890s*

Declan Doyle and Colm Rourke had never entirely forgotten their vow that they would one day go up to the devil's watch-tower and beard the mysterious, sinister Nicholas Sheehan in his lair. At odd intervals over the years they reminded one another of it. Wouldn't it be a fine thing to do, they said, and wouldn't it impress all the girls in Kilglenn and Kilderry too, and maybe even beyond.

But it was not until they were both nearly nineteen that they actually made good their boast, although as Declan said, it was not for the lack of wanting that they put it off so long. Colm said if truth were to be told, they did not actually put it off, rather it put them off. There were always so many other things they had to be doing. There were tasks in each of their homes – Colm's father had died a few years earlier, so he had to help with carrying and fetching and daily errands. Declan, who had a full complement of parents, was server at Mass each Sunday, which meant attending extra religious classes. They were both in the church choir which meant a practice every Thursday so they could whoop out the *Kyrie* at High Mass while the rest of the congregation was surreptitiously sleeping off the poteen taken in Fintan Reilly's bar the night before or laying bets on how long Father O'Brian's sermon would last.

And there was school every day in Kilderry so they would not grow up like tinkers' children without a scrap of book-learning to their name. They went there on the back of Fintan's cart, which he took to Kilderry every morning to replenish his bar after the exigencies of the previous night, apart from Mondays since not even Fintan dared open his bar on Sundays. Declan's father had promised to look out for a couple of bicycles for next spring so the two boys could cycle to school and back home, because Declan's mother did not like him to be riding on a cart that stank of last night's poteen and the gin Fintan kept for the hussies who enjoyed drinking it.

But no matter how they got there, both families were agreed that Declan and Colm must know how to read and write and to know a bit about history and geography. They had to learn some Latin as well, said the monks who ran the little school, and never mind about Latin being a dead language. It was not dead as far as the Church was concerned; in fact it was the universal language of Catholics. Imagine if they were to find themselves in a foreign country some day, and not know its language? How would they go on about confession in that situation? But if they could speak Latin, they could confess their sins in Latin and the priest – and never mind if he was French or German or Italian or anything else – would understand them.

'Be damned to confessing sins in a foreign country, I'd be too busy committing the sins to care,' said Colm, and Declan grinned and agreed it'd be great altogether to see a bit of the world.

Colm was good at mathematics and understanding about mechanical things. Declan shone in the classes for reading and writing. He was a dreamer, Colm sometimes said, to which Declan always retorted that didn't the world need a few dreamers, and it a wicked place.

'I'd like to be wicked,' said Colm, his eyes glowing. 'I'd like to create scandals and outrages, and I'd like to be talked about from here to – to England and America.'

But of the three children, growing up in Kilglenn, it was neither Colm nor Declan who created the scandal. It was Colm's cousin Romilly.

The evening was one of the silent scented evenings that sometimes came to Kilglenn at that time of the year. Everywhere was drenched in soft violet and indigo light, and the ocean was murmuring to itself instead of roaring gustily – the sounds so soft you could believe the creatures of the legends were singing inside them. On a night like this, if you stood on a particular point on the Moher Cliffs you could persuade yourself you were glimpsing the *sidhe* dancing on the water's surface – the ancient faery people who had chill inhuman blood in their veins, and who would pounce on the souls of men and drag them down to their world for ever.

'I think I'd go with them without having to be pounced on,' Colm said, as he and Declan stood looking out to the shimmering wastes.

'It's Homer's wine-dark sea tonight,' said Declan, staring across the water's surface.

'Wine was never that gloomy colour.'

'Your trouble is you've no romance in your soul.'

'I have plenty of romance,' began Colm hotly. 'In fact—' He broke off and turned to look back at the path that wound back down to the village. 'Someone's coming up the path,' he said.

It was unusual for anyone to venture out to this part of Kilglenn. Most people said it was too lonely and too steep, and the spray from the ocean was enough to give anyone a terrible dose of the pneumonia, but after a few drinks at Fintan's, they also reminded one another that the devil had once walked those cliffs. You couldn't trust him not to still do so if the mood took him – especially just when everyone had finally been relaxing and thinking he had left Kilglenn for richer pastures.

But tonight it was not the devil's footsteps Declan and Colm could hear coming towards them through the warm, scented May twilight. It was Colm's cousin, Romilly.

Her hair was dishevelled and streaming out behind her like copper silk, and her small face was tear-smudged. She ran up to them, gasping for breath, clutching Colm's hands.

'What's happened? Romilly, what's wrong?'

'Sit down and tell us,' said Declan, fishing in his pocket for a handkerchief.

'I was mad ever to agree,' said Romilly, sobbing into the handkerchief. 'I know I was mad. But he was persuasive, you know. The silver tongue of the devil, isn't that what they all say about him?'

'Say about who? Rom, stop crying and tell us properly.'

The story came out in hiccupping sobs, with frequent recourses to Declan's handkerchief, and many self-reproaches. She had been walking on the cliff side that very afternoon, said Romilly. Yes, she knew it was a stupid thing to be going up to that stretch of the cliff, but there were times you wanted to be on your own, away from everyone and everything.

This was understandable. Romilly had had to live with a series of her father's people ever since her parents died in the influenza outbreak four years back. Even Declan's mother, who disapproved of most girls on principle, said it was a disgrace the way Romilly Rourke was passed around like a lost parcel.

Anyway, said Romilly, wiping away a fresh batch of tears, she had gone up to the cliff side and that was where she had met him.

For a moment the two boys thought after all this was going to be a new episode in the story of the devil walking the Moher Cliffs, but in fact it was not the devil whom Romilly had encountered, although Declan said afterwards it might have been the devil's apostle.

It was Nicholas Sheehan. The disgraced priest who lived in mysterious seclusion in the old watchtower; the rebel hermit and the sinner (opinions were always divided on that point), whom legend said had challenged the devil to a chess game, and had won.

'He was walking on the cliffs as well,' said Romilly. 'It would have been rude not to say good afternoon, so I did. And we were quite near to the watchtower path, and he started talking to me about it. How it was built by a High King of Tara on the highest point he could find to watch for enemies. But how it was made very grand to impress the ladies of the court.'

'Nick Sheehan would know about trying to impress ladies,' said Colm caustically, at which Romilly began to cry all over again.

Father Sheehan – always supposing he still had any right to that title – had apparently suggested Romilly come up to the watchtower there and then. From the topmost window there was a marvellous view, he said. Why, on a clear day such as this one, you could almost imagine you were seeing all the way across to America. And even if they could not see America, Miss Rourke could take a look at the inside of the watchtower. Some of the stones were at least a thousand years old, and said by some to possess the magical arts of the long-ago High Kings. And there were books – all kind of curious and strange books, and some of those were believed to possess magical powers as well.

Declan and Colm exchanged a look, but did not speak.

'So I went,' said Romilly.

'You did? You went all the way up the path to the tower?'

'I did.'

'And . . . you went inside?' said Declan. Neither of the boys knew anyone who had actually gone inside the watchtower.

'I did,' said Romilly again. 'But it's no use asking me what it's like, because all I can remember is a room with light coming in through slitted windows – the kind of light you never saw before, so thin and pure you'd imagine you could cup it in your hands. And there were chairs and tables and everywhere was hung with silk and velvet. But I don't remember much more because he gave me a glass of wine and when I drank it I felt a bit – I don't know how to describe it – as if my mind didn't belong to my body any longer. And the next thing I knew we were lying on a bed – all velvets and silks, you'd never see anything finer if you toured the world. Cushions with gold tassels and all.'

'Oh, Jesus,' said Colm. 'Never mind the cushions, Romilly, tell me you got up and came home and that old villain didn't do anything to you.'

'I didn't come home,' said Romilly, beginning to cry all over again. 'I sat on the bed and he got on to it next to me, and he took off my clothes and then he took off his own clothes – well, I mean he took some off and unbuttoned others so he could—'

'We don't need to know that part,' said Declan hastily, not able to bear the image of Nick Sheehan, who must be forty at least, for God's sake, removing and unbuttoning in order to enable him to take Romilly's virginity.

For the virginity, it was now plain, had been well and truly taken.

'It hurt,' said Romilly, wrapping her arms around her body and shivering. 'I didn't know it'd hurt. You'd think they'd tell us that, wouldn't you? When we're being told we mustn't do it before we're married, I mean. You'd think they'd warn us it hurts, so we'd never want to do it anyway. It hurt a lot.'

As she said this she sent a sideways glance at the two boys – it would have been overstating it to call the glance sly, but they had the brief uncomfortable impression that Romilly was looking to see how they were taking her story and whether they were ready to proffer sympathy.

But clearly this was grossly unfair because obviously Romilly had suffered the ultimate disgrace for a girl. Declan and Colm sat for a long time with the sun setting in wild splendour over the ocean, Romilly telling the story over and over again. They both tried not to notice that more details were being added with each retelling.

'I won't stay in Kilglenn now,' said Romilly, sitting forward on the grass and hugging her knees with her arms. 'I can't.'

'Why? No one need ever know what happened,' said Declan.

'But what if there's a child? There might be. Because,' said Romilly with a display of knowledge that was as embarrassing to the two boys as it was unexpected, 'he didn't stop doing it to me before he . . . you know, the part that makes a baby.'

'Oh, Jesus,' said Colm, and Romilly, with unprecedented sharpness, said:

'I wish you wouldn't blaspheme so much, Colm. It's a sin to blaspheme.'

'It's a sin to rape innocent girls,' said Colm. 'That's enough to make the saints blaspheme.'

'And it's no use saying no one need know,' said Romilly. '*He* knows. I'll never be able to look him in the eye after today.'

'You don't need to look him in the eye. You don't need ever to see him,' said Declan.

'You can't run away,' said Colm. 'Where would you go? What about money?'

'I'd go to England,' said Romilly. 'And I can do it, because Nicholas Sheehan gave me some presents. Not money because he doesn't have money. But he has jewelled cups and silver platters and things like that.' It came out defiantly. 'He gave me some. He said I could sell them for a lot of money, and that I was a good and pretty girl and I deserved to have a reward.'

Colm, his eyes furious, said, 'I won't let you go.'

'You can't stop me. No one will miss me – I'm supposed to move on to the next lot of family next week anyhow. They'll just think I've gone early, and they won't bother to find out. I dare say they'll be glad I've gone, because I don't really fit anywhere, do I?'

'Yes, but you can't just go, Rom—'

'I can. I'll leave a note saying that's what I've done,' said Romilly. 'And I'll go on Sunday when everyone's at Mass.'

'I'm not letting her go,' said Colm, after they had walked with Romilly to her house and made sure she had gone inside primed with a story about tumbling down on the cliff path to account for her tear-stained face and general dishevelment.

'How will you stop her?'

'I'll confront bloody Nick Sheehan, the old villain,' said Colm, his eyes lighting up. 'That's what I'll do. I'll force him to leave Kilglenn for good. Then Romilly can stay.'

'How would you force him to leave?' said Declan.

'I'll say if he doesn't go, I'll bring Father O'Brian and the entire village out to the watchtower to throw him out,' said Colm, his eyes glowing with angry fervour. 'Like when they used to march a harlot out of the town with the rough music playing.'

The word 'harlot' was not often used nowadays and nobody had heard rough music played in Kilglenn for at least fifty years. Fintan, when the poteen got to him, sometimes spun a tale of how, as a boy, he had helped run a painted Jezebel out of Kilglenn, and described how the banging of saucepans and tinkers' pots had been as satisfying a sound as Gabriel blowing his trumpet on Judgement Day. Everyone enjoyed this story, although most people felt that for Fintan to berate painted Jezebels was a clear case of poacher turned gamekeeper, for the old rascal had broken just about every commandment during his life, with particular attention to the seventh.

'And I tell you what,' went on Colm, 'if Sheehan wasn't defrocked and excommunicated all those years ago, then he would be now if the truth got out. But,' he said, 'I'd rather put him to rout myself.'

'You're going up to the watchtower to confront him?'

'I am.'

'Then,' said Declan, 'I'm coming with you.'

They went the next morning, which was Saturday and which was, as Declan said, a time when anyone might be anywhere and no one would be particularly looking for them. Declan's mother said it was sad altogether when a boy could not be staying at home, and must be off stravaiging into the village, dinnerless. When Declan said he hadn't any appetite today, she scooped an apple and a wedge of freshly baked soda bread from the table and made him pocket both.

The path winding up to the watchtower was steep and narrow. Colm and Declan had walked past it hundreds of times, but neither of them had ever climbed to the very top of it.

The gentle May warmth no longer cast a scented balm on the air and the sky held the bruised darkness that heralded a storm. Far below, the Atlantic flung itself against the cliffs, and if the *sidhe* were abroad today they were in a wild and eldritch mood.

For the first half of the climb the watchtower was hidden from view by the rock face, but as they rounded a curve in the path, it reared up, a black and forbidding column against the sky.

'It looks,' said Declan, pausing to stare at it, 'as if it's leaning forward to inspect us, d'you think that?'

'You read too many books,' said Colm, but he too looked uneasily at the stark silhouette.

'Someone's looking down out of that window,' said Declan.

'It'll be Nick Sheehan, crouching up there like a spider watching a couple of flies approach his lair.'

'There's a door at the centre,' said Declan as they drew nearer.

'Did you think your man flew in and out of the place by the windows like a winged demon?' demanded Colm. 'Or that it was the door-less tower where Rapunzel was imprisoned?'

'I thought I was the one who read too many books,' said Declan.

The door was a low one, slightly pointed at the top like a church door, set deep into the stone walls, the surface black with age, but the huge ring handle gleaming in the sulky storm-light. As they drew nearer, the door opened, doing so with a slow deliberation that held such menace Declan thought it would not take much to send them helter-skelter back down the slope and be damned to being revenged. Then he

remembered they were doing this for Romilly and that Father
Sheehan was a libertine and a seducer of young girls, and he
took a deep breath, and went forward at Colm's side. Even
so, for a wild moment he thought he would not be surprised
if they found themselves confronted with Lucifer himself,
holding the door wide and bidding them, with honeyed and
sinister persuasiveness, to step inside.

It was not Lucifer who was standing in the doorway of the
watchtower, of course, although on closer inspection it might,
as Declan had once said, be one of his apostles.

Nicholas Sheehan. The man who, according to local legend,
had once been a devout priest, but who some deep dark cause
had forced to this lonely eyrie.

At first they thought he was younger than they had expected,
but as they drew nearer they revised this opinion, and thought
he was considerably older. Colm said afterwards that it was
impossible to even guess his age, and he might be anything
from thirty to sixty. His hair was dark and his face lean and
even slightly austere. There was the impression that he might
enjoy good music and wine and interesting conversation, and
this was the most disconcerting thing yet, because if you have
ascribed the role of unprincipled seducer and devil-befriender
to someone, you do not want to discover that person has an
appreciation of the good and gentle things in life.

'Good day to you,' said Nicholas Sheehan, and smiled so
charmingly that Declan and Colm almost smiled back. But
the smile doesn't reach his eyes, thought Declan. They're the
weariest eyes I ever saw.

'You're a long way from Kilglenn,' said Father Sheehan,
leaning against the door frame of the ancient watchtower. 'And
it's a fair old haul up that path. Will you come inside and take
a drink with me?'

'That's very trusting of you,' said Colm, after a moment,
and this time the smile did reach Sheehan's eyes.

'Oh, I'm not trusting in the least,' he said. 'But I know who
you are, so I'm taking a chance. You're Romilly Rourke's
cousin Colm, and you're his good friend Declan Doyle. A very
likely pair of boyos, I'd say, although you'll be stifled and
repressed by the outlook of the villagers, I don't doubt. Do

they still gather in Fintan Reilly's bar of an evening to put the world to rights, and believe themselves rebels and firebrands?' He stood back and indicated to them to come in. As they did so, he said, 'I don't imagine you're here to plunder my worldly goods and chattels, but in case you have that in mind, I should mention you'd be wasting your time.'

'Because you have hell's weapons in your armoury?' demanded Colm.

'My, what a very dramatic young man you are,' said Father Sheehan, looking at Colm with more interest. 'But I'm sorry to disappoint you, Colm. I haven't so much as a pitchfork stashed away. It's simply that I gave up possessing goods and chattels long ago.'

# FIVE

For a man who had given up worldly possessions, Father Sheehan seemed to live in considerable comfort. The stone walls inside the watchtower had been softened with tapestries of soft blues and greens and with ornate mirrors. Silken rugs lay on the floor, their colours dimmed by age, but glowing richly against the ancient oak and stone.

The minute Declan and Colm were inside they had the sensation of stepping neck-deep into a past that was very dark and chilling. They shared a thought: are we mad to be doing this? Then the memory of Romilly sobbing and distraught and threatening to leave Kilglenn came back, and they both followed Sheehan to an octagonal room where books lined the walls and several velvet-covered chairs were drawn up to a massive hearth. Even though it was May, the afternoon was dark and a fire burned, casting mysterious crimson shadows. Through the narrow windows came threads of deep blue light from the ocean, edging the firelight with violet.

'Sit down,' said Sheehan, and took a careless seat in one of the chairs, facing them. The glow from the fire washed over him, so that for a moment he was a creature of shadows and fire. 'A glass of wine?' Without waiting for their reply, he reached for a slender-necked decanter on a side table and poured three glasses.

Colm and Declan had hardly ever drunk wine, and they were certainly unused to alcohol of any kind at this time of the day. But Colm took the glass with slightly forced nonchalance and Declan followed suit. The wine was rich and potent, and they had the feeling that the scented firelight might have soaked into it.

'I'm thinking,' said Sheehan, leaning back in his chair, the fingers of his hand curled lazily round the stem of his wine glass, 'that this visit is connected with your little cousin. What a beautiful girl. Hasn't she a fine charm? And as persuasive as a witch on Beltane.'

'Persuasive?' said Colm sharply. 'Weren't you the one who was persuasive with her? In fact,' he said, setting down the wine glass and leaning forward, 'weren't you a whole lot more than persuasive, Father Sheehan?'

'You know I no longer have the right to that title,' said Sheehan, politely.

'They stripped it from you,' said Colm.

'No. I stripped it from myself.'

'You lost your belief?' said Declan, curious despite himself.

'I lost some beliefs. But you didn't come here to discuss beliefs.'

'We came to . . . to bring you to account over what you did to my cousin Romilly.' Declan saw Colm's eyes flicker as he said this and knew Colm must have heard how brash the words and the tone sounded compared to Sheehan's soft courtesies.

'I did nothing to your cousin Romilly. And if I weren't such a gentleman,' said Nick Sheehan, thoughtfully, 'I'd tell you that she went away very disappointed indeed.'

'You're saying she seduced you?' demanded Declan.

'I'm saying she tried. But I'm a little too old to be lured by sly innocents.'

'You're a black-hearted liar,' said Colm angrily.

'I promise you I am not. Your waif-like Romilly made it perfectly clear what she wanted. I made it clear I wasn't interested. I wasn't especially flattered by the approach,' said Sheehan and paused to drink more wine. 'Her real motive was money, of course.'

'You can't know what her motives were,' said Colm.

'Women usually do want money. Or are you both still too young to know that?'

'Did you give her any money?'

'I gave her objects of value that could be turned into money. She forced my hand,' said Sheehan. 'She threatened to tell people I had raped her, and I wasn't prepared to risk that. My solitude – my life here – is important to me. So I gave her more or less what she wanted.'

Anger had spiked into both boys' minds at the mocking implication that they were too young, but hard on its heels came the memory of Romilly saying, 'Nicholas Sheehan gave me presents. He said I could sell them.' Alongside that was the image of her expression and how she had looked at them through her tears as if to assess how they were receiving her story.

Declan said, 'Did you tell her she was a good and pretty girl?'

'Is that what she said? No. I told her she was a sly little liar, and she would one day get her just deserts.'

'I don't believe you,' said Colm, but there was a note of doubt in his voice. 'I think you seduced her and there needs to be a reckoning between us.'

'What kind of reckoning do you propose?'

'That you leave Kilglenn for good.'

'Aren't you the most dramatic young man ever, Colm Rourke?' said Sheehan. 'I'm not leaving this place.' Something flickered behind his eyes that neither of the boys could identify. He said, 'And you've only Romilly's word against mine for what happened.'

Colm leaned forward. 'The legend says you're a gambling man,' he said. 'If that's right, I see how we can resolve this with honour on both sides.'

'What had you in mind?'

'A game of chance. The winner to set the forfeit.'

Sheehan studied him. Then he said, 'Was it perhaps a game of chess you had in mind?'

With the words something seemed to shiver in the quiet room with its muted light, but Colm said firmly, 'Yes. Yes, it was.'

'You know the legend of the chess set?'

'I know one of them. And I'll play you for it,' said Colm. 'If I win, we'll agree that you dishonoured my cousin. You'll leave here for good. And I take the chess set.'

'And if I win?'

'I'll apologize and ensure my cousin doesn't repeat her story. The chessmen will stay with you.'

'The chessmen,' said Sheehan, 'will go where they choose.

You and I won't have any say in it.' He frowned, and Declan, eyeing him, thought Sheehan would never agree.

Then Sheehan stood up. 'Come with me,' he said.

In the stone entrance hall was a carved screen, which Sheehan moved aside to reveal a small door. There was a flight of stone steps immediately inside, very worn at the centre and leading into pitch darkness.

'I'll have to go ahead of you,' said Sheehan. 'The room is deep into the ground, and the steps are uneven. There's hardly any natural light, so I'll light lamps and you follow me.'

As they stood together at the head of the steps, waiting for the flare of light from below, Declan said in a furious whisper, 'Colm, you can't do this.'

'I can. Didn't we always vow we'd come up here one day and challenge Sheehan to a chess game and win the devil's powers off him?'

'We were children, for pity's sake. Can you even play chess?'

'I can,' said Colm, his jaw set stubbornly.

'But he'll trick you.'

'He will not. He's all show. No substance.'

'Yes, but this is the chess set that—'

'That's just an old legend and Sheehan probably spread it around to make himself more interesting. So will you shut up?'

'But—'

'He's got the lamps lit,' said Colm as light flared below them, and he began to descend the steps. After a moment Declan followed.

The steps spiralled round and were treacherously narrow. At the bottom, a door had been propped open, and beyond it was a stone-lined room. Colm and Declan had been expecting a conventional cellar, but this chamber was situated on the open side of the cliff face and one section of wall had a tiny barred window, barely two feet square, looking straight on to the ocean. Dull light came through it and there was the sound of the sea moaning against the rocks.

'You're in one of Ireland's deepest pockets of memory,' said Sheehan, who had set three oil lamps around the room. 'This place is drenched in ancient memories – sometimes, on a still night, it's almost possible to hear them. There are chords within the mind, you know. If you know how to pluck them they go on resonating for far longer than you'd imagine.'

At the centre of the room was a small round table with two chairs drawn up to it. Nicholas Sheehan tilted one of the lamps slightly and light fell directly on to the table's surface. Colm and Declan caught their breath, for set out on the table, reflecting fathoms deep in the polished surface, was the sinister chess set from the legend.

It was the most beautiful and yet also the most repellent thing either of them had ever seen. The black pieces were ebony and jet, studded with tiny iridescent chips of something they did not recognize, the pawns about five inches high, the kings and queens two or three inches more. The white figures were ivory, crusted with what looked like tiny pearls. The carved armour gleamed and the crowns sparkled and it was easy to think the figures moved in the lamplight – that a fold of a king's cloak twitched, that a prancing knight tightened his rein.

For a moment no one spoke, then Sheehan said softly, 'Yes, they are beautiful, aren't they? The white pieces are ivory and white jade, with seed pearls. The black are ebony and black jade with black diamonds. But it's said they bring ill luck,' he said, and Declan suddenly had the impression that Sheehan was afraid.

'I'll risk that.' Colm was staring at the chess figures, and Declan was aware of a growing unease because Colm's eyes held something he had never seen before. But Colm seated himself at the table, and Nicholas Sheehan took the chair facing him.

'Declan, are you going to stay?'

'I am,' said Declan to Sheehan, and sat down where he could see the faces of the two combatants.

'And,' said Colm, with an edge to his voice, 'we'll both take another glass of wine.'

Storm clouds were gathering outside as they began to play, and the light from the lamps cast pools of light. But outside of those pools, Declan had the increasing feeling that something hid in the thick shadows and that it watched from sly narrow eyes.

Sheehan's expression was unreadable. He played the black pieces, and when Colm captured his bishop, Sheehan shrugged and said, 'A weak piece. Of little account. In Persian tradition, the piece was originally an elephant. Later, the Europeans called it *Aufin*. *Aufin* is related to a French word for fool. It's curious how language merges one with another, isn't it, and produces totally different words and meanings? But in that case the transformation was appropriate, for most bishops I ever met were fools anyway.'

Colm said, 'Chess is a Persian game, isn't it?'

'Who knows? Some tell how the God Euphron created it, or that it began as a dice-playing game at the Siege of Troy. But most legends place its origins in India, although it was supposed to be part of the princely education of Persian nobility.'

'You're very knowledgeable,' said Colm, with reluctant admiration.

'I learned a little – a very little – from the man who owned this set before me. He possessed far more knowledge than I ever will,' said Sheehan.

When Sheehan's King was placed in jeopardy, Colm gave a soft hoot of triumph, and Sheehan said, 'Yes, that's a telling move. But you should not feel too pleased with yourself. The King is the most important piece, but it's the Queen who is the most powerful.'

But as the black pieces were taken with measured inexorability, Colm and Declan had the impression that Sheehan no longer cared if he won or lost. Whether he was suddenly tired of the old legend and wanted to put an end to it, they had no idea, but at length the black Queen was cornered. As Colm reached out to lift the ebony figure from the board, the tiny jewelled eyes in the carved head caught the light and seemed to glint evilly. Colm hesitated. Then he shrugged and his fingers closed round the figure.

Sheehan and Colm looked at one another for a long moment. Then Sheehan said, 'Congratulations, Colm. A game well played. I imagine you're about to demand I keep our bargain.'

'I am.'

'Leave Kilglenn? Leave this tower?'

'That was the agreement.'

'A gentleman's agreement only. And,' said Sheehan, 'it's a long while since I was regarded as a gentleman.'

Colm said, 'You're reneging on the deal?'

'An ugly word.'

'Well?'

'I'm not leaving this place,' said Sheehan. 'I can't.'

As the words fell on the old room, something seemed to enter it – something that was not part of the ocean or the greasy lamplight, but that hissed its way through the black bars of the tiny window and scalded its way round the old walls.

'Then by God, I'll make you!'

'Colm, no!' Declan started forward, but Colm was already on his feet, his fists clenched, and Declan had the astonishing impression that the hissing anger had poured into Colm and glared from his eyes.

Sheehan threw up a hand to defend himself, backing away. In doing so, he stumbled against the chess table and fell. His head hit the stone floor with a sickening crunch and his neck lolled at a dreadful angle. There was a gasping exhalation of breath, then his eyes rolled upwards and he was still.

The scalding anger drained from the room as quickly as it had come, and Colm stood staring down at the prone figure, white-faced, his eyes no longer holding the terrible glare.

'He's dead,' said Declan in panic. 'Mother of God, he's dead and it's your fault, you bloody madman.'

'He's shamming,' said Colm, but there was a note of uncertainty in his voice. 'Feel for a heartbeat – it'll be pounding away like a tinker's drum. Well?' he said, as Declan knelt down and thrust a hand inside Nicholas Sheehan's jacket.

'Nothing. Wait though – a mirror.'

'What in God's name . . . ?'

'You put a mirror to somebody's lips to see are they breathing. If they are, it mists the mirror. Fetch that glass from the wall there.'

'I'm telling you he'll sit up in a minute and laugh at us,'

said Colm, but he unhooked the small oval mirror from the wall and between them they lowered it over Sheehan's face.

'Nothing,' said Declan presently. 'He's not breathing. He's dead.'

'It's my fault,' said Colm, staring at Sheehan's body, in horror. 'Only, I didn't mean to kill him, I swear to all the saints. I didn't so much as touch him, Declan, you know that.'

'I do know. But would anyone else?' said Declan.

'They'll hang me for a murderer.'

'Of course they won't.'

'He's a priest, for God's sake! Of course they will! What do I do?'

'I don't know.'

'Well, *think*. Can we leave him here and not know anything? Will he be missed?'

'He might be missed after a few days,' said Declan, trying to think clearly. 'He's noticeable. If he's around in Kilglenn or even Kilderry, people always remember seeing him because of the old story about the chessmen.'

The chessmen. They both glanced uneasily at the carved figures.

'And,' said Declan, speaking reluctantly, 'for all he set himself up as a . . . a hermit, I think he has visitors here at times. People seek him out. My father once said some of the young men considering entering the Church come to talk to him. Colm, his body will be found, and people will know he was killed. There's a socking great bruise on his head.'

'Where he hit it on the ground.'

'Yes, but would people think someone had hit him with a fist?'

'Well, you had nothing to do with it,' said Colm firmly.

'Will you shut up? I'm as much a part of this as you. Let's think what to do. Were we seen coming up here, d'you think?'

'We might have been.' Colm was still looking down at Sheehan's body. It lay where it had fallen, the ocean light mingling eerily with the lamplight, casting strangely coloured shadows over it. 'They'll piece it together,' he said. 'Once the body's found the *Garda* will work it all out. Evidence. Clues.'

They both knew this was a real danger. Fintan's Bar

sometimes had a publication called *Strand Magazine* which they read after the others had finished with it, devouring the exploits of the Baker Street detective called Sherlock Holmes. Almost all of Mr Holmes' crimes took place in England, but the methods employed by the English police to track down a murderer would not be much different from the ones the *Garda* would use in Ireland.

'You're right,' said Declan. 'They'll question everyone. They'll know we were here.'

'Not if we destroy the evidence,' said Colm. 'All of it – including Sheehan's body.'

'How?'

'There's only one way,' said Colm.

# SIX

Their minds had always fitted together so well that they scarcely needed to consult each other as they worked. Leaving Sheehan's body where it was, they dragged a heavy oak chest out of the room. Then they closed the door on the room and pushed the chest hard against it.

'That's fine,' said Colm, after they had tested it. 'It's wedging the door shut. No one will be able to get in there until it's too late.'

They had left one oil lamp inside, but they carried the other two up the steps. In the tapestry-hung room where Sheehan had poured the wine, they tumbled books from the shelves, choosing them at random and using them to build a small bonfire at the centre of the room.

'You realize we could be destroying valuable books?' said Declan, hesitating.

'If we don't, something more precious and valuable than books might end in being destroyed,' said Colm. 'Me.'

'True, O King.'

'And *don't* quote the Old Testament at me!'

'Sorry. Will we drag some of those tapestries down while we're about it?'

They did so, and surveyed the heap of books and tapestries critically.

'I think that's as good as we'll get,' said Colm.

'And everything's as dry as kindling; it'll go up like the deepest cavern of hell.'

'I hope so. This room's directly over the underground room so everything down there should burn.' He looked frightened, then said, 'But in the long run, we're all going to burn,' and tipped the oil from the lamps over the bonfire. 'Get ready to run as if the devil's chasing you,' he said, and Declan struck the tinder.

As the glowing tinder fell on to the bonfire and flames burst upwards, Colm cried, 'Run!'

'And slam the doors as we go,' gasped Declan, tumbling across the hall to the door. 'It'll keep the fire contained for a while and we need that underground room to *burn*.'

They got outside and skidded breathlessly down the first few yards of the path, expecting every minute to hear cries and to see people running up the cliff path, ready to douse the fire. But no one appeared and a quarter of the way down they stopped to look back.

'Nothing's happening,' said Colm, staring up at the black monolith of the tower.

'Yes – look, there's smoke coming through the bricks on the left.'

'Only a few wisps, though. Will we go back to make sure it's burning up?'

'They'll be annoyed at home if we're late,' said Declan doubtfully.

'They'll be more than annoyed if I'm hanged for Sheehan's murder. I'll go on my own if you want.'

'No, I'll come too.'

They went back up the path, skirting the tower's front and making a cautious way around the cliff face. There was not exactly a way across the open face of this part of the Moher Cliffs, but there was a series of crevices and jutting rock spurs that made it possible to swarm partly across. Colm and Declan had clambered over these cliffs almost since they could walk, and they knew the way as well as they knew their own gardens. Even so, negotiating them was hazardous and they did not speak until they were close to the base of the watchtower.

'It *is* burning,' said Colm, on a note of relief. 'See over there. There're flames coming out from between the stones.'

'And you can smell the smoke,' said Declan. 'It's funny that you don't see the barred window of that underground room from here, isn't it? All the times we've been out here, and we've never once seen it.'

'It'll be beyond that spur of rock,' said Colm. 'See there, where it overhangs? We've never tried to get round there.'

'We don't need to get round it now, do we?' The spur of rock was large and it thrust menacingly out of the rocks.

'No, because the fire's burning up properly now; you can see the glow . . .' Colm broke off and turned to stare at Declan. The dull crimson glow mingled with the light of the approaching storm, casting a shadow over his face. 'Did you hear that?'

'It was the sea,' said Declan after a moment.

'It sounded like somebody shouting,' said Colm.

'Someone who saw the fire? Raising the alarm?'

'I think it came from inside the tower,' said Colm.

They looked upwards, fear clutching them. The watchtower reared up into the bruised sky, the black stones already tinged with angry red.

'Was it Sheehan?' said Declan. 'Oh God, could he still be alive in there?'

'We thought he was dead,' said Colm, but he too sounded uncertain.

'But what if he wasn't? After all . . .' Declan broke off because this time they both heard the cry, and there was no mistaking it. It was Sheehan's voice and he was shouting for help.

'*Help me . . .*'

'What do we do?' said Colm. 'Can we get him out?'

'We'll have to try.' Declan began scrambling towards the jutting piece of rock, with the barred window just out of sight beyond it.

'No!' said Colm. 'We'd be better to go back up to the tower and get him out that way.'

'There's no time!' said Declan angrily, and even as he spoke a column of flame shot upwards. 'The fire'll be raging – we'd never get to that underground room. We'll have to get him out through the sea window.'

But they were both remembering that the window was only two feet square, with three thick iron bars. A cat could not get through the space, let alone a grown man.

'We'll have to try, though,' said Declan. 'The fire might have loosened the bars.'

Negotiating the rock spur was difficult, but there were foot-holds and crevices and also thick clumps of rock vegetation to cling to. The wind shrieked around them and tore at their hair, and they were both drenched from the sea spray, but eventually they got round the rock. A few feet ahead was the window to the underground room.

Nicholas Sheehan was peering through it, his face slicked with sweat and his eyes wild with terror.

'We'll get you out!' shouted Declan. His words were snatched away by the sea, but he thought Sheehan heard.

'The door's wedged,' said Sheehan. 'I can't get out of here. You must get help.'

'There isn't time. We'll try to knock out the bars and get you out this way.'

'You'll never do it. You bloody villain, Colm Rourke, you thought you'd left me for dead, didn't you?' The words came raggedly but they were filled with hatred and fear.

'Yes,' panted Colm. 'But we'll put it right – I swear we will.'

They were on each side of the barred window now, but when they grasped the bars, intending to pull on them, Declan yelped with pain.

'They're as hot as a griddle,' he said, gasping.

'Of course they are, you fool, this whole room's heating up,' cried Sheehan. 'The stone walls are acting as a conductor to the fire – this room's turning into a dry oven. If you don't get me out I'm going to bake to death. For Christ's sake, do something!'

'I'll go for help,' said Colm.

'There isn't time! Oh Jesus, it's getting hotter by the minute. Oh God, I never meant to die like this!'

'You won't die,' said Colm. 'We'll get you out.'

'Then bloody do it!'

Working on the side of the cliff face, in the gathering darkness shot through with fire streaks, was appallingly difficult, but they managed to fashion a rope from Declan's sweater and Colm's scarf, and to tie it round one of the bars. But the bars were glowing so hot their hands blistered, and the first attempt to secure the makeshift rope caused the wool to shrivel.

'Again!' cried Sheehan. 'Wait, use this as well.' His hands shaking, he passed them a length of cord – Declan thought he had torn it from one of the tapestries.

This time the makeshift rope held and they were able to get purchase on the bars and pull.

'It's still no use,' gasped Colm after several minutes. 'They're stuck fast.'

Sheehan was gasping and sobbing, and waves of intense heat were belching out from the room. Declan and Colm were starting to realize with horror that they were not going to succeed. Nicholas Sheehan was going to be slowly roasted alive.

It was already happening. Sheehan's skin was flushed and shiny, and he was breathing harshly and painfully. Then, quite suddenly, he said, in a clearer voice than he had yet used, 'You won't succeed. I'm going to die. And it'll be a dreadful death—'

'No, it'll be fine,' cried Declan, still furiously working to loosen one of the iron bars.

'People will have seen the fire,' said Colm eagerly, 'and they'll be coming out here.'

'It'll be too late. You aren't going to get me out. But there's one thing you can do – and this is a request from a dying man . . .'

'What—?'

'Absolve my soul from all its sins.'

They stared at him, not understanding.

'No,' said Colm. 'You need a priest, and we'll never get one out here in time.'

'There's another way – it might be an empty superstition, but it's one of the oldest beliefs known.' Sheehan was standing as close to the window as he could; his hair was drenched with sweat and his eyes were violently bloodshot. 'And it might save me from damnation—'

Without thinking, Declan said, 'Then you did do it? The stories are true about you beating the devil.'

'Let the legend live,' said Sheehan, and incredibly a smile twisted his face so that for a moment they both saw the urbane, slightly mocking man they had met hours earlier. 'And if it's proof you want . . .' He thrust a hand through the bars, seeming hardly to notice that the fierce heat from the iron burned his fingers. 'Take what's left.'

'What . . . ?' Declan began, then saw it was the black King from the chess set.

'Take it and do what I'm asking,' said Sheehan urgently. 'I daren't die with my sins all still with me. I *daren't*. Don't you know the devil never keeps his side of a bargain?'

Declan hesitated, and it was Colm who nodded and reached out a hand to take the carved figure. Declan thought he shuddered as his fingers closed over it.

Sheehan was doubling over, gasping and moaning. Mingled with the sweat pouring down his face were drops of thick yellow fluid. Exactly, thought Declan with horror, like when you bake an apple in the oven and the skin starts to split and the juices leak out. Then with what was clearly an immense effort, Sheehan said, 'The old ritual – the ritual performed before Christianity even began. The ritual that's in the Old Testament – you've had the monks' teaching, you must know it. The Hebrew ritual of the scapegoat?'

'Yes – Aaron confessed all the sins of the Children of Israel over the head of a live goat,' said Declan. 'Then they sent the goat into the wilderness to die, believing it bore all their sins.'

'It's in Leviticus as well,' said Sheehan. 'The sins of one are transferred to another. Do that for me now. Take on the burden of my sins.'

'But – how?'

'They'd do it with bread and wine,' said Sheehan. 'But if the stories are right, any piece of food and drop of liquid will serve.'

Declan said, 'I have an apple. And a wedge of soda bread.'

'Apples have juice. And bread is the staff of life. Do it, Declan.'

'Me?'

'Colm's already half tainted with murder. The sin-eater has to be as innocent as possible. But oh God, hurry,' said Sheehan. 'I'll be beyond sanity very soon.'

'Declan, you can't,' said Colm in an urgent whisper. 'This is wrong.'

'But he's going to die. He's facing screaming agony. He *knows* he is. So if this makes him feel better, it can't be so wrong. And he's a priest, or he was once. Wouldn't that mean he knows what he's talking about?'

'Wouldn't the devil quote Scriptures for his own ends?' retorted Colm. 'Declan, this isn't a Catholic ritual – it might not even be Christian. And supposing it – um – works? You don't know what his sins are. You don't know what you'd be taking on your soul.'

'I'll confess tomorrow. My sins and his.'

'Do it!' screamed Sheehan. 'At least let me know I won't die in mortal sin! Oh God, I'm burning! My stomach . . . My guts are on fire . . .'

In a strained, helpless voice, Declan said, 'Tell me what to do.'

In the end it was simple enough.

Declan and Colm managed to slice a small piece of the apple, and to crumble the soda bread which they passed through the bars. Sheehan grabbed the fragments of food and in a struggling, dried-out voice, sobbed out his sins. He spoke half in English, half in Latin, but his words were so blurred with agony and terror that the boys could not hear many of them.

Then Sheehan began to chant the Act of Contrition.

'*Confiteor Deo omnipotenti, istis Sanctis et omnibus Sanctis et tibi frater, quia peccavi in cogitatione, in locutione, in opere, in pollutione mentis et corporis. Ideo precor te, ora pro me.*'

The familiar Latin fell raggedly on the fire-streaked darkness, and for a moment it almost seemed as if the shrieking wind seized the words and tore them mockingly to shreds.

'The food,' gasped Sheehan. 'Take it from me. The sins will go from me with it.'

Declan hesitated, but when Sheehan thrust the already-discolouring sliver of apple and the drying bread back through the bars, he took them, although he was uneasily aware of the dark echoes of the Mass, and he knew Colm was, too. The iron staves were so intensely hot by this time that he burned his hand, and cried out from the pain. But it would be a pinprick compared to what Nicholas Sheehan was already suffering.

'Eat!' cried Sheehan. 'You must eat it!' and Declan, shivering despite the glowing heat from the tower, nodded and crammed the food into his mouth. He gagged a couple of times and for a dreadful moment thought he would actually be sick, but he managed to swallow most of it. Then he half fell against the cliff face, gasping.

Colm said urgently, 'We have to go back now.'

'We can't leave him.'

'Declan, this cliff face is so hot we'll soon roast to death ourselves,' said Colm, but he said it in a low voice so Sheehan would not hear.

Declan looked back into the room. Sheehan was no longer standing near the window; they could just see him lying in a dreadful huddle on the ground at the room's centre. His hair was dried and most of it had fallen out, and he seemed to be curling in on himself.

'Look at his hands,' said Colm. 'D'you see his fingernails?'

Sheehan's hands were curled into claws, the nails blackened. Mercifully they could not see his face, but they could see the skin of his neck was dark and leathery-looking, and the image of a piece of pork roasting in an oven came sickeningly to them. This time it was Colm who turned away, retching. When the spasm passed, he turned back, and his face looked suddenly old, as if the flesh had shrunk from the bones. He said, 'Declan, we *have* to go now,' and this time Declan nodded.

They began a cautious journey back around the rock spur and across the cliff face. They had reached the path when, from within the glowing watchtower, they heard Sheehan begin to scream.

They sat together, huddled on the ground, knowing they would be missed at their homes, but unable to leave. The tower was still burning, but the stones were too thick and too stubborn to actually crumble. The fire would burn itself out, and the watchtower, rumoured to have been built by the ancient Kings of Ireland, would go on standing, a blackened ruin.

Presently, Declan said, 'He's not screaming now, is he?'

'No.'

'He'll be dead.'

'Yes. Will we say a prayer for him?'

'All right.'

Self-consciously they chanted the paternoster, and then began to make their way home.

'Did you throw away that chess figure?' said Declan suddenly.

'I'll do it later. When no one's around.' Colm's voice sounded distant, but Declan was relieved that his face no longer had the dry, shrunken look. He was still staring at the tower. 'There was a strange thing,' he said. 'When Sheehan passed the figure through the bars, I thought his hand closed round mine.'

'Did it?'

'No,' said Colm. 'For when I looked at him, I saw both his hands were wrapped around his body – like you do when you're in bad pain.' He looked at Declan from the corners of his eyes. 'But something reached out from that room and clasped my hand,' he said. 'Something very small – nearly as small as a baby's hand would be. But leathery feeling. Dry. As dry as old parchment.'

'You imagined it,' said Declan. 'Or it really was Sheehan's hand you felt, but it was – um – already partly burned. It'd feel dry and small.'

'It'd be that, wouldn't it?' said Colm, eagerly. He seemed to relax a little, then he said, 'Did you feel the sins go into you?'

'No,' said Declan.

'I didn't think you did. But you'll have to find a priest to confess to. Because if you die with all Sheehan's sins on you, you'll go straight to hell.'

*The present*

Coming out of Declan's world was like coming up through fathoms of thick swirling green water. Benedict was aware of jagged lights somewhere far above his head, like glinting sunlight on sea. That's Holly Lodge, he thought in confusion. That's where I belong. I should try to get back there.

But it seemed a very long way, and it took every shred of his strength and resolve to reach upwards. Then the scents and the shapes of Holly Lodge closed around him and he realized he had been lying on the floor where he must have fallen. His head ached and the light, coming through the tall windows, struck painfully across his eyes. He winced and put up a hand to shield them. Nobody had ever said how very different the light had been a hundred and twenty years ago. But of course no one would, thought Benedict. They wouldn't know. Unless you had actually been there and seen it . . .

The scent of the burning watchtower was still in his nostrils, and horridly mingled with it was that other dreadful scent that might have been roasting meat . . . He shuddered and fought down a lurch of nausea, then, moving cautiously, attempted to sit up. He was dizzy, but the sick feeling was passing. Using the side of the desk for ballast, he tried to stand up, but the dizziness overwhelmed him and he fell back, grasping at the desk's edge to save himself. The drop-down desk flap tilted and the desk partly overbalanced. Several of the small drawers flew open, and the sheaf of newspaper cuttings about the Mesmer Murderer slid to the ground. A shower of old pens and notepaper came with them.

And something else. Something that fell to the ground with a soft thud and lay inches from Benedict's hand.

A carved figure, some eight or ten inches high, dulled with the dust of years, but unmistakably fashioned from a smooth black substance. Ebony, thought Benedict, staring at it. The figure was studded with tiny glinting black gems and beads of something that might be jet. There were the folds of a cloak around it, and the sharp outline of a crown encircled the head. In one hand was a slender staff, tipped with a further crown.

The black king from the devil's chess set. The figure that the dying Nicholas Sheehan had given to Declan and Colm over a century ago.

Benedict reached out to it and, as his hand closed around it, he thought he felt tiny fingers curling around his. Fingers that were almost small enough to belong to a baby, but that were as dry as old parchment.

The darkness started to close over him once again, but before it did so, someone bent over him, and Declan's strong blue eyes looked down into his.

# SEVEN

The French windows opened on to what was clearly a dining room. It smelled a bit damp, but Nell, who was fairly used to entering old houses in her work, had encountered a lot worse.

She expected Benedict Doyle to come down to greet her, but he did not, so she went through the dining room into a big shadowy hall, and called out to him.

'Hello? I got in all right. I'm Nell West – Nina's friend, about the antiques.'

There was still no response, although she had the feeling there was someone quite nearby, listening. This was disconcerting and probably simply nerves, so Nell walked across the hall, deliberately clattering her footsteps to make extra noise. She waited for a few moments, but when he still did not appear she opened all the doors on the ground floor and looked into each room. Nothing moved in any of them, unless you counted a few drifting cobwebs, and the impression of an army of spiders indignantly scuttling away from the sudden ingress of light. There did not seem to be anything of particular interest in any of them, but Nina had said Holly Lodge had been rented for a number of years, so probably the main stuff was stored behind a locked door somewhere. Nell paused in a smaller room that might have been a study, running her hand over the dulled surface of a mahogany desk, wanting to restore the grain to life.

It was already growing dark and shadows were crawling out from the corners. She would switch on the next light she came to and hope the electricity was on. She still did not understand why the man she had seen had not come down to meet her. She went back to the hall and started up the wide stairway. There was a big landing, with a second flight of stairs at the far end. He must be up there on the second floor. Nell called out again.

'Hello? Are you here? Is it all right to come up?'

Her words echoed eerily and there was still no response. She glanced at the row of closed doors. Perhaps the man was in one of those rooms and perhaps he really had not heard her. She was about to open the first, when a movement from the second flight of stairs made her jump. But it could only be Benedict so Nell went purposefully towards the stairs, wishing this house was not so full of shadows.

The stairs turned sharply to the left and, as she negotiated this turn, an uncertain light came in through a narrow window. It slanted across the unconscious body of a young man with dark hair lying on the half-landing. Bending over him was a second, older-looking man.

Nell froze, a shaft of panic slicing through her, then tensed her muscles to run back down the stairs and out to the safety of the street. But almost in the same moment she saw it was not after all the classic scenario of a householder attacked and the attacker preparing to finish his victim off. Whoever the older man was, he had loosened the unconscious boy's collar, clearly attempting to revive him. But Nell still hesitated, and, as if aware of her apprehension, the man half-turned to look at her. Her first impression that he was too old to be Benedict Doyle had been right; he was probably in his mid-thirties and there was a brief impression of a rather pale, lean face. His face was still partly in deep shadow, but there was the definite glint of very vivid blue eyes.

'What's happened?' said Nell, wishing he would say something. 'I'm Nell West. I'm a friend of Nina's. Is this Benedict? Has he fainted? Have you called a doctor – an ambulance?'

The man made a brief gesture with one hand that might have meant anything, and bent over Benedict again, obviously more concerned with him than with Nina's friend.

Nell said, 'He's out cold, isn't he? Ought I to dial nine nine nine?'

He frowned, still bending over Benedict, then nodded.

'My phone's downstairs in my bag,' said Nell, relieved to have something definite to do, and to be summoning help. 'I'll go down and make the call. Um – he's breathing and everything is he?' But she could already see the slight rise and fall

of the unconscious young man's chest. Perhaps he had fallen
down the stairs and knocked himself out, or perhaps he was
an epileptic or something like that.

She went quickly back to the ground floor, and made the
call. It was annoying not to be able to provide any details, but
the fact that someone was unconscious seemed to trigger an
instant response.

'They'll be with you as fast as possible,' said the disem-
bodied voice. 'Traffic permitting. But they'll put on the sirens
for unconsciousness. Are you there on your own? D'you want
to stay on the line until the paramedics get there?'

'No, that's all right,' said Nell. 'There's someone else here.'

'Don't move the patient at all,' said the voice. 'Just put a
blanket over him.'

'Yes, I'll do that. Thank you very much.'

She went back to the foot of the stairs, and called up. 'The
ambulance is on its way. They said not to move him, but to
cover him up. I'll see if I can find a blanket or a rug.'

She opened several doors on the first floor before finding
a big airing cupboard. Taking out a thick blanket, she went
back upstairs. The unknown man seemed to have vanished;
probably he had gone downstairs to open the front door for
the ambulance, and most likely he had called out to tell her
but she had not heard. This house seemed to have the curious
quality of smothering sound. Nell put the blanket over the
still-unconscious Benedict, and sat down on the floor, taking
his hand in hers. Her touch seemed to reach him, because
after a moment his fingers tightened around hers and his eyes
opened. He looked up at her and Nell saw he had the same
vivid blue eyes as the older man, although at the moment
they were confused.

Nell said quickly, 'You're quite safe, but you fainted or
something, so we're getting you checked out. I'm Nell West
– Nina's friend.'

His gaze went beyond her. 'Where's Declan?'

Declan must be the older man. 'He's gone down to let the
paramedics in,' said Nell.

'He was here . . .' His voice sounded a bit slurred; Nell did
not know if it was how he normally spoke. He frowned, then

said, 'The fire – oh God, we were trying to stop the fire – have they done that yet?'

'There's no fire,' said Nell, slightly puzzled but not unduly so. 'You're in Holly Lodge. I think you fainted or fell down the stairs.'

'I didn't fall. At least I don't think I did . . . There was a fire – the watchtower. It was burning – and he was inside and we couldn't get him out – oh God, he screamed so much . . .'

'Who screamed? Is someone trapped in a fire?'

'Did someone get to him in time?' said Benedict. 'Did they save him?' His hands came out to Nell and the blue eyes were filled with fear.

'Everything's fine,' said Nell. 'You don't need to worry about anything.' She heard, with relief, the sound of an ambulance outside, and then of people coming up the stairs.

She stepped back as the two paramedics bent over Benedict, and sat on the top stair to wait while they took his pulse and heartbeat.

'ECG?' asked the younger of the two.

'Did he have any chest pains?' said the other to Nell.

'I've no idea. He was virtually unconscious when I found him.'

'We'll do an ECG anyway – fetch it from the van, will you? I don't think it's necessary though. BP's a bit low, but not to cause too much concern. What did you say his name was?'

'Benedict,' said Nell.

'Benedict, have you any pain anywhere?' said the paramedic. 'No? That's good. Can you follow my finger if I hold it up? Yes, that's fine.' He looked round for Nell. 'Vital signs all more or less normal,' he said. 'Pupils equal and reactive. He doesn't seem to have been drinking, although he's a bit unco-ordinated. We'll take him into A&E – they'll do blood tests, and keep an eye on him for a few hours. If he fell down these stairs there might be some concussion. What's his medical history? Is there any epilepsy? Or diabetes?'

'Or does he take drugs of any kind, do you know?' asked the younger one, who had come back with the portable ECG.

'I don't know anything about him,' said Nell. 'I've never met him before today. You'd have to ask – Benedict, did you say it was Declan who was here?'

'Declan,' said Benedict. 'Yes, he was here.' His voice still sounded slightly slurred.

'Who's Declan?' asked the paramedic.

'Didn't he let you in?' said Nell, glancing up at him.

'No one let us in. The front door was open – we just came straight up.'

'I don't know who he is,' said Nell, 'but he was here when I arrived. I think he must be a relative. He has the same vivid blue eyes as Benedict.'

The older paramedic looked at her in astonishment. 'This man has brown eyes,' he said. 'Look.'

With a stir of fear, Nell saw that he was right. Benedict Doyle's eyes were brown.

After they had gone, Nell sat for a while in the dining room.

Her mind was in turmoil. How could someone's eye colour change like that? She was sure she had not been mistaken. Benedict's eyes had been vivid clear blue when she first knelt by him: the colour had made her think of things like gentian and lapis lazuli, or the vibrant Prussian blue beloved of painters. Could it conceivably have been tinted contact lenses, which had later dropped out? But the other man's eyes had been the same.

The other man. Benedict had called him Declan. Nell had lost track of him and he had not seemed to be around when Benedict, still confused and disoriented, was carried down the stairs. He had not got into the ambulance, but he might have had his own car and followed, although there had not been a car parked on the drive when she arrived. The possibility that he really had been a housebreaker flickered on Nell's mind again, but she dismissed it. In any case, Benedict had seemed to know him – he had referred to him as Declan. So Declan might simply have gone unobtrusively away, not wanting to be involved. If so, it was not very polite, but some people were fazed by illness. Perhaps Benedict really did have epilepsy, which not everyone could deal with. But whatever he had done and whoever he was, Nell had better let Nina know what had happened to Benedict.

'Oh Lord, that's dreadful,' said Nina, answering her phone

with the usual breathless air that implied she had been in the middle of something fiercely important and was racing to meet half a dozen unspecified deadlines. 'Oh, the poor lamb. I expect they took him to the Whittington or the Royal Free, didn't they, so I'll check which one and dash out to see him at once – well, almost at once, because I'm just putting together a wedding buffet for a hundred people – it's her third wedding, you'd think she'd settle for smoked salmon sandwiches and a slice of cake, wouldn't you, but no, it's got to be ice sculptures and the most elaborate buffet you ever heard of and . . . Did they say what might be wrong with Benedict?'

'No, but they said his vital signs all checked out all right,' said Nell who had been waiting for Nina to pause for breath. 'They did ask about epilepsy or diabetes.'

'Well, if he's got either of those things it's the first I've heard,' said Nina. 'And I should think I'd know, wouldn't you, on account of being a kind of elder sister and the poor love's next of kin—'

'It looked more to me as if he'd simply missed his footing on those second-floor stairs and knocked himself out when he fell,' said Nell, hoping she was not giving false reassurance or painting an inaccurate picture. 'They're very narrow, aren't they?'

'Are they? I've only ever been to that house once and I don't remember going upstairs at all. But it sounds as if it's a good thing you turned up, or Benedict might have been lying there for hours.'

'Well, there was the other—'

'Nell, darling, I'll have to go, because if I'm to get to the hospital to see what's going on and then get back for this frightful over-the-top wedding food. Honestly, why I ever started a catering business, I can't imagine. But I'll call you later and let you know about Benedict. I should think you're right about him falling downstairs and knocking himself out.'

It was too late to start on the inventory now; Nell would have to arrange a return visit. But she had better make sure everywhere was secure before leaving – that windows were all closed and latched, and, if the electricity was on, that no heaters had been left on. She could bolt the French window, then go out by the front door which had a Yale lock and could be slammed. Walking through the dark house, she was glad to think that in about ten minutes she would be among people and shoppers and crowded trains.

The electricity was on, but most of the bulbs seemed to have blown. But the hall light worked and provided enough light for her to glance into all the downstairs rooms and then ascend the main staircase to the first floor. Luckily the landing light worked as well. Nell checked the bedrooms, then looked at the small stairs leading to the second floor. She did not need to go up there. Or did she? It was more likely that Benedict had been coming down from that floor when he fell or passed out and that meant Nell had better check up there as well in case he had left something behind. Wallet or keys or something.

She went up to the half-landing where he had been lying. It did look as if he had dropped something which the ambulance men had not noticed – near the skirting board was something small and dark. Keys? No, too big for keys. A mobile phone?

It was not a phone. It was a black carved chess piece, about ten inches high, either the King or the Queen. Looked at more closely it was the King: there was a definite masculine look to the features. 'And there's a rather unpleasant snarl about your mouth and slant to your eyes,' said Nell to the graven face. 'I hope you weren't modelled on a living person, but if you were, I wouldn't want to meet the original.'

She bent down to pick it up, and as her fingers closed around it a small tremor seemed to go through the house. Nell glanced through the small window of the half landing, because it sounded as if a huge pantechnicon had driven past. Or perhaps a plane had flown overhead, a bit low.

She took the chess piece to the window and sat down on the window seat to examine it. It was beautifully fashioned. There was a satiny sheen to the black surface and it felt heavy enough to be ebony. Were the tiny glinting chips scattered over the king's robes jet? Could they even be black diamonds?

But despite the sheen, the figure felt dry and rough against her skin and Nell found it rather repulsive. Still, a complete, undamaged chess set in ebony and jet would fetch a terrific figure. Ebony and black diamonds would send it into a much more rarefied category. And what would the white pieces be made from? A longing to know if the rest of the set was here seized her and she glanced at her watch. It was already after five. It would be mad to go up to the top floor – she would almost certainly have to grope around in the dark – but she looked back at the carved figure and thought: What if the whole set is up there? It would not take more than a few moments to go up these stairs and if none of the lights worked she really would call it a day. She dropped the figure into her shoulder bag. She would tell Nina what she had found and say she would like to get the piece examined by a specialist.

She went back up the stairs. As she reached the fourth stair the floorboards above her creaked loudly and Nell's heart jumped, then she reminded herself that old stairs often had the way of creaking erratically.

The second-floor landing was bigger than she had expected, and although the bulb had blown here as well, a narrow window overlooked the side of the house and slivers of light came in from a street lamp. There were four more rooms; Nell, who was starting to feel distinctly uneasy, thought she would just glance into each one. She was annoyed to realize she was glancing over her shoulder every few minutes, but she was starting to have the feeling that someone had crept up the stairs after her, and was standing just out of sight.

The light switch did not work in the first room she opened, but it was possible to see several large packing cases stacked against the wall. She eyed them longingly, then put her bag down on the floor. If the lids came off she would take the briefest of looks at the contents, then she really would leave.

It was disappointing to discover the tops of all the cases were firmly nailed down although it was not really surprising. Next time she would bring pliers to prise out the nails. She was about to go back out to the landing when there was a movement at the other end of the room – blurred and indistinct but unmistakably a movement. It was almost as if something that had been standing in the shadows had stepped forward.

Nell stood very still and turned her head slowly. Standing

at the far end of the room, half-hidden by the packing cases, was the outline of a dark figure. She gasped, one hand going to her mouth in the classic fear gesture, then saw with a rush of relief that the movement came from within a big oval mirror over a dressing table. All she had seen was her own reflection in the dusty glass. Stupid.

She bent down to pick up her bag, expecting to see the reflected figure move with her. But it did not. It remained motionless. Nell straightened up slowly, her eyes on the indistinct outline, her skin starting to prickle with fear. Most likely she had simply missed seeing the reflection move with her, but—

Slowly and deliberately, facing the mirror head-on, she lifted her right hand above her head. Please move with me, she said silently. Please be an ordinary reflection.

But the figure did not move. It's not my reflection, thought Nell, her heart racing. But I won't panic: perhaps there's a long coat hanging from a hook somewhere, and that's what I'm seeing. She looked about her, but the room was bare, save for the packing cases and the old dressing table. Was someone standing in direct line with the mirror? Where, though? Still moving slowly, she turned her head until she was looking at the half-open door. Through the narrow space she saw with cold terror a dark-clad man standing on the landing.

He's been watching me, she thought. He doesn't realize the mirror's picking up his reflection – he doesn't realize I know he's there. And I'm on my own, and there's no one within screaming distance . . . What do I do? Can I summon help? Police? What if there's an innocent explanation, though? But surely an innocent person would have called out to make his presence known. Nell slid a hand into her bag, and her fingers closed reassuringly around the phone in its side pocket. As she did so, there was a soft creak from the landing and the door swung slowly inwards. Nell gasped and backed away to the wall, feeling for the nine on the phone's keypad, but her hand was shaking so much it slipped from her grasp and when she groped in the bag, her fingers only encountered the chess piece.

The door opened all the way, and the figure stood on the threshold, the light from the lower landing and the street lamp behind it. Even so Nell recognized him. It was the man she had seen earlier – the man who had been bending over Benedict Doyle. The man with the vivid blue eyes.

He did not come into the room: he remained on the landing, three-quarters in the shadows. Nell tried to calculate whether she could get past him and down the stairs without getting too close. No. Then the best thing to do was act as if there was nothing wrong.

She said, 'Thank goodness it's you. You're Declan, aren't you? Benedict said so. I'm Nell West. I didn't realize you were still here – I thought you had gone with Benedict in the ambulance.' She thought she would have to get downstairs, even if she had to push him down two flights.

'I'm about to leave,' she said. 'I haven't managed to make any notes for the inventory, but I can come back another day. After New Year.'

'When?' His voice was soft and muffled.

'Probably the week after. Say the eighteenth,' said Nell, more or less at random, but thinking that Hilary Term would have started at Oxford, and life would be more or less back to normal.

'Yes. Come on the eighteenth.' The words were as insubstantial as if someone had breathed the letters on to a misted glass, but as they died away, Nell stopped feeling frightened. There was nothing alarming or threatening about the man after all. If he would step a little more into the light he would probably turn out to be rather nice-looking, in fact.

She said, 'The eighteenth. Yes, all right.'

His face was still partly in the shadows, but Nell could see the glint of blue from his eyes. She thought he smiled briefly, then he was gone.

Nell thought she would not tell Michael about the man or the meeting on January 18th, although she would tell him about Holly Lodge and Benedict. He would want to hear what the house was like and whether the contents had been interesting or valuable. Beth was spending the night with a school friend who was having a Christmas party, so Michael had offered to cook supper for himself and Nell. She was pleased about this;

she liked Michael's rooms at Oriel College – she liked the untidiness of the books he always had strewn around and the way the window of his study overlooked a tiny quadrangle which was sun-drenched in summer and crusted with icing-sugar frost in winter.

She suspected, though, that they might end up ordering pizzas for their meal, because the last time Michael had tried to cook he had ended in blowing all the fuses on the entire floor, and Wilberforce the cat had decamped in disgust to the buttery where he had disgraced Michael yet again by eating an entire turbot, intended for an Oxford Gaudy lunch.

# EIGHT

'It was a trick of the light,' said Michael Flint, seated opposite Nell in his rooms in Oriel College. 'People's eyes don't change from blue to brown in the . . . well, in the blink of an eyelid.'

'It wasn't a trick of the light. When I first found him, Benedict Doyle had the most vivid blue eyes I've ever seen.'

Nell was curled up in her favourite chair, sipping wine with apparent composure. But there was still a faintly scared look around her own eyes and, seeing this, Michael was glad he had suggested cooking supper. He had laid the small drop-leaf table and had opened a bottle of sharp white wine which they were sharing. The meal would be ready in about half an hour; he thought it was as foolproof as it could be. He had bought salmon steaks, which he had wrapped in foil with a sliver of butter and lemon juice, and had bought salad ingredients to go with them. This surely could not go wrong, although it was remarkable how often cooking did. If things did not burn they came out nearly raw, or something fused or blew up within the cooker itself.

Michael had once tried to make vichyssoise and had put a number of ingredients in a blender, which had exploded halfway through the process, showering half-mushed potatoes and leeks everywhere. Unfortunately, Wilberforce had been sitting on the window sill at the time and had received most of the contents. He had been so disgusted he had vanished for two days, but, as Nell's Beth had said afterwards, this would be a really cool thing to include in the new book about Wilberforce, didn't Michael think so? So Michael had dutifully written a chapter in which Wilberforce, wearing a chef's hat slightly too big for him, attended a series of cookery lessons, until the mice, with whom Wilberforce waged ongoing and unsuccessful battles, gleefully tipped the pepper pot into the stew.

At the moment, the real Wilberforce was in the kitchen, keeping a watchful eye on the cooker, where the salmon was cooking according to schedule. The bowl of salad was in the fridge, and Michael could give his attention to Nell's odd experience in Benedict Doyle's house.

'Will you go back to the house to draw up the inventory?' he asked. He liked seeing Nell here; he liked the way she always kicked off her shoes and curled her feet under her in the deep armchair by the fireplace. She still had on the jacket she had worn for London – it was golden brown and it brought out the copper lights in her hair.

'Yes, I think I'll have to. Apart from anything else, there's this,' said Nell, producing the chess piece.

'That looks valuable.' Michael did not say he didn't much like the slightly sneering face on the carved figure. He set it down on a low table and considered it.

'It does, doesn't it? I'll have to get it looked at properly, though. I found it after Benedict was taken to the hospital. It's the reason I went up to the second floor – to see if I could find the rest of the set. I didn't, though.'

'No, and from the sound of it, it's probably as well, in fact— Oh bother, that's someone at the door.'

It was Michael's friend Owen Bracegirdle from the History faculty.

'Sorry, I didn't realize you had a guest – oh, it's Nell. Hello, Nell, how nice you look. I won't intrude, I see you're about to eat, I'll just say hello and vanish into the night like a . . . Well, if you insist, I'll have a quick glass of wine, thank you very much.'

Owen had come to find out if Michael was going to the Dean's Christmas lunch tomorrow, and who Michael was supporting for the election of Professor of Poetry.

'I am going to the Dean's lunch, and Nell's coming as well this year,' said Michael, who was looking forward to walking into the Dean's long dining room with Nell. 'But I'm not supporting anyone for the poetry professorship; in fact I don't even know who the nominees are.'

Owen knew, of course, and he knew all the details of each candidate. He loved college gossip and entered into it as enthusiastically as a Tudor courtier swapping backstairs intrigue. But tonight, probably in deference to Nell's presence, he forbore to launch into one of his mildly scandalous speeches. He drank his wine, observed that Michael always had good taste in plonk, and got up to take his leave.

'I've got to read some first-year essays on the First Jacobite Rebellion, scrubby lot.'

'The Jacobite rebels?'

'The first years. So I'll melt into the ether and . . . Where on earth did that come from?'

He was staring at the chess piece, which was still glaring from the low table with disdainful malevolence.

'It's a chess piece,' said Nell a bit defensively.

'I can see that.'

'I found it when I was doing an inventory of the contents of an old house earlier today. I'm hoping I'll unearth the rest of the set.'

'It's not something I'd want to have sneering from the mantelpiece,' said Owen. 'Can I look at it? Thanks.' He picked it up, turning it over in his hands. 'Admit it, it really is a bit sinister, isn't it?' he said.

'A bit.'

'Wilberforce didn't like it much,' said Michael. 'He glared at it, spat like a demon, then decamped to the kitchen.'

'That was because he could smell food cooking,' said Nell. 'And if it's valuable, it doesn't matter how sinister it is, or how many times Wilberforce spits at it.'

'I've got a feeling I've seen something a bit like it some-where else,' said Owen. 'But I can't think where.' He put the chess piece back, then said, 'Michael, I hate to say this, but there's a smell of burning coming from the kitchen.'

'Oh God, it's the salmon.'

The salmon was not a complete lost cause because Wilberforce scoffed it in one sitting. Michael and Nell had salad and bread and cheese.

'I'm sorry,' said Michael, helplessly.

'It's fine, honestly. I love bread and cheese anyway.' As if to prove the point, Nell sliced another wedge of Double Gloucester and reached for the butter dish.

'Yes, but I wanted to give you a really nice meal and . . . Well, anyway, there's fruit for pudding and one of those squidgy cakes from that bakery in the High,' said Michael.

'Blow the fruit and squidgy cakes, let's take the remains of the wine to bed.' Nell said this with such abruptness that Michael, who had been cutting more bread, looked up, startled.

'You're being very direct tonight, you shameless hussy.'

'D'you mind?' She looked at him from the corners of her eyes as if suddenly unsure of his response.

He smiled at her. 'Refill the wine glasses and come here, and I'll show you how much I mind.'

'Michael,' said Owen's voice on the phone next morning, 'are you immersed in something Victorian and romantic at the moment – or even in something twenty-first century and romantic?'

Michael was not immersed in anything remotely Victorian or romantic. He had just received an email from his editor at the publishing house to say they were about three thousand words short on the new book, so they would like Michael to come up with an extra adventure for Wilberforce. There was no immediate panic, she said, italicizing the word 'immediate'. Perhaps he could put together something over his long Christmas holiday.

When Owen phoned, Michael was trying to think what Wilberforce could do in three thousand words that he had not already done in the first book. He said, 'I promised to meet Nell at the porter's lodge at twelve fifteen so I can take her in to the Dean's lunch, but I'm free for the next hour. Why?'

'Can you come along to my room? I can't explain this over the phone.'

Owen enjoyed believing that phone conversations were insecure, despite everyone telling him it was only royalty and football stars whose phones were tapped. He said he spent most of his days studying nests of intrigue at Tudor courts and secret societies plotting to restore the Stuarts (if not the Plantagenets) to England's throne, so he was allowed to be slightly neurotic about eavesdroppers. Last year a group of his students, gleefully influenced by this outlook, had written a satirical sketch for the OUDs, in which the concept of telephones was discovered three hundred years early, resulting in the foiling of the entire French Revolution by a text message and the subsequent continuation of the Bourbon line to the present day, and also in Guy Fawkes managing to blow up Parliament after all because somebody's number was engaged.

'Can't you give me a clue?'

'I've found something about that macabre chess piece Nell had last evening,' said Owen, and the image of the malevolently sneering chess piece rose up vividly in Michael's mind. Something seemed to prickle across the back of his neck, and he thought: *I don't want any part of this. I don't want Nell to have any part of it, either.*

But this was absurd, so he said, 'I'll be there in ten minutes.'

'I knew I'd seen that chess king before,' said Owen, opening the door. 'And I was right. Sit down, if you can find a space in this muddle.'

Michael did so, and Owen picked up a slightly mildewed book and brandished it.

'I'd set a group of second years an essay on the background to the birth of Home Rule in Ireland,' he said. 'And one of them came up with the fact that the eighth Earl of Kilderry led a group of local men in one of the Fenian Risings against the British. Well, I'd never heard of Kilderry, let alone its having an Earl all to itself, so I was a bit suspicious – they aren't above making these things up purely for the hell of getting one up on the lecturer. So I looked it up.'

'And had he made it up?'

'No, he had not. Don't you hate it when your students wrong-foot you like that? Although I suppose it doesn't happen to you; an Elizabethan sonnet is an Elizabethan sonnet for all time. Anyway,' said Owen briskly and before Michael could argue this intriguing subject, 'round about 1900 somebody wandered around the west of Ireland, collecting stories for an anthology. I followed the source to its root and unearthed the actual book, and the Earl of Kilderry did exist. The middle to late 1800s it was, and it seems he was a roistering old sinner.'

'What were his sins?'

'Drink, women, thieving, every kind of debauchery. Reading between the lines there was probably the odd murder, too. Even allowing for the Irish habit of exaggeration he seems to have lived a very fruity life. There's a brief biog of him here,' said Owen, reaching for the book. 'Listen, I'll read the opening.

'"During the middle years of the nineteenth century, the eighth Earl of Kilderry was notorious in Kilderry itself and also the surrounding villages. He was known locally as the Wicked Earl, and maidservants at Kilderry Castle [*editor's note: castle abandoned in the 1880s*] would tell how he sent for them to come to his bedchamber, sometimes singly, but more often in twos and threes, where they would be forced to pleasure the Earl in whatever way occurred to him. He was also known to be a devotee of the ancient British tradition of the *droit de seigneur*, exercising a feudal right to deflower all virgins the night before they went to their marriage bed. Despite being a scion of an old and honourable line—" Sorry about that snobby touch, Michael, I told you this was all written around 1900, so it . . . Where was I?'

'Scion of an old and honourable line.'

'Oh yes. "Despite that, the Wicked Earl had misappropriated considerable sums of money, by theft, forgery, and fraud, but it did him little good in the end, for by 1880 Kilderry Castle was a virtual ruin." One gets,' said Owen, in parenthesis, 'a marvellous image of this bawdy old sinner moving from room to room in his tumbledown ancestral home, trying to stay one step ahead of leaking roofs and death watch beetle, absent-mindedly rogering anything that strays in his path as he does so.'

'That's the downfall of many a stately home,' said Michael solemnly.

'Rogering?'

'Death watch beetle.'

'Too true.' Owen grinned, then recommenced reading. '"Perhaps the most curious tale about Gerald Kilderry is told by a former servant of the Kilderry family, who was still living in Kilglenn at the end of the nineteenth century."'

He broke off and looked at his watch. 'You'd better read the next part for yourself,' he said. 'It's apparently a first-hand account from a maidservant who was at Kilderry Castle for a number of years – quite good primary source stuff if it's genuine. I've got to get changed before we set off for the bunfight – did you know I'm saying grace at the lunch this year?'

'How are you saying it?' asked Michael, taking the book. Oriel College had a tradition at formal Hall of reciting an ancient Latin grace ascribed to Erasmus, and the present Dean was trying to establish his own small sub-tradition by choosing a different member of the college to say grace at his own Christmas lunch. A modest rivalry had grown up to see who could produce the most unusual form; last year had been a Greek Orthodox version which, as somebody pointed out later, was all very well, but had only been comprehensible to the Modern Language scholars.

'I've found a really ancient form that the source swears was used at Hever Castle when Ann Boleyn was a girl,' said Owen gleefully. 'And it certainly has an early Tudor ring to it.'

'That ought to rock them in the aisles.'

'Yes, and I need to run over it again because I don't want it to sound forsoothly.'

He vanished into the adjoining bedroom, and Michael sat down by the window and began to read.

# NINE

When I was a girl most people went up to the castle into the service of the Kilderry family. I was twelve when I went, and it was when the old Earl, who most people called the Wicked Earl, was there, although I never called him that in case he got to hear of it.

People said the castle was the worst ruin in Ireland, but coming from a cottage with twelve of us, it seemed a palace to me. I thought the massive grey walls and the tangled gardens were like something out of a fairy story, although the mice overran the sculleries and the constant dripping of water where the roof leaked would drive you mad if you let it. The Master had no money to repair the roofs because he spent it all chasing women or fighting the British. So we set traps for the mice and put buckets to catch the water when the rain came in, though you had to remember where everything was, or you'd step on a mousetrap in the dark and nearly lose a toe, or trip over a bucket and send it clanging down a flight of steps, with a sound fit to wake the dead before judgement day. About the British we did nothing at all. We left that to the likes of the Master and his friends, although the cook used to go up to the turret and wave the frying pan and cheer when they marched off for a battle.

I had to sweep and polish the library every week. Rows and rows of books there were – I used to touch them thinking one day I might understand the symbols on the paper. When the Master wasn't away, hiding out from angry husbands or plotting confusion to the British, he sat in that room in the evening. It was a grand room: the logs burned up in the hearth so everywhere was scented with peat, and in the candlelight you never noticed the shredded fabric of the curtains where the mice chewed them, or the bullet holes in the walls where the Master had once shot a man he said was a British spy, although I never knew the truth of that.

If the Master was in a room you never really noticed anyone or anything except him anyway, for he had the way of filling up the entire place just by being there. People said he wasn't handsome, but once you saw him you never looked at anyone else. He had eyes that you could imagine were searching for your soul, and that they would eat it if they found it.'

*Eyes that would eat your soul . . .* That was a disturbing phrase, whatever your beliefs. Michael broke off his reading for a moment and from the doorway Owen said, 'All right?'

'Perfectly. It's very vivid this, isn't it?'

'I love that energetic way the Irish have of speaking – and of writing,' said Owen. 'But you have to bear in mind that they're the storytellers of the world. And if some of them were invited to recount their bits of legend and lore for a book, they'd have a high old time.'

'I'll allow for exaggeration,' said Michael, and read on.

The unknown maidservant had apparently told the book's compiler that the one thing no one could ever overlook in the library at Kilderry Castle was a set of carved pieces for a game called chess.

'I was supposed to dust them every week, but I never did, for they glared so fiercely from their carved faces you'd think it was the devil peering out of the bits of wood and stone. The first time I saw them I ran from the room.

People called the Master the Wicked Earl, but he could be generous to his own people. One or two of the female servants had trouble and in any other household they'd have been thrown out, but the Earl never did that. 'Ah, Mary,' he'd say, 'hadn't you the self-control to say "no"?' Or, he'd say, 'Oh, Fidelia, did you have to be taking your pleasures so carelessly?'

And then he'd make some provision for the babies born that way, and Mary and Fidelia would continue in

his service, and life would go on much as before. Those
of us who had a young man knew we shouldn't do those
things that made babies, but hadn't we the example of
the Earl himself before us, and him bedding any number
of fine ladies over the years and likely siring many a son
or daughter outside of wedlock.

And hadn't some of the young men who came courting
us such charm you couldn't resist them? When I walked
with Fintan Reilly through the lanes, and he slid his arm
round my waist, I'd pray to the saints not to succumb
and lose all my virginity in one go.

There came a night at Kilderry Castle when the wind
screeched across the Moher Cliffs like tormented
banshees. It was a week before Christmas, and there was
snow flurrying inside the wind. We all huddled round the
scullery fire and when a loud knocking came at the door
we jumped, for you wouldn't expect anyone to be abroad
on such a night. The butler opened the door, and it was
a priest asking to see the Master – a man from somewhere
near Galway, so the butler told us. They say Galway's a
fine city, although I was never there. But we all agreed
that wasn't it strange for a man of God to be calling on
the Master, but the cook said the devil made strange
bedfellows, it was nothing do with us, and wasn't it time
we had our cocoa.

Next morning I found that the priest had stayed the
night with the Master, both of them in the library with
the candles burning low and the fire sunk to embers. I
went in to open the curtains at seven o'clock as I always
did, and there they were, hunched over the table with the
chess pieces. It had been snowing, and the cold snow-
light streamed into the room. The Master was white and
drawn and shrivelled-looking as if he'd spent one of his
wicked nights – as if he'd spent a month of wicked nights
all in a row – but the priest looked as calm as if he was
about to say Mass. He was younger than I had thought
from the butler's words – mid-twenties, perhaps – and
he had the most beautiful clear grey eyes I ever saw.

The library was in a shocking state, with empty brandy

bottles and glasses, and cigar stubs where they'd flung them carelessly into the fire, and it was God's mercy they hadn't burned the whole castle to cinders. While I was tidying up, tiptoeing around so as not to be noticed, the Master said, very softly, 'You won't get it, you know.'

'Won't I, though? I'll have your devil's chess set one way or another, Kilderry.' He had a nice voice, like silk or a cat's fur.

The Master laughed. He said, 'D'you know, it would please me to think of a priest possessing Lucifer's chess set. Or would they excommunicate you?' He studied the priest for a moment. 'You know that the devil's power's said to come with those pieces?'

'Didn't I grow up knowing the legend?' said the priest.

'I dare say you did,' said the Master. 'But if you do ever get them, you should remember that the devil's luck comes with them. That's what I've had all these years,' he said, bitterly.

'I see that,' said the priest, looking round the tattered library. 'But the devil's bargains were always hollow ones. Will we play on?'

'We will,' said the Master, and so they did, all through that day.

The servants sat in the scullery, not knowing whether the guest should be offered food. The Master often went without food during the day, but hospitality for visitors was a strict rule. But just after midday he rang for more brandy and, as an afterthought, said they'd have some food as well, so, along with the brandy, the butler took one of cook's game pies, together with bread and cold chicken.

'Are they still playing chess?' asked the cook when he returned.

'They are. It's my opinion that the priest is determined to get that chess set by fair means or foul.'

'The Master won't let him have it,' said the cook. 'He sets powerful store by that set.'

'The Master,' said the butler acidly, 'likes people to think he was once in company with the devil, and that he won the devil's own chessmen from him. But at the moment he wouldn't notice if the entire contents of the castle were to be stolen under his very nose, for he's as drunk as I ever remember him being.'

'Is the priest drunk as well?' I asked, a bit timidly, for although you hear of priests taking too much drink, it's not something you talk about.

'Alert as a cat at a mouse hole,' said the butler sourly. 'You'd swear he hadn't touched a drop.'

Just after three o'clock, with the wind shrieking down the chimneys and sending smoke into all the rooms, the library bell rang. When I went along to answer it, the Master was slumped back in his chair, and you'd be hard put to tell if he was drunk, dead, or merely asleep.

The priest looked white and tired, but he smiled at me, although it was a smile he had to force from the dregs of his strength.

'My guest is leaving, Eithne,' said the Master, his eyes still closed, his speech slurred. 'Get out of here,' he said, not unkindly, but waving a hand in dismissal.

The priest's black cape was in the window alcove, so I went to fetch it. It was as I crossed the room that I saw something which has stayed with me ever since.

On the chimney breast hung a large oval mirror in a gold frame. It reflected almost the whole of the room and I knew it well for it was one of my tasks to polish it, although it was so smoke-smeared from the years of wood fires that if you spent seven years cleaning it with seven mops it would still never come clean.

The mirror reflected almost the whole room and it reflected the table with the chess set. I always tried not to look at those chess figures in the mirror, for somehow they were even more fearsome the wrong way round. But on this day I'm speaking of, I did look. And here's the nightmare. The chessmen looked back at me with living faces and eyes that could see.

I know it sounds as if I'd been at the Master's brandy myself, but as God's my witness it's the truth. Those figures in the mirror had living breathing faces and

glinting crimson eyes, and if ever I looked at the faces
of demons from hell's darkest cavern, I did so on that
afternoon. When I turned back into the room, they were
ordinary wooden figures once again.

I don't know if the Master or the priest saw those
reflections. The priest said, 'Thank you, Eithne,' as I
handed him his cape, and the Master, his eyes still closed,
said, 'I dare say I shan't see you again.'

The priest looked at him for a moment. Then he said,
'I wouldn't be too sure of that, Kilderry.' Then he gave
me his smile again and went out.

*Eithne*, thought Michael, coming up out of the atmosphere of
the ramshackle old Irish castle for a moment. Knowing the
girl's name made her suddenly vivid and real. Eithne, who as
a young girl had gone fearfully to the tanglewood, Sleeping-
Beauty castle and been so afraid of the chess figures she had
run from the room.

He read on.

I always believed that time when the priest was at the
castle woke something in the carved figures. For that
same night, as I was going up to my bed, I thought I
heard something creeping up after me. My room was at
the very top of the castle so the stairs were narrow and
steep and twisty. I had a candle to see my way, and I
whipped round at once, holding up the candle to see
down the stairwell. The shadows moved slightly, and
although I couldn't see anything, I could hear something
breathing – a creaking, dry breathing it was, the sound
you'd get if you had a lump of old yellow leather instead
of lungs.

I ran the rest of the way up the stairs and how I didn't
drop the candle and burn the whole of Kilderry Castle
to the ground I'll never know. But I got into my room
and slammed the door shut – although when did a
slammed door ever keep out the devil if he had a mind
to enter? Still, I pulled the latch into place and dragged
a chest across as barricade, and wound my rosary around

the latch. Then I sat on my bed with my crucifix in my hands, my eyes on the door.

It never moved, that door. Nothing rattled the handle, and nothing tried to push against it. But I knew something was there. It stayed there almost the entire night – I heard its leathery breathing, and twice the glimmer of light around the edges of the door changed, as if something was moving around out there. Whatever it was, it knew what I had seen in the mirror, and it wanted to get at me. To stop me from telling the tale, would it be? I don't know, for I haven't the learning, but I've always thought that's what it was.

A little before dawn I fell asleep. When I woke it was to the memory of strange dreams and shadowy beings. Something was holding my hand as I lay in the bed – I didn't mind that. It's a comforting thing to have your hand held. I thought of my small sister at home with the rest of my family. She used to crawl into my bed and hold my hand if she had a nightmare.

But then, little by little, I came more awake and I knew it wasn't my sister's hand. It was too small. And it felt dry and rough – and the fingers were tipped with tiny hard nails . . .

I leapt out of bed and ran from the room, sobbing and gasping, and tumbled into the bedroom of one of the other maids. I said I had had a dreadful nightmare, and I spent what was left of the night there.

They all thought it was a nightmare – the cook teased me about it a bit, saying what did I expect, walking out with that Fintan Reilly, a man to give a girl nightmares any day of the week!

And perhaps it really was a nightmare, the feel of that small wizened hand clasping mine. I accepted the teasing and smiled for it was good-natured and affectionate, and I tried to think that what had happened really had been a nightmare. But later that day, I made sure to be the one to help cook with the scrubbing of the scullery floor, so as to scour my hands free of the feeling of that hand clasping mine. And that was the night I knew I would have to make sure the chess set was destroyed, although I did not, at that time, know how it could be done.

Anyone who reads the fine book that's to be written about old memories of Ireland might think my story nothing but a piece of foolishness. Eyes that would eat your soul, chess sets belonging to the devil that watched from mirrors . . . People might think me no better than the tinkers who tell wild tales to impress simple folk.

It's all God's truth, though. I saw what I saw. As for impressing people – well, I never wanted to impress anyone, unless it might have been Fintan Reilly . . .

And perhaps we did what we shouldn't have done one night (even several nights), Fintan and me, but then again, perhaps we didn't. It's a mortal sin to do that unless you're married, but the truth's for no one to know except me and Fintan and the good Lord. And even though Fintan's long gone, I don't forget him. And if I sometimes believe my daughter looks at me with Fintan's eyes, and if my son is a bit too fond of a tankard of poteen of a night, well, that's a piece of foolishness I don't mind being accused of.

The account ended there, but the book's editor had added a brief footnote. Michael read it with interest.

The legend of the devil's chess set owned by Gerald Kilderry, the Eighth Earl, is one of the many vagrant Irish legends circulating on the west coast in the nineteenth century. It does seem as if the Wicked Earl really did possess a remarkably fine and unusual set of chessmen, but they apparently vanished around the late 1870s. Of 'the priest from Galway' there seems to be no mention anywhere, save in Eithne's tale. However, several sketches and woodcuts were made of Kilderry Castle and some of its rooms, which were preserved in some Galway archives. [See two sketches overleaf of the library as it was during the eighth Earl's life.]

Michael turned the page, and the sketches leapt out at him. Whoever had done them had gone to considerable trouble, for the details were very clear. The library was fairly typical of its kind: high-ceilinged and with the walls lined with books – probably most of them bought by the yard. In the first sketch the chess set was only suggested, but in the second it was in the foreground, set out on a round table inlaid with the squares of a chessboard. The figures had been carefully drawn with meticulous attention to detail. Their faces were slant-eyed and sly, and it was not difficult to accept that a young serving girl living in an Irish backwater had believed they might climb down from their table and go prowling through the dark gusty corridors of a ruinous castle, or slip into a bed and clasp the hand of a sleeper.

Michael sat looking at them for a very long time. Because the king was the exact replica of the piece Nell had brought home from Benedict Doyle's house.

The macabre core of the tale could not possibly be true, of course. Eithne had no doubt existed, and it seemed that Kilderry Castle and the Wicked Earl and his chess set had also existed. But that was as far as it went. The story of the devil bartering chess pieces with humans for sinister reasons of his own would be a legend spun by the imaginative, dramatic Irish, who loved a good tale and never allowed the absence of facts to stand in the way of a story. This particular story was the plot of the old Faust legend in a different guise – *Dr Faustus* and Mephistopheles and the ill-starred Marguerite – and it was a plot that had made its appearance in a dozen darkly romantic works of fiction over the last four centuries.

*But just supposing*, said a small voice in Michael's mind, *that there's a grain of truth in it somewhere? You dismissed an ancient legend once before, remember?* He frowned and pushed several cold memories firmly away. To tangle with one grisly myth, as he and Nell had done in Shropshire, could be regarded as misfortune – even just about believable. But to tangle with a second was downright incredible. And this particular legend was so off the wall it could not possibly contain any reality.

Even so, he was annoyed to realize that Eithne's tale had disconcerted him, to the extent that he spent most of the Dean's lunch trying to decide whether or not to tell Nell about it. He wanted to do so, but he baulked at upsetting her. And there was a strong possibility that the piece she had found was just a copy of the original. How likely was it that a fragment of an ancient Irish chess set had found its way to an innocent-sounding house in Highbury? Not likely at all, thought Michael determinedly. And even if it was the original king from the macabre set, it was probably not worth a row of beans without the other pieces.

Nell had said she would get the chess piece assessed by a specialist, so it was probably sensible to keep quiet until she had done so. Then Michael could pick a suitable moment to relate the story to her, although he could not think what would constitute a suitable moment for telling somebody that a chess piece was supposed to have belonged to the devil – and that the last time it had been used appeared to be during a match between a wicked Irish Earl and an enigmatic-sounding nineteenth-century priest.

The Dean's Christmas lunch ran its customary and convivial course, treading the usual path between slightly pompous traditionalism which gave way to subdued raucousness by the time the brandy circulated.

Nell appeared to enjoy herself. Michael was grateful to her for having taken the trouble to look so striking: she had on the copper-coloured jacket she had worn for her London trip, with an amber pendant and earrings. Her hair was brushed to a shining cap and she listened to everything with the eager absorption that Michael always found so attractive. It looked as if the Dean found it attractive, too; at least twice during the pre-lunch drinks he leaned forward to pat her shoulder. The third time he did it, Nell caught Michael's eye and gave him a half-wink.

Owen's solemn recital of the fifteenth-century form of grace was received with the respect proper to the occasion, although Michael afterwards heard several of Owen's more acerbic colleagues muttering that wouldn't you know Professor Bracegirdle would come up with something so bloody obscure nobody could check its provenance.

It was nearly four o'clock when the meal ended. Nell

arranged to meet Michael next day for lunch at one of their favourite trattorias, then went off to collect Beth from the school friend's house where she had been staying. Michael felt slightly at a loss, until he was swept along by Owen and several members of the History faculty who were bound for what they said was a wine-tasting event, but Owen said would be an excuse to get potted. Nonsense, of course Michael must accompany them, they said, cheerfully. They were going on to a Greek restaurant afterwards to blot up the vino.

Owen's view turned out to be right, and what with the wine-tasting and the moussaka that followed, it was after midnight when Michael got back to his rooms. He was let in by the porter, who had been lying in wait to recount Wilberforce's latest piece of devilry.

Wilberforce, it appeared, had gone to sleep unnoticed on the bed of a nervous first year. Nobody knew how he had got in, because nobody ever knew how Wilberforce got in anywhere. But it seemed that when he tried to get off the bed he had found himself so entangled in the bedclothes he had reared up under the sheets with an angry yowl. The student, who was writing an essay on the Victorian Gothicists and had gone to bed just after eleven with a copy of *The Castle of Otranto*, had been so deeply immersed in the world of phantoms and apparitions, he had thought a ghost had come to gibber at him, and had dashed on to the landing in a panic and yelled for help, resulting in several of his neighbours mounting a grand ghost hunt. No, said the porter crossly, he had no idea whether anyone actually believed there was a ghost; what he did know was that there had been cavortings across the quad after midnight, and six people were due to see the Dean next day, never mind it nearly being Christmas, college rules was college rules, Dr Flint.

Michael, called to account next morning, did his best to apologize, and was tetchily told by the Dean, who was fighting a hangover, that if he could not control his turbulent cat, Wilberforce might have to be banned from College for good.

'I'll lace his milk with bromide,' promised Michael, and retired to his room, where he spent three hours detailing the fictional Wilberforce's exploration of a haunted house, to which the gleeful and inventive mice had lured him, dressing up as white-sheeted ghosts to stalk him through the cobweb-draped rooms. This seemed to take care of the requested three thousand words, and he emailed the document to his editor so it could be dealt with before the world closed down for Christmas. After this he went off to his lunch with Nell, which was followed by a shopping expedition to equip Beth for her forthcoming trip to America where she was going to spend two weeks with Michael's god-daughter in Maryland.

As Christmas drew nearer, Nell seemed to have what Michael thought of as her inward look. He usually put this down to something having triggered an unexpected memory of her dead husband. He never pried, but he sometimes wondered if she would ever get over his death. It was nearly three years since Brad West had been killed in a motorway pile-up, but three years was not so very long, and Christmas could be difficult and sad for bereaved people.

The day before Christmas Eve, Michael received an email from his editor to say that much as she had enjoyed Wilberforce's outing with the ghosts, she thought it was a bit too scary for seven year olds, and please could Michael think up a different adventure because they still had that three-thousand-word space to fill by the second week of January.

'You'll think of something,' said Nell, when Michael reported this. 'You always do. Or Wilberforce will provide copy. Did I tell you I'm meeting Nina Doyle after Christmas? She thought I might like to meet Benedict – I mean properly meet him. Which I would, of course.'

'How is he?' Michael's mind switched from Wilberforce to the chess set.

'Bored with being kept in hospital, according to Nina. They haven't found what's wrong yet; they just keep doing dozens of tests. I hope he doesn't have to stay in hospital over Christmas. It won't be very festive for him.'

'It won't be very festive for us if I don't manage to bash out three thousand words on that pestilential Wilberforce.'

# TEN

Benedict's Christmas was very far from festive. He had been allowed out of hospital, but he must not, said the doctors firmly, be on his own, until they had got to the root of this. Was there someone he could stay with?

'He can stay with me,' said Nina, sweeping aside Benedict's suggestion that he could go back to the house in Reading where at least two of his fellow students would probably be around. 'No, don't argue, Benedict, there's a spare bedroom in my flat, and I can keep an eye on you.'

Benedict did not want an eye keeping on him, at least not by Nina who would read up on all the things that might be wrong with him, and offer a new diagnosis every day. He wanted to get back to a semblance of normality, to join in any Christmas parties that might be going, and to get back to his work. He particularly wanted to make a start on his criminology essay and the hunt for interesting Victorian criminals to use as its base. The thought flickered that he had found a very interesting Victorian criminal in his own family, but he pushed this away.

But he was allowed home on Christmas Eve only on the strict understanding that he would be staying in his cousin's spare room. Four students sharing a ramshackle house near Reading University did not, it appeared, constitute the kind of aftercare the infirmary was prepared to countenance.

Before leaving, there was a discussion with the consultant neurologist who had been overseeing his case, which Nina insisted on attending. Benedict, fuzzy from the drugs they were giving him and feeling as if he was not quite connecting with the rest of the world, had not had the energy to ban her from the consulting room.

'We still need to do more rounds of tests and will mon you for a few weeks, but as you know we've been able out anything actually physiological,' said the neu

'Yes.' Benedict had been massively grateful to the doctor who had told him this two days earlier.

'At the moment we're tentatively ascribing your condition to a form of dissociative personality disorder.'

At first the words danced crazily and meaninglessly in Benedict's brain, but then they arranged themselves in a more comprehensible pattern. This means Declan isn't real, he thought, a huge relief unfolding inside him. He's something I've conjured up because I've got this thing, this illness. He had not heard of dissociative personality disorder and it sounded alarming, but it was nowhere near as alarming as believing his great-grandfather's spirit had haunted him since he was eight years old.

Nina said, rather sharply, 'D'you mean schizophrenia? Split personality?

'Schizophrenia and split personality are somewhat different,' said the consultant. 'Perhaps a more easily understood term in this case is multiple personality.' He glanced at Benedict and said, 'It sounds terrifying, doesn't it?'

'It does, a bit.' Not as terrifying as ghosts though, thought Benedict. He said aloud, 'The word "multiple" is worrying.'

'It doesn't need to be.' The neurologist, who had a slightly creased face that looked as if he had stolen it from somebody much older, said, 'We're still filling in details, but I'm fairly sure DPD will be the eventual diagnosis.' He glanced down at his folder of notes. 'How much do you remember of that day you came in here?'

'Hardly anything. It's mostly a blur.' It was as well Benedict was not wired up to any of the terrifying machines they had been using to identify his illness, because this was a whopping lie. He clearly remembered being in Holly Lodge that ʼ    d feeling his dead great-grandfather – or what      vas his great-grandfather – pull him down into      Ireland. But none of it was real, he thought.       r Colm, or that Irish village or Nicholas

      han. There was the chess set, he thought, in      ʼ *I found the black king at Holly Lodge.* But      explanation for that, as well – perhaps he had seen the chess set that day of his parents' funeral, and woven the memory into the fantasies.

Even so, he did not want to tell anyone the extraordinary depth of those encounters, so he said firmly, 'I don't remember any of it. And you've kept me tanked up on sedatives and tranquillizers and God knows what since I got here, so I haven't really been able to think about anything very much.'

The doctor made a gesture as if to say this was to be expected. 'It's sometimes useful to trace what we call the alter ego – the second self – to its source,' he said. 'To find out where it's come from or what sparked it into life. You talked quite a lot about Ireland that first day. You weren't entirely conscious, but you were quite lucid. You believed you were actually there – the west coast, I should think it was. And you talked about meeting a priest who died in a fire.'

Benedict felt as if something had punched him in the throat. I told them all that, he thought. All those details . . . But he only said, 'I don't remember any of that.'

'Have you ever lived in Ireland?' asked the doctor. 'Or even stayed there for a holiday?'

'He's never been to Ireland at all,' put in Nina, bossily. 'At least, not unless he's sneaked over there without anyone knowing.'

'I haven't,' said Benedict shortly.

'Have you had this kind of experience before?' asked the neurologist. 'Ever? Even very slightly?'

This was difficult, because Benedict had no idea how much their graphs and computers might have found out. But it was clearly important that they had all the information, so he said, guardedly, 'Maybe one or two extremely vivid dreams.'

The neurologist studied him for a moment, then said, 'Yes, I see,' and Benedict thought he did see – that he understood Benedict had had other experiences but did not want to talk about them. He suddenly liked the man very much for respecting this.

'If we're going to accept DPD as our diagnosis,' said the neurologist, 'it seems as if your alter ego hails from Ireland. In fact he – it sounds like a "he" by the way – apparently knows Ireland quite well.'

He did know it well, thought Benedict. He lived there until he was about twenty. No, I mustn't think like that – none of it was real. But oh, God, how much did I tell them when I was zonked on their loathsome pills? He forced himself to listen to Nina who was demanding to know how Benedict would know about a country he had never visited.

'Oh, books, films, television,' said the consultant. 'Absorbed by the subconscious mind over the years.'

This was instantly reassuring. That's how all this has happened, thought Benedict. Even the chess piece – maybe even that photograph of the Mesmer Murderer in those old newspapers. I saw them the day of the funeral and didn't remember. He said, 'That's interesting about the subconscious mind. It's one of the arguments put forward to disprove reincarnation, isn't it? To debunk the descriptions of what people believe are past lives dredged up under hypnosis.'

'Yes. As for your case – when I said your alter ego seemed to know Ireland, I should have said he knows *an* Ireland. It mightn't be an accurate picture – it'll be the picture you have of it.'

'Taken from my own mind?'

'Yes. The human brain is remarkable. We don't understand more than a tiny part of it,' said the doctor. 'But we do know that with DPD the mind can fashion fragments of facts – half-remembered memories and experiences – and use them to clothe the alter ego. Usually unconsciously. But make no mistake, these second selves have very distinct personalities and if you do have this condition, Benedict, you'll believe very strongly that your own alter ego exists somewhere in the world – or maybe has existed sometime in the recent past. And you'll certainly question our diagnosis, even if you don't do so openly.' He smiled. 'But also remember that this diagnosis isn't definite yet. We're keeping a very open mind, and it's important you do the same.' He paused, then said, with slight reluctance, 'All the same, you've certainly displayed what are called auditory hallucinations of other personalities, and that's typical of the condition.'

'Oh God.' This was Nina. Benedict looked at her, and thought: *this might terrify you, but for me it's liberation. I feel*

*like going off and celebrating – getting drunk from sheer relief.*
*I feel like giving this wonderful neurologist with the crumpled*
*face a thousand pounds in gratitude.*

The crumpled-face neurologist was saying that dissociative personality disorder did not need to ruin anyone's life. 'DPD is a condition that's controllable – within certain parameters, that is.'

'You're telling me you couldn't get rid of . . . of this alter ego,' said Benedict, carefully. 'But that you could probably keep the volume tuned to "low". Have I understood that right?'

'Yes, you have. Although it's more a matter of teaching you how to keep him tuned to a low setting,' said the doctor.

I've done that for years, thought Benedict. But if we can turn it even lower, that would be a bonus.

Nina suddenly said, 'What about his eyes? Nell West – that's the friend who found him – said they changed colour.'

'Yes, they did. Brown to blue. Actually, sufferers from this condition do sometimes display different physical states while in the grip of—'

'An attack?' said Benedict, and the doctor smiled.

'I was going to say in the grip of the alter ego,' he said. 'But that sounds a bit macabre, doesn't it? Some EEG tests done on patients – sorry, Miss Doyle, EEG is electroencephalography – have recorded brain scans showing changes in blood-flow patterns. Changes at the moment the switch between the personalities happens. Sometimes blood sugar levels change, as well. We didn't see that with you, Benedict, but we did see the change in eye colour. It happened twice in the first twenty-four hours. It's a curious symptom and quite unusual – I've never personally seen it before, but I've talked to colleagues working in this field, and it's not unknown.'

'But what causes this illness?' Nina's tone was challenging and slightly suspicious.

'It doesn't necessarily need a trigger, although there's a fair body of evidence to indicate that a childhood trauma can contribute. Or even,' said the neurologist, his voice carefully expressionless, 'some form of abuse.'

Benedict said at once, 'I've never been abused.'

'But there was trauma,' said the doctor. 'Your parents died when you were young. Eight years old, wasn't it?'

'Yes, and that was massive – the worst thing that can happen to any child. I was devastated for a very long time. Of course I was. But I thought I recovered fairly well.'

'We all thought so,' added Nina.

'I missed them for years,' said Benedict, speaking a bit unwillingly, because he did not like having his emotions probed so rigorously. 'I still do sometimes. I'd have liked them to see that I managed to get to university, for instance. But the . . . the pain of loss got less as the years went along. I lived with my aunt – that was Nina's mother – and she was very kind, very loving and supportive. Always so proud if I achieved things. I truly don't think she ever made any distinction between Nina and me.'

'She didn't,' said Nina. 'And as far as I was concerned you were – you still are – my brother.'

'Thanks,' said Benedict, a bit awkwardly. 'But you see what I'm saying? It was a happy background. I had all the normal family things.'

'How about school?'

'I quite liked school. I wasn't bullied or anything. And I like university now. I'm reading criminology and law – criminology especially is fascinating. I've got friends, a fairly good social life – not wild partying or clubbing, but it's lively enough.'

'Girlfriends? Or,' said the doctor, sounding a bit too casual, 'boyfriends?'

Benedict supposed they had to tread carefully with sexuality, and he guessed the doctor was wondering if there was any conflict there. He said, 'There's been one or two girlfriends. No one serious yet, but I live in hope.' This seemed to strike a lighter note and he felt slightly better. 'I honestly think I've had a relatively normal life,' he said firmly.

'If you're being honest – and I think you are – it sounds as if you *have* had a relatively normal life,' said the doctor. 'And there's no reason why you shouldn't continue to do so.'

'Thank you,' said Benedict.

\*      \*      \*

But putting a sane and logical name to Declan's invasion of Benedict's mind did not banish Declan himself. Declan and that misty world he inhabited remained on the edges of his mind. But it's all right, Benedict thought. It's just this complicated mental imbalance.

'The pills will help for the moment,' the neurologist had said, and at first Benedict took them obediently. But he had an uneasy feeling that something had torn down what defences he had and that Declan, no matter how unreal he might be, was finding it easier to reach him. This conviction increased over the Christmas week in Nina's flat. *You're closer to me than I like*, he said silently to Declan.

Staying with Nina was easier and more relaxing than he had expected. She did not pry as much as he had feared, although she mentioned Declan once or twice, referring to vague memories of how he was said to have been a bit of a charmer. 'So I suppose it's not unusual you should latch on to him as an alter ego. Have you thought of talking to any of the great-aunts to find out a bit more about him?'

'I'm not sure if it would be the right thing to do. It might sort of feed the whole thing.'

'Oh yes, so it might,' said Nina, 'how intelligent of you. Oh, and while I think about it, would you mind terribly if we don't join the family Christmas dinner this year, because I've got so much to do, you wouldn't believe.'

Benedict was deeply grateful for any excuse that would mean he did not have to see the family, most of whom would want to know how he was and what he had been doing and whether he was going to sell Holly Lodge. Nina was booked to provide two dinner parties and a buffet supper for people who did not want, or had not time, to cook for their guests, and Benedict was pressed into service to peel potatoes or chop parsley. It was vaguely soothing; it reminded him of how he and Nina used to make toffee when they were children, until the saucepan exploded one day, showering the walls with caramelized sugar and Aunt Lyn had been furious.

But when, on the day after Boxing Day, Nina said she had invited Nell West for a drink so she and Benedict could meet properly, Benedict was aware of a stab of panic. Nell would

need to talk about Holly Lodge, and he did not want to even
think about the place. But he would have to do something
about the house and its contents, and Nell West had apparently
found him flat out unconscious in the house, called the ambulance and probably saved his life. Benedict had sent her a note
of thanks, but she was owed a bit more than a few lines scrib-
bled from a hospital bed. So he said, in an offhand way, that
he would look forward to meeting her.

'She said something about finding a chess piece while she
was there,' said Nina.

The chess piece. The black carved figure that Declan and
Colm had taken from the dying Nicholas Sheehan, and that
Benedict had found in the desk at Holly Lodge. The memory
of how Declan and Colm crouched on the cliff face while
Sheehan slowly roasted alive rose up vividly.

'I didn't know there was a chess set in the house, did you?'
Nina was saying.

'No,' said Benedict. Then, 'D'you mind if I shut myself in
my room for an hour or so? I ought to sort out some of my
holiday work for next term.'

He managed to reach his room before Declan's claws sunk
all the way into his mind, and before Declan's misty, wild
Irish world – the world that did not exist – pulled him down
once again.

# ELEVEN

*Ireland 1890s*

I t was not until Declan and Colm were nineteen that their dream of leaving Kilglenn suddenly became possible.

Colm's mother died just before his twentieth birthday, and he told Declan that there was no longer anything to keep him in Kilglenn. 'And I'll have to move out of the house anyway.'

'Why? Isn't a man's house his own forever?'

'Yes, but the house wasn't my ma's in the first place,' said Colm. 'It was rented and the black-hearted landlord won't let me have it in her place. He says he had enough rent arrears from the Rourke family to last him a lifetime. But I don't care, and anyway Fintan's letting me have the shack for the time being.'

'You can't live in the shack,' said Declan, horrified. 'It's falling to pieces. It's a shanty house. A tumbledown hut stuck on top of an earth mound.'

'It's either that or the hedge behind Fintan's Bar,' said Colm carelessly.

'But you can't live there. Listen, I'll talk to my father – you could share my room and—'

'I could not share your room, or anybody else's room. I'm not taking charity, not even from you,' said Colm angrily.

'All right, the shack it is,' said Declan. 'When will you move in?'

'Tomorrow. If I'm not gone by midday the evil landlord says he'll carry me out bodily.'

'Let's make sure you're gone before that then. Will we take a few things from the house to make the shack a bit more homelike?'

'Yes, and we'll do it before the villainous English landlord gets his claws on anything,' said Colm.

'You sound as if you're about to revive the old Kilderry Rebellions,' said Declan.

'If the Wicked Earl of Kilderry can fight the British, so can I.'

Between them they made the shack as comfortable as they could, but, as Declan said to his parents that night, it was still a one-room cottage on an earth mound.

'And damp as a river, I shouldn't wonder,' said his mother, and went off to look out a couple of blankets, because even that rascal Colm Rourke could not be allowed to freeze to death in a tumbledown hut that Fintan should have pulled down years ago. Declan's father said he would help knock a few nails into the ramshackle roof of the place to help keep out the rain.

'Ramshackle's the word,' said Mrs Doyle. 'That whole family was ramshackle, and the worst of the lot was Romilly Rourke, for if ever there was a Giddy Gertrude—'

'Does Colm ever hear from her?' asked his father, because if Declan's mother once got started on the giddiness of girls they would not have their supper until midnight.

'I don't think so.'

'I don't hold with girls stravaiging off to London,' said Declan's mother, coming in with the blankets. 'It's a wicked place, London. Colm won't hear from that hussy again.'

But as if in mocking irony, the very next week Colm did hear from Romilly.

'I've had a letter,' he said, as he and Declan sat in the shack. They had whitewashed the walls and tacked up some curtains Declan's mother had donated, and Colm had said Declan was to treat the place as his own. If, for instance, there was a girl he ever wanted to bring here . . .

'Some chance,' said Declan, grinning, but he liked the idea of having this place as a kind of second home where his parents would not know what he was up to. He and Colm knew they would not intrude on each other's privacy.

It was raining and Colm had built a fire in the tiny hearth. They were sprawled on the battered couch and there was a rag rug in front of the fire.

'I've brought some of Fintan's whisky,' said Declan. 'That'll keep out the cold even more than the fire, although Fintan made me swear on my immortal soul I wouldn't tell anyone he sold it to me. What with me only being nineteen and not supposed to buy alcohol.'

'Did you tell him your immortal soul was already in pawn to the devil anyway, on account of Nick Sheehan's sins?' asked Colm.

'I did not. Just as you didn't tell anyone you have the sin of Nick Sheehan's death on your own soul,' retorted Declan.

They looked at one another.

'We've never talked about it, have we?' said Colm. 'All these years, and all the good friendship, and we've never once talked about that day. Whether we ought to have done something different or whether we could have got him out. Or,' he said, very softly, 'whether we ever confessed to any of it.'

'Do you want to talk about it now?'

'No,' said Colm, not looking at Declan.

'Nor do I. Can I hear what Romilly wrote or are you going to brood on sin all afternoon?'

'I'll read the letter,' said Colm.

Dearest Colm,

Did you think you'd never hear from me again, after I ran out of Kilglenn as fast as if the demons of hell were chasing me? I expect you knew you would one day though, for we were always as close as two pieces of quicksilver that had to come together again in the end.

Oh, Colm, I'm in such terrible trouble and I can't think of anyone else to turn to. I'm frightened for my life and if you won't help me I don't know what will become of me. You always said you'd come to London – you and Declan Doyle both said it – so I'm asking if you'll come now. *Now.* At once. Truly, I wouldn't ask if it wasn't necessary. If ever you had a loving thought for me, please do what I'm asking you.

I'm praying to all the saints that this will reach you. Yes, I do still pray to the saints, although I don't think any of them listen to me and I don't think any of them can help me.

Romilly.

PS. If Declan Doyle comes with you, that would be great.'

As Colm stopped reading and laid down the single sheet of paper, a tiny breath of wind blew into the old chimney, stirring up the fire so that it glowed red, as if dozens of pairs of baleful eyes had suddenly opened and were glaring into the room.

At last, Declan said, 'Do we go?'

'To London? I always meant to.' Colm waited, not speaking, staring into the fire.

At last, Declan said, 'If you go, I'll come with you.'

'Will you?' It came out eagerly and gratefully.

'Of course I'll come. My parents will object—'

'But,' said Colm, his eyes shining as they used to when they were much younger and wove wild adventures, 'couldn't you just leave without telling them? Secretly.'

'By dead of night—'

'And a letter left on the kitchen table, explaining. You'd have to do that. It's what people always do when they go off to find their fortunes or rescue a maiden in distress. Not,' said Colm, wryly, 'that this is a maiden, precisely. But it's a . . . a quest, isn't it?'

'It is. Are we really going to do it?'

'Yes.'

The immediacy of the adventure – the adventure they had wanted since they were boys and never entirely believed would happen – was suddenly real and thrilling and terrifying.

'What will we do for money?' asked Colm suddenly.

'I can manage the fare on the ferry.'

'I can, too. Just about.'

'How far would it be from the ferry to London?'

'I don't know. The ferry docks at Holyhead, and I'd say it'll be a fair old journey from there. We might have to work our way to London, but I've heard you can take jobs for just a few hours. Cafes and bars – washing-up and the like. It'd only be for a few days. I'd sleep in ditches for Romilly. God, I'd *clean* ditches for her.'

'So would I. Romilly doesn't say what the trouble is, does she?'

'No, and for all I know it's anything from an illegitimate

child to involvement with a gang of criminals. Don't look at me like that, you hear of such things in London.'

'But will we be able to find where she's living?' said Declan, doubtfully. 'London's a big old place.'

'She's put the address on the letter,' said Colm, picking it up again.

'What is it?'

'It sounds very grand. The house is called Holly Lodge, and it's in North London.'

*The present*

Somewhere nearby, music was playing – loud insistent music that pounded jarringly on Benedict's ears. He wanted it to stop, but it did not. Declan's world splintered painfully, and he was abruptly and confusingly back in the sharp modernism of Nina's flat, with Nina clattering saucepans in the kitchen and the radio blaring.

But the words Romilly Rourke had written in her frantic, scrappy letter more than a hundred years ago – the words Colm had read out in the peat-scented, fire-lit cottage – were more real than Nina's flat. The address on the letter that Colm had read out burned deep into his brain.

Holly Lodge, North London.

It's only another of the fragments, thought Benedict. It's what the neurologist said about the brain shaping odd memories to clothe the alter ego.

But supposing it wasn't. Supposing they existed, those two naive Irish boys. Supposing they came to that long-ago London with its gas-lit streets and its raucous tumble of people and the clatter of carriages and hansom cabs over cobbled streets?

*We did come to London, Benedict, and a remarkable place we found it . . .*

Benedict stared across at the oval mirror on the small dressing table. Something stirred in its depths, and his heart lurched.

You're there, aren't you, he thought. But that mirror's in direct line to the window, and it's a sunny day, and you don't like the light, do you, great-grandfather . . . ?

*Oh, Benedict,* said the faint fragile whisper. *If only you knew why I don't like the light . . . If only you knew what it is that I have to hide from the prying gaze of everyone . . .*

Murder, thought Benedict. That's what you have to hide. But what dark corner of my mind has that fragment come from? Why am I making my alter ego a killer? A killer who was never brought to justice?

*Ah, but I had justice in the end, Benedict, and it's a justice you wouldn't want to hear about. And it started innocently enough. We came to London to find Romilly . . .*

Romilly, thought Benedict, feeling Declan's world tugging at him. The red-haired waif who looked so innocent the saints would trust her, but who was bold as a tomcat beneath.

'You lived in that tiny house – the shack.' The image of the tiny dwelling came again, like old cine footage, uncertain and blurred, but recognizable.

*Yes, the shack.* There was the impression of sadness – of an ache of loss. He loved that cottage, thought Benedict.

*We should never have left it and we should never have left Kilglenn. But we came to London, and whatever dreams we might have had of your London, nothing had prepared us for the reality . . .*

*London, 1890s*

Declan said, and Colm agreed, that whatever wild dreams they might have had of England and London, the reality beat the dreams into a cocked hat.

They did not, as Colm had half-seriously prophesied, actually have to sleep in ditches, but there were a couple of nights when they slept in houses so crowded and so dirty Declan said ditches might have been preferable.

'Heaving with unwashed humanity,' said Colm, as they left the second of these. 'Wouldn't you die for the scents of Kilderry – the ocean and the grass? But we're almost there, and travelling like this – begging lifts, working as we go – shouldn't take more than two days, so that man told me.'

It was an early evening when at last they walked into the city, and the sun was setting. The River Thames was directly ahead with, beyond it, the palace of Westminster, and there was a moment when the dying sun tipped the edges of the buildings with gold and seemed to set the river alight. For several enchanted moments they almost believed the glowing light was tangible – that it was molten gold pouring down over the stones and timbers and glass, and that it would lie in glistening pools on the pavements.

'Golden pavements after all,' said Declan, very softly, as they stood still, staring at it.

'Not really, of course.'

'Oh no.'

But the image of their childhood dreams was strongly with them, and there was an unreal quality to this final part of their journey, almost as if they might be entering a magical land where anything might happen and where whatever did happen would be wonderful.

As Colm said much later, the pity was that the feeling had not lasted.

At first the sheer size and noise and the crowds of people confused them and, curiously, it was Colm who faltered under the onslaught of London. But then Declan said they should remember this was the fabled city of their childhood dreams, and fabled cities were there to be conquered.

'You're right,' said Colm, squaring his shoulders. 'We're on a quest, and we'll find our way around this place somehow.'

'We'll start by asking directions to Holly Lodge,' said Declan, firmly.

In the event, they had to ask several times, but in the end they found Holly Lodge, which was a large house in a street of large houses.

'I hadn't expected it to be so grand,' said Colm. 'Rich people live here, d'you think?'

'I do. Or,' said Declan, critically, 'people who were once rich, but aren't so much now.'

'Yes. But,' said Colm, frowning, 'what will Romilly be doing here?'

'Working? A housemaid?' Declan said it doubtfully, because it was difficult to think of Romilly being servile, and yet what other work would there be for her? He did not say this, however, nor did he say that now they were actually here, in the fabled city of golden opportunities, it did not seem as if there would be much work for themselves, either.

They had not worked out a plan for when they actually reached Holly Lodge; they had simply concentrated all their energies on getting there.

This time it was Declan who faltered. He looked doubtfully up at the house and said, 'What do we do now?'

'We go up to the door right away, and ply the door knocker and I ask can I see my cousin. What could be wrong about that?'

'Nothing in the world,' said Declan.

They were both hoping that Romilly would open the door to them, but she did not. Instead they were confronted by a rather large lady with a fleshy face and curves imperfectly concealed by a scarlet gown. There was a moment when neither of the boys knew what to say, then the lady gave a slow smile, patted her improbably auburn hair with a be-ringed hand, and said, 'My my, two new gentlemen. Young ones, as well. Looks like my Christmas 'as come early this year. Come inside, dear, and get acquainted with the ladies of the house.'

'Oh, God,' said Colm. 'It's a bloody knocking shop.'

Of all the things they had been expecting, this was the very last. They sat awkwardly in a large downstairs room with overstuffed sofas and flock wallpaper, and their hostess introduced herself as Flossie Totteridge – 'Mrs Totteridge, I'm a widow woman'. She pressed upon them a series of refreshments, starting with Madeira, which she said the house kept specifically for the older gentlemen who visited, to sherry, which they might say was more of an afternoon drink, all the way down to gin, which was what the girls usually favoured.

'We won't take anything, thank you,' said Colm. 'We just want to know about my cousin, Romilly Rourke. To see her if we can. Is she here? Because she wrote to me—'

'She was here, but she ain't here now, more's the pity, because the gentlemen liked her.'

'I see,' said Colm, and although his voice was perfectly ordinary, Declan could feel that he was raw with pain at having learned Romilly had been a prostitute. He thought they were both raw with pain.

'All to do with her being Irish,' said Flossie Totteridge. 'Goes down well, Irish.' She sent an appraising look at the two boys, particularly lingering on Colm.

'Where did she go?' said Colm, and Declan heard, with apprehension, that Colm's voice had taken on a softer note.

Flossie Totteridge heard it as well, and sat up a little straighter. 'I couldn't say,' she said. 'I did hear she'd taken a room somewhere, but I don't remember where.'

'Would you try?' said Colm, and now there was no doubt about the tone of his voice.

'It's no good, it's gone. I'm a poor hand at remembering. It might have been Canning Town, but then again it might not.'

This meant nothing. Canning Town might have been anywhere in the world.

Declan said, 'Would any of the . . . the girls know?'

'They might.' A speculative gleam came into Mrs Totteridge's eye. ''Course, their time's very valuable to me. I have to think of that. Gentlemen pay to spend time with my girls.'

Neither Colm nor Declan had any idea what a prostitute would cost, but the knowledge that they barely had enough for a night's lodging passed between them.

'But we might come to an arrangement,' said Flossie. 'With you being Romilly's family, as it were.' She reached out a pudgy hand and laid it over Colm's.

Colm sat very still and then, to Declan's disbelief, took her hand and smiled into her eyes. 'What kind of arrangement had you in mind?' he said.

'Bit o' company, maybe. An hour or so. It gets lonely here at times, and I was always partial to a bit of Irish.'

Something flickered behind Colm's eyes. 'That sounds a very reasonable idea,' he said. 'We could come back tomorrow. Would that give you time to question the girls?'

'Come in the afternoon,' said Flossie. 'Afternoons are the time I get lonely, if you take my meaning.'

'I do,' said Colm. 'Afternoon it is.'

Somehow he and Declan got themselves out of the house, and back on to the street.

'You can't go back there,' said Declan, as they walked towards the cluster of shops and the smaller houses where they might find a cheap night's lodging. 'Colm, you can't.'

'I must. That's where Romilly was living when she wrote that letter about being frightened. It's the only link I have to her.'

'But that woman – those girls . . .'

'You think I can't cope with one or two whores?'

'Of course I don't think that.'

They walked along the wide London street, scanning all the windows for notices advertising lodgings, resignedly going past the uncompromising ones that said 'No Irish', both trying to come to terms with the knowledge of how Romilly had been living all these weeks.

As they finally picked out a modest but clean-looking house that announced itself as having 'Clean, comfortable lodgings for single, working gentlemen', Declan knew that Colm would stop at very little to find Romilly and put right whatever had gone so dreadfully wrong in her life.

He realized that he, too, would stop at very little when it came to Romilly Rourke.

# TWELVE

M ichael was rather relieved when the main part of
Christmas was over and he could start thinking about
the forthcoming term. He had a very promising batch
of first-year students, and he thought there were a couple of
double-first possibilities among the final years. He had prepared
some of his next term's work, and had also written a new
episode of Wilberforce to replace the rejected haunted house
incident. The tutorials for his students included the influence
of Andrew Marvell's anti-monarchist sentiments on his later
poetry; the Wilberforce episode included the mice wiring
Wilberforce up to the electricity circuit after he had absent-
mindedly sat on a cable and fused the lights.

Michael thought his final years would enjoy discussing
Marvell's rallying call to take up arms against the Stuart kings,
and he thought the mice's latest ploy would make for some
good illustrations of Wilberforce with his fur standing on end.
It would also serve as a warning to his youthful readers that
it was dangerous to meddle with electricity. He sorted the
Marvell notes into the appropriate folder, emailed the new
Wilberforce chapter to his editor, and was aware of a pleasing
sense of having completed some worthwhile work.

Immediately after Christmas he and Nell had put Beth on
the plane for her American trip to Michael's Maryland friends
and his god-daughter. Beth would go to school with Ellie for
three weeks, then return home for the remainder of the term
at her English school. She was looking forward to seeing Ellie,
wide-eyed with delight at the enormity of embarking on this
grown-up adventure, and charmed to meet the stewardess who
would oversee her journey and deliver her into the hands of
Jack and Liz Harper at the other end. She was also almost
speechless with pride over the brand-new notebook computer

which had been a Christmas present; she had promised to email Nell every day on it, and she made Michael promise to send her the newest Wilberforce chapter so she and Ellie could read it.

Michael took Nell out to dinner that night and later, in bed, she cried and clung to him.

'It's the first time I've been parted from Beth since Brad died,' she said. 'I feel as if I've lost her.'

'Oh, Nell, of course you haven't lost her.'

'I know that really – logically. But things do become lost,' said Nell. 'I lost Brad, and now I've lost Beth, even though it's only for a while and . . . Michael, I won't lose you, will I?'

It was so rare for her to display this kind of sudden and intense emotion and she sounded so much like Beth seeking reassurance that Michael's heart turned over. He put his arms round her. 'You won't lose me, my dear love.'

'You called me that right at the start,' said Nell. 'I do like to hear you say it. And of course I lose you some of the time, and that's natural. When you're absorbed in Andrew Marvell or Byron for instance – you aren't really in the present day at all. That's fine – it's what you are. And I like you looking like one of the nineteenth-century romantics, and I like hearing about all the things you work out for your students.'

'But none of that's *losing* me, any more than I lose you when you're absorbed in Chippendale or Hepplewhite.'

'I wish I could get absorbed in Chippendale,' said Nell, clearly feeling better. 'If I found a set of his chairs or a desk I'd be so absorbed I probably wouldn't speak for days. I'd love to find something really rare.' There was a pause and Michael thought: now she'll say something about that macabre chess piece from Benedict Doyle's house.

But she did not. She smiled suddenly, and said, 'Sorry for the high drama. I'll try not to do it again. I know it fazes you a bit. You're more at home with the emotional yearnings of eighteenth-century poets, really, aren't you? The ones who languished over locks of hair or draped themselves over marble vaults.'

'I can usually explain the languishings of the romantic poets quite well to my students,' said Michael, rather apologetically. 'What I can't do is help them with their own entanglements.'

'That's because they're part of the modern "Your place or mine?" culture,' said Nell. 'They probably don't go in for sonnets or elegies.'

'I think the girls might quite like a few sonnets. Do you know,' said Michael, getting out of bed to refill their wine glasses, 'far more girls than boys turn up in my study, to ask if I can explain a particular aspect of a poem or a sonnet to them.'

Nell said, 'Do they really?' and there was such amusement in her voice that Michael looked at her doubtfully. But she only said, in a more serious tone, 'It's all right, isn't it? I mean – we're all right, aren't we?'

'Yes,' said Michael. 'I think we're very all right.'

She grinned and her eyes slanted so that she was no longer an insecure waif; she was a very mischievous imp.

'Would you like to prove that with a demonstration?' she said.

'What a beautiful idea,' said Michael, and got back into bed.

But two days later, the air of abstraction was back. Nell was not exactly distant, but her eyes seemed to be focused on something that was either deep in her mind or hundreds of miles away. Distant horizons, thought Michael. What's that line about my soul longing to touch the dim distance? That's how she looks – as if she's longing to touch a dim distance. Am I going to lose her to a memory or a ghost?

But a few days after Christmas Nell asked, a bit diffidently, if Michael would like to come with her to visit Benedict Doyle.

'He's staying with Nina, and I ought to go and see him – if nothing else to meet him properly and talk about what we do with the contents of that house. But I think it might be a bit easier if you were there, as well.'

'Of course I'll come.' Michael was pleased to be asked.

'You'll probably like Nina – you can't always get a word in when she's in full pelt, but she's quite good company and she means well. She wants to meet you anyway.'

'Does she?' said Michael, surprised.

'Well, I may have mentioned you to her,' said Nell,

offhandedly. 'So she's curious. Don't smile like that; you look like Wilberforce when he's stolen somebody's fish supper.'

'Have they got a diagnosis for Benedict yet?' asked Michael, suppressing the smile.

'Not quite, but Nina says they're favouring – let me get this right – dissociative personality disorder. It sounds a bit sinister, doesn't it?'

'It sounds extremely sinister. What on earth is it?'

'I think it's sort of schizophrenia by another name.'

'Other personalities seeming to take over?'

'Yes – one personality in particularly, apparently.'

'What kind of personality?'

'I didn't like to ask.'

Benedict Doyle appeared to be a perfectly ordinary young man with intelligent eyes and a sudden, very sweet, smile. He was not dissimilar to a good many of Michael's own students and Michael liked him. Benedict seemed pleased to meet Michael and grateful at being able to thank Nell properly for rescuing him at Holly Lodge.

'I don't remember much about it,' he said, but Michael, who had become accustomed to looking at students' eyes in case they were taking drugs, saw that Benedict's eyes slid away when he said this. That was a lie, he thought, and glanced at Nell to see if she had noticed.

But she only said, 'I didn't do anything except call the para-medics. You were unconscious when I got there.'

'Was I? All the time?'

'You did sort of half come round while we waited for the paramedics,' said Nell. 'But you didn't say much.'

'Didn't I? I'm sorry you had a wasted journey, Nell. Will you be able to go back there?'

'Yes, I'd like to. I think there might be a few interesting things,' said Nell. 'I didn't get the chance to look at anything in any detail – oh, except for a chess piece I found.'

There was no doubt about Benedict's reaction this time. Michael thought it was as if the planes of his face shifted, and as if a different person was sitting there. He said, 'A chess piece?'

'Yes. I'm going to get it properly appraised, if that's all right with you,' said Nell. Michael could not tell if she was aware of the change in Benedict. 'If the whole set is there it might be worth quite a lot of money. I've only found the king so far, though.'

Benedict said, 'But the king is the most important,' and Michael looked at him sharply, because his voice had suddenly sounded different. Softer, silkier. Irish? thought Michael. Is this the other persona taking him over? Is this how it happens? He was aware of a faint unease.

Nell said, 'Do you like what you're reading at university?' and Michael realized she had heard the different voice as well, and that the question was meant to bring Benedict back to some kind of reality. 'Criminology, isn't it?'

'Criminology and law. Yes, I do. It's a very wide subject, but it's really interesting.'

It's all right, thought Michael. He's sounding like himself again.

'I've been doing some research on individual crimes in the late-nineteenth century,' said Benedict.

'I should think that would be a rich seam to explore,' said Nell, sounding interested.

'It was a wild old place, London,' said Benedict. 'You'd never know the half of it, not until you walked through those streets and saw the people . . .' He looked at them as if he was assessing them, and Michael caught the glint of blue in his eyes. No, surely it was only the light in here. But his unease deepened.

He said, carefully, 'Benedict, if I can help at any time—'

'With the criminology course?'

'With anything,' said Michael. He fished in his pocket for a card. 'Here's my phone number. Ring me if you want to.'

Benedict said, in a voice so low Michael only just caught the words, 'No one can help me.' Then the door of the flat was flung noisily open, and a breezy voice called out apologies for being late, but the shops had been full to overflowing with people buying the most frightful junk in the sales – and honestly, if the world was due to end and the four horsemen of the apocalypse were waiting to ride down Oxford Street people would still queue up to get a bargain in the January sales.

The glint of blue in Benedict's eyes – if, indeed, it had ever been there – faded. He's all right, thought Michael again. Or is he?

'What did you think of him?' asked Nell as they waited for the train back to Oxford.

'I think he's very confused,' said Michael, guardedly. 'I hope they can put him right, though. He's clearly intelligent – he could have a very good career ahead. Did you believe him when he said he couldn't remember what happened in the house that day?'

'Not entirely. I think he remembers more than he's letting on, but he's frightened to admit it. I'm glad you gave him your phone number,' she said suddenly.

'Yes, so am I. I don't suppose he'll call. Do you have to go back to Holly Lodge?'

'Yes, I expect so. I haven't fixed anything definite, though. Here's our train.'

Nell had detested lying to Michael – she detested lying to anyone – but somehow it had been impossible to tell him she would be returning to Holly Lodge.

*Come on the 18th . . .*

The words of the unknown man – the man Benedict had called Declan – had stayed with her. She had thought she would mention him to Nina, but she had not. It's because Nina was caught up with being concerned about Benedict, thought Nell, staring through the train window. But she knew, deep down, it was because she did not want Declan to be given an ordinary identity. She did not want to hear that he was a second cousin, or someone's brother-in-law, or that he worked in an insurance office or taught geography. She wanted him to remain mysterious and slightly sinister, which was entirely absurd – it was like a teenager infatuated with a character in a TV soap opera or a film. She had noted the date down in her diary although she had been annoyed to realize she had used red ink, and sketched the outline of a chess piece around the figure eighteen. How sad is that, thought Nell.

They got a taxi from the station, which dropped Nell by the arched entrance to Quire Court; Michael waited to make sure she got across to her own shop safely, then the taxi chugged off into the night.

Nell did not mind coming back to the court when it was dark and quiet. She liked Quire Court very much. There was a small printing business whose origins went back to the 1700s and from which the courtyard took its name; a second-hand bookshop which was probably inevitable, a silversmith, and a florist. They all coexisted very amiably, and Nell and the silversmith were hoping to have a joint exhibition of their best pieces next summer. The printer would supply posters at cost price and the florist would help with decorations.

She paused before going into her own shop, liking the mellow stonework and the mullioned windows, and the way the lights from Turl Street painted harlequin patterns everywhere. Michael had once said if only you knew the right way to look at the shadows of Quire Court, you might catch a glimpse of the people who had lived and worked there – like seeing coloured cellophane cut-outs, he said. Nell smiled, remembering this. Dear Michael. He was one of the very best things that had happened to her since Brad's death.

Tonight, she had the feeling that Michael's cellophane ghosts might be near, and with the thought, faint sounds reached her. She looked around, puzzled, because the court-yard was deserted. The sounds came again, this time closer, as if something was walking across the stones – something so light and so insubstantial its footsteps were as fragile as spun glass . . .

*Or as fragile as the footsteps of creatures who tread with a boneless print and leave no footprints . . .*

The words were so distinct that for a moment Nell thought they had been said aloud. But there was no one here. She looked about her. Behind her was the reassuring buzz of traffic and the calls of people setting off for their evening and groups of students heading for the pubs and bars. Ahead of her, in Quire Court, was an older Oxford, and for the first time that older Oxford did not feel reassuring. She shivered, and unlocked the shop.

Once inside, the familiar, reassuring scents of old wood and beeswax closed round her. It's all right, she thought, locking the door. It was probably nothing more sinister than a pair of teenagers using a dark corner of the courtyard for a spot of furtive sex. At the very worst it would have been a couple of burglars plotting a break-in. Nell reminded herself that all the shops, including her own, had efficient and extremely loud alarm systems, and went through to the back room which she used as an office. She would see if there was an email from Beth, then she would photograph the chess piece in order to mail the details to one or two of her contacts.

Beth had sent a happy email, full of all the things she and Ellie Harper had been doing. Nell read it with enjoyment. Liz, Ellie's mother, had emailed as well, saying the girls were having a great time and they were loving having Beth to stay. She also sent a photo of Beth and Ellie in the garden of the Harpers' Maryland home. Beth was wearing a crazy sun hat which Liz must have given her, and she was laughing and squinting slightly against the sun. Her father used to narrow his eyes in exactly the same way. Nell touched the screen with the tip of her finger, as if by doing so she could touch Beth and through her reach Brad, then frowned and dashed off a bright email to Beth and another to Liz Harper.

She crossed to the safe, which stood in a rather dark corner, and unlocked it, swinging back the thick door, then reaching inside, feeling for the chess piece. There was a moment of apprehension because the figure, which she had wrapped in soft cotton waste, did not seem to be there. It must be, though; she remembered locking it away. She was just telling herself there was no need to panic, when, from within the darkness of the safe, a hand – small, dry, *scaly* – closed around hers.

Nell cried out and shot away from the safe, nursing her hand as if she had scalded it, her eyes on the safe. Terror engulfed her in sickening waves. Something had got in there. An animal – maybe a rat. But rats did not clasp your hand in that dreadful human way; rats did not have small rough fingers with nails at the tips that dug into your skin . . .

The safe door was still half open, and she had to break out of this frozen terror and slam it hard, turning the lock before whatever was in there could get out. Then she would get help. But from who? Police? RSPCA? Nell had a wild image of herself saying, 'Something's hiding in my safe and it's just clutched my hand.'

Whatever was in there was not moving. Dare she switch on the overhead light? No, that might alarm whatever it was. She went nearer, moving slowly, and with a shaking hand, grasped the edge of the door. In doing so, she stepped to one side of the desk lamp, and its light fell across the safe. The only things in there were the wrapped chess figure, exactly as she had left it, a small box containing some Victorian jewellery she had recently bought, and the digital camera, which she usually left there for safety. There was nothing else – absolutely nothing. There was no way a hand could have reached out and taken hers. Except that it had.

She looked round the office. Had it darted out of the safe, and was now skulking in a corner? But she had not taken her eyes from the safe, she knew that.

Her hand felt odd, as if it had been slightly burned, and she held it under the lamp, expecting to see some indication of what had happened – indentations, even, from that dreadfully small hand that might have been a baby's, except that a baby's hand would not feel dry and shrivelled. But her own hand was unmarked. Had she imagined it? Could it have been some kind of nerve spasm? There was something called neuropathy – an elderly aunt of Brad's had had it and Nell thought it gave you quite unpleasant crawling sensations over your skin.

The best thing was to continue as if nothing had happened. She unwrapped the chess piece and set it on a small table, against a plain section of wall. Studying it again, she thought she might have been wrong about the eyes being jet; there was a distinct crimson glow to them. Rubies? Surely not.

She switched on the overhead light. In its glare, the chess piece threw its own shadow on the wall; the shadow was several times larger than the actual piece, and the outlines were sharply defined. Nell moved round the table so as not to pick up the shadow on the photos. She took half a dozen shots, some of them close-ups of the details, some using the flash. The chess piece's eyes glittered – they *were* red. I don't like you, said Nell, pausing for the flash to recharge. I don't know how old you are – you might be anything from a hundred years old to five hundred. I don't care if you're a thousand years old and worth ten thousand pounds, I still don't like you.

She squared the camera's viewfinder again, and as she did so something happened that made her heartbeat skip with fear. The shadow had moved. Nell took a step back, still holding the camera. The shadow could not have moved, of course; it was only that she had moved around to get shots of the details from all angles.

But as she stared at it, the shadow's head began to turn, very slowly. It's turning away from the light, thought Nell, one hand going to her throat in the classic gesture of fear and defence. It doesn't like the light. There was a glint of crimson from the eyes, and then Nell gasped and almost laughed aloud in relief. The shadow had not moved at all; what she had seen was the mirror on the near wall picking up the light when she moved. Your trouble, my girl, said Nell severely, is that you listen too much when Michael starts spinning his romantic tales. She was aware of a sudden longing to hear Michael's voice. Would he have eaten yet? He had tentatively suggested they have a bite to eat somewhere, but she had declined because of wanting an early night. Should she phone him to suggest he came over to share a meal? No, she would not be such a wimp.

She locked everything away, and went across the small walled garden. There was a small annexe at the rear; a previous owner had fitted it out as small, but perfectly adequate living accommodation. Nell would have preferred to live separately from the shop, but although she had sold her Shropshire antique premises quite profitably, property prices in Oxford were terrifyingly high, so for the time being she was compromising.

She was unlocking the annexe door when the sounds she had heard earlier in the court came again. It's nothing, thought Nell. Just the footsteps of someone crossing the court.

*But there are footsteps that it's sometimes better not to hear . . .*

The whispering faded, but before it did so, the words came again.

*The eighteenth . . . Don't forget . . .*

Nell half fell into the tiny hall, slamming the door and turning the lock. Imagination, that was all it had been. She drew a shaky breath, switched on the light, and went into the low-ceilinged sitting room. Everywhere felt safe and ordinary, and the rooms which she and Beth had arranged so carefully were welcoming and familiar. Brad's photo regarded her quizzically from its place on the bookshelves and Nell experienced an uncharacteristic spurt of anger towards it. 'Why aren't you here to stop me being frightened to death by shadows?' she said to his image. 'If you were here I wouldn't take any notice of peculiar shadows or whispering voices. Or of scaly hands clasping mine . . .' On that thought she went into the kitchen and spent several minutes washing her hands and scrubbing the nails. Then she put some pasta to heat, and poured a glass of wine while it did so.

After food and drink she felt better. There would be a logical explanation for what had happened. Simple tiredness even – it had been quite a long day. The feeling of that sinisterly small hand would be cramp or muscle spasm, and the sounds could have had any number of innocent causes. Sounds travelled in a peculiar way late at night, and the court might be some kind of freak echo chamber.

*The eighteenth . . .* The words whispered through her mind again.

I won't go, of course, thought Nell. I will have to go back to Holly Lodge and I'll have to do that fairly soon, but I'm blowed if I'll go on that particular day.

But she knew she would.

# THIRTEEN

B enedict knew that when Michael Flint had made that offer of help, he had not meant with the criminology essay. He knew Dr Flint had somehow sensed Declan's presence.

*Of course he didn't. Don't be stupid, Benedict.*

'I'm not,' said Benedict. 'But I'm not listening to you any longer. You don't exist.'

*Don't I? Can you be sure? Can you be sure you know the truth about me?*

'What is the truth?' said Benedict, softly.

*Ah, truth. "What is truth, asked Jesting Pilate, and would not stay for an answer." Francis Bacon said that. I could probably quote the whole section if you wanted to hear it. You wouldn't have me marked as a scholar, would you, but we had to learn a fair amount of the classics when I was a boy. The monks taught us – they thought it prepared us for the big bad world, although I'd have to say they'd have done better to give us a few clues about how to deal with the temptations lying in wait for the innocent.*

Benedict said impatiently, 'Stop showing off. I know exactly what you're doing – you're rummaging around in my mind as if it's a—'

'Ragbag?'

'—and coming up with things I learned or read years ago. Those people – Nicholas Sheehan and all the rest – they aren't real. They never lived. This is all just a projection of some deeply buried guilt I have, which might even explain all that sin-eating stuff . . .' He broke off, frowning, struggling with this new idea, then said, uncertainly, 'But what am I guilty about?'

*It's not your guilt, Benedict. It's mine. Because Nick Sheehan existed and I existed, as well. If you don't believe it, look for my birth certificate. And, of course, my death certificate.*

'That wouldn't prove anything.'

*Wouldn't it?* A jab of bitterness and anger pierced Benedict's mind, and the surface of the dressing-table mirror shivered slightly as if water had trickled down over it. Benedict could see his own reflection, but overlaying it was that indistinct figure with its long dark coat, and the familiar way it had of standing a little way off, only partly facing the light.

'Why won't you ever face me completely?' he said, and with the words felt his mind start to splinter as it had done that day in Holly Lodge. It was as if dazzling spears of light were slicing deep into his brain, tearing open that strange unreal world where his great-grandfather walked. He's doing it again, thought Benedict in panic. He wants me in his own world and he's pulling me into it.

And for the second time it was London that was opening up in his mind. London in the 1890s, with its crowded, noisy, gas-lit streets. London in the days when, according to those old newspaper articles, a murderer had prowled the streets and had slaughtered five people.

The Mesmer Murderer who had never been brought to justice and who had the face of Benedict's alter ego.

*London, 1890s*

Neither Declan nor Colm really wanted to return to Holly Lodge, but, as Colm pointed out over breakfast in their modest lodgings, it was the only way to find Romilly.

'And didn't we come to London to do just that?' he demanded.

'Didn't we come to make our own fortunes as well?' countered Declan.

'We'll do that afterwards,' said Colm.

Holly Lodge, seen by full daylight, was larger than it had seemed the previous day.

'And a lot more dissolute, wouldn't you say?' asked Colm.

'Yes, but that's probably because today we know what kind of a house it is. Actually,' said Declan a bit awkwardly, 'I've never seen a brothel, have you?'

'You don't get many brothels in Kilderry,' said Colm noncommittally. 'Will we knock on the door or are we standing here for the rest of the day, debating the sins of London town?'

'I've had a word with one of the girls,' said Flossie Totteridge, ushering them into the same over-furnished drawing room. In the afternoon sunlight her hair was more insistently red. 'And it was definitely Canning Town where your cousin went. I told you I thought it was, didn't I? Sit down – oh, not there, those chairs are wretchedly uncomfortable. Belonged to my husband's family, and they had the ugliest taste . . . Anyway, it was Canning Town, for sure.' Mrs Totteridge came to sit by Colm on the horsehair sofa. 'You wouldn't know Canning Town, being just off the boat,' she said. 'And it's a bit rough. But there's nothing wrong with the rough, I always say. In the right place.' Declan saw with a mixture of embarrassment and repulsion that her hand came out to lie with intimate sugges- tion on Colm's thigh. He'll brush it politely off, thought Declan.

But Colm did not. He put his own hand over it, and leaned closer to Flossie. 'You said we could talk to any of the girls,' he said, in his silkiest voice. 'Could we do that now? And afterwards I could take that drink with you – the one you mentioned yesterday. I've been thinking about that ever since.'

Mrs Totteridge hunched a shoulder coyly and said, 'I'd be agreeable. But get the business about your cousin dealt with first. Second floor back and her name's Cerise.'

'God, is it really?' said Colm, caught off guard.

'It's her professional name. She does a bit of acting. I don't ask questions.'

'And after all,' said Colm, 'what's in a name?'

The lady whose professional name was Cerise was consider- ably younger than the house's owner, but the boys thought she was no less venal. She occupied a comfortable, rather untidy room on the first floor, and she curled up on the bed like a plump kitten, and said she was ever so pleased to help with their search for their cousin.

'I don't know if I can tell you very much, although Canning Town was where she was going, I do know that.'

'Would you know the name of the street?' asked Colm, sitting on the edge of the bed. 'For we don't know London at all well.'

'We're only just over from Ireland,' put in Declan, who did not want to admit this, but felt it was time he got into the conversation.

'Oh, Ireland. Oh, fancy. Well, Romilly talked about a room in Canning Town,' said Cerise, examining her nails with careful attention. 'But I don't know exactly where, I'm sure.'

'Isn't there anyone who would know? Any of the other girls?'

'Catch them knowing anything,' said Cerise, with a toss of her head. 'You could try Mr Bullfinch.'

'Who's Mr Bullfinch?'

'Gentleman who helps some of us out of trouble, from time to time.' Cerise made the gesture of shrugging. 'I gave Rom his address.'

Within the shabby room, smelling of sex and cheap perfume, the attention of both the boys sharpened. Colm said, sharply, 'My cousin was in trouble? What kind of trouble?'

'Lor' if you don't know what kind of trouble us girls get into sometimes, you must be green,' said Cerise, with a little trill of half-pitying laughter. 'Usual kind of trouble, dear. Either you get a dose of glim – that's the pox to you – or you find you're up the duff. A kid. Rom was at least eight weeks gone when she left here. Said she'd prayed for a release from it – something about beads and the Holy Mother.'

'The rosary,' said Declan.

'Whatever it was, it didn't do no good. Well, I said to her, love, I said, you won't find beads and praying will help you. You try the gin and hot bath, I said, and if that don't work – which it didn't – you go off to Mr Bullfinch. He'll sort you out quick as a dose of castor oil, I said, and I gave her his address.'

'Mr Bullfinch is an abortionist,' said Declan, half-questioningly.

'Don't you go calling him that,' said Cerise at once. 'Or you'll land in a different kind of trouble on your own account. He deals in pills for female irregularities, that's all. And if the pills don't work—'

'There are other things he does,' said Colm.

'I never said so and nor will he. But if you want him, you'll find him in Canning Town. Clock Street, down by the old river steps. You can't miss it. I'd take you there myself if I wasn't expecting one of my regulars in an hour.'

'You know him, this Bullfinch?'

'Blimey, dear, 'course I do. We all do,' said Cerise, care-lessly. 'And he don't half charge you, the old miser. Flossie'll sometimes help with a bit of a loan if we need it, though.'

'Did she help Romilly?' Declan heard that this came out too eagerly, but he thought they were both hoping to hear Romilly had been given practical help – money certainly, perhaps assistance with finding somewhere to live. Even just friendship.

But Cerise only said, 'Flossie didn't do nothing for Rom. I don't think she liked Rom, much. She never said so, but I heard her tell somebody Rom should've known better'n to get knapped so soon and if she left, it was good riddance to bad rubbish. But Romilly'll be all right. I sent her to Mr Bullfinch and he'll see she's all right.'

As they went down the stairs, Colm stopped at a small half-landing and said quietly, 'Declan, that girl referred to regulars.'

'Regular men who come to the house? Would they have that?'

'It sounded like it. Oh, we're so bloody ignorant!' said Colm angrily. 'You'd think the monks might have taught us a bit about the bad old world and all the wicked evils lying in wait, instead of stuffing us to the gills with Latin and penitence and how not to commit simony or sneeze during Mass.'

'Anyway, about regular men at the house?' said Declan, because once Colm got on to the subject of what the monks had taught he would go on for hours and they could not stand here whispering on the stairs.

'Let's say Romilly did have regular men,' said Colm. 'I hate saying it, but she might. They'd have liked her, wouldn't they? Maybe find her a bit unusual, and come back a second time and a third. If we could find one of those men, he might know where she went.'

'Flossie Totteridge would know who the men were,' said Declan.

'She would, wouldn't she? We'll have to go back after all. Damn, I'd hoped we could vanish into the night like a couple of ghosts, but it'll have to be faced. Do we toss a coin for it?'

'We do not,' said Declan firmly. 'For one thing it's clear

you're the one Mrs Totteridge wanted, and for another, any coins we've still got are going on tonight's supper.'

Mrs Totteridge appeared to be waiting for them anyway. She sat next to Colm, who said Cerise had been helpful, but had not known where his cousin was, either.

'But my cousin would have had regular callers, would she?'

'She might,' said Flossie. 'Yes, I do recall one or two gentlemen who asked for her, special like. One in particular. Looked like a little plucked fowl in a waistcoat, and tried to talk like a toff. Didn't fool me, I can spot Cheapside a mile off.'

'You'd remember his name, though, this little plucked fowl?' said Colm, picking out the sole recognizable reference in this. 'You'd know who comes and goes here, and how often.'

'You'd maybe even keep notes,' put in Declan, and received a cold stare.

'No notes,' said Flossie. 'Never anything written down. Complete discretion, that's what's promised.'

'But you know this little fowl's name?'

'Are you thinking you'll talk to him?'

'Yes. But we'd be discreet, as well,' said Declan. 'Could we go to his place of work?'

'That might be acceptable,' said Flossie. 'But if it ever comes out I told you, you'd be the losers.' Her eyes hardened. 'I have friends as wouldn't stand for me being rooked,' she said.

'We understand,' said Colm. 'We won't give you away.'

'Mrs Totteridge's eyes flickered to where Declan sat and Colm instantly said, 'You can just tell me, and I swear by all the saints I won't breathe a word to anyone.'

'Even him?' said Flossie looking at Declan.

'Specially not him, even though he's as close as a clam. But he's not staying,' said Colm. 'He has business to attend to just along the street.'

His eyes held a look that Declan had seen a number of times in the shack when Colm was about to embark on a sexual adventure. It was not a look he had expected to see in a London brothel, with an ageing madam stroking Colm's leg with unmistakable invitation. But he got up and said, 'Colm, will I see you back at the lodgings? An hour, say?'

'Make it two,' said Flossie Totteridge, and her hand slid between Colm's thighs. Over her head, Colm caught Declan's eye and shrugged resignedly.

'The little plucked fowl is called Mr Arnold Trumbull,' said Colm. 'He works in a printing firm at Islington, wherever that is. Tottery Floss thinks he's the manager, although I practically had to swear on my immortal soul that I wouldn't divulge that information to anyone.'

'You've just divulged it to me.'

'Yes, but you're as close as a clam. So then she made it very clear she expected me to—'

'I don't want to know,' said Declan, hastily.

'Good, because I don't want to relive it. Will we go to Islington? I don't know where it is, but we can get one of those omnibus carriages, apparently.'

Mr Arnold Trumbull's printing company was housed in a tall building squashed between other tall buildings. There was a smell of ink and paper. Mr Trumbull himself was a wispy gentleman, with a thin neck encased in a high wing collar, and rimless spectacles.

'We're here to get information about my cousin,' said Colm abruptly. 'We understand you knew her. Her name's Romilly Rourke and she was one of the girls at Holly Lodge. And you,' he said, in a tone full of contempt, 'were one of the men who paid to go to bed with her.'

Mr Trumbull, who had risen to his feet to greet them, now tottered back to his chair.

'That's a terrible thing to say,' he said. 'I shouldn't be surprised if it isn't slander. I'm a respectable businessman, a lay-preacher at St Botolph's. And my sister is a pillar of the local community, known for her charitable works—'

'Mr Trumbull,' said Colm, perching on the edge of the desk, 'we don't care how many prostitutes you've had. We're simply trying to find Romilly. Once we know where she is, we'll leave you to your lay-preaching and your charitable works and all the rest of it. But it would be a pity,' he said, 'if it became known that such a respectable gentleman regularly visited a brothel. St Botolph's, did you say? That'd be nearby, would it?'

Colm's veiled threat struck home. Speaking in a half-mumble, Arnold Trumbull admitted there had been an acquaintance with Miss Rourke – Romilly. But he supposed a man was allowed a bit of companionship of an evening – particularly when living with a sister who spent her days polishing furniture and her nights working for the relief of Superannuated Widows or Distressed Gentlewomen. And,' said Mr Trumbull, in an injured tone, when the house smelled constantly of boiled cabbage and pig's head. 'Those being cheap and filling foods, on account of my sister donating most of the housekeeping to her charities.'

'How often did you go to see Romilly?' asked Declan, sidestepping these domesticities.

Arnold Trumbull said huffily that being a man of regular habits he had gone to Holly Lodge on the first Tuesday of every month. 'And I always paid my dues. And when Romilly had her trouble, I accepted responsibility like a gentleman. I gave her money. Ten guineas.'

Declan and Colm stared at him. Colm said furiously, 'So you were the one who got her pregnant. For pity's sake, man, this is England, where you can walk into a shop and buy anti-conception aids for the asking!'

Arnold Trumbull, crimson with embarrassment, said he had tried to do that, indeed he had. 'I scoured the shops around St Stephen's Road – a large population of merchant seamen there, so it seemed a likely place – and I found a shop where there were several boxes of the items. But I couldn't face actually asking for a . . . So I fled the shop.'

'Never mind what you did, where's Romilly now?' Colm leaned across the desk, and for a moment it seemed as if Arnold Trumbull's pale eyes would manage to stare down Colm's angry glare. But he was no match for Colm. He blinked and said, in a sulky mumble, that he believed Romilly had taken rooms in a house in the East End.

'Where?'

'Bidder Lane, Canning Town.'

# FOURTEEN

*London, 1890s*

C anning Town, in the murky light of a fading afternoon, was drearier than Colm and Declan could have believed possible. The streets were narrow and rows of wizened houses huddled together as if for warmth or reassurance. There were narrow alleyways at intervals between the houses which might lead anywhere or nowhere. A solitary dog barked somewhere, and several times they heard angry voices or wailing babies from within the buildings. There were a few people about, mostly men, shabby and slightly furtive-looking, or shambling with the unsteady footsteps of the inebriated. The few women they saw had ragged shawls over their heads and bowed backs. They cast incurious glances at the two boys, and scuttled on.

A faint mist lay everywhere, and Declan shivered and turned up his coat collar. 'Romilly can't be living here, can she?'

'Little Trumbull said so.' Colm paused at the intersection of two streets, and indicated a smoke-blackened sign.

'Clock Street,' said Declan. 'The abortionist's lair.'

'I wouldn't, myself, have put it so dramatically. But let's take a look.'

They had both been expecting Clock Street, where the unknown Mr Bullfinch plied his grisly trade, to be a sinister place, but there were only the same narrow houses, the same grey hopelessness. At the far end were warehouses with grimed bricks and blind, glassless windows.

'We're nearly at the quayside,' said Declan. 'Can you hear the river sounds?'

'I don't know about hearing the river; I can smell it,' said Colm, disgustedly. 'It's like a wet coughing infection. If Romilly's living here, she'll be dead of typhoid within a month.'

'There's a flight of stone steps over there,' said Declan. 'That girl at Holly Lodge – Cerise – said Bullfinch lived near the river steps.'

'He can't make much money from what he does, or he'd have moved away long since,' said Colm. 'Are we going to confront Bullfinch? He'd probably be able to tell us where Bidder Lane is – even which house Romilly's living in.'

'Let's see if we can find it for ourselves,' said Declan, unwilling to march up to an abortionist's house and demand to know the whereabouts of one of his clients.

Bidder Lane, when they found it, was no better and no worse than the other streets.

'But which house?' said Colm, standing still and looking about him.

'We'll knock on all the doors until we find her. Somebody'll know her,' said Declan.

In the event, the fourth house they tried provided the information. 'Romilly Rourke,' said the slatternly women. 'Irish like you? Then it's Number Forty, down there.'

'You know her?'

'Not to say know. Can't miss her, though, not with that hair.'

When they knocked on the door of Number 40 it swung open. A smell of stale cooking and old damp gusted out and beyond the door was a narrow hall with a steep flight of stairs.

Colm called out, but there was no response and they looked at one another, neither wanting to go inside, but aware that having got this close to Romilly they could not go back.

The house did not look as if anyone had cared about it for years. Their footsteps rang out in the silence, and when Declan opened the doors of the two downstairs rooms the hinges screeched as if they were not accustomed to being used. There was a sour-smelling scullery at the back of the house with a cat-ridden square of garden beyond, and a grisly-looking wooden structure at the foot, which they supposed was an earth closet.

'Shared with at least six other houses,' said Declan, pointing. 'I thought we were poor in Kilglenn, but it was a different kind of poverty. And there are hundreds of people living like this in London, probably thousands—' He broke off and they both turned to the stair. From above them came a faint cry, followed by a weak tapping.

Colm was halfway up the stairs before the sounds had died away, Declan hard on his heels. They opened two doors on to sad, empty rooms, then the third.

The first thing to assault their senses was the stench. It was like bad meat, like something dead for a very long time. Colm recoiled and Declan clapped a hand over his mouth, and for a moment both had to fight a compulsion to run back down to the street.

For a moment they thought that the figure sprawled on the bed was not Romilly after all. This was someone much older, someone husked dry of life and hope and delight . . . And yet the stringy hair had once been bright copper, and the waxen skin had been like porcelain . . .

A thread-like voice said, 'Hello, Colm. You took your time getting here . . .'

She was lying amidst blood-soaked sheets, and on a marble washstand was a basin, covered with a stained cloth.

Colm said, 'Oh, Jesus, Rom, what happened to you?' To Declan's shame Colm was already seated on the edge of the bed, reaching for the thin hands, apparently heedless of the mess. He swallowed hard, then followed suit, sitting on the other side, reaching for Romilly's other hand. Once it had been smooth and soft; now it felt like sandpaper and although he had expected it to be cold, it was not: it was as if the bones beneath were burning their way through what little flesh was left.

'Bloody butcher,' said Romilly, and even amidst the horror of the room, this was a small extra pinprick of shock because Romilly had never used bad language in Kilglenn.

'We know you were . . . going to have a child,' said Declan, awkwardly.

'I was, but I didn't intend to go through with it,' said Romilly. 'So I thought, I'll get rid of it while it's nothing more than a speck.' Neither Colm nor Declan said anything, and Romilly said, angrily, 'Listen, I know it's a mortal sin and I'll fry in hell . . . But can you see me with a kid? I'd hold it wrong way up half the time. And how was I supposed to feed it and clothe it when I've hardly been able to feed and clothe myself?' She broke off, twisting in the bed as if trying to escape pain. 'But wouldn't you know I'd get even that wrong?' she said. 'Wouldn't you know that man would prod around too sharply and tear something?'

'What man?'

'Bullfinch. Butcher Bullfinch, some of them call him,' said Romilly, and the name came out on a gasp. 'Only I didn't know that until afterwards. They all said – Cerise and old Floss – both said he'd be all right.'

'Bullfinch did this to you? Injured you?'

'Yes.' She moved restlessly in the bed again and Declan and Colm looked helplessly at each other. Neither had the least idea what to do

Declan said, 'Romilly, is there help we can get?'

'The woman downstairs is doing that,' said Romilly. 'She's gone to find Bullfinch.'

'Bullfinch? Rom, we can't let him near you again!'

'She said he should put right what he did.'

'But you need a real doctor—'

'Declan, I can't afford a real doctor!' said Romilly. 'This isn't Kilglenn. Doctors here charge for what they do. And I haven't a brass farthing in the world.'

'I'll get a doctor,' said Colm, standing up. 'We'll find the money. Tell me where—' He broke off as a door banged below, and footsteps came up the stairs.

''Oo are you?' demanded a hard-faced female wearing a man's cap.

'Romilly's cousins from Ireland,' said Colm. 'Who are you?'

'I'm 'er landlady, and if you're her cousins, why din't you come sooner like she wanted?'

'We came as soon as we knew,' said Declan. 'Did you bring help?'

'Bullfinch won't come, the perishing old sinner. Says he can't do nothing and it ain't his fault. Frightened I'll shop him to the rozzers, more like.' She saw their look of bewilderment and said, 'Tell the p'lice what he done. Don't you have p'lice where you come from?'

'Yes, but—'

'I don't know what they do in your country, but they're 'ard as a brick wall when it comes to abortion here,' said the woman. 'And we don't want no trouble.' Then, in a sharper voice, 'Rom, you're bleeding again, aincha?'

'I think so . . .'

'Don't stand about like a couple o' useless pricks,' said the woman, turning to the two boys. 'One of you get downstairs and find cloths and towels. We'll see if we can cheat old man death by ourselves.'

In the nightmare hours that followed, Declan and Colm lost all sense of time. It was only when Romilly's landlady lit candles and set them around the room that they realized night had fallen.

At first they thought Romilly was going to bleed to death, and the woman clearly thought so as well. She ordered Colm to lift the end of the narrow bed and she and Declan slid house bricks under it, so that Romilly's head was lower than her body. Beyond embarrassment, they helped to wad thick towels between Romilly's legs in an attempt to staunch the flow.

The thick greasiness of the burning tallow candles mingled sickeningly with the stench of blood and sweat, and Romilly was moaning with pain, hunching over in the bed, clutching her lower stomach. Declan said in a low voice, 'If she was still bleeding, wouldn't she have lost all the blood by now?'

'She ain't bleeding,' said the woman, watching the huddled figure on the bed. 'Not to speak of, anyways. I reckon it's a poison that got in when that butcher skewered her with his filthy needles.' She glanced at him. 'You ever cut your finger and saw it turn bad and fill up with pus? So you have to jab it open to drain away the poison?'

'Yes.'

'That's what's wrong with her now. I seen it before with girls who had this done. But the poison's inside, so we can't do nothing to drain it away.'

'Could a doctor?'

'Dunno. But even if he saved her, she'd be off to prison straight after.'

Colm said, 'I'd rather she was alive in prison than dead in this room.'

Shortly before midnight Romilly seemed to sink into a kind of stupor; her skin was hot and dry, and weals broke out in patches. She seemed unaware of where she was and when Colm took her hand and told her she would soon be well, she stared at him with no recognition.

Speaking very quietly, Declan said, 'Colm – should we get a priest to her?'

They stared at one another, the tenets of their upbringing strongly with them. You did not, if it could be avoided, allow someone to die without confessing and receiving absolution.

'Yes,' said Colm. 'Yes, we should.'

'Do you know where we can get a priest?' said Declan, turning to the woman.

'I never have no truck with Romans,' said the landlady, closing her mouth like a rat trap. Declan and Colm looked at one another. Declan could hear Colm's thought as clearly as if they had been spoken. What you did on the cliffs of Moher in a lashing storm, you can do again here.

'No,' said Declan in a low, furious voice. 'She deserves the proper ritual.'

'Then I'll go and find a priest,' said Colm. 'There must be a church around somewhere.'

'You ain't got time for that,' said the landlady. 'She ain't got long.'

They sat on each side of the bed, holding Romilly's hands, feeling helpless and angry. As a distant church clock chimed twelve, Romilly fell back, and a dreadful choking cough came from her lips.

'She's going,' said the landlady. 'Nothing we can do now.'

*Oh yes there is* . . . Declan said, 'Would you pour me some water from the jug.'

'And fetch a piece of bread,' said Colm.

They bent over the bed, and the landlady stood at the foot, watching them. After about five minutes, she said, 'She's gone.'

'I know,' said Colm.

'What was that you said to her?' She looked at Declan, who hesitated.

Colm said, 'He was just chanting an old prayer we have.'

They managed to arrange a funeral at a small, rather bleak church a few streets away, and there was a brief, impersonal service, which took the last of their carefully hoarded money. Neither of them had any idea what they were going to do next. Declan was distraught at Romilly's death, but Colm swung between bitter grief and a black raging fury that Declan found frightening. Twice he went off by himself, hunching his shoulders when Declan would have accompanied him. Declan had no idea where he went – he thought he probably just walked the streets, trying to come to terms with Romilly's squalid death.

After the funeral they returned to their lodgings. They would be given an early supper and also breakfast tomorrow morning, but after that they would be expected to pay their reckoning. Neither of them knew how they would do it.

Colm had spoken very little since Romilly's death, but as a thin spiteful rain began to beat against the windows, he suddenly said, 'So this is how our wonderful dreams of making a golden fortune in London town end. In a shabby bedroom, hungry and destitute.'

Shortly after two o'clock, Declan found himself thinking they had just over four hours to get through before supper was served downstairs. Neither of them had been able to eat much breakfast because of facing Romilly's funeral, and they had not been able to afford a midday meal after it. He was starting to feel slightly sick and a bit light-headed with hunger.

A nearby church clock was chiming the half hour, when Colm suddenly stood up and said, 'I'm going out.'

'Where . . . ?' But Colm had already gone, the street door downstairs banging.

Declan grabbed his jacket from the bed and went down the stairs after him. When he reached the street there was no sign of Colm. He stood irresolute for a moment, then turned up his collar and began to walk through the driving rain towards the east. Towards Canning Town and the Church of St Stephen where Romilly was buried.

*The present*

Benedict fought his way free of the clinging cobwebs of Declan's world, and little by little became aware that he was in Nina's flat.

He felt sick and light-headed – exactly as Declan felt when he followed Colm out into the London streets all those years ago, he thought. But that wasn't real. *I've got to remember that this is all simply a quirk of my own mind.*

But he could feel that dark alter ego's claws still embedded deep in his mind, and fighting free of them took such a massive mental effort, he thought at first he was not going to manage it. This time, thought Benedict in panic, he's going to take me over forever. But even as the thought formed, he was aware of a surge of defiance. I won't let him, he thought. Whether any of that was real or not, I'm not going to stay in that world. I don't want to see what happens next – I don't even want to know about it. Because the murders are about to begin. He's going to the East End tonight – to Canning Town and to the old river steps.

Declan Doyle was about to start killing all the people he believed had brought about Romilly's death.

Michael was absorbed in his Andrew Marvell notes when the phone rang.

A slightly hesitant voice said, 'Dr Flint? Michael Flint? It's Benedict Doyle. I don't know if you remember me, but—'

'Of course I remember you,' said Michael at once. 'How are you?'

'A bit mixed. You said if I needed help . . . I dare say you're frantically busy, but . . .'

Michael consigned the Marvell notes to the back of his desk and said, 'I'm not frantically busy at all.'

Benedict sat in Michael's study with the view over the tiny, tucked-away quadrangle, and said, 'It's very good of you to spare the time.'

'You said on the phone you weren't exactly recovering.'

'I'm not. I don't know how much Nina told you—'

'Only the basics,' said Michael, not wanting the boy to be embarrassed. 'That you seem to have plugged your mind in to a different time and place.'

'Oh, OK. Well, they're calling it – this thing I have – these visions of people living in another time – a form of dissociative personality disorder. It sounds grim, doesn't it?'

'Not necessarily. Half my students have some peculiarity or other. Particularly,' said Michael, choosing his words carefully, 'if they've been taking something slightly exotic.'

'I've never done drugs,' said Benedict at once. Then, with a half-grin, 'Well, OK, I've smoked the occasional joint. Only grass, though.'

Michael said, 'I'd have been a bit sceptical if you'd said you hadn't tried anything. But I shouldn't think dissociative personality would be caused by the odd spliff.'

'You do understand, don't you?' said Benedict gratefully, and Michael saw his use of the slang term had been reassuring. 'I thought you might. My cousin's very kind, but she's a bit—'

'A bit removed from student life?'

'Yes. And the doctors were very good, but it doesn't occur to them that there might be another explanation for these visions. I don't really think there is,' said Benedict firmly. 'I think the diagnosis is right. But the things I see – people and incidents – are so real. This personality they call an alter ego – his name's Declan – I feel the emotions he feels.' He frowned, then said, 'I thought if I could disprove these people – if I could . . .'

'Find there was no record of any of the people or places?'

'Yes,' he said eagerly. 'Declan was my great-grandfather's name, so I'm identifying the . . . the alter ego with him. And he did exist, of course. But there are other people with him. I do know you can't prove a negative,' he said, earnestly, 'but I think it would be reassuring if a search – a real scholarly, organized search – didn't find any evidence of their existence. I think I could just about cope with Declan waltzing into my mind occasionally if I knew he wasn't real. But it's this halfway state I'm finding so hard. Only I don't know really how to go about making a search.'

'Isn't there anyone at Reading who would start you off?'

said Michael. 'I'm not making a polite excuse – I'd like to help if I can – but I don't want to tread on any toes. Your own tutors, for instance?'

'I'd rather no one at Reading knew,' said Benedict. 'Well, not unless they have to. I'm hoping to go back in a week or so and I don't want them to look at me sideways or wonder if I'm suddenly going to turn into Mr Hyde or the wolfman.'

'I can understand that,' said Michael. 'I think you'd better tell me a bit more. Can I make some notes? I promise to eat them afterwards so nobody will know. Or,' he said, glancing towards the window sill, 'I'll feed them to Wilberforce.'

With his usual instinct for timing, Wilberforce yawned and got up to walk across to the fire at this point, and Benedict smiled. Seeing that he had relaxed, Michael said, 'Take me through the whole saga. Start at the beginning, go on until you reach the end, then stop.'

With an air of a swimmer finally deciding to plunge into treacherous waters Benedict took a deep breath and said, 'The beginning is two boys growing up on the west coast of Ireland.'

# FIFTEEN

I t was a remarkable story. As it unfolded, in Benedict's rather hesitant words, Michael thought one of the really remarkable things was the logical, sequential nature of it. Declan Doyle and Colm Rourke's childhood – their youthful infatuation with the red-headed Romilly as they grew up; the appalling incident with the renegade priest in the old watch-tower – could Benedict really have dredged all that out of his subconscious? Could anyone? Michael reminded himself that he knew hardly anything about the subconscious mind. He reminded himself that he knew hardly anything about Benedict Doyle, either.

As he listened carefully, occasionally making a note of a name or a place, he thought: but there's the chess set. Nell found that single piece – the king – and Owen found a reference to it, or to something that looked like it. And Eithne, all those years ago, had believed it was deeply evil.

When Benedict reached the part about Nicholas Sheehan's death, he faltered, and seemed to find it difficult to go on. He accepted Michael's offer of coffee, and drank it gratefully, then resumed his story. This time Michael found himself pulled deeper into the world of Colm Rourke and Declan Doyle, and into the Ireland of the late nineteenth century, and he found it an unexpectedly attractive world. Benedict's voice was more assured now, soft and measured, with some of the consonants slightly blurred. Nice, thought Michael. The room was very still. Wilberforce was snoozing on his favourite window sill, and strong winter sunshine slanted in. A fly, fooled by the warmth into thinking it was spring, buzzed lazily against the window.

Michael put down his pen and leaned back in his chair. There was a mirror in direct line: it faced a row of bookshelves on the opposite wall and he liked sitting here and seeing the books' reflections, with the lettering on the spines reversed as if they had changed into a secret or magical language. But as Benedict's story unfolded, he began to realize he was not seeing the reversed images of the books as clearly as usual. He blinked, thinking it was the sunlight, but it made no difference. Something was obscuring the books' reflections, something that was trying to take shape . . . It must be Benedict's alter ego, he thought. It's forming – this is what he sees . . .

He turned his head towards the window, half expecting to see that Wilberforce was uncurling from his snooze, or that a large bird had perched outside and was casting a freak reflection. But there was nothing and, when he looked back at the mirror, there were the rows of books, ordinary and familiar again and perfectly clear.

Benedict ended his story with Romilly's death in London's East End, and with Colm vanishing into the rain-drenched London streets, Declan following. He sat back, looking drained and exhausted, and reached for the coffee jug again.

'That's an extraordinary tale,' said Michael softly. His voice sounded odd, as if it did not quite belong in the room, and he sat up a little straighter, hoping to dissolve the clinging mists of the Irish ghosts. He noticed vaguely that the fly had stopped its rhythmic buzzing. 'I can't decide if it sounds like a form of dark romantic fiction or simply the—'

'Ravings of a disturbed mind?'

'You don't strike me as especially disturbed.' He reached for his pen again. 'Benedict, if those other people did exist it should be possible to find a record of them. And the places – the church where Romilly Rourke was buried, for instance. Can you remember any other details – any clues in the house, maybe? Papers, documents?'

He thought there was a slight pause before Benedict answered, as if he was trying to make up his mind about something. Then he said, 'No. Nothing. There were a few boxes I didn't open, but I think they were all household stuff – glassware and china. The things Nell was going to look at.'

'Yes, I see.' Michael sensed an evasion, but he did not press further. He thought for a moment, then said, 'Benedict, I would like to help you if I can, but before we do anything I think we need to clear it with your doctors.'

'Do we? Yes, of course we do. They might say if any of
the people had lived, it would sort of feed the . . . the
condition.'

'Or that if they didn't exist, you might go into a panic and
end up worse off. I think you should ask that specialist if he'll
OK a bit of research. Explain I'm only wanting to help – that
it's meant to squash a wild idea you have that these events
might actually have happened.'

'If I could do that,' said Benedict slowly, 'I think I could
concentrate on beating this thing – or learning to live with it.'

'That sounds very sensible. Say that to your specialist, too.
And make it clear that I'll abide by his advice. If he says we
don't do it, then I'm afraid we don't. You've got my card,
haven't you? He can write to me or phone or email – whatever's easiest. And if he does agree, I promise I'll do what I
can.'

'You'll help me to find Colm and Romilly and all the rest?'

'Yes,' said Michael slowly. 'Yes, I will. I don't think I'll be
able to do much until the new term has got itself under way
– it's always a fairly crowded time and it'll be several days
before things start trundling along under their own steam – but
after that I'll start searching.'

Benedict nodded, as if relieved, then said, 'Dr Flint—'

'If we're going to be on ghost-hunting terms, you'd better
make it Michael.'

'Michael, Nell West said she'd go back to Holly Lodge. To
look over the rest of the furniture and stuff.'

'Yes.'

'I don't think she should do that,' said Benedict.

'Why not?'

Benedict paused, and Michael felt the silence start to become
charged, as if something – some hidden force – was starting
to thrum.

'Because he's there,' said Benedict at last. His voice was
very soft.

'Who? Who's there, Benedict?'

Benedict's hands gripped the arms of the chair so hard the
knuckles turned white, and he leaned against the chair back,
turning his head from side to side, as people with aching necks

sometimes do to ease stiff muscles. His eyes were half closed and Michael received the impression of inner struggle.

There was a faint movement within the mirror, then Benedict opened his eyes and Michael felt the same cold prickle of apprehension he had experienced in Nina Doyle's flat. Benedict's eyes were vividly, unmistakably, blue. When he spoke, Michael's apprehension spiralled into real fear, because it was the voice he had heard that day in Nina's flat.

'We both know who's inside that house, don't we?' said the voice that was not Benedict's.

There was a brief darting movement from the mirror, and this time, unable to help himself, Michael turned his head to look. For a split second the outline of a man looked back. A man who wore a dark coat from another era and who had turned up the collar to hide his face.

'I've been given guarded approval by the specialist,' said Michael to Owen Bracegirdle, three days later. He was focusing on the practicalities of the task and ignoring that fleeting image he had seen. It would have been auto-suggestion or some sort of self-hypnosis – the room had been warm and there had been that dazzle of light from the low-lying winter sun, and the classic soporific buzz of a fly against a window pane. It could even have been a form of telepathy – Benedict could have been believing so strongly in the presence of Declan that he had projected an actual image of him which Michael had picked up.

'The specialist emailed me saying there was no reason why we shouldn't try to track down one or two of the names in Benedict's story,' he said to Owen. 'I got the impression he had been down this route with patients before, though: as if people with this condition won't accept the diagnosis until they've made absolutely sure they aren't a victim of some peculiar kind of Biblical possession or a reincarnation takeover or something.'

'Understandable. I think I'd rather believe I was being possessed by the spirit of my great aunt Jemima, than accept my brain was flawed,' said Owen.

'He added a caveat. If I came up against anything I wasn't

happy with – or anything that might be a clue to Benedict's condition – I was to refer back to him.'

'Cautious lot, medics,' said Owen. 'Same as historians.'

'Well, don't be cautious now. Benedict knows I'm talking to you, by the way, and he's perfectly happy about it. And I need your help – this kind of research is more your field of expertise than mine.'

'Hmmm. It's an intriguing project, Michael.'

'Yes, but I suspect I'm on slightly questionable ground with it.'

'Why?'

'He's somebody else's student,' said Michael.

'Yes, but he approached you of his own volition, and you've cleared it with his doctors, and anyway, he's over eighteen and in his right mind – more or less.'

'That's true. So where do I start? Do I go after the chess-men's origins? He knows Nell found that single piece, but I haven't mentioned that story you found about the Earl of Kilderry.'

'If I were you, I'd leave the chessmen to Nell,' said Owen. 'Have you told her about this new development?'

'No.' Michael had still not sorted out in his mind why he had not done this.

'The old principle of divide and rule? But whatever it is,' said Owen, 'it's always a good idea to pursue two separate lines of research – more than two if you can. Don't influence Nell's enquiries, not until you hear what her contact comes up with. Meantime, go after other leads.'

'There are several possible ones, aren't there?' said Michael.

'There are indeed. I suppose this place – Kilglenn – exists, does it?'

'It does. It's not much more than a speck on the map, but it exists, exactly where Benedict's alter ego said. It's on the edge of the west coast, near the Cliffs of Moher. But that doesn't necessarily prove or disprove anything, though.'

'No.' Owen considered for a moment, then said, 'It's a colourful cast of characters he describes, isn't it?'

'Too colourful for them to be real?' Michael himself had had the uneasy feeling that Benedict's people might have come straight from the pages of a novel or stepped down from a film screen.

'I'm not sure. It's all a bit neat, isn't it? Facts are usually untidy. Real events are uneven. What about that church where Romilly's supposed to be buried? St Stephen's in Canning Town, wasn't it? Is there actually a St Stephen's there?'

'I don't know. It's one of the areas that was severely bombed in the Second World War. It's just warehouses now.'

'Ah. Pity. All right, what else have you got?'

Owen sounded exactly the way he sounded when he was prodding his students to think for themselves. Michael supposed he often sounded the same to his own students, but it felt strange to be on the other side of the desk.

He said, 'The ownership of Holly Lodge has to be a good possibility. Benedict's going to see if he can get a copy of the Title Deeds from the solicitor. Hopefully there'll be some of the house's history – including the name of that brothel-keeper among them.' He broke off and said, wryly, 'Do you know, Owen, when I came to Oxford it never occurred to me I'd be chasing brothel-keepers.'

'I shouldn't let that worry you; I'll bet Oxford's no stranger to brothels and their keepers. You're bearing in mind, are you, that you might not have the lady's real name?'

'I am. "Flossie Totteridge" almost smacks of a Dickens' creation, doesn't it?'

'If not Restoration comedy,' said Owen. 'But people have had odder names. She might not have actually owned the place, though. She might have been renting it. Or it might have belonged to a pimp.'

'I don't think,' said Michael, 'that Benedict told me everything. I think there was more about Romilly that he wasn't disclosing. But what he did tell me spooked me quite a lot.'

'You're too easily spooked,' said Owen breezily, and Michael thought: *but you'd be spooked if you'd seen a dark-clad figure looking out at you from your own mirror.* 'I thought you were quite at home with spooks anyway,' Owen went on. 'Didn't you encounter something a bit peculiar at that old house in Shropshire last year?'

'Yes, but that was in another country and besides the wench is dead,' said Michael irresistibly.

'And keep your bloody sonnets for your adoring female students.'

'It's not a sonnet; it's Marlowe,' said Michael.

'I don't care if it's Groucho Marx. Now listen, Michael, there's one very strong lead you seem to be overlooking.'

'What?'

'Trace the priest.'

'My God, yes, of course,' said Michael. 'Nicholas Sheehan.'

'Well, he wasn't named in that account we found about the Earl of Kilderry, was he?' said Owen. 'But didn't the wicked Earl play chess with a priest from Galway, using the "devil's chess set"?'

'Yes. And it was the set itself the priest was after. It was a bit Gothic, that tale – the wind screeching round the ruinous castle, and the priest appearing out of the blizzard.'

'Well, let's suppose there was a grain of truth in it. Let's suppose the priest might have been Nicholas Sheehan. Does that fit with this account of the enigmatic gentleman living in the watchtower?'

'It could,' said Michael. 'The dates are about right. Could the priest be traced? Either as a nameless Galway priest in the 1860s or 1870s, or as Father Nicholas Sheehan living in a watchtower around 1890?'

'He might be traceable. There's the equivalent of Crockford's Directory – it covers the Catholic Church and Ireland. Hold on, I think I've got a copy.' He got up to scan his shelves, and Michael waited. 'Thought so,' said Owen, pouncing. 'The Irish Almanac and Official Directory of the United Kingdom of Great Britain and Ireland. Compiled by one Alexander Thom and published pretty much every year for – well, certainly for the last half of the nineteenth century, which is all we're bothered about. It contains ecclesiastical directories for major religions – including Roman Catholics in Ireland, although I shouldn't have thought there were many other religions in Ireland. I can't remember where I got this and I certainly can't remember why. It probably won't be the right year – it's 1895.'

'Too late for Nicholas Sheehan,' said Michael, but leafing

the pages anyway. 'It sounded as if he'd been in Kilglenn for at least ten years by the 1890s.'

'You might have to look in several editions, but if Sheehan really was a priest he ought to be listed in Thom's Almanac. Especially if he had a parish of his own at any time.'

'It sounded as if he'd been defrocked,' said Michael doubtfully.

'It wouldn't matter if he'd been excommunicated and consigned to the outer darknesses of Hell,' said Owen. 'Once he was printed in Thom's Almanac he couldn't be unprinted.'

'Can I borrow this?'

'Certainly.' Owen reached for the wine he had opened earlier and refilled their glasses. 'Of course,' he said blandly, 'if all else fails, you could simply brave the rigours of the Irish Sea and go to Kilglenn and see if it's got a burned-out watchtower. Or any families living there called Rourke or Doyle.'

'Rourkes and Doyles are most likely ten a penny in Ireland,' said Michael. 'And the watchtower is probably a tourist centre by now. In any case I can't spare the time at the moment. It's the start of the new term – and I've got an editor's deadline to meet.'

'OUP or Wilberforce?'

'Wilberforce,' said Michael. 'I had to rewrite the haunted house scenes because they thought it was too frightening for seven year olds.'

'You could go to Ireland at Easter or half-term,' said Owen. 'Take Nell.'

'Have you ever been to Ireland?' said Michael to Nell, over a plate of pasta in the small trattoria that had become one of their favourite eating places. She looked up, as if the question had startled her, and he said, 'I sometimes have to remind myself that there are a lot of things I don't know about you. One of the things I don't know is whether you've been to Ireland.'

'I haven't, as it happens. Why?'

'Only that I thought about going there this spring,' said Michael, offhandedly. 'Just for a few days. It was only a half-idea, though. I thought it might be nice to see the west coast.

Would you like to come with me? We could go at half-term if we can fit round Beth. We can take the ferry, or we could fly over and hire a car there.'

'It's supposed to be a lovely part of Ireland,' said Nell. 'Yes, it might be nice sometime. Maybe at Easter if the shop isn't too busy. Did I tell you I'm hoping to set up an antique evening with Henry Jessel at the silversmith's? This wine's nice, isn't it? Could I have another glass?'

Nell hoped she had deflected Michael's suggestion about Ireland with sufficient tact. There had been a moment when she had wanted nothing more than to say yes, of course she would love to go to Ireland with him – a moment when she had seen the two of them bucketing across the wild Irish landscape in a hire car, perhaps getting lost but not caring, enjoying the company of the people they would meet and the food they would eat, sleeping in remote inns . . .

But then the images vanished as if an invisible hand had wiped mist from a windowpane, and she could only hear that silk and velvet voice telling her to come back to Holly Lodge . . .

*When?* he had said. And when Nell had said the eighteenth, he had said, *Yes, come on the eighteenth.*

One week to go, thought Nell. Seven days, that's all.

# SIXTEEN

Benedict had told Michael Flint almost everything about Declan and Colm. He had described in detail what had happened in the Kilderry watchtower, and how the two boys had later gone to London to find Romilly. But he had not told him how they had tried to trace the men who had been her clients, and he had not said his great-grandfather had been a killer who slaughtered five people and escaped justice.

When Michael said, 'Did you find anything in the house – Holly Lodge – that we could use? Any letters or documents that might have dates or names?' Benedict simply said no, there had been nothing. The lie made him feel guilty, so to cover it up, he said, 'I thought I'd get the Title Deeds for Holly Lodge from the solicitor, though.'

'Yes, that would be a good lead,' said Michael. 'And since Holly Lodge is your house, you're presumably entitled to ask for the Deeds – or at least photocopies of them.' He paused, then said, 'But it's a pity there's nothing in that house that will give us other clues.'

Clues. Such as newspaper cuttings describing a vicious serial killer with Declan's face?

'It is a pity, isn't it?' said Benedict.

Nina had been all set to accompany him to his next consultation with the neurologist, until she discovered it was a day when she was booked to provide a celebration lunch for a firm who had just won a PR Award. So she had gone breezily off to Soho that morning, amidst explanations about collecting two live lobsters on the way. Benedict ought not to be surprised if he heard of a traffic hold-up in Charing Cross Road, as a result of the lobsters trying to escape their fate en route.

Benedict, guiltily grateful to the PR company, was therefore able to attend the consultation on his own. He was not really

surprised when the neurologist recommended he delay his
return to Reading University a little longer.

'I'd rather you remain on sick leave until we're sure we are
dealing with DPD,' he said. 'Let this Oxford friend delve
around a bit to see if any names or places match up. After
that we can think about how we proceed. We still have to get
the balance of medication right, for instance. You're only on
mild tranquillizers at the moment, which is really an interim
measure.'

'You don't think Dr Flint will find anything, do you?' said
Benedict, taking the neurologist back to the real issue.

'I think,' said the man carefully, 'that it's unlikely this
particular alter ego – or any of the people surrounding him
– will turn out to be based on fact. They rarely do, Benedict.
But,' he added kindly, 'I'm still keeping an open mind.'

Benedict had not expected anything else, but he was disappointed at not being allowed back to university. He wanted to
surround himself with normality as soon as possible: he wanted
to be in his room in the friendly, untidy house, where the other
students would be grumbling about essays, exchanging gossip,
and complaining about their tutors.

When he returned from the hospital the flat was empty,
which probably meant Nina was still engaged in combat with
the lobsters in the depths of Old Compton Street. This gave
him a clear field to phone the solicitors handling Holly Lodge,
to ask if he could have a set of photocopies of the Title
Deeds. No, he said, he did not need the whole shooting match
and he thought he had better not have the originals, which
would be safer in the solicitors' keeping. But if he could
have a copy of the Abstract of Title and of all the convey-
ances? Well, yes, he did mean dating back to when the house
was built, and if there was a Land Registry certificate . . . ?
No, there was no need to post it, he would call. Would
tomorrow be all right?

As he rang off he had the feeling that he was thrusting his
hands deep into a past that might be better left undisturbed,
and he was aware that Declan's world was starting to thrum
on the rim of his mind, like a powerful engine revving up.
For the first time, there was a physical pain connected to it,

not precisely a headache, but the sensation of pressure on a bruise.

*Would you just let me in for a few moments, Benedict*, said Declan's voice in his mind. (Or was it in his mind? Wasn't it whispering in to the quiet bedroom?)

*Let me explain to you how it happened . . .*

I don't want to hear, said Benedict. You don't exist except in my own mind – and maybe a bit in my family's memories. You're a chimera and I don't want anything to do with you. I don't want to know about the murders or Romilly or any of those other people.

*But aren't you trying to prove that all those people existed? Aren't you trying to track down the plucked fowl in the waistcoat this very minute? God, he was a poor specimen of a man, that one . . .*

'He didn't deserve to be murdered, whatever he was,' said Benedict angrily, and this time he spoke aloud. His words lay loudly and harshly on the air.

For a moment he thought the sudden burst of anger had driven Declan back, and he waited, not daring to hope he could have succeeded so easily. But then the familiar ripple went through his mind, and his great-grandfather said sadly, *No, Benedict, no one deserves that.*

The painful pressure increased on Benedict's mind, and a dreadful apprehension started to unfold. This is it, he thought. He's set out most of his story for me – the childhood in Ireland, the encounter with Nicholas Sheehan – but now we've reached the killings, and he's going to force me to see them all happening. Five people . . . Whatever's real or unreal about this, those murders happened – they were reported in the newspapers. And I'll have to stand and watch while they die and there'll be nothing I can do – nothing I can do to save any of them . . .

*London, 1890s*

When Colm banged out of the bedroom at the lodging house, Declan assumed he was going to Romilly's grave – that heart-breakingly new grave that looked like a deep wound in the churchyard of St Stephen's. That morning, after the funeral service, Colm had said he could not bear to leave her here, in this grey, unfriendly place, where she knew no one, and Declan had had to take his arm and pull him along the church path. Surely if Colm was going anywhere, it would be there? He reached for his own jacket, turned up the collar, and went down the stairs and out into the rain-drenched streets.

But even though he was only minutes behind Colm, there was no sign of him, and Declan paused, irresolute. St Stephen's Church was a fair distance and he had no money for an omnibus. He would have to walk. It would take a long time and he was not sure of the way, but Colm would be walking as well so Declan would probably catch him up. He set off.

There was no sign of Colm, but he found his way to Canning Town in the end, getting lost a couple of times and asking passers-by to direct him. They were incurious, these London people; they had their own lives and their own worries, and they were not interested in an Irish boy trying to find a church. Declan, his jacket already rain-soaked, his scarf sodden and his hair wet, had never felt so alone in his whole life.

When finally he reached St Stephen's the daylight was draining from the day and he was aching in every bone from a mixture of hunger and exhaustion. Several times he had to stop and lean against a wall because he felt sick and dizzy, and people passing by glanced disapprovingly at him. Declan realized they thought he was drunk, which was a wild irony when he had not even the money for an omnibus.

The cemetery was deserted and it did not look as if anyone had approached Romilly's grave since the morning. Declan hunched up his shoulders against the cold, then went inside the church, grateful for the warmth and the chance to sit for a while on one of the pews. He had expected to find the church reassuring, but the faint scent of incense on the air and the massive silence in the church was painfully reminiscent of Kilglenn.

St Stephen's clock chimed six and there were movements from beyond the vestry. Evensong, thought Declan. Or at least some kind of evening service. He could not face it. He could not kneel in a church and chant the prayers that had been the fabric of his life – not when Romilly had died so brutally; not when he had again recited the sin-eating ritual over her dying body. But I'll confess it all, he thought. When all this is over, then I'll confess.

He went out of the church, his mind still on Colm. Might Colm be in Bidder Lane and the house where Romilly had died? Declan began to make his way there, but it took longer than he expected, because waves of dizziness swept over his head with a horrid pulsating rhythm.

Bidder Lane, seen in the sodden dusk light, was a bleak place, and the house where Romilly had died had a deserted look. When Declan knocked on the door there was no response. He peered through the downstairs windows. Of the two rooms visible, one had a couple of kitchen chairs and a deal table, the other had a sagging sofa and a bundle of old newspapers.

Despite the cold, he was starting to have the feeling that he was burning up inside – almost as if his bones were slowly heating up and as if the marrow in them might eventually start to boil. Had Father Sheehan felt this at the start of his terrible death on the Moher Cliffs? But Declan did not want Nicholas Sheehan's ghost gibbering at him, and he forced himself to keep walking, trying to ignore the grinding pain and the sick throbbing in his head.

He reached the intersection of Bidder Lane and Clock Street, where the man Bullfinch lived. Some of the street lamps had been lit by this time, and in the blurred light from them, he saw the unmistakable figure of Colm crossing the road, walking away from him. Declan was aware of instant relief, because Colm would help him to get back to their lodging house. He called out but Colm seemed to be too far away to hear, and so Declan went after him. Colm had vanished, but there was a break between two of the houses, and Declan made for this. As he got nearer he heard the river sounds – soft hoots from the barges, the occasional call of a man's voice, footsteps echoing eerily on the wet cobblestones. There was no sign of Colm, and everywhere was deserted. Declan could smell the dank river smell and see lights from moored river-craft. He went forward again, his footsteps ringing sharply on the wet cobbles, stepping carefully between scatterings of debris: odd lengths of rope and sodden bits of unidentifiable rubbish. Mist swirled around him, seeping into his throat and making him cough.

Directly ahead was a flight of stone steps. He went down them, and paused at the foot. A second flight went all the way down to the river itself, but he had reached a jutting shelf that extended along the quayside wall. About fifteen or twenty yards along was a massive circular hole with a brick surround, cut into the quay wall. It looked like the opening to a tunnel. Declan had no idea what it was. He stepped on to the lower steps, but his foot skidded on a pile of debris, sodden and slippery. He grabbed at the handrail, but pitched forward.

He fell in a helpless jumble of flailing arms and legs, banging against the hard edges of the stone steps. Through the tumbling confusion he managed to think he must be almost at the foot and that at worst this would mean a few bruises. Then his head banged against a jutting section of bricks; the world exploded in sick dizzying lights, and blackness closed down.

He clawed his way back to consciousness, at first aware only of the ache in his head and the fact that he was lying on something hard and uncomfortable. Then memory began to unroll in thin ribbons, and he remembered walking along Bidder Lane and Clock Street, trying to find Colm. There had been the river sounds – he could still hear them. He could still smell the river, as well, and there must be a tavern nearby because he could hear laughter and piano music.

He sat up, wincing from the pain where he had banged his head, still feeling shivery. But he seemed to be in one piece, at any rate, and he leaned back against the brick wall, waiting for his senses to return properly. He was not sure if he would manage to get back to the lodgings, but if only he could find Colm . . . Somewhere nearby a church clock chimed and Declan counted the chimes and was startled when the total was eight. It had only been a little after three when he set out to follow Colm and it had been six o'clock when he left St Stephen's. Had he lain here for two hours? His head throbbed and his skin felt as if a thousand red-hot needles were jabbing into it.

Near the top of the steps was the pile of rubbish he had

slipped on. A coil of sodden rope and a few unidentifiable rags. There was a second, similar pile of rubbish lying at the foot of the steps, quite near him. It looked like a bundle of old clothes.

It was not old clothes at all. It was a person – an unconscious man lying in a huddle on the ground. Probably it was a sailor, too drunk to stand up, or a tramp who had lain down to sleep. *Out here?* said Declan's mind, disbelievingly. *With rain sheeting down for the last eight or ten hours?* He went forward, a bit unsteadily, and bent over the prone figure.

Oh God. Oh Jesus, Mary and Joseph, this could not be real. It was part of a nightmare – an illusion from knocking himself out earlier. But Declan knew it was not. This was real; it was a man, a jowl-faced man with thin sandy hair and pale, podgy hands. The hands were held out as if to ward off an attack, and the eyes were wide and glaring with terror and agony. Blood pooled under the body, glistening in the light from a street lamp. Still wet, thought Declan. Is he still bleeding? Is it possible he's still alive? He thrust one hand inside the man's jacket, feeling for a heartbeat. As he did so, a scarf tucked into the coat slid off. Declan gasped and recoiled. The man's throat had been slit – a deep, gaping gash that showed white glints – muscle, sinews . . .

He turned away, retching. When he'd recovered and looked at the body again he was conscious of an extraordinary feeling of pity that this was all any human being was made of. Skin and muscle, and life-breath that could whistle out of you at the touch of a knife's blade.

I'm so sorry for you, said Declan, very softly to the unknown man. You're lying there in your own blood and it's raining and lonely and your blood's trickled into the puddles.

He took off his jacket and laid it across the man's body, covering up the gaping throat wound. Then he stood up and looked about him, thinking he would have to find help – dead bodies had to be reported to the police – but not knowing where to go. It was then that footsteps sounded at the head of the steps and a figure appeared through the darkness.

Colm's voice said, 'Declan, what have you done?'

Somehow Colm got Declan back to the lodging house, and wrapped a blanket round him. From somewhere he produced a mug of tea, laced with brandy.

'I don't remember much,' said Declan, sipping the tea gratefully. 'I went out to find you, only then I felt ill. I thought you might have gone back to Romilly's grave,' he said, 'but you weren't there, so I went to the house in Bidder Lane. Then I skidded on the wet river steps and knocked myself out.' He cupped his hands round the mug of tea, letting the warmth seep into his fingers. 'Colm – that man I found. We should tell someone.'

'We should not,' said Colm, at once. 'You know who it was, do you?'

'Who . . . ?'

'It's Bullfinch,' said Colm. Then, as Declan looked at him, his mind still foggy from the events of the day, unable to think who Bullfinch was, Colm said, impatiently, 'The abortionist. The man responsible for Romilly's death. And if anyone finds out you were there with his body, they'll ask some very difficult questions.'

Declan found it difficult to take this in. He was slightly warmer, but his head was still opening and shutting on waves of pain, and he felt light-headed from exhaustion. He said, 'How do you know it was Bullfinch?'

'There was a wallet lying on the steps when I found you,' said Colm. 'It was near the body. I thought it was yours so I put it in my pocket. But it isn't yours.' He indicated a small leather wallet lying on the bed. Declan saw with a shudder that it was dark with dried blood.

'There's a letter inside,' said Colm. 'Addressed to Harold Bullfinch at Clock Street. And if you think there'll be two Bullfinches living in that street . . .' He leaned forward. 'Declan, if anyone knows you were there tonight, they'll think you murdered Bullfinch out of revenge for Romilly's death. You can't tell anyone about finding his body – you do see that?'

'Yes,' said Declan slowly. 'Yes, I do see that. What do we do?'

'We leave here at once, that's what we do. We find somewhere else to stay.'

'Where? We haven't any money.'

'Yes we have.' The sudden grin lifted Colm's face. 'Bullfinch's money in his wallet.'

'We can't use that.'

'We can.' Colm got off the bed and went to the window, to peer out. 'It's stopped raining,' he said. 'And I can hear a clock chiming two. If we go now we'll just vanish into the night and no one will be any the wiser.' He looked back at Declan, and something about him sharpened suddenly. 'There isn't anything you left there, is there? Nothing that could cause anyone to connect him with us?

'No,' said Declan, then stopped. 'Oh God.'

'What? Declan, what?'

'My jacket,' said Declan. 'I put it over him.'

'Truly? Mother of God, you're raving mad. Why would you do such a thing?' said Colm, a note of anger in his voice.

'I don't know. He was lying there all bloody and dead and rained on. I wanted to cover him up,' said Declan defensively.

'Was there anything in your jacket with your name on? Letters? Your own wallet?'

'Yes,' said Declan, at last. 'Oh God, yes there was. The ferry ticket – it had my name on it. And we brought birth certificates with us if you remember – we didn't know if we might need them for anything over here.'

'You *fool*,' said Colm. 'Oh God, you madman.' He stood up. 'We'll have to go back for it,' he said. 'Before it's found.'

'But I didn't kill Bullfinch,' said Declan.

Colm turned round and looked at Declan very directly. In a very soft voice, he said, 'Can you be sure of that?'

Declan said, 'Yes. Yes, I can.' But even to his own ears his voice sounded false.

'I left you here just before three o'clock,' said Colm. 'And it was nearly nine when I found you. What were you doing all those hours?'

'If it comes to that, what were you?'

Suspicion flared in the small room, then Colm said, 'Don't be stupid. If you must know, I was at Holly Lodge. With the Totteridge.'

'Were you really? How sordid.'

'I'll be as sordid as I like. Especially,' said Colm, 'if it means getting out of this fleapit and getting my hands on some real money. Declan, this isn't what we came to London for.' He made an angry, impatient gesture, taking in the cheap shabby room. 'Rotten rooms like this, and scraping up the money for the next meal. You're sick from hunger – that's why you feel so ill. When did you last eat?'

'Breakfast this morning,' said Declan. 'And I didn't eat more than a couple of mouthfuls then.'

'I had a very nice supper with the Totteridge. Smoked eels, oyster and beef pie, then some kind of pudding the likes of which I'd never seen. She sent out for it and it was brought to the house and set down before us. She's rich, that one, Declan, and if she's handled right . . .' He gave a wry grin. 'D'you feel well enough to come with me to get your jacket now? We'll use some of Bullfinch's money and get a hansom cab.'

'I'll come,' said Declan, who did not feel well enough to so much as walk down to the street and who would prefer not to touch a farthing of Bullfinch's money. But he could not leave Colm to do this and they did not have any money left of their own.

'We'll buy a couple of penny pies and hot potatoes on the way so you don't collapse from lack of sustenance. And while we eat we'll pray the body hasn't been found.'

*The present*

But it was found, thought Benedict. It was the first of the murders, and it *was* found, and although the case didn't get much publicity – probably because it was overshadowed by Jack and his butcher's knife – Harold Bullfinch was the first of the Mesmer Murders.

# SEVENTEEN

**B**enedict collected the photocopies of Holly Lodge's Title Deeds from the solicitors next morning while Nina was delivering fifty stuffed pigeon breasts and a sushi platter to Russell Square for the cocktail party opening of a new art gallery.

Coming out of the solicitors' offices, the large envelope tucked firmly under one arm, he hesitated about returning to the flat. Nina would not mean to pry, but if she realized he had the deeds to Holly Lodge, she would want to discuss it and speculate on its former owners. Benedict wanted to speculate on its former owners as well, but not with Nina leaning over his shoulder.

The thought of going out to Holly Lodge nudged his mind. The key was on his key ring; he could go out there now and study the deeds entirely uninterrupted, and at some point he could phone Nina to say he had met a friend and not to expect him back until later.

Moving with decision, he headed for Tottenham Road tube. He suspected this was as much about proving to himself he was not afraid of the place as anything else, but he would do it anyway. In any case, whether Declan was an alter ego or a full-blown ghost, he had been able to reach Benedict just as easily in Nina's flat as he had in Holly Lodge.

On the way there he tried to dilute Holly Lodge's eeriness by turning it into an over-the-top setting for a horror film. This cartoonish mental image pleased him so much he whiled away the rest of the journey by sketching in a few details. Vapour trickling along the ground and a scantily clad heroine appearing out of the mists, pursued by some nameless evil. Yes, he would have his shrieking heroine; especially since there had not been any scantily clad females in any of his visions so far, unless you counted Romilly Rourke, which

Benedict was not inclined to do. Not that Romilly had
existed. Not that any of them had existed.

*But we did, Benedict . . . You know we did . . .*

Holly Lodge looked perfectly ordinary. It's all right, thought
Benedict, pausing at the gate and looking up at it. There's
nothing here. Or is there? For a heart-stopping second he
thought something darted across an upstairs window, then
realized it was just the reflection of a cloud. And ghosts could
not actually hurt people – they could frighten them, but nothing
worse.

*Are you sure about that, Benedict? What about your
parents . . . ? Your grandfather . . . ? How do you suppose
they really died in that blizzard . . . ?*

They skidded on the icy roads, said Benedict. But the
memory of his father saying, 'Benedict must never go to that
house,' came back to him.

*Did they skid, Benedict? Or did they swerve their motor
car to avoid hitting someone they thought was standing in the
centre of the road . . . ? Someone who seemed to be walking
towards them . . . Someone who wore a long dark coat, the
collar turned up to hide the face . . .*

I'm not listening, said Benedict to Declan in his mind. You
aren't real. With a tremendous mental effort he pushed Declan
away and went into the house. The minute he stepped through
the door the atmosphere of old memories and new hauntings
closed around him. Then, prompted perhaps by the same impulse
that compels a person to probe an aching tooth with a tongue
tip, he half closed his eyes and deliberately tried to see the big
hall as it might have been in his great-grandfather's day . . .

For a moment it was there, like a double-exposed photograph, or an old cine film projected on to a living background.
Gas lamps burning, flock wallpaper, cumbersome plants in
brass pots . . . A raddled woman presiding over a small harem
of kitten-faced hussies with painted cheeks and rouged lips,
who lay on beds ready to perform any exotic tasks the
gentlemen might require . . . And the scents – smoke from
coal fires and tallow candles, and the body sweat of people
for whom daily baths and deodorants were unknown. Benedict
had just time to think that the romantic view of the Victorians

and the Edwardians never seemed to encompass stale sweat or breath tainted by lack of dentists, when the vagrant pictures dissolved and there was nothing but the slightly damp smell of a house too long empty.

He crossed the hall, glanced in each of the downstairs rooms, then ascended the stairs. Here was the half-landing where Declan and Colm had their whispered conversation after visiting Cerise's room. Which room had that been? Which room had been Romilly's? No means of knowing.

In the second-floor room, the bureau with the press cuttings was exactly as he had left it, the desk flap down, the jumble of pens and old calendars and envelopes strewn on the floor from his previous visit. He had half fallen, he remembered; that had been because Declan dragged him out to the watch-tower and he had heard the screams of agony as Nicholas Sheehan died, and smelled human flesh and old stones slowly burning. Dreadful.

The newspaper cuttings were among the spilled debris; his great-grandfather's face stared up at him from one of the yellowing scraps, under the heading 'MESMER MURDERER ESCAPES'.

'I'm ignoring you,' Benedict said to him, putting down the envelope with the Title Deeds and scooping up the newspaper cuttings and scattered papers. The pens and calendars could be taken out to the dustbins, but he could not bring himself to destroy the accounts of the Mesmer Murders, although nor could he bear to reread them. He folded them carefully so as not to tear the brittle paper, and put them in a spare envelope which he placed at the back of the desk.

There had been three cuttings – he remembered that quite clearly. But a fourth lay near the wall, as if it had been dislodged from the desk when he had tumbled into that sinister uncon-sciousness. Benedict hesitated, then saw it was much more recent than the 1890s pieces, so it could not have anything to do with Declan. It would be quite safe to read it.

The cutting was dated twelve years earlier and had been clipped from what looked like a semi-provincial newspaper, covering this part of North London. It was an account of the inquest findings on the death of his parents and his grandfather.

With the sense that a different shard of the past was spiking into his mind, Benedict began to read.

**TRIPLE DEATH TRAGEDY**
**Small inner mystery within multiple fatality**
A verdict of death by misadventure was today recorded on the three people who died in a dramatic road smash at the height of the recent freezing blizzards that brought most of the country to a standstill last month.

Jonathan Doyle (34), his wife Emma (31), and Jonathan's father, Patrick (82), died when the car being driven by Jonathan skidded from the road and crashed into a brick wall. No other vehicles were involved, and the coroner said it could be assumed, with reasonable certainty, that the treacherous conditions were the cause of the crash.

However, two witnesses who had been travelling some distance behind the Doyles' car, stated, independently, that they had seen a pedestrian in the road, who had seemed to be walking towards the doomed car. Both described the figure as male, wearing a long dark coat.

'I thought he must be drunk,' said one of the witnesses. 'He seemed to weave in and out of the blizzard, very uncertainly.'

The second witness told our reporter afterwards that she thought the man might have been confused or have mental problems. 'Because no one in their right mind would walk down the centre of a main road in a raging blizzard, would they?' she said. 'No one would even be out in that weather if they could help it. We were only travelling ourselves because my daughter had just had her first child.'

The coroner told the court that police had tried to trace the unknown man, but had not been able to do so. No hospitals, nursing homes or retirement homes had reports of a patient missing, and there had been no accidents involving a pedestrian in the area.

The small inner mystery of the unknown man who appears to have caused these three deaths, then to have vanished, remains unsolved.

Benedict stared at the cutting, his mind tumbling with confusion. They saw him, he thought. Those two people saw Declan. I'm not ill – I'm not suffering from that dissociative personality condition – I'm being bloody haunted! It *can't* be coincidence. It must have been Declan. He deliberately caused them to swerve and crash. But why?

For the first time he reached for Declan with his mind, but there was nothing. And that's exactly like you! thought Benedict angrily. To step back into whatever shadowy world you inhabit, just when I start asking awkward questions. But I'm still not taking this as proof that you're haunting me. I'll need more than this.

He put the cutting in the envelope with the others, then, with an air of decision, took the solicitor's package of Holly Lodge's deeds from his bag. If he was going to look for proof, he would start with the house and its owners.

The legal phrases and familiar headings steadied him. This is what I know, thought Benedict. This is the kind of thing I've been studying for the last two years. Property law and the rights of ownership and the complexities of land transfer.

Holly Lodge, it seemed, had been built in 1820. There was a record of the purchase of some land by a Mr Simcox, described as an importer of fine teas. Benedict imagined a genial gentleman, making a modest success in business, building himself a fine new house in a smart part of London, indulgently tolerant of his wife's aspirations.

A proliferation of later Simcoxes seemed to have inherited the place after the importer's death, but they appeared to be a weakly breed, because there were five separate deeds of transfer, and each time a note was appending saying, 'On the death of Alfred – on the demise of Octavius – of Leviticus – the freehold messuage and lands known as Holly Lodge in the district of Highbury, County of London, were transferred absolutely . . .'

Benedict liked seeing how a house was passed down in a family or – in this case – passed across, from elder brother to younger brother, or perhaps cousin. It was interesting as well to see reference to the old geographical boundaries of London

– there had been no Inner London in those days. He spared a
moment to consider this, then turned to the next document.

This was an H.M. Land Registry certificate, stating that the
land on which Holly Lodge stood had been registered in 1870
when the last of the Simcoxes had sold the house to a Mr
Aloysius Totteridge, described as an accountant. Clipped to
this was a further transfer of title, dated 1888, recording that
on the death of Aloysius, his entire estate, including Holly
Lodge, had passed to his widow.

Mrs Florence Totteridge.

So she was real, thought Benedict, sitting back. The raddled
harridan who ushered hopeful and priapic gentlemen to the
bedrooms of Cerise and Romilly and several others, was real.
But does that mean the rest of it's real? That stuff about sin-
eating and the watchtower?

The murders had been real, though. Declan had already
killed one man, and if those newspaper accounts could be
trusted, there were four more still to be killed.

He closed the bureau, thrust the Deeds back into his bag
and went down the stairs and out into the street.

Michael's Oxford career to date had not included tracking down
elusive Irish priests, whose provenance seemed dubious and
whose probity was certainly questionable, but if Father Nicholas
Sheehan had existed, it should be possible to find him. If he
could not do so at Oxford, where research into arcane byways
of the past was the norm, he might as well give up.

The start of Oriel College's Hilary Term was, as he had told
Benedict, a bit crowded. Michael was caught up with ener-
gizing his students after the exigencies of their various
Christmas festivities, and with the demands of his editor for
Wilberforce's various adventures, and it was a week before
he could focus properly on Benedict's story.

He began by way of Oxford's Theology Faculty, strayed
into the Ian Ramsey and the MacDonald Research Centres as
a matter of course, (both of which proved to be dead ends),
and found his way to the Faculty's library in St Giles. He
liked St Giles and he liked the library, which had a pleasingly
unassuming air.

It was eleven o'clock. He would work for two hours, then have lunch in one of the nearby restaurants that scattered this part of Oxford. Several had looked interesting – he and Nell might have a meal here sometime.

The time passed without him noticing it. He was not on very familiar ground, and he wound a tangled path through learned treatises on the Old Testament, the New Testament, and on Doctrines and Ethics of various flavours and persuasions. It was all no doubt deeply interesting, but it was not what he wanted. He wanted books listing ordained priests – almanacs and year books and directories. Even privately printed memoirs from obscure and long-defunct parishes and people.

Then, shortly after twelve, he found a bookcase tucked in a corner of one of the rooms with twelve editions of Thom's Irish Almanacs. They reposed on the lowest shelf, neatly stacked in date order, and the dates ranged from 1860 to 1899. If Nicholas Sheehan had existed, according to Owen he would be recorded in Thom. Michael seized the books, disturbing a cloud of dust and dispossessing half a dozen indignant spiders of their homes, and carried them, armful by armful, to the quiet reading room before they could vanish and render Nicholas Sheehan as ethereal as ever.

At first he thought he was not going to find anything. He leafed through pages upon pages of entries, poring over the small print until his eyes ached. The lists were arranged alphabetically, which was one mercy, and there were columns showing the date of each priest's ordination, the place where he had actually been ordained and, in a few cases, a name indicating who the presiding bishop had been.

By the time Michael reached the 1860s, he was almost prepared to give up, and he was certainly in a mood to throw the estimable Alexander Thom and his entire works across the floor.

And then, quite suddenly, there it was. Nicholas Luke Sheehan. Admitted to St Patrick's Monastery near Galway in 1870, where his Abbot had been Fergal McMahon. In September 1874, Nicholas Sheehan had been admitted to Holy Orders by Bishop John Delaney.

He existed, thought Michael. And it all fits – the dates, the name. But one of the basic rules of research was to find at least two primary sources, so he made notes of everything, then headed for the index section. This was mostly on computer, and Michael keyed in a request for any material on Abbot Fergal McMahon of St Patrick's Monastery, and Bishop John Delaney.

There was nothing on the Bishop, but the request for the Abbot turned up one entry.

*Memoirs of an Irish Monastic Life. Fergal McMahon, Order of St Benedict. Father Abbot of St Patrick's Monastery, in the County of Galway. Privately printed by the Irish Catholic Press, 1904.*

The book won't be here, thought Michael, scribbling down the reference numbers. It'll be long since pulped. Or it'll be on long-term loan to some absent-minded academic who's studying nineteenth-century Irish Catholicism, and lost it weeks ago. Or – here's a likelier scenario – it won't be the right Fergal McMahon, because how many Fergals and how many McMahons must there be in Ireland? And how many monasteries dedicated to St Patrick! But what if it *is* the right person? What if this is the man who knew Nicholas Sheehan and saw him through training for the priesthood? And then, in later life, wrote his memoirs, perhaps referring to some of the ordinands in his care? No, he thought. It won't be. Of course it won't.

But it was. There in the flyleaf was a short introduction written by Abbot Fergal himself.

'In my life of service to God I came across many interesting people and events,' the Abbot had written. 'I believe it to be but a small indulgence to make a record of my life before He calls me, and trust I have done so with brevity, modesty and clarity and that my memories will be of value and interest.

'A cautionary note: the tale related in Chapter Ten of these pages is anonymous as to the name of the participant. However, it is a true tale and should serve as a warning to the inquisitive. The devil's lures are everywhere.'

Michael turned to Chapter Ten. As was customary for that era, there was a subheading, describing the section's contents. This read: 'My difficult decision over one of my ordinands

– N.S.'s ill-starred association with the man known as the Wicked Earl of Kilderry'.

Michael read this twice, foraged in his wallet for his reader's ticket, and checked the book out on loan. After this he carried Fergal McMahon and his monastic memories back to Oriel College.

His rooms were cold because he had forgotten to switch on the thermostat. He remedied this, put the Abbot's memoirs temporarily in a drawer where Wilberforce could not get at them, and closed the door on the world. Then he checked his diary, seeing with relief that he had no tutorials until five that evening, and headed for the kitchen to heat some soup for a belated lunch. While it was warming up, he lured Wilberforce off a pile of third-year essays on stanzaic form by means of opening a tin of Wilberforce's favourite cat food. After this, he sat down at his desk and took Fergal McMahon's book from the drawer.

It took all of his carefully acquired academic discipline not to turn straight to Chapter Ten and the tale of N.S. and the Wicked Earl. Instead, forcing his mind to a scholarly detachment, he opened the book at the start, putting a notebook and pen to hand so he could write down any pertinent names or places.

To the accompaniment of Wilberforce wolfing down jellied tuna and herring chunks, he began to read Fergal McMahon's memoirs.

# EIGHTEEN

'It was a great source of pleasure that the small, quite obscure monastery I helped found grew to be such a wonderful place for God's work,' wrote Fergal McMahon. 'On the day in the early 1860s when we first opened the doors, our total funds amounted to one shilling [editor's note: an Irish shilling is equivalent to a British shilling], but years later, during the Great Famine, we were able to help many unfortunate people.'

The writing was vivid and lively, although Michael found the depictions of the Great Famine somewhat depressing. The Abbot conscientiously described for his readers the memories of his youth – the grey, hopeless faces of the farmers and what he referred to as 'the peasantry', as they saw their crops fail year after year. Michael had just reached a description of the pervasive stench of potatoes rotting in the ground – 'And the putrefaction fumes strong enough to stay in your nostrils for days' – when there was a sound of angry hissing from the kitchen and the smell of burning. He dived into the kitchen to rescue the pan of soup, which he had forgotten about, and which had boiled down to an unpleasant brown mess, with mushrooms stuck to the sides. Michael swore, switched off the cooker, left the pan to cool, and returned to Fergal who was now describing the exodus of so many Irish families, and applying considerably more optimism.

'They went off to seek their fortunes in other lands, and there'd generally be a bit of a *craic* the night before they set off,' wrote the Abbot, and Michael was about to search his shelves for a Celtic dictionary, because *craic* sounded like a lobster recipe which surely could not be right, when he realized it was an Irish word for party.

'Jars of poteen always circulated freely,' explained Fergal, who sounded as if he might have partaken fairly robustly of the poteen himself. 'And most of it supplied by that rascal Fintan Reilly from Kilglenn.'

Fintan again, thought Michael. Eithne mentioned him, as well – in fact it sounded as if she'd had a love affair with him, not to mention a couple of children. This was not conclusive – Ireland's west coast was probably littered with people named Fintan – but Declan's story had also referred to Fintan, so this seemed to provide another shred of evidence in favour of Benedict's odd visions being real.

'But no one much cared if they were caught drinking poteen, and them off to Dublin the next day, bound for England on the Liverpool ferry, although they'd have a dreadful old journey below decks in steerage. They didn't care about that though, for their sights were set on the glittering cities of America. Ah, America – "Wide as Shakespeare's soul, sublime as Milton's immemorial theme, and rich as Chaucer's speech",' wrote Fergal, enclosing the sentence in quotation marks so that Michael, delighted with the Abbot's exuberant rhetoric, wrote the words down to trace to their source later.

'It was not everyone who was bound for America, though,' continued the Abbot. 'The streets of London, paved with the fabled gold of legend, also drew my countrymen. I was never in London in my life, although I believe it was a fine sight with all the splendid streets and shops and palaces, and the Queen riding past in her carriage.

'St Patrick's Monastery was growing apace and after four years we were delighted we could open a seminary for young men called to serve God as priests. There was much contentment in shaping these eager souls, some scarcely more than eighteen, for service in God.

'And then the young man I shall refer to only as N.S. came to us in 1870, and although I could not have known it at the time, his arrival heralded the reawakening of an ancient evil.'

'N.S,' thought Michael. Will it be Nicholas Sheehan or not? It must be. He read on.

It was Autumn when N.S. came to St Patrick's. A bronze October morning, scented with rain and chrysanthemums – the kind of morning when I always felt God was smiling.

I never knew N.S's parentage, but we all thought he was from the old aristocracy. A bastard son of some ancient line, perhaps. Not that these things matter.

He was a good-looking boy, dark-haired, with a glint of arrogance about him, and eyes the colour of the ocean – that clear grey you so seldom see, rimmed with black. But the day he walked through our doors, I thought, "Oh my, we're going to have trouble with this one."

Even so, for the four years of his studies he was a diligent and biddable student. But I think – no, I am sure – that there were nights when he slipped out of the monastery and made his way to one of the little nearby towns. Ladies were what he sought, of course, and with the way he looked, I dare say he'd have little trouble attracting them. Ah well, once upon a time I was not entirely blameless in that direction myself. As a young man in the seminary in Dublin, I, too, struggled with the vow of chastity, and I did not always win the fight.

As well as charm and good looks, N.S. possessed imagination, and that's a dangerous thing in a priest. A little is fine and good. Too much and your man starts to believe in the medieval tales of demons, and of horned and cloven creatures crawling and trawling the world for souls. Those creatures were made-up stories – weapons to keep people within the Church's teachings, of course. I never believed in them myself.

I believe in evil, though. It was planted in the world long before men walked in it, and it's still there, deeply buried but lethal, like the iron-jawed snares farmers set for predators. Take a wrong step, and *snap!* you're caught in Satan's mantrap. He's a sneaky, subtle creature, the Prince of Darkness, and his evil can tear lives apart and shred souls.

It was Fintan Reilly who started the black chain of events. Whether Fintan could actually read or write I never knew, and perhaps it doesn't matter, for he could paint a picture with words the like of which you never heard. And on a night in 1878, when I was still a relatively young man, Fintan painted a picture that harrowed up my soul to its very marrow.'

Michael, coming up out of Fergal McMahon's world, was starting to suspect that the Abbot might have missed his vocation – that he should have pursued a career writing nineteenth-century gothic fiction. So far there was nothing in the memoirs that provided any working facts – no place names or firm dates that could be tracked to their source. He was undecided whether to show this account to Benedict Doyle. He did not precisely think Fergal was making this up, but he was keeping in mind Owen Bracegirdle's comment about the Irish being the storytellers of the world.

But it was half past four, and unless he wanted to be late for his five o'clock tutorial, he would have to put Fergal aside for the next two hours. He shut the book in the desk, then remembered he had not eaten since breakfast, so he crammed a wedge of cheese and a couple of biscuits into his mouth, after which he assembled his notes and his thoughts. He had set up a small discussion group of first years and today they were going to consider the use of diaries and letters as narrative in nineteenth-century literature. They were a bright, enthusiastic bunch and it was a lively session, although a note of high comedy was provided halfway through by Wilberforce finding the unwashed pan of mushroom soup and dislodging several plates in order to get at the remains. The plates fell off the drainer, precipitating Wilberforce into the washing-up bowl, much to his annoyance. He retired crossly to the radiator shelf to dry off, and Michael swept up the broken plates and returned to the analysis of Ann Brontë and Wilkie Collins.

The students left shortly after six. Michael threw away the ruined saucepan, and returned to the Abbot and the entry into his story of Fintan Reilly.

Fintan, it appeared, had the habit of turning up at St Patrick's unexpectedly, generally when he was broke, hungry, running from an irate husband, father or brother, or – on a couple of memorable occasions – running from the law. And there had been a particular night midway through a tempestuous November evening in 1878 when he had arrived at the monastery, his appearance unannounced, as it always was.

'A dark and wild night it was, with the rain lashing against the windows and rattling them like the bones of the restless dead, and the wind screeching across the ocean like the voices of souls trapped in purgatory,' wrote the Abbot, and Michael read this with delight. Oh, Fergal, *why* didn't you take to writing purple fiction, he thought. Or maybe you did. Maybe you were really Bram Stoker or Sheridan Le Fanu. He considered this concept of allotting shadow personas to well-known novelists for a moment in case it might make an interesting essay subject for his students, then resumed reading.

> We had two guests that night, for N.S. was visiting us as well. N.S. had left us three or four years previously, to take a curacy in a parish on the outskirts of Galway. He had written to me, describing his work with enthusiasm, and I was starting to hope my early fears about him had been unfounded. This was the first time he had returned to St Patrick's, however.
>
> It was after supper when Fintan unfolded his tale. Fintan always told a tale when he was given food; he considered it a form of payment, I think.
>
> 'I've a tale to spin,' says Fintan, on this November night, and there was a small, pleased murmur. The ordinands – we had six at the time – looked up hopefully.
>
> 'Once upon a time, and a very long time it was,' says Fintan, 'the devil, walking the world in his greedy, prideful way, thought he'd put some of his powers of persuasion into the rocks and stones and gems of the world. "Aha", thinks he, "there'll come a time when men will chisel out these rocks and stones, and make objects to adorn their houses and their shelves. And I'll be inside those things, and that'll be yet another way for me to get into their souls."'
>
> Here Fintan paused and took a refreshing draught of the mulled wine at his elbow. (Readers will be familiar with St Paul's dictum about a little wine for the stomach's

sake, although to be fair, Fintan's measures could not be called little.)

'I've a friend now, in service at Kilderry Castle,' says Fintan. 'A very particular friend she is, and a good girl, diligent and willing.' This was a perfectly acceptable remark for any man to make; the trouble was that Fintan accompanied his words with a sly wink to the monk seated next to him. The monk happened to be our cellerar, Brother Cuthbert, who was seventy-five if he was a day, and although he'd know in theory about willing girls, he'd been in the monastery for fifty years, so the practice would be a dim memory.

'My girl at Kilderry Castle has a deep concern,' said Fintan, and for the first time since I ever knew him, his voice had a serious ring to it.

Somebody further down the table observed that there would always be a deep concern about anyone inside Kilderry Castle, for wasn't the Earl known as the boldest sinner ever.

This was putting it kindly, for the Black Earl, as he was often called (although not in his hearing) was said by some to have trafficked with the devil. People said that, like Faust, he had sold his soul to Satan for power over men and women. Mesmerism, they call it nowadays, and it's a subtle power and one you'd certainly expect Satan to have in his gift.

'That's as maybe,' says Fintan, leaning forward with his elbows on the table. 'But the Earl's been good enough to my girl and he's been good enough to other servants as well.'

There was a slightly awkward silence at this, for Gerald Kilderry's particular brand of 'goodness' was generally believed to take a very particular form, although if only half the rumours about him were true you'd at least have to admire the man's energy.

'So now,' says Fintan, 'there's this room in Kilderry Castle lined with books and manuscripts and all manner of fine things for learned gentlemen to browse among of an evening. And in that room, also, is a set of chessmen

– you'll all know the game of chess, of course, you being learned people, never mind monks.'

A murmur of assent. I saw N.S. lean forward, his eyes bright and alert.

'The chessmen,' says Fintan, lowering his voice the better to infuse it with a thrilling note, 'were hewn from those very rocks that old Satan threaded through with his evil charm – and it's a charm that will talk men into doing whatever Satan wants. Imagine how it might be if an ordinary human got hold of that power. If men – even women – were able to crook a finger and point to a victim and say, "You. You come to me on such and such a date, at such and such a time".' He demonstrated by crooking his own finger and several of the monks looked startled.

'Those chessmen,' goes on Fintan, 'are as black and as bad as Satan's own horns. And there they sit, in the library at Kilderry Castle, and Satan's power trapped within them.

'And my girl at the castle tells how there are times when the Black Earl has sat in that room any length of time, that his eyes take on a look that terrifies them all. A hungry look,' said Fintan. 'As if his eyes could eat a man's soul.'

He sat back and surveyed his audience, clearly pleased at the effect his words had created. For good measure (he could never resist the extra flourish), he said, 'And you'll remember, all of you, that Kilderry Castle is no more than three miles from this very building.'

It would be untrue to say we believed Fintan's story, but it would also be untrue to say we disbelieved it. There are curious things in the world – you chance on them from time to time. Objects or houses – even people – that possess extraordinary powers.

After supper, Brother Cuthbert and I retired to my study, and Fintan followed us.

'There's more to tell,' he said, seating himself comfortably in a chair.

'I thought there might be. Speak out, Fintan.'

'Father Abbot, my girl in Kilderry Castle says the

chess pieces are frightening them all to death.' His face was serious, and for once there was no trace of his customary flippancy.

'In what way?' asked Brother Cuthbert.

'There's always been nights when some of the servants have seen the shadows of the chess figures creeping along the castle corridors, and peering out from behind a curtain,' said Fintan. 'But while the chessmen were unused – while they stood quietly on their table – nothing ever happened. But a few months back, the Earl used the chess set. A man came to the castle and challenged Kilderry and the two of them sat playing for hours and hours. My girl believes that during those hours something woke in the figures – something that had slumbered more or less harmlessly for a very long time. And now – you'll think this is absurd – but she's in fear and terror for her sanity and her soul. And for the souls of others.' He studied us for a moment. 'I see the mention of souls hits you in the consciences,' he said. 'I thought it would.'

'You thought right,' said I drily. 'What is it you're wanting from us, Fintan?'

His eyes gleamed. 'I've promised my girl that I'd ask would some of you come up to the castle when the Earl's away.'

'Why?' This was Brother Cuthbert.

'To destroy the chessmen and vanquish the devil's power, of course.'

As the good Lord is my witness, when Fintan said this, a cold, dry breath of wind ruffled its way across the small, fire-lit room and I felt it brush my skin like icy claws.

I said, firmly, 'Fintan, if you're suggesting we perform an exorcism . . .' I broke off, frowning. 'That isn't something that can be undertaken lightly. We'd need the Bishop's permission at the very least.'

'There's no need for exorcism,' said Fintan. 'All I want is for you to come up to the castle with me and burn that devilish chess set so we can tip the ashes into the ocean forever.' He regarded us. 'And tonight,' he said, 'the Earl is away, and the castle empty.'

Cuthbert and I sat over the dying fire, discussing what to do.

'Do we believe that rogue?' I said. 'For he's the world's most extravagant storyteller.'

'I believe him,' said Cuthbert. 'People forget the devil is extremely clever – they also forget that he's extremely ancient. When he lays his plans he doesn't think in terms of a few years, you know; he thinks of the age of an entire world. And he adapts to the worlds he prowls. There's the popular image of him as a persuasive gentleman with horns and a forked tail, but if he went around today looking like that, people would think he was dressed-up for a costume ball.'

I said, 'Cuthbert, you constantly amaze me. What would you know about costume balls?'

'I wasn't always a monk,' said Cuthbert, injured. 'I've had my small adventures, Father Abbot. And I know Fintan Reilly's an unlikely instrument for the good Lord to choose, but if he really has stumbled upon an ancient pocket of evil, it's for us to help him fight it.'

As he said this, a breath of wind gusted down the chimney and stirred the glowing peat fire in the hearth. I said, with more assurance than I was feeling, 'I think we'd better go up to Kilderry Castle and see this chess set for ourselves. But it's a task for younger men.'

Cuthbert, slightly aggrieved, said he hoped he could still say a prayer over a fragment of evil as effectively as ever.

'Yes, but it's three miles to Kilderry Castle and a steep haul up the hill, and you with the arthritis in both knees,' I said. 'So I suggest—'

It was at that point someone tapped softly on the door.

It was N.S. He came in with an air of faint apology, and took the seat offered him.

'I won't prevaricate, Father Abbot,' he said. 'It's about Fintan Reilly's story.'

'Yes?'

'Are you going out to Kilderry Castle to destroy that chess set?'

The directness of this disconcerted me somewhat. 'I don't know,' I said, slowly. 'Why do you want to know so particularly?'

'If you do,' he said, ignoring my question, 'Would you take me with you?'

'You? Why would we take you?'

N.S. stared into the fire. 'I have some knowledge of that old legend, Father.'

'But,' said Cuthbert, 'you surely don't believe Fintan's story?'

'Evil exists,' said N.S. 'And if you mean to confront that particular evil, you should have with you someone who understands it.'

'Do you understand it?'

'No. But I've encountered it.' He looked up at me. 'Father Abbot,' he said. 'I was the man who played that chess game with the Black Earl of Kilderry. I was the one who woke the evil in those figures.'

It was an uncomfortable journey we made to Kilderry Castle the next night, and it was not made easier by the blizzard that was raging everywhere.

N.S. and I were wrapped up against the cold; Fintan, a hardy soul, wore only his customary greatcoat with the deep inner pockets. A poacher's coat, of course, but I'd have to admit that if a plump hare or two found its way to the monastery kitchens, or a side of salmon appeared on our table, we accepted them and asked no questions.

Fintan had acquired a small cart with a donkey to pull it – when asked whence it came, he murmured vaguely about it belonging to a pedlar who had been glad to loan it for a day or two. It was a rickety old thing; Brother Cuthbert, standing at the monastery door to bid us farewell, was shocked to his toes to think of Father Abbot riding abroad on such a contraption.

'You'll be jolted like an unset junket after ten feet,'

he said, 'and your insides scrambled out of recognition, I shouldn't wonder. It's not fitting, Father Abbot.'

'It's not fitting that the Earl of Kilderry should be harbouring the devil's arts,' said I. 'I shan't mind a bit of jolting in God's work.'

'It's a short enough ride anyway,' said N.S.

But it turned out that Fintan – or possibly the pedlar – had spread a thick rug on the cart's floor and the journey was not, in the event, too uncomfortable.

I carried the large crucifix from our chapel, and we each had a phial of holy water, blessed by the Archbishop on his last visit. I had the missal bestowed on the monastery at its opening and had marked the Ninety-First Psalm – *"Whosoever dwelleth under the defence of the most High shall abide under the shadow of the Almighty . . ."* It's a powerful prayer against Satan's minions, that prayer.

Fintan carried an ancient blunderbuss which his grandfather had used at Waterloo. He appeared to think that if discharged in the face of any evil adversaries that might be prowling the castle, it would banish them there and then. Cuthbert, seeing it, said it did not look as if it had been fired since Waterloo and he would be surprised if it made more than a splutter.

It was almost eleven o'clock when we finally reached Kilderry Castle, and very dark it was, with the moon behind clouds most of the time.

Kilderry Castle stands on a small hilltop – it's a brooding, squat place, with frowning battlements and mullioned stonework adorned with gargoyles. I think former Earls liked to keep a watch for enemies sneaking up the hillside, and fire off arrows at them. On the crest of this thought I said, 'Fintan, you are sure Himself of Kilderry is away at the moment?'

'I am,' said Fintan, who was hunched over the reins, encouraging the little donkey by means of various epithets.

'He's often away,' said N.S. casually.

As we went through a belt of trees, a sharp spiteful wind stirred the leafless branches, causing them to reach down as if they intended to snatch up any stray enemies of the Lords of Kilderry. A faint dank mist rose from the ground, and I shivered. Beside me, N.S. drew the hood of his cloak over his head.

'We'll leave the cart here,' said Fintan, when we were about two-thirds of the way up. He sprang down and tethered the donkey's reins to a tree stump covered with a thick mat of ivy. 'The path's not wide enough for the cart from here. Will I bring the carpet bag with me?'

'Why would we need that?'

'To conceal the blunderbuss,' said Fintan, as if it should be obvious. 'For I'm not shouldering it and carrying it up there for all to see.'

'Bring the bag,' I said.

As we walked warily up the slope, the old castle lay deep in shadow, although several times I thought lights glinted in the narrow windows. As we climbed the steep slope I thought something huffed its sulphurous breath into my face, and a low voice, like the crackling of brittle leaves or snapping bones, whispered in my ear.

"*Better to go back while you still can*," said this voice. "*For you won't beat the One you're going to confront . . .*"

'Oh yes I will,' I said, very softly, and N.S. glanced at me in surprise.

Kilderry Castle, when finally we stood in its courtyard, was the most ramshackle place I ever saw in my life. Ivy covered parts of the grey walls and weeds thrust up between huge cracks in the courtyard. The gargoyles leered down like very demons themselves.

Beside me, N.S. said, very softly, 'It's as if there's something sick and evil dwelling in there, and it's oozed its malignancy through the stones until they're decayed and rotten.'

(The reader will see from that remark why I ascribe too much imagination to N.S.)

There was a massive portcullis at the centre of the castle's front, its great iron teeth clamped firmly down. A rusting bell twist hung down at one side. It was a relief when Fintan indicated a more conventional door set into the outer wall further along. 'Eithne said she would leave that door unbolted for us,' he said.

'But you should be careful,' put in N.S. 'For there's a murder hole just inside.'

'A . . . ?'

'An opening in the ceiling for the inhabitants to use for shooting at unwanted guests, or even for pouring boiling liquid on to them. The Kilderrys,' said N.S. rather drily, 'believe in defending what's theirs.'

'Dear God. Fintan, are you sure the Earl's away?'

'Didn't I tell you already he was?' said Fintan. 'There'll be nothing lying in wait.'

But there was.

# NINETEEN

I am not very accustomed to entering castles. I am certainly not accustomed to doing so in darkness, in company with a rapscallion poacher armed with a blunderbuss, and with the intention of sending a fragment of the devil's powers to the rightabout. But it had to be done.

I'd have to report, though, that N.S. went through the door as if he had done so a number of times before, and as casually as if he was entering the henhouse at St Patrick's. Fintan, who cared nothing for any man's rank, did the same. I followed.

The minute we were inside Kilderry Castle I knew Fintan had been wrong about there being nothing waiting for us. Something was there all right, and the instant we were over the threshold it was as if it woke and lifted a monstrous scaly head to stare at us.

N.S. said, 'This way,' and led us through dim passages, some of which were lit by greasily burning candles, others almost completely dark. Once, he paused as if listening, and I said, 'D'you hear something?'

'Don't you hear it?' he said. 'Like a fleshless whispering.'

'No,' I said a little too loudly, but I had heard it, of course. And with the sounds was the fleeting impression of small shapes, too small to be human, too large to be animals, scuttling back and forth, their eyes glinting red. But that might have been due to my disordered imagination, for by that time I was ready to believe that the demons of the pit – every last one of them – were amassing their dark forces to fight us off.

The reader will forgive me if this sounds like the sin of pride. I did not really believe Satan would send his entire army to fight our tiny band. Of course I did not.

But at this point, I do feel I should issue for my readers the warning that to engage deliberately with any kind of evil adversary is immensely dangerous. As for trading with Satan, which was what the Earl was said to have done to get the chessmen – well, that *never* bodes well. If Satan doesn't renege on the bargain in a particularly unpleasant way, he demands his share of the payment long before the term of the deal is reached. Either way you end up losing your immortal soul. There's maybe some of you will whoop with mirth at the concept of such a bargain – maybe even at the concept of an immortal soul – but there are some strange and fateful things in the world.

Fintan's Eithne met us at the door of the library. A slight little thing she was, with soft brown hair and wide, scared eyes. I noticed that Fintan took her hand and pressed it, and when he spoke to her he did so very considerately.

'You be away to your bed now,' he said. 'Father Abbot and the rest of us will see to this bit of badness, and tomorrow you can forget all about it.'

She sent a frightened look at N.S. 'Eithne,' he said, softly. 'Didn't I say I'd be back for those devil figures? And so I am, for I'm a man of my word.'

'Say your prayers devoutly tonight, and tomorrow you'll be safe,' I said.

'Yes. Thank you,' she said, bobbed a half-curtsey, and scurried away.

The Earl of Kilderry's library was large and high-ceilinged, and it might have been impressive if it had not been in such a disgraceful condition. The sections of walls not covered by books were discoloured and damp-stained, and mirrors and old portraits hung on the walls – most of them crazily askew. The portraits were so smoke-blackened it was impossible to make out any features, and the mirrors so dim with years of wood smoke and candle grease I'd defy anyone to see a reflection in them. There was a not unpleasant scent of peat and cigars.

The chess set stood on a small round table near the fire,

and small as it was, it dominated the whole of the room. I said, with as much authority as I could muster, 'We'll throw the lot in the fire and burn them to ashes. You'll both join me in prayer while we do it.'

'And then we'll be off,' said Fintan, who was setting light to the wall candles, using a taper thrust into the embers of the dying fire. As the candles flickered into life, I had the strong impression that the figures moved – that they flinched from the light. And then – and this is God's own truth – as the fire and the candles burned up more strongly, the shadows seemed to swell and to link hands and prance round us in macabre symmetry.

I began intoning the powerful and beautiful Ninety-First Psalm and there was instant reassurance and comfort from the familiar phrases, and in hearing N.S. join his voice with mine. Still chanting the prayer, I began to walk towards the table.

Twice, intoning the prayer, I had to raise my voice because it seemed as if something was pressing down on it and smothering it, but I managed to continue.

'*Whosoever dwelleth under the defence of the most High shall abide under the shadow of the Almighty . . . I will say unto the Lord, Thou art my hope and my stronghold: my God in Him I will trust . . .*'

I had reached the part that promises, *He shall deliver thee from the snare of the hunters and from the noisome pestilence*, and N.S. and I were both reaching for the chess pieces, when something very strange happened to me. From wanting – intending – to burn the chess pieces, I suddenly knew I could not. They were so beautiful, so intricate. I thought: someone must have spent many, many hours fashioning these pieces. How cruel to cast them into the flames.

At my side, N.S. said, very softly, 'Father Abbot.'

'What is it?' I said, whipping round.

'Look at the mirror,' he said.

'What? I see nothing.'

'The reflections of the chess figures are alive. And they're watching us.'

This was impossible, of course. And yet it was true. In the room the chess figures were still and inanimate. In the mirror there was movement. A horse, ridden by a knight, tossed its carven mane, the head of a bishop half turned, and one of the kings tightened a hand around a sword. And the eyes of all of them gleamed with unmistakable life.

I began to shake so violently I dropped the crucifix I had been holding. N.S. retrieved it, but I had the dreadful thought that it would be of no protection.

*For it's only two sticks of wood nailed together, after all . . .*

'Go on with the prayer,' urged Fintan, but I was struggling to breathe and something was tightening painfully around my chest. It was with deep gratitude that I heard N.S. resume the prayer. *'He shall defend thee under his wings and thou shalt be safe under his feathers: his faithfulness and truth shall be thy shield and buckler . . .'* He broke off and said, in a low urgent voice, 'Father Abbot, don't look at their reflections. Just throw them on the flames. Do it *now*.'

'I can't,' I said. 'God help me, I can't.'

'You must.' But he, too, seemed unable to touch the figures. Then he said, 'Tip up the table. Slide them into the bag. But don't look at their eyes.'

But when we tried this, the table felt as if it was made of lead or as if some invisible giant held it down. We struggled and sweated, but to no avail, and I became aware that the shadows had stopped moving, and they were standing in a line, as if preparing to face an attack. Then at last – I think it was N.S.'s younger strength that did it – we managed to tilt the table just enough and the figures tumbled into the deep bag. I threw the small crucifix in with them, and Fintan snapped the hasp shut. Clutching the bag, we ran from the Earl of Kilderry's library.

The three of us, together with Brother Cuthbert, sat together in my study. I had produced a bottle of brandy and we had all had a goodly measure.

It was N.S. who said, 'Father Abbot, you can't keep those things here.' He glanced to the corner of the room, where the bag lay quiet and lumpen, but still somehow imbued with malevolence. 'I'll take them,' he said. 'It's my responsibility. My family's responsibility.'

'You're a Kilderry?' I said, but I think I already knew he was.

'I am. Not openly recognized or acknowledged as such, but I grew up knowing the legend of the chess pieces. I came to hate and fear them, and I was determined to destroy them. That's why, earlier this year, I tried to win them from Gerald Kilderry. And I believe,' he said, his expression intent, 'that those figures need to be imprisoned in some very remote place where the evil has nothing on which it can feed. Nothing at all – not prayer nor ritual. Not even people. Because evil needs to be fed in order to grow, Father Abbot.'

'We'll burn them,' I said. I did not like N.S.'s words about evil being fed, although there were – and are – several reputable sources to support that concept.

'They'll fight you,' said N.S. at once. 'And they'll probably win. They're so old, they've overpowered stronger adversaries than us down the centuries. And it wouldn't necessarily be a . . . a physical fight, Father Abbot. They would trickle their poison into your mind and corrode your soul and you wouldn't even realize it was happening.'

'He's right,' said Fintan. 'They almost overpowered us in that library.'

'I couldn't destroy them,' I said, half to myself. 'When it came to it, I couldn't do it. I could only think it would be a wanton cruel waste of someone's intricate work.'

'I felt that,' said Fintan.

'But,' said N.S. 'if the evil can be weakened – starved – then it might be possible to destroy them.'

'That could take years.'

'I'd wait years,' said N.S. 'I'd seal them up and keep watch over them.'

'But where would you go?' This was Cuthbert.

'There's an old watchtower on the Moher Cliffs. It's

a lonely, remote place – hardly anyone goes near. I'd seal up the figures inside that tower. And I'd be their guardian.'

'You'd leave your Galway Parish?'

'I would.'

'But you can't simply withdraw from the world for an unknown time,' I said. 'No, if they're to be sealed up, it must be here. This is one of God's houses – steeped in layers of prayer and goodness, and if anything can cause an evil to wither, it's surely that.'

'I believe they can invert prayer to their own means,' said N.S. 'I don't understand it, but I think it's like turning a white bag inside out, so that you only see the black lining.'

The black lining . . . It was remarkable what images that conjured up. After a moment Cuthbert said, in a determinedly practical voice, 'How would you live?'

'That rather depends on you,' said N.S. 'In this monastery are a number of small, easily carried objects of considerable value. Mass vessels, gold and silver cups and chalices, candlesticks, silk wall hangings and altar cloths. Things I could sell in some large anonymous place, such as Galway.'

'Then,' I said, standing up, 'we'd better start deciding what you can take.'

For the first time since entering the Church, that night I ended up so drunk I couldn't walk. Fintan had to help me to my bed.

'It's a shocking thing,' he said, 'when a dissolute tinker like myself has to assist a venerable abbot of the Irish Church to his room.'

'You'll be in my prayers every night.'

'Be damned to the prayers, put me in your Will,' said the irrepressible Fintan. 'And I'll open a great little bar somewhere hereabouts and live a dissolute life so that everyone for miles will enjoy themselves disapproving of me.'

'And Eithne?'

'Ah, Eithne. There's a girl, now. There's a grand bit

of comfort to be got from a night with her. I dare say I oughtn't to say that to a monk.'

'I've known the odd bit of comfort myself as a young man,' I said.

'I dare say. What about your man who came with us tonight? He'll have known more than the odd bit of comfort,' said Fintan. 'I'd say he'll struggle to follow the path of celibacy.'

'We all have our struggles. But he's promised to make sure those evil things are safely sealed up.'

'Will they stay sealed up, d'you think?'

'I don't see why not. They seem to have been harmless inside Kilderry Castle all those years.'

'They're evil,' said Fintan. 'They're leaking evil like – like a dripping gutter. What if someone were to take them out into the world one day?'

'No one will,' said I, and I climbed into bed and sank into a drunken sleep for which I did heavy penance next morning in the form of a mind-splitting headache.

And so N.S., that slightly arrogant young priest, probable scion of the Kilderry line, took the chessmen away.

We had a final word before he left St Patrick's.

'Last night,' I said, 'you mentioned starving the chessmen of everything – even of prayer. Does that mean . . . ?'

'It means I will have to cut myself off from God,' he said, and, without saying anything more, he turned on his heel and walked away.

It pained me then and it still pains me to think of him living in that hermit-like seclusion in the old watchtower on the Cliffs of Moher, not daring to open up that channel in his mind through which comes God's blessed love and understanding.

I shall pray for him every day. And I shall pray that the power of the devil's chessmen will quietly wither and die.

But will it . . . ?

The story ended there, although the book itself went on for another page and a half, with Fergal McMahon adding a conscientious homily about divine and man-made retribution and atoning for sin.

Michael had been so deeply immersed in Fergal's world that when the phone rang it startled him so much he dropped the book on Wilberforce, who let out an indignant yowl.

The phone call was from Nell. She wondered if Michael would like to have supper at her flat the following evening.

'It's tomorrow I'm in London, sorting out the inventory at Holly Lodge,' she said.

'I know it is. What train are you catching?'

'Well, actually,' said Nell, 'I thought I might as well go up tonight. I can get the seven forty-five or the six past eight train and Nina says I can stay with her. It would mean I could make an early start. That might even allow time for me to get that chess piece valued.'

'Good idea. Shall I pick up a takeaway tomorrow so you don't have to cook when you get back?'

'That would be nice.'

'Chinese? Indian? Fish and chips?'

'Chinese, please.' She appeared to hesitate, then in a slightly too-casual voice said, 'Michael, would it be possible for you to meet me off the train tomorrow? I'll probably get the one that gets in at quarter to seven. We could pick up the food on the way to Quire Court.'

'I think I can,' said Michael, reaching for his diary. 'Yes. I've got a couple of tutorials in the morning, but that's all.' It was not like Nell to ask for a lift from the station; she hated being dependent on anyone else and on the few occasions Michael had offered to meet her from a train journey she had always said she was perfectly capable of hopping in a taxi or walking across to the bus station. He did not want to ask outright if anything was wrong, so to give her a let-out he said, 'I expect you might have a lot of stuff to lug back.'

She did not take the let-out. She said, 'It's not that. It's just that I don't want to go into the court on my own in the dark. I thought someone was prowling around a few nights ago.'

'Oh God, was there?' Michael's thoughts switched from the

spectral threat of the chess piece to the more temporal one of burglars and muggers. 'Have you reported it?

There was a perceptible hesitation, then she said, 'Yes, but it was such a vague sighting they weren't inclined to send out the cavalry. The on-duty sergeant logged it and said they would ask the duty patrol car to drive round during the evening, but that's all.'

'Would you like to bring your things over here and stay for a few nights?'

'And shock your students?' The familiar note of irony was back in her voice.

'You could creep out at dawn,' said Michael, smiling. 'Like a Feydeau farce. But how about if I stay with you for a few nights? As a security guard, I mean.'

'Would you wear a uniform?'

'Would you like me to?'

'It depends on the uniform,' she said, and chuckled.

'No, but seriously, I could sleep in Beth's room if you'd prefer, and I could be the one to do the sneaking out at dawn. I should think Quire Court's seen its fair share of furtive lovers over the centuries anyway. Tiptoeing over the cobblestones among the flowerpots.'

'You'd trip over the flowerpots and set off the shop alarms,' said Nell. 'And that would be more like a Carry On film than a French farce. No, I'll be perfectly safe, it was only that once and I haven't heard anything since. I'm probably overreacting.'

'I'll see you tomorrow.'

'Yes.' There was a pause. 'Michael – you will be there, won't you?'

'At the station?'

'Well . . .' She paused, and something seemed to shiver on the air between them.

'My dear love,' said Michael softly, 'I'll always be there.'

Michael was vaguely worried by Nell's mention of a prowler. He was even more worried when he thought about the semi-isolation of Quire Court. It was so quiet, so enclosed in its own gentle atmosphere that it did not seem a place that would be targeted by vandals or burglars. Tomorrow evening he would take a look at the locks and bolts on the doors of the flat behind the shop.

What about the other threat, though? The chess piece. Unless Fergal McMahon's memoirs were false – nineteenth-century Gothic fiction presented in an unexpected way – the Abbot and his gang had clearly believed the chess set held a very dark power. And Fergal's account of the thirty-two shadows performing their own dance macabre in a dim old library was extraordinarily chilling, no matter what one believed.

Michael glanced back at the book's publication date: 1904. Presumably Fergal had been dead by then, but it was entirely possible that he had simply stashed the memoirs away, and they had not come to light until many years later. Perhaps some member of Fergal's family – a niece or nephew – had found them and wanted the world to know the old boy's strange story. Or the Church might have suppressed the memoirs, of course. Michael thought, with a touch of irony, that the Catholic Church was probably second to none when it came to hiding what it considered to be contentious or disreputable incidents.

How much danger might Nell be in from that single chess figure? For pity's sake, thought Michael angrily, it's a lump of wood with a few semi-precious stones stuck on to it!

He made himself a toasted sandwich, poured a glass of wine to go with it, and carried the tray through to his desk. Opening the latest Wilberforce file he worked solidly for the next two hours and by eleven o'clock had almost written an entire chapter. He diligently saved the work to a memory stick, which Nell's Beth had given him for Christmas, tied up in a huge scarlet ribbon. Last December the real Wilberforce had sat on the computer keyboard while Michael was pouring a cup of coffee, and had activated the log-off key. The computer had obediently shut itself down and Michael had lost four pages intended as an insert for the American publishing house, which had recounted Wilberforce's exploits at a Thanksgiving turkey dinner, when Wilberforce had fallen into the cranberry sauce and it had died his whiskers crimson. Ellie, thousands of miles away in Maryland, had loved this, and Beth had said they could not risk losing any of Wilberforce again, so a memory stick would be a really cool present.

Michael reread the chapter he had just written and thought it was not bad. But before he let his editor see it, he would email it to Beth and Ellie. They loved being in on the birth of a new Wilberforce exploit and they would be completely honest about whether it made a good story.

As he got into bed, he wondered if Benedict Doyle had traced any of the people in his story. He had been going to get the Title Deeds to Holly Lodge – perhaps he would ring to let Michael know about that.

Lying in bed, his mind was full of fragments of Benedict's curious story and the vivid collection of people who seemed to have been its major players. It was an extraordinary tale.

He began to drift into sleep, and as he did so, a half-memory nudged uneasily at his mind. He was toppling over into sleep when it clicked fully into place. It was of Benedict sitting in Michael's study that day, the sinister glint of blue in his brown eyes, saying Nell should not go to Holly Lodge.

*Because we both know who's inside that house*, Benedict had said and his voice had once again held the soft Irish overlay.

# TWENTY

**N**ell enjoyed the evening at Nina's flat. Nina had made a huge risotto which they ate in the large friendly kitchen, together with the bottle of Chablis which Nell had brought. Nina rattled on in her customary inconsequential way, Benedict putting in the occasional word, and Nell listened with amusement. But several layers down, she was aware of an undercurrent of excitement. *Only a few hours left, then I'll see him again*, her mind kept saying. *I'll find out who he is. I'll find out what he is.* But this last thought twisted the excitement into such a wrench of apprehension that she pushed it away and focused on what Nina was saying about how people thought you could successfully transport beef Wellington for thirty people halfway across London without the pastry going soggy, could you believe it?

Benedict seemed entirely normal. He teased Nina about the risotto, and helped cut up ciabatta bread to hand round. Afterwards Nina shooed Nell and Benedict into the sitting room while she made coffee, and Nell asked Benedict about the criminology studies.

'At the moment I'm researching for an essay on old Victorian cases,' he said.

'You mentioned that last time I was here. It sounds interesting.'

'It is. I'm trying to find some really unusual crimes from the late 1800s – the 1890s particularly. Ones that weren't publicized – ones we don't know about today.' He glanced at her hesitantly, then, as if realizing she was genuinely interested, said, 'To start with, I thought I'd re-examine them, comparing the police methods with today's forensic science. But then I thought that if I could unearth some really good ones, I'd try to find oblique references to them in the fiction of that time. I don't mean obvious things like the Artful Dodger representing all the pickpockets in Alsatia, or Mr Hyde being Jack the Ripper—'

'Mr Hyde wasn't Jack the Ripper, was he?' said Nina, coming in with the coffee pot, and sounding startled.

'No, that's just an illustration of what I mean.'

'Where on earth was Alsatia? Oh bother, I've forgotten the milk. And I made some *petits fours*—' She vanished to the kitchen again.

'Where is Alsatia?' said Nell.

'It was in Whitefriars,' said Benedict. 'Roughly speaking, the Fleet Street area across to the Thames. It was sort of a sanctuary place for thieves and general ruffians and crooks.'

'And now it's home to newspapers and journalists,' said Nell, deadpan, and was pleased when he grinned and instantly said, 'Yes. So what's new?'

'I like your essay idea. And it's such a colourful era, as well. The minute you mention the 1890s, you see all the images.'

'The street life,' said Benedict. 'The hot food sellers and the beggars and toffs, and the ordinary clerks and workers. Apothecaries' shops with huge glass flagons in the windows, and little dusty drapers' shops and barrow boys. It would smell different then, and it would certainly sound different. London's always noisy, but it'd have been noisy in a different way. Hansom cabs rattling over the cobblestones, and people shouting and quarrelling, and the hoot of barges from the river, and the sound of overstrung, out-of-tune pianos played in smoky pubs—'

He broke off, and Nell said warmly, 'And one of the fascinations is that it's still just about touchable, that era. Our grandparents would remember their grandparents or even their parents talking about it. And we've got photographs from those years. Voices, as well. Those scratchy old recordings. But go back a bit earlier, and there's only what was written down. We'll never know what people really looked like.'

'Yes,' said Benedict, with a kind of eager gratitude for her interest. 'And we'll never know what they sounded like, either. In ordinary everyday speech, I mean.'

'Because language changes,' said Nell, thoughtfully.

'Yes. Not just because we use different expressions. We don't pronounce words as people did a hundred – even fifty – years ago.'

'That's true. You only have to watch one of those old 1930s or 1940s British films to hear that. Tell me some more about your essay.'

'Well, the thing is that an author writing today might have a character mentioning a current murder trial that readers would recognize and know about. Even today if you say Ruth Ellis, most people know she was the last woman to be hanged.'

'Or Fred and Rosemary West and the macabre patio in Gloucester.'

'Yes. But those references in a book probably wouldn't mean anything to somebody reading it in a hundred years' time,' said Benedict. 'So it's the lost cases of the 1890s I'm going for, then I'll see if they're mentioned in the fiction of the day.'

'Weren't there books that used to be termed the Newgate Novels?' asked Nell.

'Yes, there were,' said Benedict, pleased. 'They were a kind of fictional counterpart of some true stories of the era. *Oliver Twist* is regarded as a Newgate Novel.'

'Yes, of course. Will you use the essay as the base for a PhD, later on?'

'It'd be nice to think I could,' said Benedict rather wistfully. 'Only I'm not sure about even doing a PhD yet.'

'Wouldn't it be a good idea? And you're so knowledgeable about that era.'

'Am I?' He frowned slightly.

'Yes, you are,' said Nell. 'You convey such a sense of it. It's extraordinary, but when you were talking about it – about the street sellers and the scents and the sounds and the river barges – I could see it all so vividly.'

She knew at once that she had said something wrong. Benedict's expression changed – so markedly that Nell was reminded of still water that had suddenly rippled beneath the surface. She felt a shiver of apprehension.

In a soft voice, Benedict said, 'I'm glad you came. I hoped you would, you know.'

It was an odd, slightly disconnected remark, and for a moment Nell could not think how to reply. But then Nina came back, and Benedict said in a completely normal, slightly tired-sounding, voice, 'Nina, d'you mind if I skip coffee and head for bed?'

'To make some notes on your essay while they're still alive in your mind?' said Nell, smiling at him, relieved that the brief disconcerting moment had passed. Perhaps it had been something to do with the illness he had – she had been enjoying talking to him so much she had almost forgotten about that.

'Well, yes, sort of,' said Benedict. He stood up. 'I expect I'll see you before you set off for Holly Lodge tomorrow though.'

Nina began to fuss about the sleeping arrangements, wanting Nell to have her own room, because it would be no trouble at all, she had put clean sheets on just that very morning, and it was not right that a guest should sleep on a futon fold-out thing, because what if it collapsed halfway through the night and precipitated Nell on to the floor—

'I'll have the futon,' offered Benedict. 'Then Nell can have my room. I don't mind being collapsed on to the floor.'

Nell said, 'For heaven's sake, both of you, I'll be fine, and the bed won't collapse and I'll even get my own duvet from the airing cupboard. Stop fussing.'

'OK,' said Benedict, but he still hesitated, and Nell suddenly thought he might be wondering if he should come with her to Holly Lodge tomorrow. Please don't let him suggest it, she thought, then felt deeply guilty, because Holly Lodge was his house after all, and he would be paying her for the work. But he merely smiled, wished her good luck with the bed, nodded to Nina, and went quietly to his own room.

Later, in the narrow but perfectly comfortable bed, Nell thought how much Michael would have enjoyed the conversation this evening. He would have been deeply interested in Benedict's proposed essay-cum-thesis, and his eyes would have smiled in gentle and amused appreciation of Nina's pelting conversation. It was nice to think of having supper with him tomorrow evening, and telling him about tonight. And by tomorrow, thought Nell, I'll have seen that man at Holly Lodge, and I'll have got him cleared from my mind. This struck her as a peculiar way to think.

She felt a bit guilty about telling Michael there had been a prowler at Quire Court, although she had not precisely lied, because she had certainly heard something peculiar the night she had photographed the chess piece. But it had not really been very frightening – all she had heard were footsteps, it was important to remember that was all it had been.

*And that sinisterly small hand*, said her mind. *Don't forget that*. Oh shut up, said Nell, and pulled the duvet over her head.

She set off for the tube straight after breakfast the next morning, leaving Nina pitting half a kilo of cherries for duck á la Montmorency.

'You'd think, wouldn't you, that they could have duck with orange, or apple stuffing for their Silver Wedding party, but no, it has to be bloody Montmorency, and no thought for how long it takes to stone cherries for sixteen people. It's been lovely having you, Nell, darling, we won't kiss or anything, on account of me being covered in cherry juice and duck fat. Let Benedict have the inventory for Holly Lodge when you can – there's no frantic rush, but it'll be interesting to know how you get on and what you find.'

'Is Benedict still in bed?'

'He got up early and went out to get the papers. He does that most mornings, but it's only at the end of the road, so you might meet him on the way back, unless he's called at the second-hand bookstore, which he often does, and once he's in there, he loses track of time.'

'Michael does that in bookshops,' said Nell.

'I *like* your Michael,' said Nina enthusiastically. 'I think he's exactly right for you, in fact, if I were you— Oh God, there's the phone, I'll bet it's that woman about the Silver Wedding *again*. Can you let yourself out, because if I don't speak to her she'll be hammering on the door like that horror story where the thing gibbers at the door in a snowstorm—'

'The Monkey's Paw,' said Nell, belatedly identifying this allusion.

'That's the one,' said Nina, and dived for the phone.

It was half past nine when Nell emerged from Highbury & Islington tube, and she collected rolls and fruit at a delicatessen

so she would not need to go out for lunch. At a newsagents'
she bought a box of light bulbs. The electricity had certainly
been on at the house last time, but most of the bulbs had gone,
and Nell was blowed if she was going to fumble around in a
darkening house on a grey January day. She would not be able
to reach many of the ceiling lights, but there had been several
table lamps which would give plenty of light.

Here was the road and the house, slightly shabby, and with
the same sad feeling of neglect, and the faint smell of damp.
She went systematically into each of the rooms before starting
work, opening cupboards and drawing back curtains. This
was not being neurotic; it was sensible to make sure an empty
old house really was empty. It was certainly not that she was
visualizing a ravening axe murderer ready to erupt from the
linen cupboard. Or, said her mind cynically, expecting a
mysterious man with vividly blue eyes to walk out of the
shadows . . . ?

But despite her resolve, she found herself standing on the
upper landing, her heart skittering with half-fearful, half-
hopeful expectancy. There was no one here, of course . . .

Or was there? Standing on the second-floor landing, she had
the impression that something moved in the room at the far
end – the room where she had been working when she saw
Declan. As she hesitated, there was a soft creaking sound from
within the room. Nell jumped, then realized the sound was too
rhythmic to be man-made; it was more the kind of sound the
house itself might make – such as a door swinging to and fro
on sagging hinges. But what would cause a door to move by
itself in a silent and still house?

'Declan . . . ? Are you here?'

Nell had not intended to say this aloud, but the words
whispered into the shadows of their own volition. Her skin
prickled with apprehension, then common sense kicked in,
because she was behaving like some wimpish heroine from
a bad horror film – tiptoeing ingenuously round the haunted
house, artlessly enquiring if anyone was here. And what would
you do, my girl, if your sinister blue-eyed Declan whispered
back at you from the shadows? *Here I am . . . I've been
waiting for you . . .*

'Rubbish,' said Nell very loudly, and went noisily and deci-
sively towards the room, opening the door wide. And of course
there was no one there, only the same packing cases as before
and the old dressing table with the oval mirror. Nell touched
the mirror's frame lightly, and it moved. At once the creaking
came again, and Nell let out a breath of relief. That was what
she had heard.

She went down to the long sitting room and started listing
the contents. Anything she could not identify or evaluate herself
would be photographed so she could check with colleagues.
Like the chess piece? Measuring a Victorian bureau, Nell
allowed herself a brief daydream in which she found the entire
set, and made a killing at Christie's or Sotheby's.

The morning was very dark and towards midday she hunted
out the table lamps and screwed in the light bulbs she had
brought. There was an old-fashioned standard lamp lying in
a corner, as well, which cast a friendly pool of light. Nell
worked on. Three quarters of her mind was absorbed in what
she was doing – categorizing what was clearly junk, setting
question marks against stuff that might be worth placing with
a good second-hand dealer, trying to put a figure against items
that would be sellable in her own shop. There was a beautiful
desk that had the elegant lines of the late 1700s, and a set of
very nice dining chairs with petit point covers. Nell wondered
if Benedict's grandfather had bought them, or if previous
owners had simply included them when selling the house.
However they came to be here, she would certainly like to
have the desk and the chairs in the window at Quire Court.

In a room overlooking the back garden were four framed
charcoal sketches of local scenes: two views of Highbury
Fields, a church, simply labelled as 'St Stephen's', and a
detailed drawing of an old music hall called Highbury Barn.
Nell liked these and she liked the links they provided to an
older Highbury. The sketches were dated 1863 and 1864, and
looked as if they had been done by an amateur artist. They
would not be worth a massive amount, but a local dealer might
take them because people living in the area would like them.

She worked for another half an hour, then went through to
the kitchen where she ate the ham rolls and the apple at the

big table. The kitchen was a large room, and although it did not have the newest designer cupboards or fittings it was perfectly acceptable. While she ate, she looked through the notes she had made so far, then fetched her Filofax so she could write names of one or two contacts against a couple of the items, for possible consultations. There was a large mahogany dining table that was too big for most people's houses, but might sell as a boardroom table.

It was very quiet, probably because this was the back of the house, although when she went through to the main part of the house, the creaking of the mirror came again from overhead. She would wedge the hinges in place later. For the moment she would finish listing the dining-room furniture in company with a cup of tea. There was tea and dried milk in the cupboards; Benedict would not mind if she took a spoonful of each.

As she filled the kettle, she was glad that she had not fallen into the trap of listening for a knock at the door or the crunch of footsteps or tyres on the drive. Declan, whoever he was, had simply been playing a game that day. *Come on the eighteenth* – for pity's sake, did he think he was a character in a slushy romance or a teen magazine story? Perhaps somebody had told him he had hypnotic eyes, or perhaps there had been some sort of squiffy bet at a Christmas party.

She switched on the kettle and left it to boil while she carried one of the table lamps into the hall, which was in semi-darkness. The shadows were raggedly edged with the deep red of the stained-glass fanlight over the door, but the lamp, plugged in and switched on, chased the shadows back to their corners. She glanced up at the stair, and tilted the lampshade slightly so that it shone up the stairs. That was better. She glanced towards the front door, then opened it and peered out. The gardens were drenched in gloomy January greyness, and it must have rained earlier, because the shrubs were dripping with moisture. But it was a perfectly ordinary, unthreatening garden with an entirely normal London street beyond. Nell closed the door. She would finish in the dining room, then make a start on the upper floors. She was not expecting to find a great deal in them, but the packing cases on the second floor must be gone through thoroughly. Would she find the rest of the chess set in one of them? She had just started to go up the stairs when a whispered voice came out of the darkness on the half-landing above her.

*I'm glad you came, Nell . . .*

He was there, standing on the half landing, lit from behind by the narrow window, looking down at her. Nell's heart performed a somersault, and excitement laced with apprehension coursed through her.

In as normal a voice as she could manage, she said, 'Hello. How did you get in?' Then, as he did not reply, she said, 'You were here the day Benedict was taken ill, weren't you? You were with him when I found him.'

Still he did not say anything. Nell waited, seeing that even standing outside the lamp's glow, he was exactly as she remembered him. The eyes, the dark hair, the way he had of tilting his head as if he was listening very intently. If he would come down just two or three stairs, she would be able to see him properly.

But he stayed where he was, and from feeling uneasy, Nell began to feel frightened, because she was in an empty house with a complete stranger, and she had no idea how he had got in. Did he have a key? Had he been hiding somewhere, waiting to creep out? That was surely not the action of a sane person and clearly it would be as well to make a polite, but swift retreat. Trying to avoid any sudden action that might spark off something unpleasant, she began to move cautiously back down to the hall, feeling for the stairs with her foot, not daring to take her eyes from the man.

There were only a few stairs to the bottom; once she was there she could be across the hall and opening the door – she had not locked it. She held on to the banister with one hand and went down two more steps. Was he going to follow her? No, he was staying on the half-landing. Good. And here was the last step. Now for a quick sprint to the door . . .

It was not the last step. She had miscalculated and there were three more to go. There was a moment when Nell tried to stop herself falling, but she fell hard against the edge of the banister, banging her head with such force that lights splintered across her vision. There was a moment of blurred dizziness, then she was aware of lying in a painful jumble on a hard tiled floor. The world was still spinning, but the jagged lights seemed to have retreated. Nell drew in a shaky breath, but the blow to her head seemed to be still echoing inside her brain, and she was not entirely sure what had happened or where she was. She tried to sit up, but the dizziness seized her again and a sickening pain shot through her ankle. Sprained ankle and bang on the head? Whatever had happened she could not lie here like this – there was something she had to do, only she could not quite pin down what it was . . .

She had been cataloguing some house contents – an old shadowy house – something for Nina Doyle, was it? Yes, Holly Lodge, that was it. Was she still in the house? She must be – she could hear a muddled sound of traffic nearby.

Nell made a huge effort and this time managed to half sit up. She was in a big hall, lying at the foot of a wide stairway with a carved banister. Shadows clustered in the corners, but a table lamp was casting a pool of light – she remembered switching that on. Had she been about to go up to the bedrooms? And fallen down the stairs? Whatever she had done, she could not possibly get to the tube like this – her ankle was sending out waves of wrenching pain and she was not sure if she could stand on it, never mind walk. Could she manage to get out to the street, though? The traffic sounded quite heavy – there would surely be taxis.

Taxis. Traffic.

It was then that Nell began to think the bang on her head might have affected her hearing, because the traffic did not sound quite right. It sounded more like wheels rattling over uneven ground than cars whizzing along a London street. In addition, she could hear voices and music, and these did not sound right, either. Oh God, thought Nell, I'm suffering from concussion or something – I'm hearing things. But there was nothing odd about hearing traffic and voices in the middle of London. Except there was something very strange about the sounds. The voices were speaking English, but it was an odd, unfamiliar English. Sharper, with different emphasis on words and different vowel sounds. It was speech that Nell thought confusedly she should recognize. If the pain in her foot would ease and if she could overcome the sick dizziness, she might be able to think more clearly.

And then quite suddenly, the spinning fragments of sound and memory fell into place, like the colours in a child's kaleidoscope, and with a cold feeling of panic Nell knew what she was hearing. It was the speech of the nineteenth century. It was the street patois that long-dead authors had reproduced for readers. She was hearing the raucous calls Charles Dickens had written for his beggars and urchins, and the speech Conan Doyle assigned to the Baker Street Irregulars when they related their findings to Sherlock Holmes . . .

No, of course it was not. She was confused from the fall and the pain of her sprained ankle, and there was probably a party of angry foreigners out there – maybe tourists whose minibus had broken down.

But the sounds came again, more vividly, and with them was the memory of something someone had said recently. Memory clicked a little more firmly into place. Benedict Doyle had talked to her about researching crime from the end of the nineteenth century and he had said London would sound different. It's always noisy, he had said, but it would have been noisy in a different way. Hansom cabs rattling over the cobblestones, and people shouting and quarrelling.

That's what I'm hearing, thought Nell. Those are wooden wheels bumping over unpaved surfaces – and horses' hooves. And that music . . .

*Overstrung, out-of-tune pianos played in smoky pubs.* It was exactly what the music sounded like. But it could not be that. It must be somebody's radio or television with a Victorian play on it. Something with particularly good sound effects. Please let it be that.

Very slowly she turned her head to the door that led to the drive and out to the street. Even the light was different. And if she could reach that door and open it, what would she see?

*Open it, Nell . . . Take a look at my world . . . Just a glimpse, where it's trickling into your mind from mine . . .*

The final shards of fragmented memory dropped into place and Nell turned to look at the stair. Declan, the man of shadows and mystery, who had somehow compelled her to come here.

He began to move down the stairs and, as he reached the lower stairs, he stepped into the edge of the light from the lamp. He drew back at once, putting up a defensive hand, but it was too late. Nell gasped, because his face, oh God, *his face* . . . What had done that to his face?

She managed to scrabble a couple of feet towards the door, because surely if she could open it and call for help, someone would hear her. Someone in that alien street? The street that was filled with the sound of horses' hooves and wooden wheels clattering over cobblestones and people shouting in a form of English that no one in the twenty-first century had heard . . .

But Declan's hands were reaching for her, and his eyes were no longer the piercing blue she remembered; they were black, huge, like the eyes of some monstrous insect . . .

He came down the last few stairs, and bent over her. As he pulled her to her feet, severe pain twisted through her injured foot, and Nell tumbled all the way down into complete unconsciousness.

# TWENTY-ONE

Benedict had intended to be back at the flat to see Nell before she set off for Holly Lodge, but on the way back from buying his newspaper he had looked in at a second-hand bookshop, where he had become absorbed in several books about Victorian street life. Among them was a dictionary of Victorian colloquialisms, titled 'Slang, Cant and Flash Phrases', which he thought might be useful for his essay on Victorian crimes. It was battered and foxed, but it was full of what appeared to be genuine nineteenth-century jargon, and Benedict bartered happily with the bookseller, whose day would have been ruined if a customer paid up without challenge, then walked slowly back to the flat, thumbing through the pages.

It meant Nell had left when he got back, but Nina was there, still putting together her Silver Wedding dinner. She told Benedict she was disgustingly behind schedule, and if he had nothing else to do, could he possibly lend a hand, because at this rate the duck à la Montmorency would not be ready for the clients' Golden Wedding, never mind the Silver one.

It was twelve o'clock before Nina finally bore the duck portions off, and Benedict switched on the laptop to work on his essay. Most of what he had written so far was still in note form, but he thought it was a fairly good outline of what he meant to do. As he started to type, he wondered how Nell was getting on at Holly Lodge and if she had found anything valuable. *Like tell-all diaries signed by Declan and dated c.1898?* his mind said cynically.

But he was not going to think about Declan. He was becoming convinced that the medical explanation was right, and that it was probably better to suffer from multiple personality disorder – and have proper pills to keep it in its place – than to suffer from some peculiar form of possession by a set of ghosts. Declan had existed, of course, and Benedict might some day track down the registration of his birth or death. But apart from finding Flossie Totteridge's name on the Title Deeds of Holly Lodge, there was nothing to indicate that anyone else in that wild tale had ever lived. And most likely Benedict had seen Flossie's name written down somewhere – probably in Holly Lodge that day of his parents' funeral – and it had lodged in his subconscious.

With last night's conversation with Nell still fresh in his mind, he set about describing the backdrop to the crimes he would be examining. How England in general and London in particular would have looked and sounded; how people would have talked. He reached for 'Slang, Cant and Flash Phrases' again, and began delightedly typing in the colourful phrases from the 1880s and 1890s, wondering what the cracksmen and magsmen and dollymops would make of today's expressions. What would they think if they heard us saying it was a night when many stars were present? thought Benedict. Or talking about emailing on a BlackBerry, or texting somebody? He smiled, and worked on, enjoying the vivid language of the Victorian streets, and the famous rhyming slang, traces of which were still around today.

*And the chaunters and the penny gaffs and mobsmen, Benedict . . .*

Chaunters. Benedict had come across references to penny gaffs which seemed to have been low-class theatres, and also of mobsmen – well-dressed swindlers. But chaunters? He reached for the book again, but the expression was not listed. Then he must have seen it or heard it somewhere else. Research was magpie-ism and serendipity anyway. He typed another couple of paragraphs, but he was feeling as if something invisible had plucked lightly at strings in his mind, and as if his mind was still thrumming gently.

Chaunters. He would do a web search in a minute. It sounded as if it might be singing.

*Singing, for sure, Benedict . . . They sang for money, the chaunters . . . The first time we heard them was down by the river, with the fog like diseased smoke so a man couldn't see his way. And we thought we were hearing the voices of the Sidhe who'd*

*call to you from beneath the sea, but it was chaunters, inside a*
*tavern, earning their supper . . .*

'Will you just sod off?' said Benedict out loud, and felt
Declan's ruffle of amusement.

*It's the truth I'm telling you*, said Declan. *And there was*
*one night down by the river . . .* The silvery threads of thought
stopped suddenly, and for the first time Benedict felt a hesitation and a withdrawal. Then Declan said, *Oh, what the hell,*
*you know most of it already . . . Listen now, on the night we*
*found Harold Bullfinch—*

'Who?' said Benedict, before he could stop himself.

*Haven't you been paying attention to anything? Harold*
*Bullfinch was the abortionist, the black-hearted villain who*
*killed Romilly . . .*

Romilly. Romilly, who had red hair and who had run away
from Kilglenn after Nicholas Sheehan seduced her in the old
watchtower on the Moher Cliffs. How could I have forgotten
Romilly? thought Benedict.

*On the night we found Bullfinch's body, the chaunters were*
*singing in the taverns by the river . . . And, oh God, Benedict,*
*it was so cold and dank in those streets, and it was so lonely*
*to stand outside the taverns . . . Wanting to go in and have a*
*bit of cheer and the company of others . . . But we didn't dare*
*do that, not till we had the jacket back . . .*

*The river fog was everywhere. It muffles everything – you*
*wouldn't know that, would you, for you've almost got rid of*
*fog in your clean modern world. But when you walked through*
*one of those old fogs you'd feel as if you'd fallen into another*
*world altogether. And it was a frightening world, Benedict,*
*you can't know how frightening it was . . .*

*London 1890s*

Declan and Colm could scarcely see their way after they left the
cab and walked through the fog-shrouded streets to where
they had left Harold Bullfinch's body.

'But we have to do this,' Colm said. 'If anyone finds your
jacket they'll know who you are and half the police in London
will be hunting you as a killer.'

'I didn't kill Bullfinch,' said Declan, but he still felt strange and unconnected to the world, which he thought was because of falling down the river steps and knocking himself out. He was not, in fact, convinced that he was entirely conscious yet; walking at Colm's side, the world had an unreal quality, in which he could only remember fragments of what had been happening during the last few hours.

And then a sliver of very recent memory dropped into place, and he said, 'Colm, you said you were at Holly Lodge all of today.'

'I was. With that voracious harpy, Floss Totteridge.'

'But I saw you,' said Declan. 'You were out here. I saw you crossing the road on the corner of Clock Street.' He stopped and turned to face Colm. The fog swirled thickly around them, but a disc of blurred light from a street gas lamp touched Colm's face with colour.

'I went to Bidder Lane,' said Colm, after a moment. 'To the house where Romilly lived.'

'Why?'

'I thought there might be some of her things there. I wasn't going to leave them for that harridan to sell. But I didn't tell you, because I didn't want you to think I was a moonstruck simpleton.'

Declan did not say they had both always been a bit moonstruck by Romilly. He said, 'Were there any of her things there?'

'A rosary and a crucifix wrapped in a bit of silk.' Colm was walking on again, his hands dug deeply into his pockets, not looking at Declan. 'I took those. Keepsakes.'

Before Declan could say anything else, he pointed to the open door of a tavern on the corner of Clock Street and Bidder Lane. The music Declan dimly remembered hearing earlier was still going on – the jangly piano and voices raised in blurred song. Someone must have thrown open the door, because the scents of smoke and ale and hot food reached them.

'God, wouldn't you sell your soul to be able to go in there and be part of all that?' said Colm, echoing Declan's thoughts as he so often did.

'I would. Like Fintan's Bar at home, where we'd be recognized and welcomed, and it'd be a grand evening. Colm, couldn't we go in . . . ?'

'We could not. We have to rescue your jacket from the abortionist's corpse before anyone finds it.' Colm spoke sharply, but he put out a hand to Declan's shoulder as he said it. 'Come on, now, we're almost at the river steps. If you pass out now, I'll throw you in the river.'

'If I pass out I'll probably fall into the river without your help.'

The river steps were as dank and eerie as Declan remembered. Here was the ledge stretching out along the quayside wall; even with the fog swirling everywhere he could make out the circular hole with the brick surround. He pointed to it, wanting to delay the moment until they had to approach Bullfinch's body.

'What would that be, d'you think?'

'An overflow outlet of an old sewer, I should think. They'd have the – what is it called? – the effluence discharging into sewer pits inside there,' said Colm. 'When it reached a certain level, it'd overflow and gush out into the river.'

'Effluence being a polite word for a load of shit?'

'When was I ever polite?' Colm had turned away from the sewer tunnel, and was looking down the steps. 'He's still there,' he said, in an expressionless voice. 'Isn't that a terrible thing for a man's body to lie sodden and dead by itself. But your jacket's there as well, that's one mercy. Are you ready to sprint down those steps and snatch it up? We'll have to be fast, because we don't want to be recognized and we don't know who might be watching.'

'Watching, where from?' said Declan, looking about him.

'Anywhere. Those warehouses, barges on the river. Will you do the sprint, or will I?'

'I'll do it,' said Declan, and thought: *I don't need to look at what's under the jacket. I don't even need to think about it.* Before he could change his mind, he was down the steps, snatching up the jacket, and racing back up again.

'Good,' said Colm, softly. 'Very good indeed.'

'What now?'

'Back to the lodging. We'll get a cab again.'

'Can we afford it?'

'Your man down there can,' said Colm.

'We're still using his money?'

'He doesn't need it,' said Colm.

They spent an uncomfortable night in the narrow lodging house. Colm appeared to sleep, but Declan lay wakeful, watching the shadows dance on the ceiling, seeing them form into the outline of a twisted hunched figure lying on river steps. I didn't do it, he thought. I didn't kill him – I'd know if I had. But every time this denial formed, trailing it like an unquiet spectre, was the question: can you be sure?

There were four other lodgers eating breakfast when they went downstairs next morning. There had been no introductions, but they had all shared meals during the last few days, and they had nodded in offhand friendship. Declan thought the men looked down on them; he thought they regarded himself and Colm as innocents, unschooled lambs who might be ripe for fleecing. Colm had said this was rubbish, and he and Declan were as good as anyone in London.

But this morning, as they sat down at the long scrubbed table, with the platters of bread and margarine and jugs of strong tea, there was no doubt that the other lodgers were looking at them.

It was one of the older men who passed them a morning newspaper – they saw it was a local publication, covering this part of North London.

'Bad affair that,' he said, and his eyes seemed to rest on Declan and Colm with curiosity.

They read the story together.

BRUTAL MURDER OF MAN IN CANNING TOWN.
The body of a middle-aged man was last night found on the river steps near the old Bidder Lane sewer. The man, whose name police have not yet released, is believed to have died during the early evening. Readers will recall how thick fog covered most of Canning Town last night – a circumstance which appears to have aided the killer in his grim work.

The victim's injuries are described as savage, and reports of a young man with dark hair, seen wandering the area at the time, have already been passed to the police by local residents. One person, living just off Clock Street, thought the young man had an Irish accent, although this has not been corroborated.

Any persons who may have information as to the possible identity of such a man, are most earnestly requested to give details to their local police station or patrolling constable.

This paper feels it is a tragic day when an honest citizen of our town cannot walk abroad without dying at the hands of what appears to be a crazed murderer. People living in the area are warned not to go out alone after dark.

Editor's Note: The Bidder Lane outlet – which runs almost parallel with Bidder Lane and the intersection of Clock Street – is one of London's older sewer tunnels. Created as part of Joseph Bazalgette's sewer network in the Sixties, it fell into disuse more than ten years ago.

'Shocking,' said Declan, passing back the paper, managing to speak normally. 'Aren't there some evil people in London?'

'No worse than in Galway, though,' said Colm. 'Have we milk on the table this morning? Would you pass it over, please?'

They were able to finish their breakfasts in relative calm, although Declan thought afterwards that bread and raspberry jam would forever afterwards taste of fear.

Back in their room, Colm said, 'We have to leave this house.'

'They're suspicious of us, aren't they? "An Irish accent" the paper said.'

'We aren't the only Irish in London, for pity's sake,' said Colm, angrily, but he was already putting their few things together. 'But we'll settle up our account here so no one can remember us for non-payers, and then we'll be off as soon as we can.'

'Where will we go?'

'Holly Lodge,' said Colm. 'Where else?'

\*    \*    \*

It was mid-afternoon when they reached Holly Lodge. Flossie Totteridge greeted them wearing a thin wrapper that imperfectly concealed her plentiful flesh, and she had either not removed the paint from her face last night, or had applied it that morning in a very bad light.

Colm said without preamble, 'Floss – we need a bed for a couple of nights.'

'Do you indeed? I don't, as a rule, let rooms to gentlemen.'

'No, but you've my cousin Romilly's room still empty, perhaps?'

'I have, as it happens.' Flossie eyed Colm. 'And, of course, circumstances alter cases.'

'Circumstances?' said Colm, with a reminiscent smile at her. False, thought Declan. Oh God, he can be so false at times.

'The circumstance of you and me having become such particular friends,' said Flossie, and Declan thought how revolting it was to see a lady of Mrs Totteridge's age and proportions displaying coyness. With obvious reluctance she removed her gaze from Colm to look at Declan. 'You'd be agreeable to sharing a room with one another, I dare say?'

'We would.'

'Sharing a bed? For there's only the one in each room, although they're good wide beds, all of them. My gentlemen callers like quality in the beds, you know.'

'Personally,' said Colm, 'I can sleep on a clothesline and never know who's alongside.'

'Then it's the second floor; third left along the passage.'

It was an impersonal, not uncomfortable room, and, as Colm said, sharing it would give him a bit of protection from the voracious Floss. 'Unless, of course, it occurs to her to take both of us on.'

'Will you not even think that,' said Declan angrily.

Colm, who had been exploring the interior of the wardrobe and opening the drawers of the tallboy, grinned and sat down on the bed. Declan perched on the window sill, staring down into the gardens. The sill was narrow and hard and something dug into his thigh and he remembered putting Bullfinch's wallet in his trouser pocket last night, and fished it out.

'How much money have we left in there?' said Colm as Declan threw the wallet on to the bed. 'And hadn't we better get rid of anything with Bullfinch's name on it?' Handling the wallet by one corner to avoid the blood, he extracted several Treasury notes, along with what looked like a couple of bills bearing Bullfinch's name and address on the envelopes.

'Let's burn those,' said Declan, seeing the envelopes.

'Yes. Because if anyone sees them—'

He stopped and they both turned as the door opened. Flossie Totteridge stood there. 'I've brought you the key to this door,' she said. 'There are locks on all the rooms.' She, in her turn, broke off, and Declan and Colm saw she was staring at the wallet and the envelopes. Harold Bullfinch's name stood out, clear as a curse. Mr Harold Bullfinch, Clock Street.

'We picked this up in the street on the way here,' said Colm, and although he spoke lightly, Declan heard the note of strain underlying his voice.

To reinforce Colm's words, he said, 'We were just saying we should take it to the police station in case it's been reported as lost.'

Flossie Totteridge was still staring at the wallet with its dreadful telltale stains. She looked as if the flesh had suddenly shrunk away from her bones. She said, 'One of Zelda's gentlemen left a midday edition of *The North London Banner.*'

Declan felt a jolt of fear. The *North London Banner* was the newspaper they had seen that morning at their lodgings.

'There's a story in it about the man whose body was found last night,' said Flossie.

'We read about that at breakfast.' It was clear from Colm's tone that he was going to brazen this out. 'An unknown man on some river steps.' He glanced at Declan and Declan signalled a warning: don't pretend to be too ignorant. Colm said, 'Canning Town, wasn't it?'

'Yes. The early editions didn't know the man's name,' said Flossie. 'But the midday one says he was identified earlier today. Harold Bullfinch of Clock Street. His landlady reported him missing, and was taken to see the body. She identified him. And,' she said, in a voice in which suspicion and shock were mingled, 'you've got his wallet.'

There was a rather dreadful silence. Then Colm said, 'In that case we should take this to the police without delay.'

'Yes, you should.'

'We'll do it now,' said Colm, getting off the bed. 'Will I look in on you later to tell you what the police say?'

'You could do that. Come at three o'clock. I'll be busy with the household matters until then, but I'll be there at three.'

'Three o'clock it will be,' said Colm.

They retrieved the newspaper, which was in the drawing room, and found the article.

CANNING TOWN MURDER VICTIM IDENTIFIED

The body of the man found on the river steps by the old Bidder Lane sewer has been identified as that of Mr Harold Bullfinch (52), of Clock Street.

Mr Bullfinch was well known in the Canning Town area and was a familiar figure in several other parts of London, largely because of his work as a travelling salesman. That work caused him to be away from his place of lodging a good deal, so it was not until early this morning that it was realized he was missing. His landlady, Mrs Ivy Podgrass, reported his absence to her local police station.

'A commercial traveller, he was,' Mrs Podgrass told our reporter, 'and never away from the house without he'd tell me where he was going and when he expected to be back. He'd 'ave to be away some nights, of course, for 'is work. Salesman in ladies' undergarments he was, if you'll excuse my mentioning it, although perfectly respectful and gentlemanly.

'A business appointment 'e said, yesterday. "Very important," he said. "I've wrote it on the kitchen calendar so I don't miss it. But I'll be back in time for supper".'

It was only when Mr Bullfinch had not returned by the following morning that Mrs Podgrass reported his absence.

'I was took up with my other lodgers all evening, so I never knew Mr Bullfinch hadn't come home until break-fast time,' she told us. 'And when it come nearly dinner time and he still 'adn't come home, I was so worried I went along of the police station. And the sergeant at the station showed me this corpus they took from Bidder Lane, all laid out in a back room on a marble slab. "Ow, that's my Mr Bullfinch, sure as sure," I said, then I come over all faint and they got me a chair and give me a cup of tea for the shock.'

Mr Bullfinch's employers, Rodblatt & Company, Ladies' Outfitters, said Harold Bullfinch was a courteous man who would be greatly missed.

Police continue to search for the dark-haired man with an Irish accent who was seen near the scene of the crime. It is believed he may have useful information to provide.

In the meantime, residents of Canning Town are warned to have a care for their safety, and not to venture forth alone after dark.

# TWENTY-TWO

'So,' said Colm, putting down the paper, 'the abortionist was courteous and gentlemanly and liked by all. Would that be a case of *nil nisi bonum*, or did the landlady really think her lodger was a commercial traveller?'

'He probably was a commercial traveller most of the time,' said Declan. 'Where are you going?'

'Floss is expecting me to take the wallet to the police,' said Colm, reaching for his coat. He had acquired a long black greatcoat from one of the lodgers in their previous house – Declan hoped he had paid for it, or at least had taken it with the owner's knowledge, but had not liked to ask. 'So I need to give the truth to that lie,' Colm said. 'I'm not actually going to the police, of course. I'll get rid of the wallet while I'm out. You stay here – I won't be long. The old trout's expecting me downstairs at three o'clock, anyway.'

After he went, Declan lay on the bed and thought how Romilly would have lain here, and how men would have lain with her. Had she hated it? Had it been the only way she could survive in London? Or had Nicholas Sheehan, all those months ago, given her a taste for sex? She had been distraught when she sobbed out the story of her rape, but there had been that moment when something that was neither innocent nor distraught had peered slyly from her eyes. As if she was looking to see if they were believing her.

The sleepless night caught up with him, and he drifted in and out of an uneasy doze, rousing when the main door opened downstairs and footsteps crossed the hall. Was that Colm returning? Declan went down to the first floor landing. It was a dark afternoon and the stairs were wreathed in shadows. Someone had lit a lamp in the hall and for the first time he wondered who kept such a big house clean. Were there servants? He was halfway down the main stairway when there was a crash of furniture from the ground floor, and a scream. He froze. Had it been simply the cry of someone who had dropped a tray of crockery? Or had there been fear in the sound?

A bedroom door behind him opened, and Cerise's voice said, 'Yes, it was a shout. Dare say it wasn't nothing to worry about, though.'

Then the cry came again, more urgent, and Cerise appeared from her room, a short, rotund gentleman in her wake.

'Did someone call for help?' said the man. He sported a walrus moustache and wore a bowler hat, as if he was determined to display his respectability in a house that was very far from respectable.

'Someone did call,' said Declan. 'I don't know where it came from, though.'

'It's probably Floss at the gin and fallen over,' said Cerise. 'She gets the horrors when she's been at the gin. Either that or somebody's broke in trying to get at her savings. She locks them away every night, but she's always expecting somebody to creep through a window and steal them.' She looked back at the man. 'You go home, Arthur,' she said. 'We'll deal with this.'

'But if it's an intruder . . .' said the walrus moustache standing at the foot of the stairs. 'I don't want to be mixed up with the police, but as a good citizen . . .'

'Never mind being a good citizen, you bugger off home,' said Cerise not unkindly.

'There's no need for you to stay,' said Declan, wanting him out of the way as quickly as possible. 'I can understand you don't want it known you were here.'

'I wouldn't want to shirk my duty,' said Arthur. 'But it's my wife, you see, well, and her mother. They wouldn't understand that a man sometimes needs . . .'

'Do you live far away?' said Declan, his eyes on the closed door of Flossie's room.

'Islington. But my place of work is near here. Tea importers on the Canonbury Road.' He said this with an air of pride, then seemed to realize he had given away information that might be better kept private and closed his mouth firmly.

'Arthur, just sod off home,' said Cerise impatiently. 'It'll be Floss at the gin again and tripped over the fender. And if it's a burglar and we need the police – nor it wouldn't be the first time they come to this house! – we'll get Wally Oliphant who patrols to the end of the road.'

'Thank you,' said Arthur, and scuttled off.

'*He* ain't much help in a crisis,' said Cerise tartly as the door closed. 'Let's make sure old Floss is all right, shall we?'

'It's very quiet,' said Declan, to whom the closed door was starting to assume the proportions of Bluebeard's chamber.

'She's probably fallen over and knocked her silly self out.' Cerise strode to the door and knocked loudly. 'Floss? You all right in there, gel?'

A door banged at the front of the house, footsteps came down the hall, and Colm's voice called out, 'Declan? What in God's name are you doing skulking around like that?'

'We heard a cry from Flossie's room,' said Declan.

'Maybe your man with the bowler hat and the moustache tried to steal her virtue. I passed him in the drive, and he was running away as if hell's devils were chasing him.'

'Catch him stealing anyone's virtue,' said Cerise derisively. 'He ain't got the wherewithal to steal anyone's anything, or not so's you'd notice.'

Colm smiled, but even in the shadowy hall Declan had the strong impression that there was something very wrong about him. He said, 'Oh, leave her to sleep it off,' and turned back to the stairs. As the light from the hall lamp fell across his face a cold hand seemed to twist in Declan's stomach. Colm's eyes, his vivid blue eyes, were suffused with a dense blackness, as if some inner darkness had bled out of his brain and stained the pupils.

Cerise saw it as well, but her reaction was very different. She said, sharply, 'Colm Rourke, you been in an opium den. And don't lie, I can see it. It's your eyes.' She tapped her own. 'Black as the devil's forehead. Like the eyes of a giant insect. Can't mistake it. Rot your brain, it will. I knew a sailor once – took opium for years, got the taste for it in China, he did. He died in screaming fear of something nobody else could see.'

Declan could not, for the moment, give this accusation any real attention. He said, 'Are we opening this door or not?'

'Yes, but keep Shanghai Charlie out of the way, for I never knew a man come out of an opium den and be use or ornament for the rest of the day.'

She pushed open the door. As it swung back Declan felt as if something had slammed into the base of his throat, because it was like looking into the black core of a nightmare and it was Bluebeard's chamber after all . . .

Flossie Totteridge lay on her back, awkwardly sprawled across a table, her hair hanging down from its pinnings. Her eyes were wide open and staring, and her lips were stretched wide – still shaped in the scream Declan had heard earlier. There was a stench of blood on the air. Like tin, thought Declan, and felt sick.

Directly beneath the silent screaming lips was what seemed to be a second mouth – a gaping glistening grin. Even from where he stood, Declan could see the glint of white in that macabre unnatural grin. There were slivers of bone, sinews . . . Sickness welled up from his stomach, but he went on looking at the nightmare. In another minute he would have to step into it – he would have to play a part in it although he had no idea yet what part that would have to be. But he thought, oh God, it's the same as that poor wretch Bullfinch, lying on the river steps. The murderer had gone away that time, leaving the rain to wash clean the stench of the blood, but this time there was no rain and the stench filled up the room. And this time the murderer had not gone away. He was standing next to Declan.

Somehow they got through the next few hours. The other girls came in at intervals, and there were shrieks of horror as the news reached them, then sobbing for 'poor old Floss, silly old bitch, never did no one any 'arm, din't deserve this'.

Colm and Declan worked out their story before they were questioned.

'We say we were together when it happened,' said Colm. 'We certainly don't tell them I was out of the house at the time, for they'll ask where I was, and I can't say I was getting rid of a wallet belonging to another murder victim.' Somehow he managed to make this bizarre statement sound entirely reasonable.

'Both of you went downstairs when you heard the cry, is that right?' said the police constable, a short time later.

'I got there first,' said Declan.

'I was a few minutes after him.'

'And you were on your own in the house, apart from Miss Cerise.' The policeman was slow of speech and portly of build, and was, in fact, the Walter Oliphant to whom Cerise had referred. 'I've got her statement.'

'The other girls were out at the time,' said Colm, 'but I think they're all back now.'

'I know they're back,' said Constable Oliphant, with considerable feeling. 'I've got them penned up in their rooms, and they're carrying on like one o'clock, sayin' deceased 'ad been like a mother to them.' He closed his notebook, and said the inspector would want to talk to Mr Rourke and Mr Doyle, but for the moment they were to remain where they were, was that clear?

'It is. Could we get a cup of tea while we wait, though?' said Colm. 'For I have a powerful thirst and it's been a long time since breakfast.'

Constable Oliphant saw no reason to deny this modest request; in fact he saw no reason why everyone in the house should not have a cup of tea. It might even, he said, plodding off to find a suitable female to set a kettle to boil, serve to shut up the wailing females.

By the time the tea had been made and a tray of mugs carried in to the wailing damsels (who demanded it be laced with gin to counteract the shock), the inspector had arrived and Colm was Colm again, his eyes normal. He was polite and articulate. Asked their reason for being in the house, he said he and Declan were renting a bed for a night or two.

'And we'd be glad if you wouldn't tell our families over in Ireland, for they'd be horrified to learn we have a cousin running a bawdy house. Well, we were horrified ourselves, weren't we, Declan? Shocked to our toes, the both of us.'

'Mrs Totteridge was your cousin?'

'It's so distant a connection I couldn't even begin to trace it,' said Colm smoothly, and Declan saw Colm was handing the inspector a mixture of truth and lies. He could not decide if this was extremely clever or worryingly sly.

'If she was a relative, however distant, accept of my condolences.'

'Thank you.'

The inspector said he was bound to point out, Mr Rourke and Mr Doyle, that he would want to talk to them again. 'There was that rumour of a man with an Irish accent seen near the scene of an earlier crime. And a very similar method of death, that was.'

'You don't really think we had anything to do with this murder?' demanded Colm incredulously. 'Because as God's our witness, we never knew the lady until this last few days.'

'I suspect everyone until I know to the contrary,' said the inspector. 'But you say you were together when you heard the cry, so for the moment I'm believing you. And if either of you killed Mrs Totteridge, I can't for the life of me see why. You hadn't met her until a few days ago and there doesn't seem any motive for you to butcher the poor soul. Quite the reverse if she was giving you free board and lodging. And whoever did this is a madman – and you both seem perfectly sane to me.'

'Oh, most of the Irish are half-mad, didn't you know that?' said Colm.

'Is that so, sir? For the moment, I'll ask you to remain here at the house. I'll get the shipping company to confirm when you arrived in London.'

'We came on the night ferry from Dublin to Liverpool,' said Colm. 'We can give you the date.'

'We worked our way to London,' put in Declan. 'We can probably tell you the towns we came through.'

'That would be helpful.' The inspector made suitable notes, then said, 'I'd have to say it's in your favour that you're still here. Most murderers, once they finish their work, make sure to be miles away. But you stayed.'

'Why wouldn't we stay?' said Colm.

'We have nothing to hide,' put in Declan.

'I think we're safe, don't you?' said Colm, later that night.

Declan mumbled a vague reply. He was finding it difficult to speak to Colm and he was finding it difficult even to look at Colm. He had no idea what to do, and he had no idea how he felt. He knew, deep within his bones and nerves and blood, that Colm had killed Flossie and also Harold Bullfinch – the latter out of anger and pain at Romilly's death – the former possibly from a different kind of anger, because she had turned Romilly from the house when she got pregnant.

But he was trying to ignore this feeling, and he was clinging to Cerise's words about opium. He did not know very much about opium-smoking, but he knew it gave people strong delusions. If Colm had committed murder from within some opium-drenched nightmare, he could not be regarded as having been in his right mind.

The next morning they discussed how long they would have to stay at Holly Lodge. Declan tentatively suggested they leave without anyone knowing – they could simply vanish into London's anonymity, he said – but Colm strongly disagreed.

'The inspector asked us to stay,' he said. 'It'd look very damning if we didn't, and anyway they might track us down, and then we'd be in real trouble.'

Declan had started to ask if the police were still in the house, when from outside their door, Cerise's voice said, 'Can I come in? I want to talk to you.'

She was wearing a loosely fitting wrapper, and she sat on the edge of the bed and said, 'I ain't going to pretend or beat about the bush. When Floss, poor old cow, was killed, I was looking out of the window of my room.'

'I thought you were with the Walrus Moustache,' said Colm.

'I was, but 'e takes a long time to get up a head of steam, if you follow me. He ain't as manly as some. So we were trying it up against the wall – he thought it might help him, and blimey, we seemed to be there hours. But my window overlooks the drive and that jutting bit that's the window of Floss's sitting room as well, so I could see it clear as clear, all the time Arthur was puffing and sweating away. And,' said Cerise, looking at them both very intently, 'no one came next or nigh Floss's window, and no one came down the drive to the house. I'd swear to that in a court of law if they asked me.'

'I still don't understand . . .' began Declan.

'No one came into the house,' said Cerise, 'because no one needed to. The killer was already inside.' She sat back. 'Now do you understand?'

There was a silence, then Colm said, 'That's an extraordinary idea.'

'Extraordinary or not, I got to thinking,' said Cerise, 'that it could mean there'd be someone in this house who'd be very grateful to me for not sayin' anything about what I saw.'

'About what you didn't see, you mean.'

'Secrets have an annoying way of getting out, don't they? Of getting told to people.'

'But if you know anything, you should tell the police,' said Colm.

'Huh, catch me tellin' that lot anything,' said Cerise at once. 'No, I was thinking more of the gentlemen who come to this 'ouse. My friend who was here at the time, for instance—'

'Arthur of the walrus moustache and the tardy manliness?'

'Don't you mock 'im. He's in a very good way of business. Tea importers down Canonbury Road. And he's likely to be made an alderman or some such. He's setting a lot of store by that. He might not want 'is wife nor his ma-in-law knowin' what he gets up to here, but it's Lombard Street to a china orange that if he thought he could 'elp the police lay a murderer by the heels, he'd do it. If I told him I believed the murderer had been inside this 'ouse all the time – maybe was still here – I think he'd feel he had to tell the rozzers. Citizen's duty, 'e'd call it.'

'Yes,' said Colm slowly. 'Yes, I see, although you're jumping to a very wild conclusion, Cerise. But whatever story you've spun for yourself, neither of us want to be part of it. We have no money and anyway we haven't done anything wrong.'

'You'd been smoking opium,' said Cerise. 'I saw it by your eyes. People can do terrible things in the grip of opium, and they don't always remember afterwards. So I wouldn't judge a man for doing somethin' – even somethin' really bad – if he'd been in an opium dream when he did it. You understand that, do you?' She waited, then, as neither of them answered, said in a harder voice, 'But as for money, old Floss had a lot, all locked away. Hundreds of pounds it must be. She di'nt trust banks – she said they rooked you ten times over.' She stood up. 'And 'ooever killed the poor old trout could've got his hands on her money at the same time,' she said. 'Which means he could give me a very generous present for keeping this partickler secret. You think about that, both of you and I'll come back later. Couple of hours maybe. I just heard St Stephen's chime one o'clock when I came up here, so I'm going downstairs for a bit of dinner. Zelda an' Ruby are bringing in some hot pies.'

As Cerise went out of the room, an insouciant swing to her rump, Declan saw with a cold chill that Colm's eyes were starting to darken to the swollen insect-black once more. He thought, *Oh, Cerise, don't go on with this, don't . . .*

*The present*

'Cerise, don't go on with this, don't . . .'

It was several moments before Benedict realized it was no longer Declan's voice he was hearing, but his own, and that he was in his own room in Nina's flat.

But Declan's thoughts were still reverberating in his mind, and he found himself whispering them. *Don't go on with this, Cerise, don't . . . Because,* thought Benedict, *if you do, you'll be his third victim – he'll need to silence you. He'll never let himself be blackmailed, and he's killed twice already.*

The newspaper articles had said all the victims except one had been found on river steps. Would Colm get Cerise out there to that disused sewer outlet? Perhaps he would ask her to meet him so he could give her the money with no prying eyes to see them.

Benedict had no idea if he was thinking logically, and he was finding it difficult to think at all, because his head was aching as badly as if it was being forced wide open then smashed closed again. He felt slightly sick, but he found Nina's paracetamol in the bathroom, and gulped down two. After this he splashed his face with cold water and felt a bit better.

Cerise had been the third victim. There had been five

altogether, according to the newspapers, and Benedict had already seen two of them killed. The abortionist Harold Bullfinch, and Flossie Totteridge. How had Colm arranged the meeting with Bullfinch?

*Stupid*, said the soft voice. *I sent the villainous old slug a note asking to meet him . . . I wrote that I had been told he could help a girl out of a 'very particular kind of trouble'. He came to the river steps like a lamb.*

And over everything lay the explosive knowledge that it had not been Declan who killed those people. It had not been Benedict's great-grandfather who stalked victims through London's fogbound streets and butchered them. It had been Colm.

And that being so, it must have been Colm who had haunted Benedict since he was eight years old. But why? What did Colm want from him?

# TWENTY-THREE

The chiming of a clock somewhere close by broke into Benedict's tumbling thoughts. The sound startled him, because it was odd to hear a clock chime; he did not remember ever hearing that in Nina's flat before.

He glanced at his watch and saw it was half past one. Then it must have been a half-hour chime he had heard. That fitted with what Cerise had said about it being one o'clock . . . No, that was Declan and Colm's world. Oh God, was he starting to confuse the two? He absolutely must not do that. But the knowledge that Cerise had given Colm and Declan two hours to make a decision thudded a tattoo in his brain.

He left a note for Nina, saying he would be back for supper, collected his coat and went out of the flat. Going down the stairs he was aware of a feeling of dislocation – almost as if his head had been divided into two. Perhaps it was the result of the paracetamol on top of the stuff the hospital people were giving him. When he got out to the street the pills seemed to be affecting his eyes as well, because the light seemed wrong. A heavy mist was muffling the traffic and shrouding the modern shop fronts, but leaving visible the older buildings. Perhaps there had been a factory fire somewhere; he would look in the local evening paper later to see.

He paused at the intersection of two roads, suddenly unsure where he was going, then remembered that of course he was going out to Canning Town, to get to Cerise before Colm killed her. No, that was in Colm's time – Cerise had been dead for a hundred years and nothing Benedict could do would help her—

The clock chimed again – two single chimes – and with the sound the compulsion returned. He had an hour to get to Canning Town. Could he do it? Surely he could. Here was the Tube entrance.

In the tube he still felt odd – not weak exactly, but not

entirely in control of his mind. Was it Colm again, pulling him even deeper into that long-ago world? He had no awareness of Colm's presence, but it was vital to remember he was in his own century and Colm and Declan had lived a hundred years ago.

At Oxford Street, where he got off to switch to an eastbound train, there seemed to be some kind of disruption. All the other passengers had alighted and seemed to be heading, very purposefully, for a different station. Benedict hesitated, then followed them, because usually if there was a diversion on the Underground, somebody always did know or had heard an announcement that the rest had not picked up. There was a long brick-lined tunnel, at the end of which echoing steps led down to a grim vaulted station smelling of something that Benedict, reaching back into childhood memories, identified after a few moments as soot. I'm going back, he thought. I'm going back into my own childhood. Or am I going even further back . . . ? He had no idea if this prospect terrified him or excited him, but when a train rattled into the station he got in without hesitation, and sat in a corner, turning up his coat collar against the cold. This had to be the maddest journey in the history of the world, but he could not get rid of the compulsion that he could somehow get to Cerise before Colm did – that he could somehow prevent Colm killing again. That was the maddest thing of all, of course; you could not unmake history. He studied the other passengers covertly. They all looked fairly ordinary, but the lighting was dim and most of them were so muffled up against the cold they could have been from any era. The few females in the carriage wore hats, but even this was not remarkable these days; girls wore all kinds of trendy pull-on hats in winter.

As the train jolted along, Benedict leaned over to wipe moisture from the window with his scarf, trying to read the names of the stations, but unable to see anything other than brick tunnels with the occasional thread of light from above. The dreamlike quality of the journey intensified, and this time it began to feel like one of those horror films where the newly dead were transported to some kind of judgement place. But this was so ridiculous a concept he refused to give it any credence. Would this slow train never reach its destination?

It was just after half past two when it pulled into the station. Was this Canning Town? Yes, there was a sign on one of the walls. Benedict had been expecting a large station – he thought it was an interchange with National Rail and also the Docklands Light Railway. But it looked as if London Underground really were diverting passengers and as if they had opened up one of the oldest underground stations they had. There was an old-fashioned booking hall, and grimy brickwork, interspersed with elaborate iron scrolls. I believe I really have gone back, thought Benedict, looking about him. No, that's absurd. It's this wretched condition – the alter ego taking over. I'll just take a look round, then I'll go home. He dared not think he might not be able to get home.

Outside the station he again had the feeling that everything was displaced. He also had the odd impression that the sky was lower than it should be. Or was it simply that it was a dark afternoon and the thick mist was still everywhere?

It was then that he saw something that seemed to split his head in two all over again. The streets were crowded, but ahead of him was a man wearing a long dark overcoat, like an old army greatcoat. The deep collar was turned up to hide his face almost completely, but when he half turned his head Benedict saw him in profile. Colm, he thought. It really is him. And he's got her with him – Cerise.

He thrust his way through the people to get nearer. He was positive it was Colm, and that it was Cerise with him, although she was not quite as Benedict had imagined: she was more slightly built and he had not thought her hair was that colour. Colm was not exactly carrying her, but he had one arm round her and she was leaning against him. Anger rose in Benedict at the disinterest of the crowds. Couldn't anyone see she was being forced to go with him?

As he crossed the road and went after the two figures, a church clock somewhere close by chimed the quarter hour.

Fifteen minutes to three. And at one o'clock Cerise had said she would give Colm a couple of hours to respond.

Michael had not been able to get rid of the memory of Benedict Doyle saying Nell should not go to Holly Lodge.

*Because we both know who's inside that house*, he had said in the voice that was so eerily not his own.

Michael refused to believe that something malevolent was inside Holly Lodge, waiting to pounce on Nell. This was part of Benedict's multiple personality thing; it was not real. But the chess set was real, said his mind. Fergal McMahon seems to have been real, as well. And Nicholas Sheehan was real too; he was ordained in 1874, and the event was recorded.

It was midday and Michael's tutorials were over for the day. He had intended to spend the afternoon preparing some notes for his second years, focusing on the Victorians' slightly contradictory custom of summarily dismissing servants who transgressed the mores of the day – usually by getting pregnant – but then helping organizations dedicated to what they termed fallen women. He wanted the students to find examples of this ambiguous attitude in the literature of the period; there were plenty of examples for them to home in on.

The trouble was that Benedict's story kept intruding. Michael found himself remembering Eithne, the serving girl at Kilderry Castle, who had got pregnant out of wedlock. That was that rogue Fintan Reilly, thought Michael, smiling. But at least the Wicked Earl of Kilderry had not turned Eithne out into the snow. Oh, blast those people from Benedict's story, why can't I forget them! And why can't I forget what Benedict said?

It would not hurt to phone Nell. A friendly, ordinary call, to ask how she was getting on. Before he could think too much about it, Michael reached for the phone and dialled her mobile.

It went straight to voicemail, but if she was wandering around various rooms, looking into cupboards and even cellars, she would probably have switched the phone off. He left a casual, cheerful, message, saying he hoped she was uncovering some good finds, and he would see her later. After this he returned to work, trying to ignore the nagging unease.

*I don't think Nell should go to Holly Lodge . . . We both know who's inside that house . . .*

'Oh hell,' said Michael aloud, and reached for the phone

again to check the times of London trains. There was one at one thirty which got in to Paddington shortly before two thirty.

On the train, he felt better. Nell would be fine and he might help her with some of the inventorying, and they would come back together and then enjoy their evening.

The taxi dropped him outside Holly Lodge. It was pretty much as Michael had visualized it: a bit gloomy, a bit neglected, with the air of having known better days. There was a light showing in one of the downstairs rooms. Michael went along the gravel drive and plied the door knocker. It echoed inside the house, but there was no sound of any movement. He tried again. Still nothing. Perhaps Nell was upstairs, or at the back of the house. She had said something about French windows, so he made his way round the side of the house. Yes, there were the French windows. Michael peered through them. There was no sign of Nell – or wait, wasn't that her jacket thrown over a chair? He knocked on the window and called out, but the house remained silent and still. Perhaps she had gone out to get some lunch. Without her jacket, though, on a bitter January day? He found his phone and tried her number, but again it went to voicemail. Then he tried the French windows, but they were locked.

He was not exactly worried, but he was a bit uneasy. He went back to the front of the house. The front door would be locked as well, but he would try it anyway. But it was not locked. The old-fashioned brass handle turned easily and smoothly.

The minute he stepped into the hall, the unease deepened. He reminded himself he did not believe in ghosts, not even after that very strange business in Shropshire when he had met Nell. But he did believe that houses could retain atmospheres – that you could sometimes sense if their inhabitants had been happy or sad or lonely. Holly Lodge held none of those emotions; what it did hold was fear, stark and unmistakable. The feeling was so strong that if it had not been for wanting to find Nell, Michael would have left as fast as possible.

There was a small table lamp glowing in the hall, and it

looked as if there was another in one of the rooms leading off it. Michael called out, hoping Nell would come out of one of the rooms, or down the stairs, laughing and saying he had given her a scare. But she did not.

He looked into the rooms at the house's front, then went through to the one with French windows. Rather guiltily, he felt in the pockets of Nell's jacket. Tube ticket, a tissue, an odd peppermint. And her phone. Michael frowned, then went into the other rooms, his footsteps echoing eerily. Everything was ordinary and unthreatening.

The kitchen was a large, reasonably modern room. A chair had been drawn up to an oak table, and there was a plate with a few crumbs on it, and an apple core. A sheet of notes in Nell's writing lay at the side, with her Filofax next to it. Michael had a mental picture of Nell eating a picnic lunch, reading her notes as she did so, perhaps checking for an address or phone number to call a colleague because she had found something outside her own province. The Filofax was open at the calendar section, and today's date was circled rather elaborately in red. In the evening section, she had written, in ordinary blue ink, 'Michael – supper'. This did not tell him anything he did not already know, and he looked round the kitchen for further ideas. Without thinking much about it, he touched the electric kettle. It was hot – in fact it was so hot it could not be long since it had boiled. Michael stared at it. This was starting to be the classic dark fairy-story scenario: the apparently empty house with sinister signs of occupancy. A door left open so the unwary traveller could lift the latch and step inside . . . And, once inside, there were lamps burning, a kettle singing on the hob . . . Michael wondered whether, if he went into the bedrooms, he would find any of the beds occupied. With the corpse-bride out of Robert Browning's poem, said his mind cynically? Or were you thinking of Goldilocks in the Three Bears' cottage? Even so, as he went up the stairs, he was remembering the eighteenth-century sonnet with the old bed that thrilled the gloom with the tales of human sorrows and delights it had witnessed over the centuries.

Thrilled gloom or not, he would check the bedrooms in case Nell had fallen and knocked herself out. Michael called out again, willing her to answer, but Holly Lodge remained silent.

Most of the rooms had nothing but discarded or dust-sheeted furniture in them, so he went up to the attic floor. The rooms here looked smaller, and the passageway linking them was narrower, but again there were only odd pieces of furniture and boxes of old curtains.

When he entered the room at the far end, he had an impression of extreme fear, and so strong was it, he almost went straight out again. There were several large packing cases, and an old-fashioned dressing table with a swing mirror stood against the wall. Was that where Benedict had glimpsed that sinister reflection that had lodged in his mind? It would not be difficult to believe a figure stood in the smoky depths, watching you.

But the room looked perfectly normal, even though the fear hung in the air like clotted strings. Pushed against one wall was a small bureau with a drop-front flap and a chair pulled up to it, and Michael sat down and tried to decide what to do. Would Benedict or Nina know where Nell was? He did not have their phone numbers, but they were probably on Nell's phone or written in the Filofax. Michael was not sure if this was a situation where he could intrude on her privacy to that extent. Was there anywhere else she might be? Had she found something in the house that had sent her hotfoot out of the house? Where, though? And would she leave the house unlocked and her jacket and phone and Filofax behind?

How about the chess set? If Benedict's story could be believed, the rest of the figures had perished in the watchtower fire that had killed Sheehan, so Nell could not have found the rest of the set. But might she have found out something about its origins? Paperwork? A letter? On this thought, Michael began to sort through the desk, tipping out the contents of the envelopes. But they seemed to contain only old household accounts, yellowing notepaper with Holly Lodge's address, and bills from local merchants. No, wait, there were a couple of old photographs. He seized on them. One was a group shot, the grainy, sepia tones of the nineteenth century, the faces of the people indistinct and the background blurred. On the back, in faded, slightly childish-looking writing, were the words '*My friends in Kilglenn.*'

Kilglenn. That edge-of-Ireland place near the stormy Cliffs of Moher, with an old watchtower where Nicholas Sheehan and Colm Rourke had played chess . . .

The other photo was clearer and looked as if it had been taken by a professional photographer. It was a posed shot of two people, head and shoulders, both very young, barely out of their teens. The man was dark-haired, and he wore the faintly embarrassed amusement of any Victorian gentleman faced with a camera. The girl came up to his shoulder. She was even younger and she had an air of fragility and innocence, but there was something in the slant of her eyes and the curve of her lips that suggested she might be capable of being very far from innocent. Her hair fell to her shoulders.

The edges of the photograph were indented with parallel lines, as if it had been in a frame for many years and the frame or the glass had cut into the paper. Michael turned it over. On the back, in a different hand to the one on the group picture, it said, '*Colm and Romilly, taken at his eighteenth birthday.*'

Colm, thought Michael. Colm Rourke, Declan's closest friend, the boy who played that fatal game of chess with Nicholas Sheehan. And Romilly, the copper-haired waif, who sobbed out a tale of seduction or rape, but looked out of the corners of her eyes as she did so, to see what effect her story was having.

Benedict was not suffering from multiple personality disorder at all. Those people he had talked about so vividly had existed – which implied the events he had described had happened. Two Irish boys had come to London, to find Colm's cousin and seek their fortunes. They must have seen it as a fairy story – a romantic adventure. Two heroes travelling to the city whose streets were paved with gold, going to the aid of the beautiful Romilly.

And which version of Romilly's story was true? Had the enigmatic Nicholas Sheehan, being lonely – even perhaps influenced by the chessmen's malevolence – really seduced her that day? Or was Sheehan's own story the truth: that

Romilly had demanded money to prevent her spreading a rape story? Had she been so desperate to leave Kilglenn she had done that? And had Sheehan, desperate to preserve the chessmen's solitude, yielded to her blackmail? Michael supposed he would never know the truth, but remembering portions of Benedict's story, thought he would not put blackmail past Romilly.

He tidied the photos back into their envelope. The fact that these people had existed was something good to tell Benedict – unless, of course, he had seen these photos for himself and folded them into his fantasies. But none of it got Michael any nearer to finding Nell.

He checked the desk again. Had he looked in all the pigeonholes and envelopes? No, there was one with yellowing newspaper cuttings. They were not likely to be relevant, but Michael was not ignoring anything.

The cuttings dated from the late 1890s, and described a series of murders committed in Canning Town by a killer the press of the day had dubbed the Mesmer Murderer. Benedict had not mentioned a murderer as being part of Declan's story, but this had been Declan's house and someone living here had wanted to preserve these articles. Michael began to read the top article. It described how the murderer had been caught, but how, on his way to face justice, had escaped. The hue and cry had been raised, and the hunt was still on. A photograph, apparently taken by an enterprising reporter with an early camera, was reproduced.

Michael unfolded the rest of the cutting and stared down at the photograph. It was smudgy but it was recognizable. Allowing for the few years' difference, the face of the Mesmer Murderer was the one in the photograph he had found earlier in this desk. Colm Rourke.

So the shining fairy-tale adventure of those two boys had turned to the poisoned fruit of so many fairy stories. The golden pavements had been dirty and unfriendly; the heroine had sold her purity for a mess of pottage and had died a sad squalid death in a slum. And one of the heroes had been branded as a multiple murderer.

There were a couple of earlier articles, which gave more

details about the victims. Michael read them carefully. Four out of the five victims seemed to have had an appointment with the killer – an appointment they had written in their diaries, circling the dates elaborately in red. And the markings in each case resembled the outline of a chess piece.

A chess piece. Lights were exploding in Michael's mind and he dropped the article and half fell down the stairs, snatching up the Filofax from the kitchen table. Yes, it was a chess piece Nell had drawn on today's page, all right. But she had said she might get the single figure valued today if she had time, so probably the little silhouette was a kind of *aide memoire*. And the Mesmer Murders had been over a hundred years ago.

But there are times when logic flees, and something else drives the mind and dictates the actions. For Michael this was one of those times. He did not try to reason that those long-ago people and long-dead tragedies could not affect the present. He only knew that Nell was missing, that she had marked her diary in exactly the same way as those other murdered people, and that he had to find her as fast as possible.

The only clue he had was Canning Town, where four of the five victims had been found, near an old sewer outlet by the docks. Canning Town was where Romilly Rourke had had a room – Benedict had described how Declan and Colm had gone there to find her, but they had been too late because she had been dying from a botched abortion.

Michael went down the stairs at top speed, and out into the street to flag down a taxi.

# TWENTY-FOUR

The afternoon was darkening when Michael reached Canning Town.

'Bit off my regular beat,' said the taxi driver when Michael asked for Bidder Lane or Clock Street. 'We can ask when we get there, though.'

But there was no Bidder Lane to be found, at least not in this part of London, and no Clock Street.

'You sure you got the address right?' said the taxi driver.

'No, I'm not,' said Michael. 'And I've never been to this part of London, either. They're just two places I've been told about. Thanks for trying, though. I think I'll be better on foot from here. I can ask local people if they know those streets, or go into a shop or a pub.'

The area, generally, was a piecemeal industrial estate, with pubs at intervals and scatterings of shops. There were gasworks and gasometers as well, and modern tower blocks jutting up into the skyline. And yet, here and there were glimpses of that older London – the London that Declan and Colm must have known. Michael could not see the river, but a dank wet smell hung everywhere, and he could hear the muffled hoots of barges. Surely Nell was not out here. But this was where that long-ago murderer had killed his victims, and Nell's diary had been marked with the same curious symbol as those victims.

*I've got to find her*, thought Michael, still in the grip of the inexplicable compulsion.

Grey mist clung to the buildings, turning them into ghost outlines. Mist of any kind played tricks with your eyes, so that you began to imagine silent figures watching you from its depths. It played tricks with your hearing as well, creating curious resonances. Several times Michael thought he heard the clatter of wheels as if someone was pushing a barrow or a large cart along, and when he paused at the intersection of two streets music reached him – jangling piano music that seemed to have no relation to today's thudding car stereos.

He had lost all sense of direction, but this appeared to be one of the older – and certainly poorer – parts of the area. There were no longer any industrial units or steel-fronted shops; instead was a street of small terraced houses with grimy facades. There was no traffic, but a few people were around, although when Michael tried to approach a woman to ask for directions she ducked her head away and scurried away from him. Two men, shabbily dressed and smelling of alcohol, came down the street, but they were walking so erratically and laughing so raucously that Michael gave them a wide berth.

A church clock, somewhere on his left, chimed three o'clock, although the mist was so thick it felt more like the middle of the night. There was a pub on the corner though, and light streamed from the windows. Probably it had been where the music had come from. He would go in and ask for directions to Bidder Lane.

As he neared the pub he saw a gap between the houses – a kind of natural alley that looked as if it led down to the quay. Michael hesitated, wondering whether to investigate and, as he did so, he saw darkly silhouetted against the river fog the shape of a man half carrying what looked like a female figure.

For the second time that day he did not stop to reason. He went after the figures at once. The man was too far away for him to see any details, except that he was wearing a long dark coat, but there was something familiar about the way the woman's hair fell to one side. Was it Nell? Michael followed, trying to decide what to do, chary of putting Nell (if it was she) into danger. Ought he to call the police? But what if it was not Nell, and there was some perfectly innocent explanation?

Ahead was a flight of stone steps; in this light they looked slimy and coils of rope and scatterings of debris lay on them. The man went down these steps and Michael, following at a cautious distance, saw they led down to the quay.

The mist was thicker here, so much so that this was almost turning into the classic walk through fog, beloved of film makers and writers of horror. He and Nell would laugh about it later; they would conjure up old black and white films and gothic novels: Fu Manchu spreading his sinister spider webs through Limehouse; Dr Jekyll metamorphosing into Mr Hyde . . . Assorted murderers stalking the shadows . . . Assorted murderers. Including a real one who had mesmerized his victims into meeting him out here?

Someone had recently sprinkled what looked like sand on the steps – perhaps to make the descent less treacherous. When Michael reached the bottom there was no sign of his quarry, and he paused, looking round. The river was still some way below him but he could make out the shapes of barges, and see lights from the bridges. He was standing on a walkway with an iron railing, and further along the walkway was an opening cut into the wall. '*The bodies were found near the old Bidder Lane sewer*,' the newspaper had said. Could that be the sewer? He looked around for the figure he had followed, and it was then that he saw the walkway bore sandy footprints, leading towards the outlet.

Michael began to walk stealthily towards the tunnel, thinking he would try to see inside, and if there was anything in the least suspicious he would call the police at once. He was within about ten feet of it when he realized that there were other footsteps walking down this fog-shrouded path.

Someone was coming stealthily along the walkway towards him.

*London 1890s*

After Cerise left the bedroom Colm walked round the room twice, and paused at the window, staring down into the gloomy gardens. Then in a completely normal voice, he said, 'What a bitch. And what a lot of nonsense she talked. I've never been in an opium den in my life and neither have you. Let's ignore her altogether. We'll go downstairs to see if there's any food to be had. I don't know about you, but I'm ravenous.'

It's all right, thought Declan, following him down the stairs. Of course he didn't kill Flossie and of course he isn't planning to kill Cerise.

Two of the girls were in the scullery, eating pies which they had brought in from a stall. There was plenty to spare, they said, slicing up the pies with careless generosity. There was bread and cheese in the larder as well.

They were discussing what they were going to do, because this house would be broken up, that was for sure. The dark-haired girl, who was called Zelda, said Flossie had no family, and the other one, who was fluffily fair and whose name was Ruby, confirmed this. But whatever happened, you could depend on it that Ruby and Zelda and the others would be told to pack their bags.

'Where will you go?' asked Colm.

'Dunno yet. Me and Zelda had an idea we might set up in rooms off Charing Cross Road. You get a good few toffs wandering down Charing Cross Road of a night.'

Zelda gave this her endorsement. A girl might do very well in that part of London. They might even end up with a posh flat, all pink satin and plush, very smart it would be.

Colm entered into the plan with gusto, saying they should have a French maid to answer the door to their gentlemen, and Ruby giggled and said go on with you, French maids, who did he take them for, Lady Muck?

As St Stephen's clock chimed two, Colm got up from the table, as casually as if he had all the time in the world, and said he would be off out for a while. 'Just round and about,' he said. 'I'll be back soon.'

As he went out, Declan saw with cold fear that his eyes were filling up with the terrible blackness again. He gave it five minutes, then collected his coat and went after Colm. It was not really a surprise to see Colm get on an omnibus with Canning Town written on its front. *He's going out to the old river steps*, Declan thought. *That's where he met Harold Bullfinch and he knows it's deserted and he won't be interrupted. He must have told Cerise to meet him there. Surely Cerise would not be so foolhardy as to meet a man she believed to be a murderer in such a lonely spot?* But Declan remembered those remarks about opium. Cerise thought Colm had acted out of an opium nightmare – that he had not been aware of what he was doing, or even remembered doing it.

*I've got to make sure*, thought Declan, and waited for another omnibus.

Bidder Lane was as dismal and dispiriting as he remembered. Grime clung to the fronts of the houses and a dirty yellow fog hung everywhere. Declan went purposefully along the street, pausing at the intersection with Clock Street, and looking wistfully towards the pub. Someone was playing the jangly piano again and a few voices were raised in somewhat beery song. He wished, as he had last time, that he could go inside and become part of a noisy, ordinary group of people, but he had to reach Colm and save Cerise. He went determinedly between the houses, and down the steps to the quay. Someone had sprinkled sand or sawdust on the steps – Declan tried not to think it would be to mop up Harold Bullfinch's blood.

But there was no sign of Colm. Then had Colm been going off on some entirely innocent task? Or was he meeting Cerise somewhere else? Declan looked about him. The mist hung over the river, and the lights of the barges were blurred discs of colour. Anyone with half a grain of sense would be indoors on an afternoon like this. No wonder this stretch of the quay-side was so deserted . . .

But it was not deserted after all. At the far end of the walkway shelf, a figure stood, silhouetted against the swirling greyness. It was Cerise – even from here Declan could see the velvet cape which she swore was tipped with mink but the other girls said was rabbit. He could make out the slightly unkempt hair, the tendrils deliberately allowed to escape from their pinnings, giving that tousled, just-got-out-of-bed appear-ance. Cerise, muffled up against the damp, dank afternoon with her bit of spurious mink, waiting with cat-faced greed for the man she thought she was going to give her money for keeping his secrets.

Declan was just thinking with relief that there was still time to save her, when a second figure stepped out of the yawning blackness of the old sewer tunnel. Colm. Declan drew breath to call a warning, but it was already too late. Colm had put an arm round Cerise, and was pulling her into the darkness. Declan heard her cry out, in surprise or fear, and he went towards them, not daring to run on the slippery ground, but moving as fast as he dared. Here was the tunnel mouth. It was little more than a circular hole with a brick surround, eight or ten feet across in all, and it looked as if it had been cut into the quay wall. Declan hesitated, then stepped into the sour blackness.

The sewer had obviously long since been abandoned, and it smelled dreadful. After the dampness of the river fog it felt close and hot. It was not as dark as he had expected; light came in from outside, and he could see the blackened bricks, and the crusted grime of years. Rank weeds thrust out from cracks in the wall and grew up from the ground and the curved ceiling, a couple of feet overhead, gleamed with moisture. There was the sound of water dripping somewhere, echoing eerily. This would be a terrible place to die.

The tunnel curved round to the right slightly, and ahead, stretching from the floor of the tunnel to its ceiling, was what must be sluice gates. The centre sections were solid, age-blackened wood; the top and bottom were thick spiked iron. At one side was a mechanism, presumably for opening the gates: an immense wheel was set horizontally into its base. If that wheel could be turned, would the old sluice gates creak into life? Declan shuddered and looked about him. It was then he saw a much smaller, narrower tunnel leading off to the left. When he went towards it, he heard a female voice calling for help.

Nell had not really thought there was any point in calling for help, because she was fairly certain she was inside a particularly horrible dream. And even if this nightmare scenario was somehow real there would not be anyone in earshot. But she called anyway.

Wherever this was, there was a strong river smell, and there was the eerie sound of water dripping nearby. It was very dark and she was lying on hard ground, half against a wall. Other than this, she was not able to focus very well on what had happened. She sat very still, her eyes closed, and memory unrolled a little, showing her Holly Lodge and the things in the various rooms she had been listing. And then she had fallen part way down the stairs – she remembered that, and she remembered she had been partly knocked out. It was when she came round the nightmare had begun. There had been something odd and frightening – something to do with strange sounds – people in the street calling in voices that did not belong to the present. Nell forced herself to concentrate, and saw in her mind the big hall at Holly Lodge, with the man coming down the stairs towards her, stepping into the lamplight so that for a single nightmare second she had seen his face . . .

As this memory opened, she sat up abruptly, then gasped as pain twisted through her foot. But the pain forced the remaining fragments to drop into place. She had been running down the stairs to escape and missed her footing on the stairs and fallen, injuring her ankle. He had bent over her, the remarkable vivid blue of his eyes becoming suffused with black . . .

*'The eyes are always such a betrayal, Nell . . . There are even some eyes that can eat your soul, did you know that . . . ?'*

The words were not quite spoken, but Nell heard them, and this time she managed to sit up. He was here, standing at what must be the tunnel entrance, just out of the light. Hiding his face, she thought, and then, with helpless sympathy, now I understand why he does that.

Fear throbbed through her, but she said, 'Where is this? Who are you?' and heard how her voice bounced off the tunnel walls and roof and came back at her mockingly.

*'Benedict Doyle would tell you I'm his alter ego – a figment of a flawed mind . . . Except that I'm a real person – at least, I was once.'*

'Declan,' said Nell, half to herself, and there was a faint ruffle of something that might have been sadness.

*'No, I'm not Declan. I'm Colm. Declan was – ah, at the very end, Declan got away from me . . .'* The words whispered into Nell's mind. This was all a nightmare, of course, or the results of concussion from falling down the stairs. At any minute she would wake up in a hospital bed, with people saying things like, 'Drink this,' and, 'Try to get some rest.'

She said, 'Why am I here?' and thought how absurd this was, because nobody argued with a dream-figure or a phantom conjured up by concussion.

'*A little because you saw me that day with Declan's descendant, Benedict . . .*'

'But – does that matter? Anyway, no one needs to know. I won't tell anyone.'

She felt his mental pounce. '*That's what the others said. "I won't tell anyone," they said. Cerise said it on this very spot all those years ago. "No one needs to know what you did," she said. "I won't tell anyone if you pay me enough".*'

'Who was Cerise?' I'll keep him talking, thought Nell. That's what they say you should do in this situation. It'll create a connection between us, and he'll let me go. Except I'm not sure that we are talking in the normal sense.

'*Cerise was a greedy little cat. She thought I had committed a crime and she tried to get money from me to stop her telling people. And I had committed the crime, Nell. So I had to shut her up.*'

'You killed her?'

'*Oh yes. Just as I killed the villains who ruined the girl I loved and brought about her death. There was a man who butchered her to get rid of a baby she was having – I killed him first. He bungled the task, and the child bled out of her, and her life bled out with it. And all the colour and life and hope went out of my life on that night.*'

'I'm sorry,' said Nell, helplessly.

'*Then I killed the man who fathered the baby in the first place. A little plucked fowl in a waistcoat, that's what he looked like. Strutting around his tiny kingdom in Islington, with his charities and his churches . . . But he had his squalid pleasure with her, with no thought for the consequences, and I couldn't let him live after that. He had to be punished – you do see that?*'

'You killed three people?' said Nell, in horror.

'*More than three. I killed a greedy rapacious female who could have helped Romilly, but threw her out on to the street. And do you know, the creature had left me her house – in a drunken moment she actually wrote out a will and left it to me.*'

'Holly Lodge,' whispered Nell.

'*Yes. Me, who had lived in a shack with an earth floor – a ramshackle place in the wilds of Ireland – to be owning a house like that.*' There was a pause. '*Last of all I killed a man who might have shopped me to the police for that murder. I only knew his Christian name. Arthur, he was called. He had a walrus moustache. I was sorry about that killing, but he had seen too much and Cerise threatened to tell him about the others . . . I couldn't risk it. When I sent a note, he came to meet me like a lamb. They all came, Nell, just as you did. The newspaper said I mesmerized my victims.*'

'Did you?' In another minute I'll make a dash for the tunnel entrance, thought Nell. If I could just get outside I could yell for help – someone will hear and come. Only I'm not sure if I can get very far on this ankle.

'*I did,*' he said. '*I had the chess piece, you see. It gave me the power.*'

For an incredible moment Nell forgot about the sinister situation she was in and stared at him. 'The chess piece? The ebony chess king?'

'*Yes. I took it from a man burning to death . . . No, that's not true, he gave it to me. The other figures burned with him, but the king survived and there was still so much power left in it. You shouldn't have taken it from the house, Nell. If you had left it there, I might have left you alone. But I had to get it back. I need it to reach Benedict.*'

'Why?' I'm tapping into Benedict's illness, thought Nell. This is all a weird form of telepathy.

'*Because I still carry the sins of the others and I must pass them on. Romilly's wouldn't be so much, but God knows what that priest in the watchtower might have done . . . I tried to reach Benedict's father – and his grandfather – but they got away from me.*'

The whispering broke off for a moment and Nell glanced towards the faint light from the tunnel entrance. Was this the moment to try to escape? She said, 'I don't understand all that about passing on sins. And why Benedict?'

'*Because it was Declan who pronounced the ritual all those years ago. An old, old ritual it is, Nell – so old you'd think it would long since have frayed to nothing. We didn't believe in it at the time – it was just meant as comfort for someone facing death.'*

'But it did work?'

*'Yes. We thought if there was any power in it at all, it would be Declan who'd take the weight of the sins. But I was the one who took them. I felt it happen, Nell. I felt the sins burn down into my soul and that's a feeling so terrible you'd never recover from it. It's like having a black stone dropped into your heart – a stone that drinks all the goodness from you and feeds on the evil. I think Declan had his own armour – perhaps simply because he was genuinely good.'* For a moment a faint amusement seemed to ruffle the darkness. *'Myself, I was never a saint,'* said Colm. *'Even in the Kilglenn days.'*

'Kilglenn?

*'Yes. A tiny sliver of a village in Ireland. So beautiful though.'*

Nell said, as firmly as she could, 'You aren't real. This is all a dream, and I'm not listening to you. I'm going to wake up – I'll *make* myself wake up – and you'll have vanished.'

*'I wish,'* said Colm, with the same deep sadness, *'it was that simple.'* He stepped forward, and the uncertain light from outside fell cruelly across his face. *'Forgive me, Nell . . .'*

Nell flinched, and then, even knowing no one would be in earshot, shouted at the top of her voice for help.

There was a flurry of movement at the opening to the tunnel, and a figure stood silhouetted against the grey wintry light.

Declan had expected the inside of the sewer tunnel to be dim, but he had not expected it to be so filled with blurred shadows. He certainly had not expected to find his vision clouded so that he felt as if he was looking through a wavy, distorted mirror. But probably the river fog had seeped into the tunnel.

He did not immediately see Colm or Cerise, but he heard them. Colm was talking to Cerise, his voice soft and low. It was the voice Colm generally used when he was luring one of his females into bed with him. Declan heard Colm say something about Kilglenn, and then something about shutting people up. He's confessing, thought Declan in horror. He's admitting to Cerise that he committed those murders

– Bullfinch and Flossie – and he's telling her he'll do the same to her. He went stealthily forward, hoping not to be heard, praying he could take Colm by surprise and shout to Cerise to make a run for it. As he got closer, he heard Colm say, 'Arthur, he was called. I couldn't risk him talking. I sent him a note and he came to meet me . . .'

Fresh horror broke within Declan. He killed that other man, he thought. The walrus moustache man who was in the house with Cerise that day. Oh God, what do I do? This is Colm, he's better than a brother to me . . . But I can't let him kill again.

No longer caring if he was heard, he ran towards the voices. In a corner of the inner tunnel, Colm was bending over a female who was lying on the ground, half against one wall. There was an extraordinary moment when Declan thought he had got this whole thing wrong, because although the man was wearing the dark great coat Colm had taken from the lodging house, he looked like a stranger.

Cerise was different, as well. Gone was the velvet cape with the dubious fur trimming, and whoever this was, she was wearing the most astonishing clothes Declan had ever seen – some kind of loose top and trousers like a man. Her hair was certainly not Cerise's scooped-up mane with its tumbling tendrils; it was shorter than Declan had ever seen a female's hair, and somehow shaped around her head. He blinked, trying to see through the distorting mists, and then saw that of course it was Cerise lying there, it was just the curious light in the tunnel.

Colm turned at Declan's appearance, and as he did so, Cerise moved in a half-scrambling way that suggested she might already be injured. As Colm lunged towards her, she went towards the outer tunnel and Declan put out a hand to help her. She seemed not to see it, though; she went past him, still limping heavily, and Declan saw that a completely unknown man was standing there.

Whoever he was, he had disturbed the river fog, because it came swirling into the tunnels, thick and smelling of oil and grime. Declan blinked, and, when it cleared, he saw with despair that after all Cerise had not got away. She was lying on the ground, her eyes wide and staring. The fur and velvet cape she had been so proud of was soaked in the blood running from her cut throat.

*The present*

Nell clung to Michael, trying not to sob with relief, but unable to prevent tears streaming down her face. When he said, 'Nell, my dear love, we'll have the explanations later, but for the moment I'm going to get you into a taxi and head for home.'

'But we need police – the man – he's still in there.'

Michael said, 'What man?' and Nell, who had been testing her damaged foot to see how well she could walk on it, looked up at him.

'The man who took me in there. He was at Holly Lodge – I think he's something to do with Benedict's family . . . Michael, what's wrong?'

Michael said, 'Nell, there was no one in the tunnel.'

As Nell stared at him, quick light footsteps came towards them along the river walkway. It was Benedict, his face white, his hair beaded with moisture from the river mist.

Michael said, 'Benedict, what on earth . . . No, never mind for the moment. Except – did I hear you following me earlier on?'

Benedict said, 'You might have done. I was following someone, but I'm not sure who it was. I don't think it was you, Michael. Whoever it was, he was carrying someone. I thought it looked pretty sinister, so I came after him.'

'I thought I was following someone as well. But there's no one here now.'

Benedict looked at Nell. 'Are you all right? What are you doing out here?'

'I don't know,' said Nell. 'I fell down the stairs at Holly Lodge, and sprained my ankle . . . Michael, stop fussing, it's only a sprain and I can probably manage to hop as far as the road and a taxi. But I think – no, I'm sure – that someone brought me out here. And if you were both following someone—'

Benedict said, half to himself, 'I was following Declan.'

'No,' said Nell at once. 'It wasn't Declan. It was Colm.'

# TWENTY-FIVE

They pieced it together sitting in Michael's rooms the next evening, pooling all their information – Benedict's images, Michael's discoveries about Fergal and Kilderry Castle, and Nell's eerie experience inside the old sewer tunnel.

'So it wasn't Declan I was seeing and hearing all these years,' said Benedict, finally. 'And Declan wasn't the Mesmer Murderer.' He looked tired, but his eyes were clear and happy.

'It doesn't sound like it,' said Michael. 'It sounds as if Declan was trying to protect Colm quite a lot of the time.'

'And Colm was under the—'

'Baleful influence of the devil's chess piece?'

'Don't mock, you heartless wench,' said Michael, smiling at Nell. 'Damn it, I will say it. Colm was under the baleful influence of the chess piece.' He refilled the wine glasses.

'Also,' said Benedict, accepting the wine, 'I think Colm was pretty much besotted with Romilly. So that was driving him as well. He hated those people who contributed to her death.' He drank his wine thoughtfully, then said, 'You can't imagine how relieved I am to know my great-grandfather wasn't a serial killer.'

'And,' said Michael, 'to know that you probably aren't suffering from that thing – dissociative personality disorder.'

'Yes, that too, although I can't begin to think how I'm going to tell the medics about all this.'

'I'd help with that if you wanted.'

'Thanks. I think I would like that. But,' said Benedict, 'I'm still not entirely clear why my parents – and my grandfather – died all those years ago. That later newspaper report I found – there was a witness who was very clear about seeing a figure in the road. It can't have been coincidence, can it? It must have been Colm.'

Nell said, 'If we're accepting the premise of all this, it seems reasonable to think Colm was trying to . . . to offload the sins he took on. It was your great-grandfather who recited the sin-eating ritual, but seemingly it was Colm who actually got the sins.' She frowned. 'I can't believe I'm saying all this.'

'Go on,' said Benedict.

'Somehow I don't think he meant Benedict's parents and grandfather to die,' said Nell. 'I think they just got in the firing line. Colm had committed those Mesmer Murders and perhaps he was ready to face the consequences of that, but—'

'But there was the added weight of those other sins,' said Benedict. 'Nicholas Sheehan and Romilly. And even though it doesn't sound as if either of them would have particularly serious sins on their consciences—'

'Sheehan had apparently turned his back on his priest's vows, and Romilly had aborted her unborn child,' said Michael. 'Colm and Declan would both see those as massive mortal sins.'

'Yes. And Colm could only offload them on to the person who recited the original ritual.'

'On Declan,' said Nell. 'Or on Declan's descendants after his death. That's fairly classic ghost behaviour.'

'And for that he needed the chessman's power,' said Michael, thoughtfully. 'So he may have been trying to keep the chess figure in Holly Lodge so he could harness its power. Benedict, did your parents know about the chess set?'

'I don't know. But I know my father believed there was something wrong inside Holly Lodge,' said Benedict. 'I remember him saying I should never go inside because "it" was still there. And my mother said, "Even after all these years?" and he said, "Yes," very positively.'

'They probably wouldn't know all we do,' said Michael. 'But a few memories could have come down through Declan. Let's not forget that Benedict's grandfather was Declan's son.'

'But look here,' said Nell, 'are we really believing a nineteenth-century ghost carried me into that tunnel? Because there was no one in there when you both turned up.'

'There wasn't, was there? And yet I'm sure I saw someone going in there,' said Benedict. 'I'd followed him for quite a long way – even on the tube. That was all a bit peculiar,' he said, sounding uncertain. 'As if I might not have been quite in the present at all.' He gave a half-grin. 'Just imagination going into overdrive, I should think. But whoever I followed had a female with him. He wasn't quite carrying her, but he nearly was.'

'I saw that as well,' said Michael. 'And someone must have taken you there, Nell.'

'Mightn't it have been a twenty-first-century villain?' said Nell. 'A burglar – someone high on drugs?'

'What would his reason be?'

'If he was high on drugs he wouldn't need a reason. Not a logical one.'

'But you listened to all that stuff about sin-eating and the chess set.'

'I'd fallen downstairs,' said Nell, defensively. 'I could have been unconscious or concussed and hallucinating.'

'But what about Benedict's story and all the confirmations we've found? All the people who existed? Fergal McMahon's memoirs for instance. They're clear enough, real enough.'

'Fergal could have been fantasizing.'

'Then how about the formidable brothel keeper? Flossie Totteridge existed. She's on the Title Deeds to Holly Lodge.'

'All right, I'll give you Flossie Totteridge. But how did the house come to belong to Declan?' demanded Nell. 'He and Colm were penniless Irish boys, seemingly.'

'That's a missing piece so far,' admitted Benedict. 'But I'm trying to track it down – Land Registry and Land Searches and whatnot. I'll find the evidence eventually.'

'How about the evidence of the chess piece?' said Michael to Nell.

'Now you're sounding like a Sherlock Holmes story. *The Evidence of the Last Chess Piece.*'

'But even without Fergal's memoirs, there's that story in Owen's book,' said Michael. 'Eithne who was a servant in Kilderry Castle.'

'You don't like that chess piece, do you?' said Benedict suddenly, to Nell.

'No. That's why I've brought it here tonight. I think it should be burned or smashed into fragments.'

'And the fragments cast to the four winds?' said Michael,

and although he spoke lightly he glanced uneasily at the small
wrapped package on the table.

'I'm being serious.'

'Actually, so am I.'

Benedict looked at Nell. 'You saw him,' he said. 'Colm, I
mean. He didn't stay in the shadows while he was with you,
did he? You saw what he looked like.'

'I'm not sure what I saw,' said Nell, in a low voice, not
looking at either of them. 'Whatever it was, I'm still going to
believe there's a logical explanation – it's just that we haven't
hit on it yet.'

Benedict said, 'I'm going to return the chess figure to where
all this began.' He looked at them, and said, 'I think it's what
Colm wants. It think it's what he's always wanted. So I'm
going to take it back to Kilglenn.'

After Benedict had gone, Michael said to Nell, 'You still
don't entirely believe, do you?'

'Not entirely.'

'Will I ever convince you that ghosts exist?'

'I don't know. But,' said Nell, smiling at him, 'I'd like you
to keep trying.'

'Would you? So would I.'

*Kilglenn, the present*

And so, thought Benedict, finally and at last, I'm going to see
the place where Declan and Colm grew up – where all those
strange and tragic things happened.

Driving the small hire car towards Kilglenn, he thought this
part of Ireland could not have changed very much since the
last years of the nineteenth century. Here, surely, was the steep
road that Fergal McMahon, together with Nicholas Sheehan
and Fintan, must have taken to Kilderry Castle that night. He
pulled into the side of the road for a moment and consulted
the map. Yes, this was where the castle had stood; there was
a tumble of ruins at the top of the small hill. Had the chess
set somehow poisoned the fabric of the castle, so that over
the years it had rotted from within? It was more likely that the
various Earls of Kilderry had simply gambled and womanized

and quarrelled their substance into nothing, until the castle had to be abandoned.

He had not been able to identify St Patrick's Monastery on any map – or, at least, he had identified so many monasteries under St Patrick's banner that it was impossible to know which would have been Fergal's.

He had not expected Kilglenn to be large enough to warrant a road sign, but when he rounded a curve in the road, there it was. 'KILGLENN, 10 KILOMETRES.'

I'm nearly there, thought Benedict, and with the thought he felt the familiar stirring within his mind.

*Nearly home, Benedict . . .*

Benedict said, 'I thought you'd be here.'

*Would I let you do this on your own . . . ?*

Benedict gave a mental shrug and drove on. Kilglenn, when he reached it, had succumbed to a degree of modernization, although essentially it was still the small backwater which two hopeful Irish boys had left all those years ago – and which a red-haired Irish girl had schemed to escape from. But there was a small supermarket and a bookstore with DVDS and CDs, and people in the little main street had mobile phones and younger ones had iPods.

At the far end was a low-roofed building with the legend *Reilly's* and a small board with the chalked information that bar food was available. Fintan, thought Benedict, slowing down. I'm glad the name's still used. He remembered Eithne's story which Michael had passed to him, and the reference to a son and daughter. He would like to think it was Fintan's great-grandson – maybe more 'greats' – who ran this bar.

Beyond Reilly's the buildings thinned out, and there was only the wild countryside and the rise of the land towards the Moher Cliffs. But as he went on again, he saw a winding little track leading off to his right and he pulled the car to the side of the road and got out. Most likely there was nothing to be seen at the end of the track.

And yet, and yet . . .

*You know what's there, Benedict*, said Colm inside his mind. *Of course you do.*

'Of course I do,' whispered Benedict, and walked up the

track, with the springy grass on each side, and the wind with
its faint taste of the ocean all around him.

The shack. The small structure might have been any half-
ruined shanty cottage, of course, but Benedict knew it was the
place where Colm had lived; where he and Declan had talked
and planned and dreamed. He had seen it through Colm's eyes
and he recognized it now.

He picked his way through the rubble. There was nothing
left of Colm's short time in this cottage; there were only
broken-up stones, ravaged by wind and rain, and shreds of
fabric that might have been rugs or curtains or clothes, or that
might simply be the debris of picnickers.

*But there are memories, Benedict . . . There are so many
memories here . . .*

Benedict sat on the edge of what must have been a hearthstone.
'Tell me,' he said. 'Finish the story for me.'

*Ah, but have we seen the ending yet, Benedict . . . ?*

For a moment something shivered on the far wall – the
outline of a man wearing a long coat with the deep collar
turned up. Benedict remained very still, and then the tumbledown room blurred, and he had the sensation that he was
looking through a very small window, thick with the dust of
decades . . . Beyond that window was a small room, lit by
flickering candlelight . . .

*London, 1890s*

When Declan looked back over the last ten days he could not
imagine how he had been able to do what he did. He certainly
could not imagine how he had had the courage for any of it.

Finding Cerise's body in the old sewer tunnel was still a
confused series of images for him. He had been so sure he
had saved Cerise – he could still see how she had scrambled
out of Colm's clutches, and made that painful, limping run to
the tunnel mouth, and the man who stood there. But when he
looked back, Cerise had been lying on the ground, her throat
gashed almost to the bone, and Colm had been standing over
her, the dripping knife in his hands, a look of such agony and
bewilderment in his eyes that Declan had known Colm had

not meant this. He had known it in his heart and his bones and his marrow. That had been when he had made the plan to get Colm away from London, no matter the cost.

He had confronted him that night in the Holly Lodge bedroom, to which they had returned because they had nowhere else to go.

'Cerise won't be missed for a while,' he said to Colm. 'There's time for us to get away. There's time for you to tell me the truth about all this.'

'I killed them,' said Colm. 'But I couldn't help it. It was as if another person came sliding under my skin, clawing its way along my hands and fingers and deep into my brain . . . God, would that be what the monks called possession?'

'I don't know. But if you are possessed,' said Declan, 'we can make a good guess where it came from.'

'The chess piece,' said Colm, light showing in his eyes for the first time for several hours. 'Jesus God, it's the bloody chess piece Sheehan gave us, isn't it?'

'Let's keep an open mind. You hated them all because of Romilly. The police might see that as good reason for you to kill them.'

'I see that. What do we do?' He sounded so frightened and so vulnerable and he looked at Declan with such trust, Declan knew he could not abandon him. He began to outline his plan, which was quite simply for them to leave Holly Lodge now, at once, and head for Liverpool and a boat for America. If they could disappear anywhere, surely they could do so in America. He had got as far as saying they should see how much money they had, when there was a loud hammering on the street door.

'Police,' said Colm, and turned white.

'Even if it is, they can't possibly have any proof,' began Declan.

'They can if they've found Flossie's will,' said Colm.

'What do you mean?'

'Last time I was with her we got a bit drunk,' said Colm. 'And she was – uh – very grateful to me. So I said – as a half joke – that it'd be nice to have a material form of her gratitude.'

'Such as?' But Declan already knew.

'She wrote it out there and then, and that girl who scrubs the kitchen came in to add her mark as a witness,' said Colm. 'All proper legal phrasing – Floss's husband was an accountant or something, and she knew how it should be worded. Declan, she's left me this house. And in the police's eyes, that'd give me a whopping great motive for killing her.'

'She left you this whole house?' said Declan, incredulously.

'She was drunk,' said Colm, impatiently. 'I was drunk, as well. Jesus Christ, wouldn't any man have to be drunk to get into bed with that one! But it was a joke – I never thought she'd take it seriously.' Downstairs they could hear the door being flung open, and several pairs of heavy feet trampling through the house. Colm flinched. 'Get me out of this,' he said. 'Declan, please . . .'

Declan dived for the window, wrenching it open. They were on the top floor and it was a sheer drop from the window to the ground. But there was a drainpipe, and if Colm would risk trying to get down it, there might be a chance . . .

But there was no time for any chances to be taken or any risks to be made. The bedroom door was flung open and three police officers came into the room, including the large and stolid Constable Oliphant who had questioned them earlier. He looked at them with bovine recognition, and it was the inspector who spoke the feared words. 'Colm Rourke, I'm arresting you for the murder of Mrs Florence Totteridge and on suspicion of four other counts of murder . . .'

As they took Colm from the room, he turned a white, desperate face to Declan, and although he did not speak, Declan knew the same thought was in their minds. Somehow, no matter the cost, Colm had to be extricated from this. Because if not, they would hang him.

At first though, he could not see how it could be done. Colm was being held in a police cell; the newspapers were having a fine old time, telling the citizens of London – and, for all Declan knew, the rest of the country as well – how the terrible Mesmer Murderer had been caught. The five murders were described in considerable detail. Declan forced himself to read everything in case he could find something that would lead to Colm being released. Perhaps he would find mention of Colm having done something when he had been indisputably somewhere else. Remembering those eagerly devoured episodes of Sherlock Holmes' exploits, Declan scoured the newspaper reports, trying to find a chink in the police's evidence.

The killings were set out in distressing and chronological detail, although none of them mentioned Colm by name – Declan supposed there would be some legal reason for this; perhaps they were not allowed to name the killer prior to the trial. But the victims seemed to be fair game.

Harold Bullfinch had been the first. He had told his landlady he had a business appointment, but his body had later been found knifed to death on river steps near the old Bidder Lane sewer outlet. Declan was wretchedly aware, as the police must be, that Bullfinch was the abortionist responsible for Romilly's death.

He expected Flossie Totteridge to be listed as the second victim, but it seemed that Mr Arnold Trumbull, a highly respected gentleman who managed a printing company in Islington and was a lay-preacher at his church, had been next.

Trumbull, thought Declan in horror. The little plucked fowl in a waistcoat. The man whose sister gave most of their money to homes for the indigent, and fed her hapless brother on pig's head and boiled cabbage. The man who had been responsible for Romilly's fateful pregnancy. *So you killed him as well, did you, Colm?* he thought, feeling sick.

Colm would hang on only half of this evidence. The judge and the jury would see it as a killing frenzy out of revenge for Romilly.

After Arnold Trumbull had come Flossie Totteridge. The name was not given; the papers merely described her as a widow who took in lodgers. She had been found with her throat cut in her own sitting room in North London. The police would not know Flossie had seen Colm and Declan with Bullfinch's bloodstained wallet, but they would see it as another piece of Romilly's story, because Flossie had turned Romilly out of the house for getting pregnant, when she might have helped her.

There was yet another unexpected victim. It was the little

man with the walrus moustache who had been at Holly Lodge
with Cerise on the afternoon of Flossie's death. Cerise had
called him Arthur. He was described as a tea importer, living
and working in Canonbury. Colm must have traced him, and
killed him for fear of what Cerise might have told him –
and for fear of what the man himself might have seen or
suspected of Flossie's death.

Cerise was the fifth of Colm's victims. She had tried to
blackmail him, thought Declan. And she, too, could have
helped Romilly.

He sat for a very long time, his mind flooded with sickening
images, dreadful doubt hammering like spikes against his brain.
Had Colm spoken the truth when he described something clawing
its way into his brain and forcing him to kill? Or had he killed
of his own free will out of revenge for Romilly's death?

He was allowed to see Colm once, and entering Newgate Gaol
was a terrible experience. It was like stepping neck-deep into
a well of black despair and Declan had to resist the compulsion to turn around and run away. The meeting took place in
a dreadfully bleak room, with Colm behind bars and two
officers present. It was impossible to say very much, so Declan
just said, 'I'll do everything I can to help you,' and Colm,
white and sunken-eyed and distraught, merely nodded.

Walking back to the small lodgings which were all he had
managed to afford after leaving Holly Lodge, Declan thought:
but what can I do? *What?*

Two days after the visit he suddenly saw how he might get
Colm away. The newspapers were still reporting on the Mesmer
Murders, and Declan read how Colm was to be taken to stand
trial at the Old Bailey Courthouse in three days' time. The
paper would tell its readers the details of the first day of the
trial that same evening.

Three days, thought Declan. They'll take him from that
prison – Newgate – in a closed carriage.

The beginnings of a plan began to unfold.

# TWENTY-SIX

I t was a simple plan – Declan tried to remember that the most successful plans were the simple ones.

On the morning of the trial, he made his way to Newgate Gaol very early. He had spent a sleepless night – he had, in fact, slept very little since Colm was arrested. A small crowd was massing to watch the excitement of a murderer being brought out, and Declan stood with them, hating them because they were relishing Colm's situation.

As eight o'clock struck from St Paul's, a kind of jeering cheer went up, and Declan saw the gates open and a closed carriage come out, drawn by two horses.

'Black Maria's here,' shouted several people, and cries of delight went through the crowd. Several people threw their hats in the air, and women nudged one another with a kind of lascivious glee, and asked was it true he was a fine, handsome young man?

Declan was relieved to see the horses drawing the closed-in carriage; he had been unsure whether the police might use a motorized vehicle, which would have made his plan impossible. His plan was frighteningly flimsy, but, if it worked, Colm would be free. If it did not, Colm would hang and probably Declan with him.

The crowd surged forward, eager to get a glimpse of the notorious Mesmer Murder. The driver urged the horses through them; the horses occasionally shied and showed the whites of their eyes, but Declan thought they were accustomed to crowds and not very much disturbed by them. As the carriage drew closer, judging his moment, he leapt forward and grabbed the bridle of the nearer horse, jerking it away from its companion. The second horse reared up at once, and the carriage slewed round, the wheels scraping and bouncing erratically. The driver leapt from his seat to calm the now-plunging and whinnying horses, and as the crowd backed away, the carriage rocked dangerously. There were shouts from inside, and the driver, trying to get the frightened horses under control, shouted, 'Get 'im out! It'll overturn – get 'im out!'

The door was opened, and two men emerged, holding Colm between them. Declan, watching his chance, saw that one of them was bruised and dazed-looking, and guessed the man had been flung against the carriage's sides as it swayed. It was now or never. He darted forward, willing Colm to respond, praying there was enough confusion to get him clear, agonizing in case Colm was handcuffed or in chains.

All his prayers were answered. There were no fetters of any kind, and Colm's eyes lit up as soon as he saw Declan. He swung a blow at the dazed officer, knocking him from his feet, then he leapt forward, and Declan grabbed his arm. Together they ran, scarcely noticing where they went, not really caring. Narrow streets, cobbled alleys, huddles of shops, barrows with fruit, vendors with chestnuts and flowers and jellied eels . . . Pounding feet came after them, with cries to stop.

'Don't stop,' gasped Colm. 'Not for anything, or I'm a dead man.'

At some stage Colm tore off the shameful prison garb so that he was wearing plain trousers and a singlet. It looked no more odd than some of the barrow boys and fruit sellers who had stripped off jackets the better to carry their heavy wares.

At first Declan thought they would never shake off their pursuers, but suddenly, in the way London has of springing its surprises, they went across a square and down an alley, and found themselves in a completely different district, near a small park. And they could no longer hear the sounds of pursuit.

'Have we done it?' demanded Colm, white-faced, his eyes blazing. 'Have we got away?'

'I think so. Let's just walk normally, so as not to attract attention.'

'Where are we, d'you think?'

'I don't know, but it doesn't matter,' said Declan. 'Because we're going to get out of London. We may have to walk most of the way, but we walked in, and we can walk out.'

'They'll be looking for me though,' said Colm. 'For both of us. Have we money?'

'Some.' Declan had brought the remains of the money from Bullfinch's wallet. He hated doing it, but he could not see any other way.

'Enough to get to Liverpool and the ferry?'

Declan paused and looked at him. 'Are we going home? I mean – back to Kilglenn?'

Colm sat down on a little low wall overlooking a patch of green. 'We are,' he said. 'But you don't have to come with me. And if I can get there I can hide out in the shack. No one will know I'm there if I'm careful.'

'But . . . why? Colm, all the world's at our disposal! I thought we'd cross to America – they say there's plenty of work to be had—'

'We thought there was plenty of work to be had here,' said Colm bitterly. 'And yes, we'll go to America afterwards. But there's something I have to do first.'

'What?' But Declan already knew.

Colm said, 'I have to get that accursed chess figure back to the watchtower.'

'Because the other pieces are there,' said Declan after a moment.

'Yes. I know they're cinders under the burned-out tower,' said Colm, before Declan could go on. 'And I don't understand it, not really. But I think it's got to be done.'

Declan said, 'But I didn't bring the chess piece. I brought all the things I thought we'd need, so we wouldn't have to go back, but I left the chess piece at Holly Lodge.'

'Then,' said Colm, 'we'll have to go back and get it.'

They argued for hours, sitting in the unknown park with London's life teeming all around them. At midday Declan bought food from a passing street vendor.

'You have no idea how good that tastes after Newgate fare,' said Colm, eating hungrily.

'Is it really bread and water they give you?'

'It tasted like it.' He finished the food and stood up. 'I'm going back to Holly Lodge,' he said. 'I'll find my way somehow. I'll meet you here as soon as I can.'

'I'll go,' said Declan. 'You daren't be seen.'

'Nor dare you. The police will know you were the one who caused the escape.'

'But no one at Holly Lodge will know that yet,' said Declan. 'So you're the one who'll wait here until I come back.'

'All right,' said Colm. 'If you see anything of Romilly's while you're there, bring that as well, would you? I think she had some photos from Kilglenn.'

'For pity's sake, I can't go rummaging through all the rooms—'

'I suppose not. But there's one very important thing—'

'Yes?'

'See if you can find the Title Deeds to the house,' said Colm. 'For I'm damned if I'm leaving without getting something out of this.'

It was vital not to feel angry or annoyed with Colm. Declan, threading his way through the streets, watchful for police, reminded himself that the request to find the deeds to Holly Lodge was reasonable – even sensible. They had hardly any money between them, and they would be fugitives for some time to come. To own a house would be a fine thing. But how could it possibly profit them? They would not dare live in it, nor would they dare sell it or rent it out. And were you allowed to profit from a crime you had committed? Declan had no knowledge of the law, but he thought it was a reasonable assumption that you were not.

Still, if he could get the Title Deeds he would do so, although he would not endanger either himself or Colm in the process.

The chess figure was another matter entirely.

Thinking furiously, Declan began to make his way across London.

In the end he simply walked openly into Holly Lodge. If anyone appeared – police or any of the girls – he would say he was collecting a couple of items of clothing he had left behind and he would be ignorant of Colm's escape.

But no one did appear. Declan heard faint sounds of crockery from the kitchens, but he was able to go up to the room he and Colm had shared. Moving quickly, listening for footsteps on the stairs, he scooped up the few odds and ends that were there. Then, taking a deep breath, he opened the bedside drawer and took out the chess piece, dropping it into his pocket. It felt heavy, as if it was dragging down the cloth of his coat.

There did not seem to be anything in the room that might have been Romilly's though, and Declan went back down the stairs. No one seemed to be around, although he could still hear someone moving around the scullery. Dare he go into Flossie's part of the house? Surely the police would have taken away all her papers and documents anyway? But Colm had been insistent, and Declan, remembering the way Colm's eyes could blaze with anger, did not feel like returning without having at least tried to find the Title Deeds. His heart thudding, he went through to the little sitting room where Flossie had died.

Everything was neat and tidy; furniture stacked to one side, a tea chest standing in the centre, containing what looked like a miscellany of Flossie's possessions. Declan made a cursory search of this, but there was nothing except ordinary household goods, a few sketches of local scenes, some china and glass ornaments. Where would papers be kept? There was a small bureau-cum-desk in one corner; it was almost certainly locked, but it was worth trying.

It was locked, but the lock was a flimsy one and it snapped fairly easily. Feeling like a housebreaker, Declan went swiftly through the papers inside it. There were letters, bills, odd receipts from various local merchants. He opened the small drawers at the back of the desk.

The Deeds were there. Several pages of thick, expensive-looking paper, tied with narrow green tape, bearing the legend: *Holly Lodge, freehold messuage and lands in the district of Highbury, County of London.*

Declan thrust the papers into the inside of his jacket and almost ran from the house.

*The present*

'So that's how you did it,' said Benedict softly, in the ruins of Colm's cottage, with the ocean-scented air blowing all round him.

*We did. And it took a long and weary time to get back up to Liverpool.*

'But you came back here?'

*We did. And for a time we thought we were safe. We thought we could hide out, and I'd take the chess figure back to the watchtower.*

'To be with the embers of the others,' said Benedict, softly.

*Yes. I wish I could explain to you about its force – about how it poured itself into me and made me feel such hatred and such malevolence.*

'I understand a little,' said Benedict, remembering parts of Fergal McMahon's memoirs.

*Do you? But you can't begin to imagine how weary these years have been. The poets write about beckoning ghosts in moonlight shades, and they wax lyrical about wizard oaks and Homer's thin airy shoals of visionary ghosts. Oh yes, Benedict, I have the learning and I have the classics at my beck and I can quote the great minds with the best, for the monks wouldn't have sent their pupils out into the world deformed and unfinished before their time . . . But the moonlight shades are lonely and desolate and as for wizard oaks, I wouldn't have them as a gift, even if I knew what they were.*

Benedict said, 'Why did you kill my parents? And my grandfather, who was Declan's son after all.'

*But isn't every man somebody's son? And I didn't mean to kill them. They were hell-bent on destroying the chess figure. They had a few shreds of its story, handed down by Declan; they knew it was something to be feared. But I knew that if it was destroyed I'd lose my only chance of reaching one of Declan's descendants, and ridding myself of the sins. It had to be one of Declan's family, because—*

'Because he was the one who set the ritual working,' said Benedict, softly.

*So you understand that, do you? When I realized your father intended to destroy the figure I tried to stop him. They were taking it to the old St Stephen's cemetery to bury it or burn it – he and your grandfather had pieced together some of the links to the past, mostly from half-memories Declan had left them. They hadn't got it quite right, but they knew enough to realize it was the source of the house's strangeness – that it was connected to the person they sometimes saw looking out of the mirrors. I had to prevent them destroying it, but I didn't intend them to die. And then afterwards there was only you, Benedict.*

'The figure in the mirror,' said Benedict, half to himself. 'So my father did see you.'

*Oh yes. But all those years ago when your great-grandfather got me out of Newgate Gaol, I wanted to destroy the chess piece – I knew it had made me a murderer. Declan didn't want to come back here – he said we'd be seen and recognized. But I persuaded him. I could always persuade him to do what I wanted. I said even if we were seen, we'd be the prodigal sons returning.*

*But once we reached this cottage, it all went dreadfully wrong and the nightmare began . . .*

*Kilglenn, 1890s*

For the first few hours of their return, Declan and Colm stayed in the shack, waiting for nightfall.

'Then we'll go up to the watchtower, and we'll cast this devil-inspired figure into the rubble,' said Colm. 'It can reunite itself with the others, and for all I care they can spend the next thousand years raising Satan's armies to invade the world.'

'I hate being here and not seeing my family,' said Declan.

'When we make our fortunes in America we'll come back and bestow largesse everywhere. What is largesse, by the way?'

'No idea, but we'll bestow it anyway.'

Darkness had not completely fallen when they set off for the watchtower. A faint glimmer came from the ocean, and the moon was rising, casting a cool silvery light.

There was a dreamlike quality to the cliff path as they climbed it, and they both remembered again the old tales of the Sidhe who could lure men to their deaths with their chill fatal singing.

The watchtower reared up above them as they came round the last curve of the path, stark and bleak against the night sky, and they both stopped and stared up at it.

'Just think,' said Declan softly, 'how we used to make up stories about it – how it was a giant's castle with a captive princess inside, or how it had been built from the magic-soaked stones of the ancient Irish Court of Tara.'

'And now,' said Colm softly, 'it's a burned-out wreck, with the bones of a renegade priest in the rubble.' He began to walk up the last few yards, then stopped. 'Can you hear that?'

'I hear nothing. And if you're starting to think this place is haunted, or the Sidhe are calling . . .' Then Declan heard it as well, and the sounds were not ghosts and they were certainly not the Sidhe.

The sounds were human. Several voices, all shouting, 'Murderer.'

They turned and saw, on the path below them, torch lights flaring through the dusk. At least twenty people – most of them men, but some women – were coming towards them.

'That's half the village of Kilglenn!' said Colm, staring at the people in fear. 'And they're coming for me.'

'But we needn't be afraid,' said Declan. 'Those are people we know – we grew up among them. My father isn't there, though,' he said, scanning the faces. 'Neither is Fintan.'

'Never mind who's not there, what do we do?'

Declan looked wildly about him, then said, 'We'll go inside the tower. If we can barricade the door against them, they might calm down after a while. Or we might be able to reason with them. Because these are people we've known since childhood!'

They tumbled across the remaining few feet to the tower and half fell against the door, gasping with relief when the handle turned and the door opened. They slammed it against the torchlit procession, and leaned back against the blackened oak, trying to regain their breath.

Even after the fire, the stone walls were so thick that the sounds of the approaching villagers was shut off, but it was so dark they could barely see anything.

'We'll have to find something to barricade the door,' said Colm.

'There's nothing. Everything's burned to cinders.'

'No, wait, there's a few bits of furniture – there's a chest over there, I think. Stay here – keep the door shut while I drag it over.'

Declan stayed where he was, holding the door's iron latch in place. He could hear Colm dragging the chest from the wall, but he could not see him. He pressed his ear to the door's surface, listening for sounds that the villagers had reached the top of the cliff path. Perhaps they were outside the door now. Or were they trying to find another way in? *Was* there another way in?

Here was Colm now. He must have got the chest across the room while Declan was listening for the villagers' approach. He had come to stand next to Declan – he was actually standing very close. Declan half turned his head and it was then that Colm reached down and took hold of Declan's hand. This was odd; it was not in the least like Colm. And Colm's hand felt wrong – it was too small, almost shrunken, and the fingers were curling round Declan's with a terrible intimacy . . .

In a voice that shook, Declan said, 'Colm? Where are you?'

'Over by the old fireplace, trying to get this press out from the wall. Why?'

Declan said, 'Something's standing next to me. And it's grasping my hand.' He recoiled, snatching his hand free and nursing it as if it had been bitten. Colm's voice, still on the other side of the tower said, 'Declan? What's wrong?'

'There's something in here with us,' said Declan, and as he spoke, the darkness slithered, and shadows reared up on the walls – grotesque shadows that might easily be figures on prancing horses, figures wielding spears, figures that wore crowns and mitres . . . There was the glint of crimson – like slanted eyes peering down from the walls, and Declan shrank back, flinging up a hand in instinctive defence. A face came swooping out of the darkness and peered down at him – a dreadful carved face, the red eyes slitted and malevolent, the lips stretched in a hungry smile.

At the top of his voice, he yelled, 'Get thee gone from me, Satan!' and there was a dry chuckle, like ancient, skinless bones being rubbed together.

Then the door burst open and the Kilglenn villagers erupted

into the tower. Cold moonlight, eerily mingled with leaping
torch flames, came jaggedly through the darkness. The shadows
with their glinting red eyes vanished, and the villagers seized
Colm and half-carried, half-dragged him out on to the cliff
side.

But Declan saw that the crimson light shone from the eyes
of the men and women he had known since he was born.

There was nothing either Declan or Colm could do.

The villagers thrust the torches in the ground, and held
Colm down.

'Murderer,' they chanted. 'Mesmer Murderer. We know who
you are.'

'Murderers have to be branded,' cried several more. 'The
mark of Cain. As it was in the beginning, so it shall be now.'

'Brand the murderer, brand him.'

'Set the mark upon him.'

*Branding irons*, thought Declan, horror engulfing him.
*They've brought branding irons, and they're heating them in
the torch flames. The newspaper stories about the Mesmer
Murderer with Colm's photographs must have reached them
– they know what he did. And they're going to burn him. I've
got to stop them*, he thought, but as he started forward, two
more of the men grabbed him and held him back.

'See what we do to murderers,' said one of them.

'We'll do it to you as well, if you try to stop us,' said
another.

Declan said, 'You can't do this. Please. You're not sane –
you're being used – can't you tell that! Can't you feel it?' He
searched frantically for words. What had Colm said it felt
like? 'Something's slid beneath your skin,' cried Declan. 'It's
clawed its way along your hands and fingers and into your
brain . . . Can't you feel that it has?'

But they threw him away from them, sending him sprawling
on the wet ground, and turned back to Colm. Through the
panic and fear, Declan had time to think that in the light of
the flaring torches, these people bore no resemblance to the
villagers he had known. He looked about him, frantically trying
to see a way of saving Colm.

But it was already too late. The villagers of Kilglenn, filled with bloodlust, were holding down Colm's arms and legs. The glowing branding irons – two of them – were raised into the night sky. Then they were brought down on to Colm's face.

# TWENTY-SEVEN

For Declan the worst part was not Colm screaming in agony; it was the dreadful stench of burning flesh – the stench they had both smelled on this hillside not very long ago.

A thin rain had started to fall, cooling the irons, and as the glow of their heat faded, the hatred and malevolence of the villagers seemed to fade. They stepped back from Colm, seeming unsure of themselves – almost seeming unaware of where they were. Some of the women started crying. In twos and threes, avoiding each others' eyes, they made their way back down the cliff path.

Somehow Declan got Colm as far as the shack, partly carrying and partly dragging him. Colm was moaning and struggling, but once inside the cottage he seemed to become calmer. Declan laid him on the battered sofa, and faced, with horror and dismay, the task of tending to Colm's burns. The branding irons had burned away almost the whole of one side of his face, searing into his cheekbone all down to the jaw.

'Eyes both intact though,' said Colm, in a thready voice. 'At least I'll see Death when he approaches.'

'You're not going to die,' said Declan angrily.

'Declan, they've burned half my face off! Why would I want to live?'

'It's not so very bad,' said Declan. He was not sure how burns should be treated, but he tore strips from his shirt and soaked them in the cold rain, then laid them over the burned flesh. But Colm was still twisting and turning as if trying to escape the pain and Declan was dreadfully aware that Colm's hands were icily cold. Could you actually die from the shock and pain of a bad burn? Please don't let him die, he thought, and stood up with decision. 'I'm going to get help from the village.'

'No one will come.'

'My mother would. My father, too.' But even as he said it, Declan was wondering if he could ask it of them. Neither of his parents had been among the torchlit group, but they would not want to be seen by the villagers as aiding a killer. And how would they feel towards Declan himself, after he had run away without warning, leaving only a note?

In miserable indecision, he built up a fire in the shack's little hearth, and drew a rug over Colm. In one of the cupboards he found half a bottle of whiskey, which he handed to Colm hoping it might dull the pain. Colm drank most of it, then relapsed into an uneasy sleep, and Declan sat on, wanting to get help, knowing there was no help to be had.

Shortly after midnight Colm seemed to rouse, and Declan sat up.

'You're feeling better?' he said, but he could already see that Colm was much worse. His eyes were wild and he seemed to be having difficulty breathing. The unmarked side of his face was taking on a waxen tinge and there was a pinched blue look to his lips. I can't lose him, thought Declan, in anguish. Only I don't know what to do.

In a weak voice, Colm said, 'What were we saying about death, Declan?'

'You're not dying,' said Declan again.

'I am. And here's the thing, Declan, I'm dying with all those sins on my soul. Mine and Romilly's, and Nicholas Sheehan's . . .' He struggled into a semi-upright position and reached for Declan's hands. The fingers, closing around Declan's, were cold, but beneath the surface the bones seemed to be on fire. 'Let's remember Romilly aborted a child and Sheehan reneged on his vows,' said Colm. 'And let's remember that I murdered five people in London . . .'

Declan said, 'Will I get a priest?' and Colm gave a half-laugh that turned into a scraping cough.

'Father O'Brian? Oh sure, he'd break his neck to come all the way up here for a sinner like me.'

'He would come,' said Declan.

'Declan, by the time you get to his house and bring him back out here, it'll be too late. Oh God, it's burning into my bones . . .' He broke off, struggling against the pain. Then he said, in a quieter voice, 'I don't want to die like this – I don't want to die at all. Life's bloody unfair, isn't it?'

'You'll get through it,' said Declan valiantly.

'But in case not . . . Declan, will you do one last thing for me?'

'What?' But a cold horror was creeping over Declan, because he already knew what Colm wanted.

'You did it twice before. Once for the priest. Then for Romilly. Do it for me, now. The ritual – the sin-eating ritual.'

Declan stared at him, his mind in tumult. After what felt like a very long time, he said, 'I can't.'

'Why can't you? You did it for those others. Aren't I your oldest friend?'

It would be impossible to say, 'Yes, but you're a murderer five times over.' Instead Declan said, again, 'I can't.'

'But you'd confess straight afterwards.' Again the pain overwhelmed him, and he hunched over, gasping.

Declan thought, *confess to murder? Five murders?* Priests hearing confession were bound by absolute secrecy, but he could not believe a priest, hearing a confession of murder, would not find some way to invoke temporal justice. And who would believe Declan was confessing on behalf of a man who was himself dead?

He said, 'Colm, let me try to get a priest to you . . .'

But Colm seemed not to hear. He said, 'Declan, if I gave you something . . . Get my jacket – don't argue, just do it.' He waited until Declan passed him the jacket, and thrust his hand into the pocket.

'What . . . ?'

'The Title Deeds to Holly Lodge,' said Colm. 'You got them out of the house, remember? And that house is mine – it was left to me fairly and legally. But you take them and take the ownership of it. Find a way of getting your name on to the – I don't know what it's called – on to the ownership part of the Deeds.'

'I'd never get away with it,' said Declan, but something had tugged at his mind, saying, wouldn't it be a marvellous thing to own a whole house . . .

'Yes, listen. You'll have to leave it a while – maybe as long as a year or even more. Then you turn up at a solicitor's office, and give them some story. Say you met someone while you were travelling and he gave you the Deeds as he lay dying. That's true enough, anyway,' said Colm, bitterly.

'But Flossie's family—'

'She didn't have any,' said Colm. He had fallen back on the sofa and his eyes were becoming distant. 'I'm telling you, you'll get away with it.'

Declan said, 'Colm, even with this, I can't do what you're asking.'

'I shan't give up,' said Colm, and broke off with a dreadful rasping cough. His hand, which Declan had taken again, seemed to be loosening. 'I promise you, Declan Doyle, I shan't give up.'

*The present*

He never did give up, thought Benedict, still seated in the soft dimness of the shack. He died here in this cottage, but he couldn't be at peace. He believed he was the one who had taken the guilt of those other sins and he believed he needed someone to repeat the ritual to remove them. And to remove his own sins, thought Benedict. All those killings . . . It's medieval and it's impossible, but he believed it.

*Declan wouldn't do it . . . He wouldn't repeat the ritual . . . Declan's son wouldn't do it, either, and nor would his grandson . . .*

Benedict said, very firmly, 'And nor will I.'

*No . . .* The word drifted through the desolation and the shadows, sadly accepting.

'Did my great-grandfather bring the chess piece back to Holly Lodge all those years ago?'

*He did. He couldn't face destroying it. He got his name transferred to the Title Deeds and he went back to London. The chess piece went with him. You know the rest.*

Aware of absurdity, Benedict said, 'Can't you – let go now?'

*I don't know. Aren't I the ghost doomed to walk the night?* The familiar irony was there.

Benedict said, 'If I were to destroy the chessman? If I take it up to the watchtower and smash it? Would that – I don't know the right expression – would it release you?'

There was a long silence, and for a moment he thought

Colm had gone. Then, *Let's try*, said Colm's voice. *Let's try that now.*

So they stood together in the burned-out watchtower, where a renegade priest had lived out a lonely existence in an attempt to contain an ancient evil, and where two boys had clung to a rock spur and listened to him die in screaming agony.

And, thought Benedict, where a set of figures that once haunted a castle library perished.

*Except for one single piece, Benedict . . .*

Benedict picked his way through the rubble and the charred debris. It was just possible to see the outline of the room that had once existed. There were even fragments of furniture that had survived the fire – he could see a small chest with a carved lid, several chairs, even a few strings of fabric that must have been curtains or rugs. The hearth was filled with grass and birds' nests and the tiny skeletons of birds themselves, but above it still hung an oval mirror, the frame black with age, the surface so smeared it gave no light and no reflection.

Benedict took the chess figure from his pocket. He had the fleeting impression that it resisted him, but he took a deep breath, and flung it hard against the stone fireplace. It described an arc through the dimness, and there was a moment when it reflected eerily in the old mirror. The shadows stirred briefly, and for the space of two heartbeats he thought shapes formed on the stones – the silhouettes of prancing horses, marching warriors, imperious figures who wore crowns or mitres . . .

Then the illusion vanished, and there was a small splintering sound, like frost icicles cracking. He saw the chess figure fracture against the stones. Tiny glinting chips flew out – some caught the silvering moonlight. The small sounds died away and the shadows were quiescent again.

Benedict said, very softly, 'Colm?'

But nothing moved within the ruined room and Benedict drew in a deep, shuddering sigh of relief. It's all right, he thought. He's gone. As he crossed to the door, something seemed to shiver within the tarnished mirror, and he turned, his heart skipping a beat. But there was nothing there, of course.

He went quickly down the hillside to his car.